AN AFFAIR OF SORCERERS

by

George C. Chesbro

Apache Beach Publications

Published by
Apache Beach Publications
Nyack, New York 10960
N.41.05.730
W.073.54.920
November 1999

This novel is a work of fiction. Any references to historical events, to real people, living or dead, or to real locales are intended only to give the fiction a setting in historical reality. Other names, characters, places, and incidents either are the product of the author's imagination or are used fictitiously, and their resemblance, if any, to real-life counterparts is entirely coincidental.

ISBN: 0-9674503-9-X

The author wishes to express his gratitude to Simon & Schuster, which published the original hard cover edition of this work.

FOR JOAN SANGER

Chapter 1

Channel 13, the PBS station in New York City, had been conducting its annual fund-raising auction, and my smart-ass brother had bought me a dozen tympani lessons with the Principal Tympanist of the New York Philharmonic; that was his idea of a practical joke. As far as I was concerned, the joke was on dear old Garth: I got rhythm. It was easy enough to practice; all I needed was a score, two pencils and a flat surface to beat on. I had a full set of kettledrums on order, and I couldn't wait to hear Garth's latest discourse on what he believed to be my obsessive need to overcompensate.

With eight lessons behind me, I already had visions of auditioning for the New Jersey Symphony; at the very least, a dwarf tympanist should guarantee them a sold-out season.

It was a Friday morning at the end of July, and I was in my uptown office. I'd finished the summer courses I'd been teaching, I had no clients and there was absolutely nothing I had to do for six weeks. Paradise Now. I planned to gorge my head on New York's cultural cornucopia and drum the rest of the summer away.

I was in the middle of the third movement of Tchaikovsky's Fifth, hoarsely *pum-pum-pumming* the main theme, tapping madly away in a big roll and impressive *crescendo,* when Dr. Peter Barnum, Chancellor of the university where I teach, knocked on my door and walked in. I finished the measure, then folded the score and dropped the pencils on top of it.

Barnum's craggy, sixty-year-old face was slightly flushed, and there were thin lines of tension around his mouth. He stopped in front of my desk and smiled tightly as he nodded toward the music score. "Are you thinking of changing departments, Dr. Frederickson?"

Barnum was an austere, distant man, and it was the first time I'd ever heard him try to be funny; it surprised me, since we usually gave each other a fairly wide berth. I had considerable respect for Barnum's administrative and fund-raising talents, but I didn't think he cared too much for me. He'd made clear in a number of faculty memos that he didn't approve of moonlighting college professors or celebrities on his staff; he knew I fitted into the first category, believed I was in imminent peril of joining the second. Also, in the past I'd suspected that he considered the idea of having a dwarf on his faculty somewhat undignified.

"I'd hoped I was getting the hang of the Criminology Department, Chancellor," I said, my tone idling in neutral gear. I rose and shook the long, bony hand he offered. It was moist. "Please sit down."

He did, nervously perching his tall, thin frame on the edge of the chair as if he were expecting someone to call him to a speaker's dais. "You're a fine professor, Dr. Frederickson," he said, clearing his throat and not quite looking at me. "Your teaching and scholarship have been uniformly excellent. I regret that we haven't been able to establish a more . . . personal relationship. I'm afraid I'm simply not very gregarious."

"You're a fine chancellor, sir," I said, puzzled by the drift of the conversation but deciding it was time to toss a blossom back. "That's all any faculty member has the right to expect from you."

"You also have an impeccable reputation as a private investigator," he said like a man who was choosing his words carefully. "It's remarkable that a man with your handi—" I doubted that he saw anything in my face, but he stopped anyway and shook his head, embarrassed. "I'm sorry," he continued curtly. "The fact is that I'd like to hire you." He raised a hand, coughed lightly behind it. "I mean as a private detective."

Another surprise; Barnum was full of surprises. I sat and stared at him for a few moments, thinking about Tchaikovsky, hoping Barnum would change his mind and go away. He didn't. "You didn't have to drive up here, Chancellor," I said at last. "I would have been happy to see you at your office." If I was going to turn him down, the least I could do was be polite.

"I know you would have," he said, waving a skeletal hand in the air as though I'd made a preposterous suggestion. "I prefer it this way. Actually, I don't want anyone to see us together." He paused, blinked nervously. "What I have to say *must* remain in the strictest confidence, Dr. Frederickson."

For a change, the air conditioning in the building was working. Still, the few strands of white hair that ringed the bald dome of Barnum's head were damp with perspiration. A vein throbbed in his neck.

"Everything my clients tell me is taken in confidence," I replied evenly. "That's the way I work."

"But you haven't said whether or not you'll help me," Barnum said warily.

"You haven't told me what it is you want, Chancellor. Until you do, I can't commit myself. In any case, whatever you have to say will go no farther than this office."

Barnum passed a hand over his eyes as if trying to erase a bad vision, then leaned back in the chair and stared absently at the nameplate on my desk. Finally he raised his eyes and looked directly at me. "I'd like you to investigate Dr. Vincent Smathers," he said thickly.

That got my undivided attention and a long, low mental whistle. I could understand Barnum's penchant for secrecy. Vincent Smathers was the university's most recent—and rarest—prize catch; an experimental behavioral psychologist who was a Nobel laureate. University chancellors didn't normally make a habit of investigating their Nobel Prize winners; the usual procedure is to create a specially endowed one-hundred-thousand-dollar chair, which was precisely what had been done for Smathers.

"What's the problem?" I asked.

"I . . . hear things," Barnum said, his face reddening.

"What things, Chancellor?"

"I'm sorry," he said archly, "but I don't wish to repeat them. At this time they must be classified as nothing more than gossipy rumors. If you do agree to conduct this investigation for me, I don't want you to begin with any preconceived notions. I know it sounds strange, but I must insist it be done this way."

Barnum paused, raised his eyebrows slightly. When I didn't say anything, he continued in a lower, even more confidential tone: "As you know, we're under increasing financial pressure. I have a responsibility to protect the university from any scandal that could hurt our student recruitment or gaining of Federal grants. I just want to make certain that everything appears . . . as it should."

"You mentioned rumors, but you talk as though something may already have happened. *Is* there anything now that doesn't appear as it should?"

"There is something . . ." He shrugged, continued after a thoughtful pause. "I don't know; perhaps I'm being overly suspicious."

"Suspicious about *what,* Chancellor? It would help if you gave me some idea of what's bothering you."

Barnum tapped his fingertips together, took a deep breath and slowly let it out. Again I hoped he was going to forget the whole thing, and again he disappointed me. When he finally spoke, his voice was somehow different—strong and even, as though only at that moment was he fully committed and prepared to live with his decision.

"Dr. Smathers brought an associate with him—Dr. Chiang Kee," the Chancellor said quietly but firmly. "Kee, in turn, brought an assistant with him, also Chinese. I'm not sure Kee's assistant can even speak English. Quite frankly, the man just doesn't look like someone with a university background."

It was my turn to shrug. "Neither do I."

Barnum's gray eyes flashed. "I assume that's meant to chastise me for almost saying you're handicapped."

"No, sir," I said evenly. "I'm saying that you, better than anyone else, should know that you get some pretty strange types on a university faculty, most of them thoroughly qualified for the work they're doing. I'm just trying to save you—or the university—some money."

Barnum cleared his throat. "Uh, how much do you charge?"

"A hundred twenty a day, plus expenses. But you haven't spent a cent yet. I like working at the university, and I get along. I'm sure *you* understand that I'd have to believe there was very good cause before I started nosing into the affairs of a colleague. It has something to do with academic freedom." I leaned forward and folded my hands on the desk. "You still don't want to tell me about the rumors?"

He shook his head. Relieved, I started to get up.

"Do you know Mr. Haley in the English Department?" Barnum asked quickly.

I said I did, reluctantly sat back down. Fred Haley and I had shared a few beers.

"Mr. Haley tells me he's seen Dr. Kee before, in Korea," Barnum continued. "As you may know, Mr. Haley was a POW. He tells me that Kee—who was using a different name then—was an enemy interrogator in charge of the brainwashing program to which all the POWs were subjected. Apparently, this Kee had a reputation for brutality—psychological as well as physical."

I was impressed. Fred Haley wasn't a man given to wild accusations: at least, he was no more paranoid than anyone else who has to live and work in New York City. On the other hand, as a former POW he'd have a very special ax to grind.

"It wouldn't be the first time a former enemy had come to work in the United States," I said. "Where would we have been without Wernher Von Braun? Kee could have changed his name to keep people from rattling the skeletons in his closet. Smathers certainly must know the background of his own associate. It's possible that everything's on the level."

"I'm fully aware of that," the Chancellor said, a note of impatience creeping into his voice. He crossed his legs quickly, nervously, then uncrossed them. "As I said, I'm concerned with appearances. There's also the matter of the one-hundred-thousand-dollar yearly endowment Dr. Smathers receives for the academic chair he holds. That represents the entire budget for his department, including salaries. While it's true that a man of Dr. Smathers' proved administrative abilities is not normally expected to—"

"You think Smathers is embezzling funds?"

"On the contrary," Barnum said wryly. "It's more likely he's *printing* money; that's the only way *I* could explain the equipment deliveries and remodeling that are going on over at Marten Hall."

"Doesn't the university audit Smathers' departmental budget?"

"Of course. But the audit covers only the money that the university provides directly, and the department budget is broken down into very broad categories. Frankly, our audit simply shows that Dr. Smathers is a very careful budgeter. Still, I wonder . . ." He paused and scratched his head, sighed. "It's hard to criticize an administrator for providing *more* within his budget than he would seem capable of. But I'm convinced he has additional sources of funds, and I'm curious as to where the extra money is coming from."

"What's he working on over there?"

"Frankly, I don't know; and I probably wouldn't understand it if I *did* know. Under the terms of his contract, he teaches one graduate seminar—which he's been doing brilliantly—and he has an absolutely free hand in research."

"Why don't you just go over and see for yourself what he's up to?"

"Because it would look irregular. Obviously, one doesn't risk stepping on the toes of a Nobel Prize winner." He licked his lips, and his gray eyes seemed to grow darker, more intense. "Look, Dr. Frederickson; I wouldn't even *care* about these financial matters if it weren't for Dr. Kee's rather questionable background, and the . . ."

"The rumors you won't tell me about," I finished for him.

"Correct," Barnum said with a quick nod.

I picked up my pencils and began tapping out a rhythm; it wasn't right, and I put the pencils aside again. "Where did Smathers come from?"

"Harvard."

"Harvard takes good care of its prizewinners, to say the least. It's hard for me to believe they wouldn't have matched any offer that was made to him. Why do you suppose they let him get away?"

Barnum's reply was a prolonged, eloquent silence. Rumors.

"What did he win his Nobel Prize for?"

"He did pioneering work in sensory deprivation. It seems Dr. Smathers is a leading authority in the field."

"Sensory deprivation," I said tentatively. "That would be artificially taking away a man's senses—sight, sound, smell, touch, taste?"

"I believe that's correct."

"To what purpose?"

"Apparently none, except to simply find out what happens. The first experiments were conducted to determine the effects. NASA was interested for a time because of the sensory deprivation that might be involved in interplanetary space travel. But they gave it up when it became evident that the experiments entailed too much risk for the volunteers; it seems you can actually induce psychosis." Barnum paused and drew himself up in his chair. "Well, Dr. Frederickson? Will you investigate Dr. Smathers for me?"

"I'll check out a few things and get back to you in a week or so."

"Thank you," he said, the curtness of his tone laced with relief. "You'll need a retainer."

I didn't want the job, didn't want the retainer; but I also didn't want to offend Barnum. The university had been good to me, and at the moment the Chancellor represented the university. I gave him a figure of two hundred and fifty dollars, then cut it in half when I saw he was writing out a personal check.

As soon as Barnum left I put the check in a drawer, picked up the phone and called a private investigator in Boston by the name of Winston Kellogg. I'd done some work—*gratis*—in New York for Kellogg on a few occasions, and it seemed a good time to cash in the IOU. I asked him to make some inquiries—nothing expensive—into Smathers' tenure at Harvard and let me know what he found out, if anything.

The phone rang while I was on my way out the door. I let it ring a few times, then went back and answered it. I was glad I had; it was Janet Monroe, a good friend. Janet was a nun, as well as a premier microbiologist. She was on indefinite leave from a small upstate Catholic college to develop special projects at the university.

"Mongo!" Janet breathed. "*There* you are. I've been trying all morning to reach you here at the school. I thought I might have to resort to prayer." It was one of her standard jokes, but now her voice had an odd ring to it. She sounded tense and breathless, as though she'd run a long distance.

"What's the matter, Janet?"

"Are you free around one this afternoon?"

I glanced at my watch; it was eleven. I was hoping to have a few words with Vincent Smathers, and maybe even wangle a tour of his facilities. It was a chore I wanted to get out of the way. "For you, dear Sister, I'm free anytime. But can we make it one thirty?"

"One thirty will be fine," Janet said quickly. "We need to talk to someone we can trust."

"We?"

"Yes. There's someone I'd like you to speak with, if you will. Unfortunately, he's on a very tight schedule."

"Who is it, Janet?"

There was a short pause. Then: "I'd—rather you find out for yourself. Can we meet in my office?"

"Sure, Janet. See you later."

"Thank you, Mongo. You're a dear, dear friend." There was a plaintive note in her voice that was uncharacteristic of the strong, vivacious woman, and it made me uneasy.

After hanging up the phone I started out the door again, then hesitated and went back to my desk. I sat down and deliberately tapped and hummed my way through the remaining measures of the third movement. When I'd finished, I rolled up the pencils in the score and put it in the bottom of a filing cabinet. I hoped I was wrong, but I had a strong feeling it would be some time before I got to the fourth movement.

Chapter 2

I picked up a hot dog and soda from a Sabrett vendor and ate in the car on my way downtown to the university. I parked in my usual spot and headed across campus toward Marten Hall, an old building which housed the Psychology Department. It was hot and muggy, close to rain. It would be a good afternoon to nap, or lounge around in a dark piano bar listening to music with a woman. I'd spend the afternoon snooping. I wished Smathers had taken the summer off; I wished *I'd* taken the summer off.

It soon became obvious that one didn't simply wander in off the campus and strike up a conversation with a Nobel Prize winner—at least, not with this particular specimen. Smathers had a ground-floor office, and his first line of defense was a large, hawk-faced woman who looked as if she'd barely escaped the last pro-football draft.

Being the only dwarf criminology professor/former circus headliner/Black Belt karate expert/licensed private investigator on campus has its advantages; most of the people at the school had at least heard of me. Counting on this modest notoriety to get me around what looked to be some sharp corners, I smiled broadly at the woman. Incredibly, the nameplate on her desk identified her as MRS. PFATT.

Mrs. Pfatt finished typing a line, then slowly looked up at me. Except for a glint of suspicion, her murky black eyes were blank. "Yes?" she asked coldly.

"Is Dr. Smathers around?"

Mrs. Pfatt stared at me for what seemed a long time; behind her thick glasses, the woman's eyes were large and unblinking. Finally, she said: "Is Dr. Smathers . . . *around?*"

"Yeah," I said. "*Around*. I'm Dr. Frederickson, and I'd like to introduce myself to my esteemed colleague."

"I'm afraid that's impossible," Mrs. Pfatt said briskly. "Dr. Smathers is a very busy man, and I know you don't have an appointment."

"Then why don't you *give* me an appointment?" I replied, raising my tone a few professional notches. "Let's call it a request for a consultation. I'm a criminologist; I'd like to talk with Dr. Smathers about certain areas where our research interests may overlap."

"Dr. Smathers has no time for consultations," she sniffed, turning her attention back to her typewriter.

"Then I'd like to speak with Dr. Kee."

"I'm *sorry,* sir," Mrs. Pfatt said indignantly, her chins quivering. "Dr. Kee will not see you either."

"How do you know unless you ask?"

"I know my job, sir," she said, and resumed typing.

Taking my leave of the charming Mrs. Pfatt, I walked down a long corridor lined on both sides with classrooms. The rooms were all empty, except for one where a makeup examination for a summer course was in progress. A few students recognized me and waved; I grinned and waved back. From what I could see, everything in Marten Hall was distressingly in order.

The building had four floors, and I started to work my way up them as casually as possible. The second floor consisted of empty classrooms, while the third was a combination of offices and laboratories, sparsely populated on a summer Friday with a few graduate researchers. I headed toward the stairway at the end of the corridor, stopped and stared. A heavy steel door had been installed across the entrance to the stairs. A warning had been stenciled in red paint on the cold gray metal.

NO ADMITTANCE

AUTHORIZED PERSONNEL ONLY

There was no reason why I couldn't come back to Marten Hall after my meeting with Janet Monroe; I simply didn't care to. To judge by Mrs. Pfatt's behavior, I could spend all summer playing hide-and-seek with Smathers and

Kee without ever coming up a winner. I was impatient to get on with the job; as a result, I did something I might not otherwise have done: used a lockpick.

Smathers should have spent less money on steel and more on the lock: I had it open in about five minutes. A narrow flight of stairs snaked up and twisted to the left. The inside of the door as well as the walls and ceiling of the stairwell had been soundproofed. It seemed a curious expense for a psychology department; mental processes just don't make that much noise.

I climbed the stairs and found myself at the end of a long corridor which had been expensively remodeled with glassed-in offices on one side and locked steel doors on the other. I decided to jimmy my way into one of the locked rooms, but first wanted to make sure that the offices on the left were empty. They were—except for the last one.

The Chinese caught me out of the corner of his eye before I could duck down out of sight. He was the original Captain Flash, out of his chair and standing in front of me in a lot less time than it would have taken his rival to find an empty phone booth.

"Uh . . . Dr. Kee?"

The man simply stared at me, which probably made him Kee's assistant. It occurred to me that I should have paid closer attention to Barnum's mini-lecture on first impressions: the man in front of me looked like a battered refugee from a tong war. Somebody had tried to use his head as a whetstone; his right cheek was a sheet of white, rippled scar tissue. He looked blind in the right eye, but the left was perfectly all right; he was glowering at me with it.

Smiling, I wished him a cheery good afternoon. He still said nothing.

"Is Dr. Smathers here?"

Still no response; he might have taken it as a Chinese insult, or maybe he just didn't care for dwarfs. I shrugged and turned around to walk away.

The Chinese was around in front of me like a cat, crouched and balanced on the balls of his feet like a prizefighter. His right hand came out and gripped my shoulder. "No go!" he yelped in lumpy English.

My watch told me I had fifteen minutes before my meeting with Janet Monroe. "Sorry," I said, slapping his hand away. "You're a brilliant conversationalist; I'd love to stay, but I've got business."

I started to step around him. He moved with me, reaching out with snake speed to grip my shoulders with both hands. His fingers started to tighten on the nerves and muscles around my collarbone. I slapped his hands away again with more force, hitting the insides of his elbows sharply with the sides of my hands. He didn't like that; he sputtered something in Chinese and took a swing at my head. I ducked under the blow and stepped into him, spinning clockwise to gain momentum, snapping my elbow into his solar plexus. I hit him a lot harder than I would have if I hadn't been slightly perturbed. He arched on his toes, the air exploding from his lungs, then crumpled to the floor, where he gasped and heaved for air like a beached fish.

"Tell Dr. Smathers that Bob Frederickson was here to see him," I said, squatting next to the man's head. Pain, surprise and hate swam in the good eye, filming it like a second skin. "Tell him I'd like to buy him a beer one of these days, when he's got the time."

Janet Monroe was waiting for me in her main laboratory. The woman was the pride of her religious order and a leading researcher in microbiology; more important to me, she was a valued friend. We'd drained a good many pots of coffee with arcane philosophical chitchat about God, gods, men's needs and deeds. Janet was a handsome woman in her early fifties. As usual, her shiny gray hair was drawn back into a flowing ponytail, which served to highlight her violet eyes and the finely sculpted, aquiline features of her face. Now she looked troubled.

"How's my favorite nun?" I asked, kissing her hand.

"Hello, Mongo," Janet said, taking my hand in both of hers and squeezing my fingers hard. She looked at me, frowned. "Are you all right? You look pale."

"Indigestion," I said, resisting the impulse to add something about Chinese food. Putting Kee's assistant on the floor hadn't really involved that much exercise, but the residual tension from the confrontation obviously still showed. "What did you want to see me about?"

She nodded toward a small office just off the laboratory. "The man I want you to meet is in there."

The man waiting for me looked like a movie star who didn't want to be recognized. When he took off his dark glasses, he still looked like a movie star; he also looked like a certain famous Southern senator who was very close to wrapping up his party's presidential nomination.

"Dr. Frederickson," he said in deep, stentorian tones that echoed faintly in the small office. "I've been doing so much reading about you in the past few days that I feel I already know you. I must say, it's a distinct pleasure. I'm Bill Younger."

"I know. Nice to meet you, Senator." I shook his large, sinewy hand. With his boyish, middle-aged face and full head of brown, razor-cut hair, Younger looked good. Except for the anxiety in his eyes, he might have been waiting to step into a televison studio.

I glanced inquisitively at Janet, but she was standing over by a window, her arms loose at her sides and her gaze fastened steadily on the floor. When I looked back at Younger, he cocked his head to one side and smiled absently, as at a memory.

"I used to take Linda—my daughter—to see you perform when you were with the circus," he said distantly. "You were Mongo the Magnificent. What an *incredible* gymnast and tumbler you were. I remember the stunt where you—"

"That was a long time ago, Senator," I interrupted gently. It had been seven years since I'd left the circus, but it seemed a hundred. "Why the background check?"

"I recommended you, Mongo," Janet quietly interjected from the other side of the room.

Younger's smile faded. "Now you're very well known as a private investigator," he said, looking at me hard as though he couldn't quite believe it. "I wanted to make certain you were also discreet. You are; your credentials are impeccable." His tone shifted slightly. "You seem to have a penchant for unusual cases."

"Unusual cases seem to have a penchant for me. You'd be amazed how few people feel the need for a dwarf private investigator."

Younger wasn't really listening. "Have you heard of Esteban Morales?"

"No."

"Perhaps I should explain," Janet said, leaving her outpost by the window and coming across the room to us. That was fine with me; the Senator seemed to be having trouble getting started. Janet stopped in front of me, continued softly: "Esteban is a healer."

"A doctor?"

"No, Mongo," Janet said, slowly shaking her head, "not a doctor. Esteban is a psychic healer. He heals with his hands . . . or maybe his mind." She paused and looked at me intently, as though trying to gauge my reaction. I must have looked startled, because she quickly added, "I know it sounds absurd, but—"

"It doesn't sound absurd," I said. Janet had no way of knowing—and I couldn't tell her—that the most unusual case I'd ever handled had involved a man by the name of Victor Rafferty. Rafferty had been able to heal—and do a great many other things—with nothing more than the power of his mind. "Go on, Janet."

"Apparently, there are supposed to be a number of good psychic healers in this country," Janet continued. "Most of the ones we *hear* about are associated with some religious group. But people who are familiar with this kind of phenomenon consider Esteban the best."

"What group is he with?"

The nun shook her head. "None that I know of. Esteban's not a *faith* healer. What he does seems to be independent of religious belief—his, or that of the person he's treating. Anyway, I received a grant to do a research project on him this summer."

"Excuse me, Janet," I said, "but working with faith healers, psychic healers or any other kind of healers seems like an odd project for a microbiologist."

"I'll explain later," she said softly. "I know Senator Younger has to return to Washington for an important committee hearing. The critical point is that Esteban is now in jail awaiting trail for murder. In fact, Garth was the arresting officer. It seems he's now working on some special squad that has to do with . . ." Her voice trailed off into embarrassed silence.

"The occult," I finished for her. For months, Garth had been heading an interborough task force working the burgeoning New York occult underground, ferreting out the con artists—and worse—who preyed on the gullible. The tympani lessons had been his response to my mercilessly kidding him about wasting the taxpayers' money chasing witches, warlocks and Satanists. But murder wasn't so funny.

Janet was slowly and rhythmically massaging her temples with the tips of her index fingers. "It seems that Esteban, as a psychic leader, is considered some kind of *occult* figure just because he's not associated with any religious group," she said with a trace of bitterness in her voice. "That's why Garth was assigned to the case."

Watching Younger, I was beginning to suspect that it could be more than Janet's recommendation that had attracted him to me. I hoped I was wrong, because he was going to be disappointed if he thought I could—or would try to—influence my brother when it came to his official business. I had a natural distrust of politicians. "Is Esteban one of your constituents?" I asked the Senator.

"Yes," he answered simply. "It so happens that he is; but that's not my reason for wanting to help him."

"What *is* your reason?"

Younger was still having trouble telling me what was on his mind. When he didn't answer right away, I turned to Janet. "Who's this Esteban accused of killing?" I asked abruptly.

"Don't you want me to tell him now?" she asked Younger. Janet's voice was very gentle, and I wondered if my impatience with the Senator was showing. I was still smarting from my tussle with the Chinese, and angry that I'd agreed to investigate Smathers in the first place; I could hardly wait for the next meeting of the faculty Ethics Committee.

"No," Younger said, his voice strangely muffled. "I can do my own talking. It's . . . just that I'm having trouble . . ." He swallowed hard, closed his eyes. "Yes, Sister," he whispered. "Would you please fill Dr. Frederickson in on the background of the case?"

I tried to sneak a glance at my watch, and Janet caught me at it. Her gaze was steady and vaguely accusatory. "Esteban is accused of killing a physician by the name of Robert Samuels," she said tightly. "Dr. Samuels worked at the university Medical Center."

"Why would Esteban want to kill Samuels?"

Janet touched her fingers to her temples again, then dropped her arms stiffly to her sides. I had the feeling she was struggling to control an enormous amount of tension. "The papers reported that Dr. Samuels filed a complaint against Esteban—practicing medicine without a license. The police think Esteban killed him because of it."

"They'd need more than suspicion to book him."

Janet nodded quickly as she sucked in a deep breath. "Esteban was found in Dr. Samuels' office—with the body. Dr. Samuels had been dead only a few minutes; his throat had been cut with a knife they found dissolving in a vial of acid." Janet's tone had been growing increasingly strained. She paused and took another deep breath. It seemed to calm her, and her words came easier.

"Mongo," she continued, "if it's true that a complaint was filed against Esteban, it wouldn't be the first time; and it certainly wouldn't have been a reason for Esteban to kill anyone. He's always taken the enmity of the medical establishment in stride."

"Esteban is *not* a killer," Senator Younger interjected from the center of the office, where he'd been nervously pacing. He stopped and pounded a fist into his palm. The sharp slap of flesh against flesh grated on my nerves, and I suddenly realized I had a headache. "The charge is absurd! Damn it, the man's spent his entire adult life *helping* people!"

"The Senator's right, Mongo," Janet said, and the nun/scientist's soft, quavering voice had a far greater impact on me than Younger's outburst. "Esteban just *couldn't* have killed anyone; and certainly not *that* way. I feel a responsibility for what's happened, because I brought Esteban here. When Senator Younger came to see me, I told him I thought you could help."

"I'm not sure *how* you think I can help, Senator," I said, turning to face the politician. "And I still don't understand why the case is so important to you."

Younger slumped into a chair behind him. He unconsciously ran a hand through his hair, then quickly smoothed it down. "You must clear Esteban," he said, looking at me with anguish in his eyes. His voice was steady, intense. "Prove that Esteban didn't do it—or that someone else did."

"That's a pretty tall order, Senator. And it could get expensive. On the other hand, you've got the entire NYPD set up to do this kind of work for nothing. It's their job."

Younger shook his head. "I want one man—you—to devote himself exclusively to this case. You work here at the university; you have contacts. You may be able to find something the police overlooked—or didn't care to look for. The police think Esteban is guilty, and we both know they aren't going to spend a lot of time investigating what they consider an open-and-shut case."

"I can't argue with that."

"This is *most* important to me, Frederickson," Younger said, jabbing his finger in the air for emphasis. "I'll double your normal fee."

"That won't be nec—"

"At least, I *must* have access to Esteban if you can't clear him. Perhaps . . . your brother could arrange that. I'd be willing to donate five thousand dollars to any cause your brother deems worthy."

The words, heavy and ugly, hung in the air. Janet looked away, embarrassed. "Uh-oh," I said quietly. "Hold on, Senator. I can see that you're a little overwrought, but if I were you I wouldn't suggest that kind of arrangement to Garth. He might interpret it as a bribe offer, and he's very touchy about those things."

"Damn it, Frederickson, it *will* be a bribe offer!" Younger's face was blanched bone white. He choked back his anger, and his next words came out in a forced, breathy whisper. "If Esteban Morales is not released, my daughter will die."

I felt a chill, and wasn't sure whether it was because I believed him or because of the possibility that a United States Senator and presidential hopeful was a lunatic. I settled for something in between and tried to regulate my tone of voice accordingly. "I don't understand, Senator."

"Really?" he said tightly. "I thought I was making myself perfectly clear." Younger was still shaken, but now he had his anger and desperation under control. He took a deep, shuddering breath and slowly let it out. "My daughter's life is totally dependent on Esteban. Linda has cystic fibrosis. As you probably know, doctors consider the disease incurable. The normal pattern is for a sufferer to die in his or her teens, usually from pulmonary complications. By the time Linda was fourteen, we'd consulted the finest specialists in the world and were given no hope; my wife and I were told that Linda would die within a year. Then we heard of Esteban, and we felt we had nothing to lose by going to him for help. He's been treating Linda in his own, very special way—for ten years. She's now twenty-four. But Linda needs him again; her lungs are filling with mucus."

I could see how the medical establishment might be made a little nervous by Esteban Morales' activities; false hope could be the most insidious of poisons. Under the best of circumstances—meaning when I didn't have a Nobel laureate to poke at—it didn't sound like the kind of case I'd be too eager to take on. If Morales was a hoaxer—or a killer—I had no desire to be the bearer of bad tidings to a man with William Younger's emotional involvement.

"How does Esteban treat your daughter, Senator?" I asked, finding myself naturally slipping into the familiar usage of the healer's first name. "With drugs?"

Younger shook his head. "Esteban just *touches* her; he moves his hands up and down her body. Sometimes he seems to be in a trance, but I don't think he is. It's . . . very hard to explain. You have to see him do it."

"How much does he charge for these treatments of his?"

Younger looked surprised. "He doesn't charge anything. I'm told that most psychic healers—the good ones, anyway—won't take money. They feel it interferes with the source of their power, whatever that may be." Younger laughed shortly, without humor. "Esteban prefers to live simply—off Social Security, a pension check and small gifts from friends. He's a retired metal-shop foreman." He smiled thinly. "Doesn't sound like your average rip-off artist, does he, Frederickson?"

It was true that Esteban didn't exactly match the mental picture I'd been sketching of him. "Senator," I said, tapping my fingertips lightly on the desk beside me, "why don't you hold a press conference and describe to the public what you feel Esteban has done for your daughter? It could do more good than hiring a private detective; coming from you, I guarantee such a statement would get the police moving."

Younger grimaced. "It could also get me locked up in a mental institution. At the least, I'd be voted out of office—perhaps recalled. My state's in the Bible Belt, you know, and there'd be a great deal of misunderstanding. Both Linda and I would be ridiculed. Esteban isn't a religious man in my constituents' sense of the word—meaning he doesn't claim to receive his powers from God. I'm not sure he even *believes* in God. Even if he did, I doubt it would make much difference." The Senator's painful grimace became a bitter smile that slowly faded. "I've found that most so-called religious people prefer their miracles . . . well aged. You'll forgive me if I sound selfish, but I'd like to try to save Linda's life without demolishing my career. I'm egotistical enough to really believe . . . I have something to offer my country. If all else fails, then I'll hold the press conference you suggest." He paused and looked at me a long time. Then he said softly, "Now will you take the job?"

The business with Smathers had just begun, and I hadn't wanted *that* job. Now, just hours later, I was being asked to take on a second investigation that looked to be stranger and more unpleasant than the first. I wasn't exactly enthralled by the prospect.

When I looked at Janet, her lips silently formed the word *"Please."* I told Younger I'd see what I could find out.

Chapter 3

"How did you become involved with Esteban?" I asked Janet as I followed her out of the office into an adjacent, smaller laboratory. Younger had left to catch the shuttle flight back to Washington, and Janet had indicated that she wanted to show me something.

"Yvonne Mercado mentioned him to me; she was the one who suggested I design a research model to study him. I did, and I got the grant."

Yvonne Mercado was another friend, although not as close as Janet. "Where did Yvonne hear about him?"

Janet shrugged. "Well, I suppose cultural anthropologists get involved with all sorts of strange types. She told me she was introduced to him in Miami while she was researching some of the Cuban refugee groups there." Janet paused and looked at me strangely. "You should talk to Yvonne. She has some provocative things to say about these healers."

"Thanks; I will. Has Esteban made you a believer?"

"Here," she said, stopping beside a marble-topped lab table. "Before I answer that, I want to show you this."

The microbiologist opened a drawer under the table and took out what appeared to be a large photographic negative. In its center was the dark outline of a hand with outstretched fingers. The tips of the fingers were surrounded by waves of color; flashes of pink, red, violet and green undulated outward to a distance of two or three inches from the hand itself. The effect was oddly beautiful, and very mysterious.

"Pretty," I said. "What is it?"

"It's a Kirlian photograph. The technique is named after a Russian who invented it a few decades ago. By the way, the Russians are far ahead of us in the field of parapsychology."

I knew: the Rafferty case again. What had started out as a lazy Friday was turning into a very strange day filled with haunting memories and racking tensions.

"They're very good at this kind of research," Janet continued quietly. "Healing, ESP, clairvoyance—that sort of thing. Kirlian photography is supposed to show what's known as the human *aura*, part of the energy that all living things radiate. The technique itself is quite simple: you put the test subject—or object—into a circuit with an unexposed photographic plate, run a small current through the circuit while the subject touches the plate with some part of the body—in this case the hand." She pointed to the print I was holding. "This is the sort of thing you end up with."

"Esteban?" I asked, tapping the print.

"No; me. That's an 'average' aura, if you will." She reached back into the drawer and withdrew another set of negatives; she studied them, then handed one to me. "This is Esteban."

The print looked no more spectacular than Janet's, and I told her so.

"You might say that's Esteban at rest; he's not thinking about healing." Janet handed me another print. "Here he is with his batteries charged."

The print startled me. The bands of color were erupting from the fingers—especially the index and middle fingers. The apogee of the waves extended beyond the borders of the print. It reminded me of pictures I'd seen of sun storms.

"You won't find that effect in the other examples," Janet continued in the same, soft tone. "Simply thinking about healing makes no difference with most people. It does with Esteban—as you can see."

"I'm impressed, Janet," I said, handing her back the prints. "What does it mean?"

Janet smiled disarmingly. "Mongo, I'm a scientist. I can only afford to deal in hard facts—*especially* when I'm working with a controversial subject like Esteban. Even the Kirlian technique is controversial; but the fact of the matter is that Esteban *does* produce one hell of a Kirlian photograph. The implication, of course, is that he can literally radiate great amounts of energy from his body—at will."

"Do you believe he can actually cure diseases?"

She took some time to consider her answer, then said, "Since you insist on putting me up against the wall, I'll say that there's no doubt in *my* mind that he can. And he's not dealing with psychosomatic disorders. Esteban has been involved with research projects at other universities. In one, a strip of skin was surgically removed from the backs of monkeys. The animals were divided into two groups. Esteban simply *handled* the monkeys in one group, and the animals in that group healed almost twice as fast as the ones he didn't handle." She paused, smiled wanly. "Plants are supposed to grow faster when he waters them."

"What did you have Esteban working on here?"

"Enzymes," Janet said with a hint of pride. "It's the perfect research model, inasmuch as there are no personalities involved. Enzymes are the basic chemicals of the body. If Esteban *could* heal, the reasoning went, he should be able to affect pure enzymes. Well, he can."

"I take it the results were good."

"Good? They were *spectacular,* Mongo. You see, irradiated—'injured'—enzymes break down at specific rates in certain chemical solutions; the less damaged they are, the slower the rate of decay. What we did was take test tubes full of enzymes supplied by a commerical lab and irradiate them. The samples Esteban handled broke down at a statistically significant *lesser* rate than the ones he didn't handle." She paused, then added: "Ninety-nine and nine-tenths percent of the population wouldn't be able to affect the enzymes one way or the other. On the other hand, a very few people seem to be able to make the enzymes break down *faster*."

"*Negative* healers?"

"Right," Janet said, smiling thinly. "Pretty spooky, huh?" Her thoughts must have shifted to the Senator and his daughter; her smile vanished. "The longer I work with science, the more strongly I'm convinced that we haven't even begun to plumb the depths of God's gifts to us. Just imagine: there seem to be people alive today with Jesus' miraculous healing gift."

"And most of the ones I've heard of try to package it like oatmeal," I said.

For a moment I was afraid I'd offended the nun, but Janet slowly nodded in agreement. "So true," she said softly.

"But this is incredible," I said. "You're saying you have a man here who may actually be able to heal sick people with some kind of natural energy, and only a handful of people have ever heard of him." I thought of Younger, his desperation and frustration. I wished he hadn't left; I'd have liked to apologize to him for my impatience and bad manners.

"It's next to impossible to get *funding* for this type of research, much less good publicity," Janet said tightly. "Believe it or not, there are a lot of religious groups opposed to this kind of research; they feel it takes away from the spiritual aspect of healing. As I told you, Esteban is considered part of the occult. Most of my colleagues are laughing up their sleeves at me."

"Wasn't acupuncture considered occult at one time?"

Janet nodded. "Yes; and you know how long it took Western scientists and doctors to get around to taking acupuncture seriously. Psychic healing just doesn't fit into the currently acceptable pattern of scientific thinking. When you do get a study done, none of the respectable journals want to publish it; they're afraid of the subject." She sighed. "But that isn't important now. What matters is that Senator Younger's daughter needs Esteban to keep her alive, and Esteban's in jail."

"Tell me about this Dr. Samuels."

Janet thought about it for a few moments. When she finally spoke, I had the impression she was choosing her words carefully. "Well, Dr. Samuels was never happy about his part in the project. Now I'm beginning to wonder about Dr. Jordon; I'm still waiting for his anecdotal reports."

"You've lost me, Janet. What did Samuels have to do with this project? Who's this Dr. Jordon, and what reports are you talking about?"

She looked at me strangely for a few seconds, then pressed her hand to her forehead. "I'm sorry," she whispered. "I thought I'd explained all that. My mind . . . I've been so upset."

"I can see that. Just take your time and tell me everything that you think could have any bearing on the case."

Janet breathed deeply, nodded. "I only needed Esteban about an hour or two a day, when he actually handled the specimens," she said, her voice very soft but steady. "The rest of the time I was involved with computer analysis of the test data. I decided it might be interesting to see what Esteban could do with real patients—under medical supervision, of course. I wanted to get a physician's point of view. I put some feelers out into the medical community and got a cold shoulder from everybody but Eric Jordon, who happened to be Robert Samuels' partner."

Janet was beginning to tremble. I took her arm and eased her into a chair. She smiled her appreciation, then continued in the same quiet voice.

"We worked out a plan where Esteban would go to their offices after finishing his work here. They'd refer certain volunteer patients to him. The volunteers were in no immediate danger, but their conditions had been diagnosed and all would eventually require hospitalization. The patients would report how they felt to the doctors after their sessions with Esteban. Both Samuels and Jordon were then supposed to prepare anecdotal reports. Not very scientific, but Dr. Jordon and I thought it would make an interesting footnote to the main research project."

"And you haven't seen any reports?"

"No. As a matter of fact, I think Jordon is stalling."

"Why stall after agreeing to participate in the project in the first place?"

"I don't know, Mongo. He may have had second thoughts after the murder; or maybe he's simply afraid his colleagues will laugh at him."

Maybe. It still seemed to me like a curious shift in attitude. One thing was certain: I'd dearly love to see the list of patients who had been referred to Esteban. The list might contain the name of someone who'd had a motive to kill Samuels and try to pin it on Esteban Morales.

"What else can you tell me about Samuels and Jordon?" I asked. "You said they were partners?"

"Yes," Janet said thoughtfully. "They were also very much involved in the modern, big-business aspect of medicine. Dr. Jordon, of course, still is. It's what a lot of doctors are doing these days: labs, ancillary patient centers, private hospitals—that sort of thing. Jordon's skills seem to be more in the area of administration, frankly." She paused, nervously smoothed back a loose strand of gray hair. "Now that I think about it, I guess Dr. Jordon would be about the last person I'd have expected to be interested in psychic healing. Anyway, there were rumors to the effect that they were going public in a few months."

"Physicians go public?"

"Sure. They build up a network of the types of facilities I mentioned, incorporate, then sell stock."

"How did the two of them get along?"

"Who knows?" Janet said distantly. "I assume they got on about as well as most business partners. They had quite different personalities, though."

"How so?"

"Samuels was the older of the two men by quite a few years. He was a much more experienced doctor, and I suspect he was attracted to Dr. Jordon in the first place because of Jordon's business acumen and administrative skills. Samuels was a good doctor, but he was . . . well, *brooding*. Absolutely no sense of humor. Jordon has a lighter side. Obviously, he was also the more adventurous of the two."

I gave it some thought, then said, "Adventurous or not, it still strikes me as odd that Jordon—from the way you describe him—would want to take the *time* to work with Esteban. He sounds like a man with a lot of irons in the fire."

"Oh, he certainly is that. I really can't explain Dr. Jordon's enthusiasm—and, as I told you, Samuels was opposed to their involvement in the project from the beginning. Dr. Samuels told me he didn't want to waste his time on what he considered superstitious nonsense. But then, when Dr. Jordon persuaded his partner to participate, I wasn't about to question the motives of either man." She hesitated, then added, "I do think Dr. Samuels' negative attitude finally affected Esteban."

"Why do you say that?"

"I'm . . . really not sure; it's just a suspicion. Toward the end of our work here, something was destroying Esteban's concentration—or *whatever* it is that he needs to do what he does. He wasn't getting the same results with the enzymes that he was getting earlier, and I was never able to find out why. I asked Esteban about it, but he made it clear that he didn't want to discuss the matter." She paused and looked at me for a long time with her moist, violet eyes. "Mongo," she continued at last, "Esteban is probably the gentlest, most loving person I've ever met—except for you. Thank you so very, very much for agreeing to help."

The tremor in Janet's voice and the tears in her eyes embarrassed me. I responded with something inane and inappropriate about recommending me to her main department head, then hurriedly left.

It was four o'clock. To that point it had been what could be described as a depressing day. I seriously considered repairing to the local pub, but was afraid I'd succumb to temptation and get gloriously drunk; with two decidedly oddball cases to juggle, I thought it might be a good idea to stay sober. I went home.

I perked up when I saw the little girl waiting for me outside my apartment. Kathy Marlowe was a small friend of mine from 4D, down the hall. Frank Marlowe, her father, was a man who'd become rich churning out hundreds of pulp novels under a dozen different pseudonyms.

Marlowe was a rather strange man, even for a writer. Brooding, almost totally self-absorbed, he was a hard man to get to know, even by New York standards, and I'd always respected his privacy. Still, the fact that I was a real-life private investigator seemed to fascinate him, and we'd managed to have a few discussions. He'd once announced, only half joking, that I'd inspired him to create a new series of paperback novels featuring a dwarf private detective. I'd heartily discouraged the idea, assuring him that no one would believe it. During the course of those few conversations, I'd come to perceive Marlowe as a complex man with complex ambitions that went far beyond anything that appeared in the simply written, fast-paced entertainments that seemed to pop out of his typewriter once every three or four weeks. He was divorced from his wife, but Kathy visited him every summer. The child and I had become fast friends.

Kathy, with her fine blond hair, dressed in a frilly white dress and holding a bright red patent leather purse that perfectly complemented her blue eyes, looked positively beatific. I laughed to myself as I recalled that it had taken me two of her seven years to convince her that I wasn't a potential playmate.

"Kathy, Kathy, Kathy!" I shouted, picking her up and

setting her down in a manner usually guaranteed to produce Instant Giggle. "How's my girl today?"

"Hello, Mr. Mongo," she said very seriously.

"Why the good clothes? You look beautiful, but I almost didn't recognize you without dirt on your nose."

Kathy still didn't smile. "I've been waiting for you, Mr. Mongo, because I want to ask you something. I went to a birthday party, but I left early so I could meet you. My daddy's at a meeting with his editor. I was afraid I wouldn't see you before he came home."

Now tears came, welling slowly in her eyes like dew on the most delicate blue flowers. I gently brushed the tears away, suddenly realizing that this was no child's game. "What do you want to ask me, Kathy?" I said, gently kissing her on the forehead.

The child sniffled, then regained control of herself in a manner that reminded me of someone much older. "My daddy says you sometimes help people for money."

"That's right, sweetheart. How can I help you?"

"I want you to get my daddy's book of shadows back," she said, her words coming in a rush. "I heard Daddy say he thinks either Daniel or Esobus took it, and I know he's real worried. He always talks to himself when he's upset. I want him to be happy like he used to be." She sniffled again, blew her tiny nose on a tissue she'd retrieved from her red purse. When she looked at me again, her eyes semed very large. "But you mustn't tell Daddy, Mr. Mongo," she continued in a small, frightened voice held together by determination. "He'd be *awful* mad at me if he knew I told anyone. But I can tell from what he says that he just has to get his book of shadows back, or something terrible will happen."

"Kathy," I said, cupping my hand under her chin, "slow down and tell me what a 'book of shadows' is. Who are Daniel and Esobus?"

But Kathy wasn't listening; she was sobbing, fumbling in her small purse. "I . . . I've got money for you," she stammered between sobs. "I've been saving my milk money."

Before I could say anything, the little girl had taken out a child's handful of nickels, dimes and pennies and pressed them into my palm. I started to give the money back, then hesitated when I heard footsteps come up behind me.

"Kathy," a thin, nasal voice said. "What are you doing here?"

The girl gave me an anguished look that was an unmistakable plea to keep her secret. Then she quickly brushed away her tears with the back of her hand and smiled up at the person standing behind me.

"Hi, Daddy! I fell and hurt myself. Mr. Mongo was trying to make me feel better."

I turned to face Frank Marlowe. He seemed much paler and thinner than when I'd last seen him, but I decided that could be my imagination; Marlowe had never looked that healthy to begin with. A tall man in his mid-thirties, he had a high, domed forehead which accentuated the dark, sunken hollows of his eye sockets. He looked like a man who was slowly caving in under some invisible but inexorable pressure.

"Hello, Mongo," Marlowe said warily.

"Hi, Frank," I said, absently slipping the coins Kathy had given me into my pocket and shaking the hand that was extended to me. "Good to see you."

"Thanks for taking care of Kathy." Marlowe looked down at his daughter and smiled warmly. "You all right now, kitten?"

Kathy nodded her head. Her milk money felt heavy in my pocket, and I felt foolish. By the time I realized that I probably had no right to help a seven-year-old keep secrets from her father, Frank Marlowe had taken his daughter's hand and was leading her off down the corridor toward their own apartment. Kathy looked back at me once, quickly, and the intensity of the plea in her face startled me.

When they were gone, I took the money Kathy had given me out of my pocket and counted it. There was fifty-seven cents. I went into my apartment, dropped the coins into a large ashtray on my coffee table and poured myself a stiff Scotch. I immediately downed that and poured another. I wanted nothing so much as to go back and start this particular Friday all over again.

Chapter 4

It was Saturday morning, but I had the feeling that someone had a strong urge to get in touch with me; and my home telephone was unlisted, the number given to friends only. Deciding that it was best to get what I assumed would be the most disagreeable part of the day out of the way first, I went downtown to my university office to give Vincent Smathers a shot at me. It didn't take the Nobel laureate long to get there; I was only halfway through coffee and a bagel when he burst into the office.

The photographs I'd seen of him didn't do justice to his solid, athletic build. He was, according to his university biography, fifty-four years old, but he looked younger. His brown hair was thinning on top, long and wavy at the sides and back. His eyes were his most striking feature—a cold emerald green. The left eye was slightly cast, making it difficult to meet his gaze. At the moment, his face was the color of chalk. Dr. Vincent Smathers was a very angry man.

He barely managed to bring himself to a halt in front of my desk. He stood before me, fists clenched, trembling with rage. "What were you doing in my private laboratory?" he growled in a deep, rasping baritone.

I swallowed the last of the bagel, washed it down with coffee, patted my mouth with a paper napkin. "I got lost looking for the men's room," I said. It was no way to talk to a Nobel winner, but I was feeling a bit surly myself.

Smathers' tongue worked its way back and forth across his lips until he finally found the words he wanted. "You're a liar!"

"Okay, okay," I said testily. "I was looking for you or Dr. Kee. I wanted to consult you on a professional matter."

He swallowed hard and finally managed to bring his

voice under control; stripped of the distorting anger, it was deep and rich—almost hypnotic. "I believe my secretary informed you that neither Dr. Kee or I have time for such matters."

"I don't like doing business with other people's secretaries. You might have extended me a little professional courtesy."

"Courtesy!" he boomed. "The door to my laboratory was locked!"

"Not when I got there," I lied. "Talk to your keeper of the keys. The door was open when I walked by, so I just went up. The next thing I knew I was face to face with Fu Manchu."

"Do you realize you could have killed that man? You might have ruptured his spleen or his heart!"

"If I'd wanted to kill him, he'd be dead," I said quietly, trying to meet Smathers' curious, off-center gaze; he seemed to be looking at me first with one eye, then with the other. "The fact of the matter is that your helper got a bit pushy. I just pushed back. If you want to pursue the matter, file a complaint. Go see the Chancellor. He might like to find out what's so damn important to you that you feel the need to keep an entire floor locked behind two inches of steel."

That backed him up. He took his hands off the top of my desk and stiffened slightly. "I don't think there's any need for that," he said carefully. His gaze rose to a spot just above my head, then snapped back to my face. "We're both professionals. I have no desire to embarrass you, and quite frankly, I can't spare the time from my work that bringing formal charges against you would entail."

"What are you working on?" I asked casually.

"I didn't come over here to discuss my work, Frederickson."

"Sorry; I was just trying to make conversation. I can't help being curious as to what kind of research requires a human watchdog like the one that came after me."

Smathers made a nervous gesture with his hand. "If you must know, Dr. Kee and I are investigating some of the more bizarre human mental aberrations. On occasion we have potentially dangerous people on that floor. *That's* the reason for the security. Our assistant obviously thought you might have been one of our subjects."

I laughed. "You get a lot of crazy dwarfs up there, Doctor?"

The scientist didn't smile. "I repeat: the man simply thought he was doing his job."

"What's behind those locked doors, Dr. Smathers?"

His green eyes flashed. Smathers' apologetic number, not that good to begin with, was over. "None of your business. *God,* you have nerve! But then, I suppose a spy needs it."

"I wasn't spying," I said evenly. "I was looking for you."

"You will *not* come up there again, Dr. Frederickson!"

We stared at each other for a few moments across the narrow expanse of my desk. I was the one who finally broke the silence. "Interesting colleague you have. Did you know that Dr. Kee was an adviser to the Peoples' Liberation Army in North Korea? I understand he was a brainwashing specialist."

"That's slanderous," Smathers said, flushing. "Who told you that?"

"What difference does it make? It's just a rumor. Haven't you heard it?"

"I wouldn't pay attention to such a story."

"If Dr. Kee was in Korea, why try to cover it up? That war's long over."

Smathers' eyes narrowed and his voice dropped in pitch. "Why this sudden interest, Frederickson?"

"I have tremendous respect for anyone who wins a Nobel Prize," I said truthfully. "I simply wanted to meet you. It turns out you're a very secretive person. Of course, if you've got something to hide—"

"I have *nothing* to hide!" Smathers snapped. He paused, thoughtfully tapped his knuckles on the top of my desk. "All right," he continued with a slight air of resignation. "I knew when I invited Kee to work with me that he'd been in the Chinese Army during the Korean War. That fact was—and is—irrelevant; there are still people who would be very upset if they knew of it, and we thought it best to keep it to ourselves. Dr. Kee is an expert in induced aberrational psychology, and the only man in the world who knows enough about the subject to be able to assist me."

"How did the two of you get together?"

"You're *interrogating* me!"

"No, I'm not," I said easily. "I'm just curious; and you *did* say that you had nothing to hide."

Smathers was uncomfortable, but apparently felt he'd already said too much to stop. "I was attending a conference in Poland," he said defensively, staring at me with his cast eye. "It was made known to me through intermediaries that Dr. Kee was available and wished to come to the United States in order to work with me. I said that I was agreeable, and he joined me soon after that."

"Interesting," I said casually. "Are you still experimenting with sensory deprivation?"

"No! Why do you ask?"

I raised my eyebrows, said quietly. "It's what you won your Nobel for. Why *shouldn't* you still be working in the field?"

"Because the research is considered dangerous, and it's no longer approved of by my colleagues." The scientist hesitated; the focus of his eyes shifted until he seemed to be looking through me. I must have pushed the right button, because he suddenly started talking rapidly, with passion. "I was surrounded by fools!" he continued heatedly. "I was on the verge of a medical breakthrough as profound as the work they gave me the Nobel for."

"A cure for the common cold?"

"Don't mock me, Frederickson," Smathers said, breath whistling through his voice. "I'd almost discovered a cure for alcoholism. Alcoholism, like drug addiction, is primarily a psychological problem; despite the gross changes that take place in the body as a result of dependence, the problem is one of the *mind*. I can literally remold a mind, erase those problems—"

"By erasing the mind," I interrupted. "I've done a little reading on sensory deprivation. To put it simply, a man goes out of his mind; to be more precise, his mind goes out of him. You take away all of a man's sensory landmarks and he'll eventually become like a baby—with no past, present or future. He becomes extremely suggestible; brainwashed, you might say."

Smathers slapped his thigh in an impatient, angry gesture. "Don't use that archaic term with me! You're being hopelessly simplistic. To begin with, the minds of the people I'm talking about have been rendered useless *any-*

way. These men and women are no good to themselves or to anyone else. So don't moralize to me!"

"The thought never crossed my mind, Doctor."

Smathers suddenly thrust his shoulders back and raised himself up ramrod straight. "You will *not* interfere in my affairs again, Frederickson," he murmured in a quiet growl. "If you do, I'll make certain you regret it. You've been warned."

He spun on his heel and strutted stiffly out of the room, slamming the door behind him. I crumpled my coffee container and tossed it toward the wastebasket. I missed.

The confrontation with Smathers out of the way, I wanted to shift cases and see Esteban Morales. I drove over to Garth's precinct station and had already parked before I remembered that he was away for the weekend. I might have been able to get in to see Esteban on my own, but I didn't want to talk to the healer until I'd spoken with Garth—and I didn't want to talk to Eric Jordon until I'd heard what Esteban had to say. That seemed to leave me the weekend—almost. I went to the 42nd Street library and checked through the newspaper files for more information on the murder of Dr. Robert Samuels, but there wasn't anything important in the papers that I hadn't already learned from Janet and Senator Younger. I took a workout at the New York Athletic Club, cooked in the sauna for a half hour, then went to a movie.

I was in the middle of the Sunday *Times* Arts and Leisure section when Winston Kellogg called me.

"Good morning, Mongo," Kellogg said in his clipped British accent that ten years of living in Boston had done nothing to alter. "I have some information for you."

"I said *inexpensive* snooping, Winston; not haphazard. What the hell can you find out about a man in a day and a half, on the weekend?"

"Oh, you'd be surprised," Winston said, a faint trace of hurt in his voice.

"Try me," I said drily, activating my desk recorder and fastening the suction-cup attachment to the telephone receiver.

"Well, after my first lead, the best information I got was from contracts *I* have in New York and L.A. Very colorful stuff." He sniffed. "You *will* pay for my phone calls, I trust?"

"C'mon, Winston. For Christ's sake, I'll pay for the calls. And I apologize for questioning the quality of your investigation. Okay?"

"Very well," he said archly. "First of all, Smathers was eased out of Harvard because he insisted on continuing a research program the administration didn't approve of. He was into something called sensory deprivation."

"It doesn't surprise me. Look, Winston; keep on digging. You can even spend some—"

"Hey, wait a minute! I haven't gotten to the *juicy* parts yet."

Rumors. I felt my stomach muscles tighten. "Go ahead." I said quietly.

"Your man's a chicken hawk."

"Jesus," I whispered. "He likes boys?"

"Oh, not just boys. He likes little girls *too*; and big boys and big girls. He may like goats and sheep, for all I know. He doesn't seem to have any particular preference."

"A real swordsman, huh?"

"That's what I'm told. One of my police sources tells me that Smathers' name turned up on a list of *very* select clientele for one of the kinkiest cathouses you've ever heard of. I'll bet it beats anything you've got in New York. Anyway, the man's got some far-out sexual tastes; kids, necrophilia—you name it and he's probably tried it."

"Winston," I said softly, "are you serious?"

"Yes, Mongo, I'm afraid I am. You'll be getting my report—and some interesting photostats—in the mail. None of this stuff I'm giving you ever made the papers because of Smathers' reputation in the scientific community; he was protected. It seems he's a specialist in kinky behavior—but he's a goddamn weirdo himself. Watch yourself, my friend; I don't know how he feels about dwarfs."

Kellogg gave me some more particulars while I sat and listened, my eyes closed, breathing rapid with tension and distaste. When he'd finished, I thanked him and hung up. I took the tape off the machine and locked it in the small safe I kept in the apartment. Then I took a hot bath; I felt dirty.

On the spur of the moment, I decided to clean out my head by spending the afternoon reading poetry and listening to Medieval music at The Cloisters. When I passed 4D, I suddenly remembered that I had a third client, of sorts—one who'd hired me for fifty-seven cents. With luck, I hoped I could get *that* matter out of the way fast. I'd ring the bell, look for an invitation from Marlowe for coffee—and hope that Kathy would tell me it had all been a joke and demand her money back. I decided I'd keep a nickel just to teach her a lesson.

If the fear was still in Kathy's eyes, I'd ask Marlowe to let me take his daughter to the movies. One way or another, I hoped to find out what was on the little girl's mind.

The exercise was wasted; there was no one home. I spent the afternoon at The Cloisters, then went down to the Village in the evening to play chess.

Someone was calling my name. It was a child's voice, crying and terrified, a small wave lapping at the shore of my consciousness.

Suddenly I was running down a long tunnel, slipping and falling on its soft, rubbery surface as I struggled to reach the small, frail figure at the other end. Kathy's image seemed to recede with each step I took, and still I ran. She was dressed in a long, flowing white gown buttoned to the neck and covered with strange, twisted shapes. Then time blinked and she was before me. As I started to reach out for her, Kathy burst into flame.

I sat bolt upright in bed, drenched in sweat. My first reaction was an immense surge of relief when I realized I had only been dreaming. Then came terror as I smelled smoke.

Or thought I smelled smoke. Part of the dream? I started to reach for my cigarettes, then froze: there *was* smoke coming from somewhere. I leaped out of bed and quickly searched the apartment, but could find nothing burning. I yanked open the door of the apartment and stepped out into the hall.

Smoke was seeping from beneath the door of Frank Marlowe's apartment.

I sprinted to the end of the hall and broke the firebox there, then ran back and tried the door to 4D. It was locked, and I didn't waste time knocking. I braced against the opposite wall, ran two steps forward, doubled up in the air and kicked out at the door, just above the lock. The door rattled on its hinges. I picked myself up off the floor and repeated the process. This time the door sprang open.

The first thing that hit me was the stench. The inside of Marlowe's apartment was filled with thick, greenish smoke and smelled like a sewer. There was a bright, furnace glow to my right, coming from the bedroom. I started toward it, then stopped when I saw Kathy lying on the couch. What she was wearing filled me with a different kind of terror; despite what seemed to be the vivid reality of the stench and heat, I was certain I had to be in my bed, still asleep.

Kathy was clothed in the same gown I'd seen in the dream.

I screwed my eyes shut, shouted at the top of my lungs and drove my left heel into my right shin. My voice sounded real, pain shot through my ankle—and Kathy was still lying unconscious on the couch when I opened my eyes.

The child was the only reality that mattered, and I pushed the dream dilemma out of my mind as I bent over her and put my ear to her chest. Her breathing seemed normal and her heartbeat was regular, but she was completely unconscious, not responsive to either my voice or my touch. I gathered her up in my arms and carried her out into the hall. I gently laid her down on the worn carpet, then hurried back into the apartment.

There was nothing I could do there. Covering my mouth and nose with a handkerchief, wincing against the furnace heat, I stood at the entrance to the bedroom and gazed in horror at the bed, which had become a funeral pyre. The naked, shriveling body of Frank Marlowe was barely discernible inside a deadly ring of greenish-white fire that was burning too bright, too steady, to be a normal blaze. It was a chemical fire.

Back out in the hall, I checked Kathy's vital signs again. They remained steady, but her eyes, when I lifted her lids, were glassy and unseeing. I shouted at one of the stunned onlookers to keep everybody away from her, then sprinted back to my apartment and threw on some clothes. The fire department still hadn't arrived by the time I got back. Ambulance service being what it is in New York City, I picked Kathy up in my arms and carried her down to the underground parking garage. I laid her across the back seat of my Volkswagen, then raced to the university Medical Center, horn blaring all the way. She was immediately admitted through Emergency, and I nervously sat down to wait.

A few hours later a young black doctor emerged from the inner sanctum. "Excuse me, Doctor," I said, grabbing his sleeve. "How's the little girl? Kathy Marlowe?"

The doctor was frail and walked with a slight limp. He had thick, curly black hair and large brownish-black eyes that weren't yet glazed over by the endless pain one encounters in a New York City hospital. His flesh tone was a glistening ebony. The name tag on his white smock identified him as Dr. Joshua Greene. At the moment, he looked somewhat surprised to see a dwarf standing in front of him.

"Who're you?"

"My name's Frederickson."

The man's large, sensitive eyes narrowed. "I think I've heard of you; or I've seen your picture someplace."

"Never mind that. I asked how the girl is."

"Are you a relative?"

"No; friend of the family. I brought her in. Her father's dead, and I don't know how to get in touch with any other member of the family."

The doctor put his hand on my shoulder and guided me to a small alcove off the main corridor. I didn't like the way he walked and held his head; it was too sad, a little too desperate.

"My name is Greene," he said quietly. "We have . . . a problem with Kathy."

"What's the matter with her?" My throat felt dry and constricted; I could barely get the words out.

Greene shrugged his frail shoulders. "We really don't know," he said, his eyes clouding. "There's no sign of smoke inhalation, which was the first thing we looked for. Since then we've run a number of tests, but they're all inconclusive. There's no sign of any physical injury. She's just . . . unconscious. She's stable at the moment, but there are indications she may not stay that way."

"You mean she hasn't regained consciousness at all?"

He shook his head. "The child is in a deep coma, and we don't know what's causing it."

"Can't you treat it?"

Greene's laugh was sharp and bitter, belied by the anguish in his eyes. "Treat *what?* Coma is only a symptom, and none of those marvelous machines we have in there can tell us what's causing it." He swallowed hard, licked his lips. "There must be something in her background—an allergy, or some obscure hereditary disease. That information is vital. If we could only contact a relative . . ."

"I'll see what I can do about finding one. What about trauma? Could severe emotional shock precipitate a coma?"

"Maybe," Greene said carefully. "But there'd have to be some other contributing factor."

"What about drugs?"

The doctor looked at me a long time, obviously thinking about the question. "There are certain drugs that can induce coma," he said at last. "But if that's the case here, we're in trouble; we haven't been able to detect any foreign substance—yet. If she was given something, we'd have to find out exactly what it was before we could reverse the effects. And I don't think we have much time." He paused and shook his head. "Why would anyone want to drug this little girl?"

I didn't know the answer to that question, any more than I knew why someone had wanted to roast her father. But I was convinced that that was the case, and I intended to *find* the answers.

"Do you still have the gown she was wearing when I brought her in?"

"The one with the odd pictures?"

"Right. Will you give it to me?"

"Why?"

"I'd rather not say right now, Doctor. But I think the symbols on that gown could mean something. If I'm right, they could provide a clue to what's wrong with Kathy."

"They're just designs," Greene said impatiently. "It's a child's nightgown. What could it possibly have to do with the girl's condition?"

"Maybe nothing. But we won't know for sure unless you give me the gown."

"I don't know," he said hesitantly. "We have . . . procedures."

"That's *your* problem, Doctor," I said tersely. "You're the one who said we might not have much time."

He thought about it for a moment, then turned away, walked quickly down the corridor and disappeared through a swinging door. He reappeared a few minutes later with the gown wrapped in a plastic bag. I glanced at my watch: it was five thirty A.M. I was suddenly very tired, my senses drugged with the kind of hypertense, nervous exhaustion that is the mind's gambit to escape from pressure.

I felt cold, numb, disoriented; but most of all I felt fear for Kathy—and that was all I would need to keep me going. That fear would burn away the fog inside my mind. It had to. Like Frost's winter wanderer, I sensed that I had miles to go before I'd sleep.

Chapter 5

A heavy rain was falling, chilling the sooty New York City dawn. I parked on the street outside Garth's West Side apartment house and walked a half block to an all-night diner at the corner. I bought coffee and hard rolls, then called my brother from a booth in the back. He finally answered on the sixth ring.

"Yeah?"

"Good morning, Lieutenant. This is a close relative calling."

"What the hell do you want, Mongo?" he asked groggily. "You have any idea what time it is?"

"Frankly, no. It's early for you, late for me. I need to talk to you."

"I've got company."

"What am I, a priest? I don't want to talk to *her;* I want to talk to *you.* C'mon, brother. Would I be out here on the street calling you at this hour of the morning if it weren't serious?"

"Damn right you would." He paused, chuckled evilly. "How are the tympani lessons going?"

"Garth, let me come up."

Something in my voice must have struck a chord. There was a pause; then: "Okay, Mongo. But if this is a joke, I'm going to kick your ass. Fair warning."

"It's no joke."

"Bring coffee."

"I've got coffee."

Garth, dressed in a robe, met me at the door to his apartment. Unshaven, his thinning, wheat-colored hair uncombed, he looked as our father had looked early mornings on our Nebraska farm where we'd grown up. Garth and I had come a long way from the Midwest, by very different routes, and had both ended up in New York within a few months of each other. We liked that, liked each other. I owed the man; he'd helped me survive a dwarf's cruel childhood and adolescence.

Without a word, Garth reached down into the bag I was carrying and took out a container of coffee. He opened it and swallowed a large mouthful of the lukewarm liquid. Finally he looked at me, yawned. "You look like hell, Mongo. Come in and sit down."

I followed him into the living room and went straight to the bar, where I poured a stiff shot of Irish whiskey into my coffee. I drained off half of it, poured in another shot. That made me feel a bit better. I took the gown out of the bag and showed it to him.

"Does this mean anything to you?" I asked.

"Occult symbols," he said, examining the garment and nodding. "It could be a witch's robe if it were a little bigger. Where did you get it?"

"The little girl who was wearing it is in the hospital right now, in a deep coma. When you check the sheets this morning, you'll find that a man by the name of Frank Marlowe burned to death in his apartment about three o'clock this morning. The girl's his daughter. I was there, and it had to be a chemical fire; it was very hot, smelled like hell and formed an almost perfect circle around the bed."

Garth, wide awake now, held up his hand to stop me. "Whoa, brother. You're saying you think somebody killed this Marlowe?"

"Right. And whoever it was did something to the girl and dressed her in that gown. I—"

"Hold it," Garth said tersely. He rose and went into the kitchen. I heard him talking on the telephone, and a few minutes later he came back into the living room. He lighted a cigarette, then tilted his head toward me in what might almost have been a nod of approval. "Stop down at the station house later, okay? We'll want a formal statement from you."

"When I get time. I was about to say that the girl's doctors don't know what's causing her coma. There doesn't seem to be anything physically wrong with her—at least nothing they've been able to detect."

"There are drugs that can put a person into a coma."

"I know. If she is drugged, the problem is identifying

the drug before she dies. Obviously, whoever drugged her didn't intend for her to die right away; she was dressed in that gown, then left outside the circle of fire where someone could find her before the blaze spread."

"Strange," Garth said quietly, pulling at his lower lip.

"Yeah. I have to find out what's going on—in a hurry."

Garth got up, pulled open the draperies and stared out into the wet morning. The vanguard of the working people was beginning to fill the city, and the hissing sound of tires on wet pavement drifted up from the streets below. "What kind of son-of-a-bitch would do that to a kid?" he growled.

"You're the one who's been working that side of the street; I was hoping you'd be able to tell me."

He turned back to me, ground out his cigarette and lighted another. He took a deep drag, then blew the smoke out with a sigh of exasperation. "I deal mostly with a lot of wackos," he said. "I get groups sitting around a stinking, decaying body for a week while they try to raise it from the dead. I get small-time bunko artists, and the idiots who get taken by their mumbo jumbo. Every once in a while I tie into something big like the Son of Sam case, where some poor bastard thinks he's possessed by demons and starts killing people. But most of the stuff I see is small potatoes—cases with losers who got tired of being screwed by the natural and hoped to do better with the supernatural. There's always someone around to oblige them. This business that you describe, if you're right about it being a setup, sounds pretty sophisticated; you've got chemicals, drugs and a locked door."

"I thought all the real weirdos were in Southern California."

"The *organized* weirdos are in Southern California. Not counting victims, New York really has two layers of people involved in the occult. There are a lot of cocktail-party fortune-tellers, of course, but there are also some very sophisticated people who are very much into what they're doing."

"What do the symbols on the gown mean—if they mean anything?"

"I don't know," Garth said, shaking his head. But I can think of a couple of people who might. The guy I'd really like you to talk to is Michael McEnroe. He's a clairvoyant, psychic and teacher who lives down in the Village; supposed to be a real saint. The problem is that he's in India." He paused, rubbed his forehead. "You might talk to John Krowl. He works out of a brownstone in Brooklyn, just across the Manhattan Bridge. I'll give him a call for you."

"What does Krowl do?"

"He reads hands and tarot cards. He used to be one of McEnroe's students until they had a falling-out of some kind. He's a very heavy fellow."

"Meaning what?"

"Meaning . . . he's *heavy,*" Garth repeated, raising his eyebrows. "Krowl seems to be able to do exactly what he claims he can do: read your past, know your present—and maybe predict your future."

"Christ, Garth, you sound as though you're starting to take this shit seriously."

He didn't smile—didn't say anything. My words seemed to have triggered a whole train of thought in him, and for the moment he was lost in it. I was about to say something else when a tall, pretty redhead with green eyes stepped into the living room. She was dressed in one of Garth's shirts. My brother introduced her as Regina Farber.

"So you're Mongo," the woman said in a throaty whisper. "I've heard so much about you!"

"At your service," I said with a bow.

"Garth talks about you all the time."

"Quiet, Regina," Garth said with a good-natured growl. "The man's conceited enough as it is."

"I've got to get along, Garth," I said, tapping the face of my watch. "How about giving this Krowl a call now? I'd like to see him as soon as possible."

"Hey, come on. It's six o'clock in the morning. You're not going anywhere until you get some food in your belly and some sleep."

"I'm in a hurry."

"Sure you are. You haven't slept all night, and you haven't eaten. You go out of here now and you're going to fall right on your dwarf ass. That's not going to do you—or the little girl—any good. You know I don't give a damn what happens to *you,* but for the sake of the girl I'd like your brain to be functioning in full gear. So you're going to have something to eat, take a bath and sleep before you go back into the arena. In the meantime, I'll see what I can find out. Okay?"

Garth was playing Mother. I decided to let him get away with it, because he was right.

"I'll make us something to eat," Regina said, gliding on her long, slender legs toward the kitchen.

Garth turned serious again. "You talk about witchcraft and Satanism," he said, lowering his voice as though he didn't want the woman in the kitchen to hear. "Ever think about Charles Manson?"

"Have I ever *thought* about Charles Manson? Yeah, I've thought about Charles Manson; it's my business to think about nice folks like that."

"I'm not sure you have," Garth said evenly. "Not really. Here's an out-and-out punk, a failed songwriter, failed you-name-it, and he—"

"He was a successful butcher."

"Yeah, but he had *power*, Mongo; enormous personal power—enough to fuck up the minds of a whole flock of kids that he got to do his killing for him."

"Weirdos. It's all psychological."

"Of *course* it's psychological." He looked at me hard, sighed. "You're missing my point."

"I'm afraid so. Even Manson didn't claim that the Devil made him do it."

"Look," he said after a pause, "let me tell you about a case I just wrapped up. Last week, a woman wandered into the station house with this outrageous story. Witchcraft was involved, so it was referred to me. Well, her story turned out to be true. For the last eight months the woman had been enslaved by a 'spiritualist' she'd gone to for advice on how to cure her epileptic daughter. The spiritualist and her boyfriend had persuaded the woman to move in with them, along with her two kids. To make a long story short, the couple had been beating up on the woman for eight months; they'd been torturing her with lighted cigarettes, beating her with paddles and wire cables."

"How'd she get away?" I asked, not really caring. I was distracted by the thought of Kathy in the hospital, but sensed that Garth was trying to tell me something he thought was important.

He shrugged. "She was never actually locked up. She

didn't have to be confined, because she was *controlled.* The couple had convinced her that they'd cast a spell and that she'd die if she tried to escape. Anyway, she was sent out to buy some groceries and a friend saw her. The friend asked her where she and the kids had been for eight months, and she blurted out the story. The neighbor convinced her that she should go to the police."

He paused, blew a smoke ring, then impatiently swept it away with his hand. "The place was quite a sight," he continued. "All red: red carpets, red walls, red altars, red candles—red everything. Satanism. Somehow, that couple had even managed to turn the woman's *kids* around; the children would *help* beat their own mother. Up to Friday—which was the last time I checked it out—the little bastards *still* preferred the spiritualist and her boyfriend over their mother. Would you call that a spell?"

I swallowed hard; my mouth felt dry, sore with fatigue and anxiety as I thought of mothers squirtgunning cyanide into their babies' mouths in Guyana. "I'd call it a horror story. And I'm still missing your point."

"Have it your way, brother. I'm trying to give you some advice: if you're going to jump into this particular pond, swim with a straight face. Believe what you want to, but never let on that you don't take these people seriously—not if you expect to find out anything. *Especially* remember that when you talk to Krowl; he'll pick up on it in a second if you try to bullshit him. Keep your usual smart-ass remarks to yourself."

"*You* take Krowl seriously, don't you?"

Garth looked uncomfortable, and he took a few moments to think about his answer. Finally, he said, "You and I come out of our background with a certain set of preconceptions that we call 'reality.' It's damn hard giving up those notions, but someone like Krowl can start you thinking. I've seen and heard some things that are hard to explain."

"Did you go to Krowl for a reading?"

"Yeah," Garth said, lighting his third cigarette. "I'd heard about him and I was curious. What can I tell you? He wiped me out. Between a palm print and a few layouts of those tarot cards, he seemed to know my whole goddamn life. I'm talking about Elizabeth and the babies' deaths, what section of the country I come from, the fact that I was a county sheriff before coming to New York, and even the year I came here. He even knew about . . . Neptune."

We stared at each other in silence, the atmosphere in the room suddenly heavy with tension. A year before, Garth had been in love with an Iranian woman by the name of Neptune Tabrizi. An investigation I'd been conducting had resulted in her death. The discovery that Neptune's love for Garth had been a lie and a betrayal had not altered the fact that he'd loved her deeply. I knew all was forgiven, but Neptune was still a subject we avoided.

"I don't have the slightest idea how he does it," Garth continued. "All I'm saying is that *something* is going on. His list of clients reads like a Who's Who of celebrities: rock and movie stars, politicians and their wives, writers and artists. And those are just the people who don't mind publicity. I have a feeling we'd both be surprised at the names of some of the shyer ones who regularly use him as an adviser."

"Interesting, but tarot cards and palm reading don't sound like the kind of thing we have with that gown."

"You're right; the symbols on the gown definitely look like witchcraft, which isn't Krowl's number. But Krowl is an expert on the occult in general."

"How soon can I get to see him?"

"I don't know. I'll call him later, then get back to you. If you're out, I'll leave a message with your service."

Regina appeared with two steaming mugs of coffee. Garth took his, then excused himself and went into the bathroom to wash up. Regina wanted to talk, and I managed to carry on a fairly decent conversation, despite the fact that I was only half-listening to what the woman had to say. I sipped at the hot coffee, resisting the impulse to splash in another slug of Irish whiskey. My lack of sleep was beginning to take its toll; my eyes smarted, and I felt disoriented—although not sleepy. I kept thinking of Kathy, dwelling on the fact that her sleep could turn out to be permanent.

Garth reappeared, shaven and with his hair combed. He glanced at Regina.

"Excuse me again," Regina said, patting me affectionately on the forearm. "I think our steaks are just about done."

"I'm impressed," I told Garth when Regina had gone. "I thought this was the age of Women's Lib."

"Regina's liberated," he said. "The fact is that she likes me, she likes cooking, and she likes to leave when I'm talking business. *You* should find yourself such a liberated girlfriend."

I drained off the rest of my coffee. "You said there were two people who might be able to help me. Who do you have in mind besides Krowl?"

Garth looked uncomfortable. "I was hoping you wouldn't ask. I may have spoken out of turn; it's a rather confidential and very special source. Why don't you talk to Krowl first and see what he can tell you?"

"C'mon, brother. There's a child's life at stake here, and I haven't exactly had time to make up a schedule of where I'm going to be, or when. I don't know how I'm going to handle this yet, so why don't you just give me the name now? I'm not going to give it to the *Daily News*."

He thought about it, finally nodded. "You know her; she's a colleague of yours. Dr. Jones."

"*Madeline* Jones. Mad Jones is an *astronomer*. What the hell does she know about the occult?"

Garth laughed. "I've got news for you. That astronomer is also an astrologer—and a good one, if you can believe there is such a thing."

"Madeline *Jones?*" I knew I was repeating myself, but I couldn't help it. The woman he was referring to just happened to be a world-renowned astronomer, a cosmologist who was a leading expert on black holes and quasars. She spent half her time teaching, the other half flying around the world to deliver papers at various conferences.

Garth nodded. "Don't ask me the details, because I don't know them. Somehow, Dr. Jones got mixed up with the occult underground here—the heavies, not the weekend dabblers. She takes a pretty wry attitude toward the whole thing when I talk to her, but I can tell you that she's respected by the people who count."

"And how does *your* horoscope look for today?" I said with a grin, then quickly held up my hand. "Sorry; I'll remember to keep a straight face."

"I'm not into astrology, brother," Garth said, annoyance creeping into his voice. "I'm just telling you that Dr. Jones has a big rep. As an astrologer, the woman's damn near a legend. Naturally, she's a little nervous about word of her extracurricular activities getting back to *your* circles."

"*My* circles?" I laughed; the whiskey was starting to affect me. "I've got enough circles to make a sphere. How'd you meet Mad?"

"Breakfast's ready!" Regina called from the kitchen.

"Apparently, she gets pretty close to her students," Garth said quietly. "Last year, one of them got mixed up with a coven that turned out to be a homosexual procuring ring. They were really doing a number on the kid. Dr. Jones heard about it through her sources, and she came to me for help. She had to expose her own occult activities to me, but she was willing to risk her academic career to save the kid. Anyway, her friends in the occult protect her—and I protect her. She's been useful as hell to me. You'd be amazed at some of the kinky things otherwise sensible kids get themselves involved in. Dr. Jones is the best snitch I've got when it comes to these spook rip-off artists. I think she takes a kind of pride in keeping the field . . . pure." Garth must have seen something in my face, because he suddenly laughed self-consciously. "Weird, I know."

"I don't know how to get in touch with her," I said. "With her schedule, Mad could be anywhere in the world."

"She's at the university for the summer. I talked to her last week about another case."

"*Garth!*" Regina called. "*Mongo!* Get in here right now or it goes in the garbage!"

We went into the kitchen and sat down at the table. Regina had prepared steak, eggs, hashed-brown potatoes and toast. I hadn't realized how ravenously hungry I was until I started eating, and I wolfed down the food along with two more cups of Regina's strong, black coffee. Then my weariness hit me and I wanted nothing more than to lay my head down on the table and close my eyes. But there was still more business to be taken care of.

"What's the story on the psychic healer you've got locked up across town?" I asked.

Garth glanced up from his coffee, surprised. "Esteban Morales?"

"That's the one. How does it look to the cops?"

"Why?"

His question put me in a bind. Garth had broken a confidence by telling me about Madeline Jones, and he wasn't going to like if it I turned coy on him. Still, I didn't want to say too much while Regina was there.

"Garth," I said, looking down into my empty coffee cup, "someone who thinks Morales is innocent has asked me to look into the case."

I glanced up in time to see Garth narrow his eyes. "That's very nice of someone," he said softly.

"My client has . . . personal reasons."

"Christ, you're a busy man."

"You don't know the third of it," I said, thinking of Smathers. "The interested party is a very heavy politician who can't afford to have his name linked with a psychic healer."

"I can understand that—particularly when the healer is accused of murder. Why is Morales so important to him?"

"It *is* very personal, Garth. Let's just say that he's as impressed by Morales as you are by John Krowl."

"Do you want me to leave?" Regina asked, reacting to my tone and starting to rise.

"It's all right," Garth said, gripping her elbow and gently pulling her back down into her chair. "I don't really have that much to say, Mongo. I think you'll be wasting your time on that one. You know the background of the case?"

"Some of it. I know Morales was involved in a research project, and his work with the two doctors was part of it. He was working with their patients."

Garth nodded. "Samuels—the M.D. he killed—had filed a complaint on him, something about practicing medicine without a license. Samuels claimed Morales had administered drugs to a patient—something he'd been specifically prohibited from doing. It was channeled to me because Morales is billed as a psychic healer."

"Why is everyone so damn sure that Morales is the killer?"

"He was found standing over the body. Samuels and Jordon met every Thursday night at their offices to go over their business affairs. Morales got there early one night and slit Samuels' throat. Dr. Jordon came in a few minutes later and found Morales with the body. Morales had dropped the knife he'd used into a vial of acid."

"Then it was Jordon who reported the murder?"

"Right."

"That I didn't know. Sounds suspicious."

Garth smiled condescendingly. "Why? Jordon wasn't anywhere he wasn't supposed to be."

"What does Morales say happened?"

"He claims he received a call from Samuels asking him to meet Samuels a few minutes before Samuels' meeting with Jordon. When he got there, he saw the body and went over to it; that's when Dr. Jordon walked in. Hell, what would you *expect* him to say?"

"Does he have a lawyer?"

"Legal Aid."

"People who know the man say he's not a killer."

Garth shrugged. "Hey, he's a real nice old fellow; but then, even nice old fellows have been known to kill."

"How much investigating are you doing?"

"We're looking into it, but there just isn't anyone else with a motive to kill Samuels."

"No one that you *know* of, and you're not likely to *find* anyone else without a little digging. A complaint isn't that strong a motive, Garth."

"Hey, what can I tell you? He was found standing next to the body."

"Can I get in to see him?"

He thought about it, said: "Let me know when you're ready. If Morales and his lawyer don't have any objections, I'll see what I can do." He paused, drummed his fingers on the table. "Personally, I like the old man; I hope you *do* find out something. But I don't think you will."

"Thanks, brother. I'm not sure when I'll get to that, but I would appreciate it if you'd check with Morales. Tell him I'd like to help, if I can."

"Fair enough."

I knew I needed sleep, but wasn't sure I could. I shaved with Garth's razor, then took a hot shower. I dressed again, then lay down on the couch. I'd intended simply to rest until a more reasonable hour when I could try to reach Madeline Jones—but I was asleep by the time I put my feet up.

Chapter 6

My sleep was filled with recurring dreams of Kathy bursting into flames. I awoke with a start, realized where I was and anxiously glanced at my watch. It was nine thirty. Despite the fact that I'd had only two hours of troubled sleep, I felt oddly invigorated; it was an unnatural, nervous energy, fueled by anxiety—but I was grateful for it. It was time to go out and do battle again.

Garth and Regina were gone. I made myself a cup of acrid instant coffee, then called the university and asked for Madeline's extension. She answered the phone herself.

"Hey, darlin'," I said. "Guess who?"

"Mongo!" she exclaimed in her sultry, breathy voice. "My God, I haven't seen you in *months.*"

"Well, that's not my fault; *I'm* not the one traipsing all over the world. I've got all the crooks I need right here in New York." I paused, lowered my voice. "Mad, I'd like to talk. Got a half hour for me?"

"Sure," she purred in a tone that always made me feel flushed. "And here I was afraid you'd forgotten all about me."

"I'll be there in a few minutes; I believe I'm going to have to take a cold shower first."

She laughed huskily, hung up.

I drove to the university, parked, then walked to the Hall of Sciences, where I found Madeline in her suite of offices. If there was order in the universe, it certainly wasn't reflected in Madeline Jones's working quarters. As usual, her office was cluttered with charts, telescope parts and other astronomical paraphernalia. A coffeepot was percolating on a hot plate on a corner of her desk, its pleasant aroma filling the room.

Madeline's hair, a natural strawberry blond in old photos she'd shown me, was now a burnished silver. She wore it long, swept back from her face in a manner that gave her a sleek, sexy look. She was pushing fifty, but daily, vigorous jogging had given her the face and body of a thirty-year-old, and she had the glittering, playful eyes of a teen-ager. She was a sensual woman, and made no effort to hide the fact; she was attractive—and energetic—enough to have carried on a string of affairs with a procession of lab assistants twenty years her junior. Madeline Jones might have been many things, but a tease wasn't one of them. I'd had more than one thinly veiled invitation from her, but had passed each time. I wasn't sure why; maybe she scared the hell out of me—or maybe I simply didn't want to jeopardize a cherished friendship.

Madeline glanced up from a celestial map she'd been studying and grinned at me as I entered the office. "Hello, Sugar," she said throatily, sea-blue eyes flashing. "Remember to take your cold shower?"

"*Please* don't test me, darlin'," I said, going across the room and kissing her hand. "*Damn,* you're a good-looking woman!"

"You look tired," she said seriously.

"I am, babe."

"Oh!" she said playfully, pointing to the package I carried under my arm. "You've brought me a present!"

"Not exactly, Mad," I replied, unwrapping the gown and handing it to her. "I'm told you might be able to tell me what these symbols mean."

Madeline tentatively took the garment from my hand and examined it. When she looked up, her eyes were veiled. "What makes you think I'd know anything about these designs?" she asked guardedly.

"Garth told me about you, Mad. Lieutenant Frederickson. Did you know he was my brother?"

"I knew," she said icily. "He had no right betraying my confidence."

It was the first time I'd ever seen her angry; somehow, it made her even more beautiful. "Garth wouldn't have done it if it weren't absolutely necessary, Mad. This is an emergency. A little girl's life could depend on what I can find out about the symbols on this gown—and how fast."

I quickly filled Madeline in on the details of what had happened during the night. As Mad listened, her face became stiff and she seemed to grow increasingly agitated.

When I told her about Kathy's condition, she raised the back of her hand to her mouth as if to stifle a cry. When I finished, she abruptly turned and walked to the opposite side of the room.

"The girl's lucky she has you as a friend, Mongo," the astronomer said very softly. "You were right; the symbols do mean something. I don't know *what's* been done to her, but something *has* been . . . done. The girl's life is definitely in danger. The gown is covered with magical vengeance and attack symbols. It's meant that she should die . . . and I think her death is meant as a warning to someone."

"You mean the girl was poisoned in order to send a *message?*"

"Yes," she said so softly that I could hardly hear her. "You might say that."

Mad's back was to me, muffling her voice even further. I walked across the room in an effort to see her face, but she turned away from me. I stopped where I was. "Can you tell from the gown *who* the warning is meant for?"

Madeline shook her head; the slight movement sent her silver hair undulating back and forth across the back of her head in shimmering waves. "No," she said. "As far as what's been done to her, witches would probably try to use something organic. There are certain herbs that could be used, like hemlock, but I don't know much about those things." She paused, then whispered, "It's so unbelievably *evil* to use a child like that."

"Mad, does the term 'book of shadows' mean anything to you?"

Now she slowly turned to look at me. There was surprise in her face. "A book of shadows is a witch's diary," she said. She sounded distracted, and the focus of her eyes slowly shifted until she was looking somewhere beyond me.

"A witch's *diary?*"

Madeline nodded. "It's a collection of spells, omens, dreams, coven rituals—anything the witch considers important. It's meant to be a record of spiritual growth."

"Can a man be a witch?"

"Most definitely," Mad said distantly. Her gaze slowly came back into focus on my face. "Anyway, a book of shadows is a witch's most precious possession. It's only seen by other members of the witch's coven—if it's shared at all."

Which seemed to mean that Frank Marlowe had been a witch. Without question, he'd been traveling in nasty company; and whoever had done him in hadn't lacked brains, nerve or skill. They'd known enough about herbs or drugs to poison Kathy with a substance that seemed to be virtually untraceable; enough about chemicals to arrange for a chemical fire by delayed combustion; finally, they'd been cool enough to lock the door behind them.

A message. But for whom?

Smart, yes; evil, definitely so. But there was something that just didn't make sense to me. Marlowe might have been strange, but I'd sensed that he was basically a decent man; I couldn't imagine him belonging to the kind of group that had probably killed him.

So far, I couldn't see how anything Madeline had told me could be of use in finding out what was wrong with Kathy. I decided to take a flyer. "Mad, do the names 'Daniel' and 'Esobus' mean anything to you?"

Mad's eyes widened and her face grew pale. *"Esobus?* Does Esobus have something to do with this?"

Her sharp reaction startled me, and I felt my stomach muscles tighten. "Possibly. Why, Mad?"

She put her hand to her brow, momentarily shielding her eyes. "It's incredible," she said in a weak, baffled tone, slowly shaking her head. " 'Esobus' is a witch name—a pseudonym. There have been rumors for months about a very powerful and evil ceremonial magician in New York using that name."

"What's a 'ceremonial magician'?"

Mad took her hand away from her face and sighed. "Mongo, what *do* you know about witches, or the occult?"

"Yesterday, I'd have made a smart remark about broomsticks and pumpkins," I said evenly. "Now I'm just listening."

Mad's eyes had gone out of focus again, and I wasn't even sure she'd heard me. "From a Christian point of view, you might describe a ceremonial magician as an upside-down priest," she said. "But it really has nothing to do with Christianity. A ceremonial magician is a priest of the occult—a master."

"A heavy witch?"

"Yes and no. Both are seekers of knowledge and power, but ceremonial magicians are really beyond witchcraft. Witches form covens. Thirteen is considered a magical number; as you probably know, it's the traditional number of witches in a coven. Witches try to work their will on the world, and they believe the coven protects them from being consumed by the very forces they're trying to summon forth."

Madeline's voice trailed off, as though she had lost her train of thought—or was thinking of something else. Her eyes looked roiled, muddy. I was about to say something when she continued: "Ceremonial magicians work alone. Witches believe that the ceremonial magician learns to control the world around him as he learns to control himself. There are some who are supposed to be able to control matter—or even create life."

"Do you believe that?"

She smiled thinly. "No, I don't believe that. But the story on Esobus is that he *destroys* life; he attempts to accumulate personal power through the conscious pursuit of evil."

"I'm not sure I follow that reasoning."

"Of course you don't; that's because you're a good person. Most of us, if we hurt somebody, are quick to say we didn't mean it. Esobus—if there is an Esobus—makes no such rationalization, and seeks no forgiveness. It's looking-glass ethics: the search for a kind of salvation through evil. Anyway, I've heard a rumor that Esobus has created what you might call a 'super coven' here in the city."

"Why?"

Madeline shrugged. "I don't know, Mongo. I think it's just a story."

"I'm impressed, Mad; you do get around. Do you have any idea what Esobus' real name is?"

She shook her head slowly and deliberately. "I doubt that Esobus even exists," she said distantly, tension in her voice. "I think he's just a legend—something for Black Arts occultists to believe in. Like God. In the end, Esobus may turn out to be the Wizard of Oz."

"This Wizard of Oz sounds pretty dangerous."

Mad looked at me a long time, as though still lost in thought. "You still haven't told me what Esobus has to do with the girl's condition," she said at last.

"On Friday, the girl told me she'd heard her father say he thought either this Esobus or someone named Daniel had stolen his book of shadows. He was worried about it. That's the reason for all these questions."

"If a ceremonial magician took this man's book of shadows, it would have to be for a very good reason," she said quietly. "It would be like a minister stealing a sacred relic from someone else's church."

"What about this Daniel? Is he a ceremonial magician too?"

"Yes," she said tautly.

"But you don't know who he is?"

"I know who he is," Mad replied after a long pause. "But he won't talk to you about this—or about anything else having to do with the occult. You'll be wasting your time. These people have a saying: 'Those who know don't talk, and those who talk don't know.' "

"You've been talking, and I think you know what you're talking about."

Madeline smiled wryly. "A child's life is at stake. Besides, it's different with me; I'm a scientist. I'm interested in the pursuit of knowledge, not personal power."

"Most of your colleagues might find some irony in that statement," I said gently.

"To say the least. But I don't worry about what my colleagues think—only what they know. What they're not aware of they can't worry about."

"You get me to this Daniel, and let me worry about striking up a conversation."

She slowly walked around behind her desk, sat down. She suddenly looked much older, and very tired. "Daniel's real name is Richard Crandall," she said in a low, strained voice. "He lives and works in Philadelphia. I don't know his home address, but this is the name and address of the bank where he's vice-president." Madeline quickly wrote down the information on a piece of paper and slid it across the desk to me. I picked up the paper and put it in my pocket.

"Daniel is the most celebrated ceremonial magician in this part of the country," Madeline continued, reaching across her desk and touching my arm. "That doesn't mean anything to you now, but it might in a few days. You'll undoubtedly find Daniel strange, but he's a *very* strong-willed and powerful man. Until now, no one outside of the most sophisticated occult circles knew of his secret spiritual life, accomplishments or reputation. You now become the exception. His identity was a kind of 'gift' offered to me in honor of my own . . . accomplishments. I'm giving you Daniel's real name because I realize you must do everything you can to save this child's life. But I have to ask you not to tell Daniel how you found out about him."

"I understand, and I won't. Do you think he's dangerous?"

"I've never met him personally. I know that he's respected—and feared—by those who do know him personally. That's something for *you* to bear in mind, my friend. My concern is that he could cut me off from my occult contacts."

"And they're important to you, aren't they?"

"You know they are," Mad said, then dropped her gaze.

I stared at the top of the scientist's head for a moment, then turned and walked toward the door. I was very conscious of the fact that every minute could count, and I was anxious to get to my car and begin the drive to Philadelphia. Yet something made me hesitate with my hand on the knob and turn back; perhaps it was the realization that I was entering a world I didn't understand at all, and was anxious about it. Madeline's *seriousness* had had an impact on me.

"Mad," I said softly, "what's this all about?"

She looked up at me and frowned, obviously lost in her own thoughts. "Excuse me?"

I smiled. "How is it you've never told me before about any of these hidden talents of yours? God knows we've sat through enough boring faculty parties together."

After a few seconds Madeline smiled thinly and seemed to relax. "What would your reaction have been if I *had* told you?"

"I'd have choked on my Scotch, of course."

"That's what I thought," Mad said wryly. She paused, tapped her desk once, then continued in a low voice. "It started as a hobby. I was *curious* about things like the statistical rise in the crime rate when there's a full moon. Astronomy evolved from astrology, you know, and astrology is ages old. I believe that anyone who rejects out of hand the tools that other men have found useful for thousands of years is a fool. The Occult is the Mother of Science, my friend."

"It seems to me that science is what *replaced* ignorance and superstition," I said evenly.

"That's true," Madeline replied easily. "Most of what you read about the occult in the popular press *is* nonsense." She paused, looked at me intently. "But not all of it is nonsense, I assure you. It's like digging for diamonds; you may have to wade through twenty tons of coal before you find even a small gem. I've been willing to get dirty."

"What if there aren't any diamonds? Maybe science has taken all there is to take from that particular mine."

"Oh, there are still diamonds there, Mongo. As far as I'm concerned, astrology—done properly—is really nothing more than the application of statistics. The question is simply stated: Can you correlate the position and movement of certain celestial objects with people's behavior? Insurance companies do almost exactly the same thing all the time; they charge rates based on a person's neighborhood, occupation, race and so on. You don't see many insurance companies going out of business, do you?" She raised her eyebrows, shrugged. "Either the trends of a person's life correlate with the predictions of his horoscope, or they don't. You'd be surprised at how often they *do* correlate. Statistics."

She paused, tilted her head to one side and looked at me inquiringly. When I said nothing, Mad opened her desk drawer and took out a series of charts and graphs. She rose, laid the papers out in front of her and motioned for me to come over. I did so, increasingly impatient to be on my way but anxious to hear everything Madeline had to say. She seemed excited now, totally absorbed in whatever it was she wanted to share with me. The charts were complex computer readouts of letters and numbers that made no sense to me whatsoever.

"This is a statistical analysis I'm working up," Madeline continued. "It will include all the horoscopes I've ever cast, as well as charts from other well-known astrologers. The subjects are letter-coded to ensure anonymity. I won't bother you with the details, but the idea is to codify specific astrological predictions in a research model that can be scientifically evaluated. If my hypothesis is correct, I'll end up with statistical proof that astrological techniques *can* be used to predict behavior."

For some reason I thought of Janet Monroe and her work with Esteban Morales. "Interesting," I said. "Where do you get your funding?"

She laughed sharply, without humor, as she replaced the charts in her desk drawer, locked it. "No one else even knows about what I'm doing here. This is my own private project."

"How do you justify your computer time?"

"I steal time from my other, 'respectable' projects. It's the only way I can do it."

"Mad, I can get into what you're saying about astrology as statistics—at least, in theory. But what about things like witchcraft?"

She thought about it for a few moments, then raised her hand and slowly drew a circle in the air with her index finger. Her blue eyes were moist, gleaming. "We live in a circle of light that we call 'Science,'" she said thoughtfully. "Obviously, *I* believe in science. Science is the most *efficient* means Man has ever found for discovering certain truths—and for *getting things done*. That doesn't mean that science is the *only* way. To say that science is efficient can never take away the wonder of what some men are able to do through self-discipline. Maybe these powers are vestigial. Perhaps there are men who still pursue—and find—secrets that our ancient ancestors knew instinctively. Let's suppose there are still unbelievably powerful forces out there in the darkness which some men have learned to tap. The term 'occult,' after all, means nothing more than secret knowledge. Understand: I'm just trying to give you a different point of view."

"Thank you, Mad," I said, assuming she was finished. "You've put me in the proper frame of mind—and I mean that sincerely."

She didn't seem to have heard me. Madeline Jones was deep in thought, and it suddenly struck me just how deeply obsessed this astronomer was with the occult. Only then did I realize that, up until a few minutes before, I had persisted in looking upon her involvement as some kind of off-the-wall professorial joke. It wasn't: Madeline Jones was deadly serious.

"Are you religious, Mongo?" she asked distantly. "I don't want to offend you."

"Say what's on your mind, Mad. You won't offend me."

"I know for a fact that most of the very scientists who would ridicule me are the stalwart members of churches or synagogues. They're intellectual schizophrenics; they just won't accept the fact that orthodox religious beliefs are every bit as 'occult' as witchcraft."

She looked through me, laughed shortly. "In Westminster Abbey, there's a mausoleum for the Black Knight," she continued in the same distant, ironic tone. "Beside the tomb is a small, typed sign advising all to pray on that spot for their relatives and loved ones in the armed services." She paused, shook her head. "*That,* my friend, is a pure example of 'sympathetic magic'—a straight steal from the occultists."

I smiled. "You'd better not let your neighborhood clergy hear you talking like that; they might want to stage a public burning."

Madeline smiled back, and I had the feeling some of the tension in her had passed. "I do get carried away, don't I? But ignorance bothers me, especially when the ignorant are so damn self-righteous." She hesitated, studied my face intently for a few moments, then continued: "Did you know that the Magi mentioned in the Gospels were probably astrologers?"

"I think I've read it somewhere."

"Our word 'magician' comes from 'magi.' The 'star' they saw in the east, if it wasn't a supernova, was probably an astrological configuration they knew how to interpret. And it led them to Jesus." She took a deep, shuddering breath. Once again her eyes were wide and bright. "Most people consider only two possibilities when they think about Jesus of Nazareth. Either he *was* the Son of God, and could thus perform miracles—or he *wasn't,* and therefore the accounts of the miracles must be false. What excites me is a *third* possibility: Jesus may have been the greatest ceremonial magician who ever lived."

"Hmmm. Sounds like a rather unusual theory." I was hoping my stab at dry humor might at least get a smile from Mad, but she was oblivious to everything but the ideas bouncing around inside her head.

"Early Christian history is permeated with astrological

symbology," she continued excitedly. "Jesus, with his disciples, numbered thirteen—the classic number of the witches' coven. The sign of the early Christians was the fish—and Jesus lived in the age of Pisces."

Madeline now lapsed into silence. I glanced at my watch. It was past eleven, and I wanted to get on the road before my body realized I was operating on only two hours of sleep. "I've got to go, Mad," I said. "Thanks for the information and advice. And don't worry: your secret's safe with me."

She looked up and nodded. "Good luck, Mongo. I hope the little girl will be all right."

Outside, the August sun was hot. I felt a chill, although I couldn't tell whether it was caused by fatigue or by fear that Madeline could be right. Perhaps there *were* powerful, dark forces that I knew nothing about and could not combat; perhaps someone was using that power to kill Kathy.

And I had stepped into the line of fire.

I told myself that that kind of thinking was silly. Still, as if in self-defense, I stood on the sidewalk for a few minutes, my head tilted back, savoring the feel of the bright, cleansing sunlight on my upturned face.

Chapter 7

I stopped at my office and called Dr. Greene at the hospital. He sounded as tired as I felt, and just as worried. Kathy had still not regained consciousness, and there'd been a change for the worse: her heart was beginning to show signs of irregular beating. Although Greene was personally supervising the various tests, with only a few hours off to sleep, the doctors and technicians still had not been able to identify the cause of Kathy's coma. I repeated to Greene what Madeline had told me about the possible use of poisonous herbs. By the time I hung up, my weariness had been replaced by acute anxiety. I ran to my car.

Within a half hour I was through the Lincoln Tunnel and on the New Jersey Turnpike, heading for Philadelphia. I cruised at seventy-five, keeping an eye on the rear-view mirror for state troopers.

The hot, white afternoon had a bracing effect on me; it was as if the heat and light formed a friendly committee of Nature welcoming me home after many hours spent wandering in a dark, nightmare cave which I'd assumed, before talking to Madeline, was reserved exclusively for the ignorant. Zooming along on the sunlit highway, I found it hard to believe I'd spent the last few hours talking about witches and witchcraft, covens, astrology and ceremonial magicians; somehow, those things just didn't sit well inside my head in the middle of the day. But then there was the strange case of Madeline Jones—a respected scientist who led a double life as an astrologer. To say that Mad was obsessed explained nothing. As far as my client and I were concerned, it was a good thing she was; Madeline had given me potentially invaluable information about the occult. Still, out in the sunlight, I found I was worried about Madeline. But I was more worried about Kathy; a little girl was dying, a victim of these eerie spinners of twisted dreams, and that was the only reality I cared about.

I got off the Turnpike at Cherry Hill, New Jersey, then drove on and crossed over the Benjamin Franklin Bridge into Philadelphia's Franklin Square.

Unlike W. C. Fields, I liked Philadelphia. Only two hours from New York City, it was at once a vast warehouse crammed floor to ceiling with fascinating history, and a place of human *ordinariness;* it was this feeling of vaguely boring nonhurry that made it, on occasion, a welcome relief from the constant, draining excitement of New York. After my painful immersion the year before in the ancient culture and politics of Iran, I'd become highly sensitized to the infancy—and wonder—of my own country's history. As a result, I'd spent a number of weekends soon after my return visiting Philadelphia's historic sites. If I hadn't been knotted tight with tension and anxiety, it probably would have felt good to be back.

The address Mad had given me was in a fashionable area of Broad Street, near the Academy of Music. The sight of Richard Crandall's place of employment only added to my sense of surreality; a bank seemed a rather odd place to find a ceremonial magician. But then, not even Madeline—for all her obvious respect and fear—had claimed that Daniel could change lead into gold. It seemed even ceremonial magicians had to eat, and it looked as though this particular specimen was eating well; as Madeline had indicated, he was sitting in the bank vice-president's chair. His nameplate was flanked by Christmas Club and Hannukah Club signs.

Crandall looked the part; that is, he looked more like a bank vice-president than a master of the occult arts—whatever such a master looked like. Maybe I'd been expecting Orson Welles in drag. At the moment, Crandall was busy talking to a customer. He looked to be over six feet, and I judged him to be in his mid-thirties. He had close-cropped, prematurely gray hair which coordinated well with his matching eyes and gray pin-striped suit.

I sat down on a banquette covered with green imitation leather and waited, feeling my anger grow. Crandall must have felt my gaze on him, because he suddenly glanced up. Our eyes held. Perhaps it was exhaustion working on my brain, but there seemed to be something startling about his steady gaze. We stared at each other for what seemed a long time, and I could feel a warm flush working its way up the back of my neck, spreading across my cheeks. Finally he looked away and resumed talking to his customer.

When Crandall had finished, I rose and walked up to his desk. He was unconcernedly leafing through a sheaf of papers. Finally he stacked them neatly on one side of his ordered desk, then looked up at me. "Yes, sir?" he said evenly. He had an announcer's voice, deep and rich.

For some reason, I felt I had lost a round in our staring contest. I was anxious to recoup, but the studied air of self-confidence in his voice was as unsettling as his piercing stare. Both made me angry. "What the hell kind of a witch name is 'Daniel'?" I asked evenly, hoping to score back. "It just doesn't have the pizzazz of, say, 'Esobus,' or even 'Old Scratch.' "

I looked for a reaction, but there wasn't any—unless an almost imperceptible quick intake of breath could be judged a reaction. His eyes didn't change at all. He let his breath out slowly, but his face remained passive, almost blank, as though he were looking straight through me. He waited a few seconds, then said softly, "Excuse me?"

"Your witch name is 'Daniel,' " I said too quickly. "Word is that you're an occult Ph.D. I want to talk to you."

Crandall's right hand dropped below the desk for a moment, then resurfaced; it looked as if I were about to lose another round. I figured I had five to ten seconds before someone responded to the silent alarm, and I intended to use every one of them.

"You listen good, you son-of-a-bitch," I said softly, leaning on his desk. "There's a little girl dying two hours away from here. I think you had something to do with it, and if you don't set me straight fast I'm going to come down on you. Hard. For openers, I'm going to make sure that the stockholders of this bank find out about your weird hobbies. If the girl dies, I'll kill you. Believe it."

The depth of my rage surprised me. Up to that moment I'd been distracted by my concern for Kathy, but now I was struck by the full import of what someone had *done* to her. My words had been propelled by a searing hatred for the sick mind or minds responsible for an innocent child's suffering.

Time was up. I could feel the bank's security guard come up behind me, and I stiffened as his hand gripped my shoulder. I looked hard at Daniel, who suddenly held up his hand.

"It's all right, John," Crandall said easily. "My knee hit the button by mistake. Dr. Frederickson is a customer."

The hand came off my shoulder. There was a mumbled apology, then the sound of receding footsteps. I never took my eyes off Daniel's face. He rose and gestured toward a door to his left. "Come with me, please," he said softly.

I followed him into a small conference room which was richly carpeted and paneled in shades of burnt orange. He closed the door, then turned to face me. "I believe you *would* try to kill me, although I don't know why," he continued softly. He had his head tilted back and was looking at me through half-closed lids, as if he were about to fall asleep. He looked almost comical, but what I found disconcerting was the fact that he made *me* feel odd; there was a sensation of heat and pressure in the pit of my stomach. I reminded myself that I'd only had two hours of sleep, and was running on reserve batteries of adrenaline and emotion.

"To kill *me*," he continued in the same, soft tone, "you'd have to know how to use the hate you feel now, then be able to conquer it and ride it to a conclusion. Can you do that? I doubt it. Very few people can."

"It's simple, Crandall; I'll just beat you to death with a broomstick. I said I wanted to ask you a few questions. Answer them right and you can go back to changing people into frogs, or whatever it is you do in your spare time."

"I will answer nothing," the gray-eyed man said casually.

Suddenly he stepped forward until he was only inches away from me. In a lightning motion, he reached down with his right hand and touched me squarely between the eyes with the tip of his third finger. It was a light tap, and yet it actually hurt; I was beginning to feel like a character out of Carlos Castaneda. Normally, my reflexes would have propelled me at him, but now, inexplicably, I found myself stepping back. I felt confused, weak and tired. I was losing rounds all over the place.

"You're to take what I say as a threat," Crandall continued casually in a voice barely above a whisper. "As you see, I know who you are; your career is familiar to me. I don't know how you came to know of me. I can't think of anyone who would dare give you information about me; but, obviously, someone did. No matter. There's absolutely nothing—*nothing!*—you can do to me. But I can . . . inflict. You'll discover that to your sorrow if you try to interfere with me in any way." He paused a few beats, then said in a slightly louder voice, "Now *you* will answer *this* question. Why did you mention the name 'Esobus'?"

"It has to do with the little girl who's dying. She told me either you or Esobus took her father's book of shadows."

Daniel blinked rapidly and took two quick steps backward. It wasn't much of a reaction, but from this man I considered it a major concession.

"Her name is Kathy Marlowe," I continued. "Her father's name is Frank Marlowe. Someone's done a bad number on that girl, and you're a major candidate. There isn't much time left, and I intend to find out what's wrong with her before she dies of it."

Crandall's impassive, stony facade suddenly began to crumble before my eyes. He opened his gray eyes wide, looked at me for a long time; his tongue darted out, licked his lips. Finally he turned and walked quickly across the room. He stopped, his back to me, and stared out a window overlooking the bank's parking lot.

"Tell me what you did to her, Crandall," I continued quietly, making no effort to keep the pleading out of my voice. "You don't seem like the kind of man who'd hurt a little girl and not regret it." I picked up the telephone receiver on the conference table next to me, held the instrument out to him. "Tell me what's wrong with her so we can call her doctor and tell him."

"I wouldn't hurt Kathy," Crandall said in a dry, croaking voice. "She's my niece."

I slowly replaced the receiver in its cradle. "What did you say?"

The man who called himself Daniel turned and looked at me strangely. His gray eyes seemed darker, his gaze even more intense. "You heard me," he said sharply. "I tell you because I want you to know I'm not responsible for Kathy's condition, and I don't want you interfering with me. Does Kathy's mother know?"

I shook my head. "I don't know how to get in touch with her. Kathy mentioned her once or twice, but I didn't really pay attention. Frank Marlowe and I were only casual acquaintances; aside from the fact that he was divorced and Kathy stayed with him during the summer, I didn't know anything about his private life. You're the first relative I've been able to find."

His eyes narrowed. "How did you become involved with this in the first place?"

"Kathy asked me to find her father's book of shadows," I said, still slightly stunned by the information that Daniel was Kathy's uncle. "Apparently, she heard her father say that either you or Esobus had stolen it."

I filled Crandall in on what had happened. He listened in silence. When I'd finished, he nodded distantly. "Thank you for saving Kathy's life," he said quietly.

"She's still in great danger. Her mother should be told right away."

"I'll take care of that, Frederickson," he murmured. He seemed totally distracted as he fumbled inside his suit jacket, produced a checkbook. "I appreciate what you've done. Let me pay—"

"I don't want your money, Crandall," I said sharply. "Your niece is my client, not you. And I still have a lot of questions. *Did* you take Frank Marlowe's book of shadows?"

It was some time before he answered. "This is an affair of sorcerers," he said at last.

"Terrific. I can't wait to use my thirty-eight-caliber wand on one of those bastards. I think it's time we called in the police."

"The police can't do anything for Kathy. Neither can you."

"But *you* can?"

"I'm the *only* one who can."

"And I say you're full of shit. You tell me Kathy's your niece, and I believe you. I also believe you didn't hurt her. But you damn well know more than you're telling me; you're plugged into this screwball scene right up to your eyeballs." I sighed with frustration and weariness. "For Christ's sake, she's your *niece* and you're playing with her life! Why don't you just tell me what this is all about so we can call in the proper authorities?"

"Stay out of this!" he hissed. "And stay away from me! I tell you there is *nothing* anyone else can do! I know what I'm talking about."

He again raised his right hand and started to move toward me; his hand was balled into a fist except for the ring finger, which was rigidly extended, pointing at my forehead.

"Touch me again and I'll crack your kneecap," I said, going into a crouch.

Crandall stopped, slowly put his hand down. That round went to me. I waited for him to say something, but he walked quickly around me and out through the office door. I followed, but he strode straight ahead and out of the bank without a backward glance. By the time I got to the street, he'd disappeared from sight. I walked to my car, got in behind the wheel and pulled out into the traffic.

I was almost sideswiped at the next corner, and it was only when I glanced in the rearview mirror that I realized I'd run a red light. I opened the window and took a deep breath; I was going to have to start paying attention to the all-too-real world around me. What with psychic healers, screwball Nobel Prize winners and homicidal witches, the previous Friday looked to have been a real loser on my horoscope.

Lack of sleep finally caught up with me an hour out of Philadelphia. The deadly monotony of the New Jersey Turnpike beat on me like a club. When I caught myself weaving back and forth between the center line and the shoulder of the road, I parked at the first rest stop, crawled into the back seat and promptly fell asleep.

I woke up at six fifteen feeling grubby but refreshed. I used a gas-station rest room to wash up, then sped into New York and went directly to the hospital. Visiting hours were over at eight thirty, but I made it by eight. Kathy was in the Intensive Care Unit, with no visitors allowed. I'd hoped to check with Dr. Greene, but I was told he wasn't available. That meant he was catching up on his sleep, which was probably more important than anything he could say to me. I left a message for him to call me at home whenever he could.

I was on my way to the elevator when I caught sight of a familiar figure sitting next to a woman in a small waiting room off the corridor. I went in. "What's the latest word on your niece?" I asked Daniel.

There was a vacant look in the ceremonial magician's eyes as he turned his head and looked at me. Without a word he rose and walked from the room, leaving me alone with the woman. She was short, maybe a foot or so taller than I was, and strikingly beautiful in a natural, totally understated way. She had to be Daniel's sister, because she had the same gray eyes, with just a touch of blue. The eyes were large and sensual, with natural long lashes. She was dressed in soft leather boots, French-cut jeans and steel-blue silk blouse. Around her neck she wore a necklace consisting of a fine gold chain supporting a dove which had been carved from ivory; the dove and silk on denim added just the right touch of vulnerable femininity. She had what looked like natural reddish-blond hair that fell neatly across her shoulders. She struck me as a person who was normally very much in control of herself. Her eyes were dry at the moment, but they were red-rimmed, and it was obvious she'd been crying before I walked in.

"You must be Robert Frederickson," the woman said, rising and offering me her hand. The hand was small and smooth and fitted easily into mine. "I'm April Marlowe; Kathy's mother."

I motioned for her to sit down again, then sat beside her. "How's Kathy?" I asked.

For a moment I thought she was going to cry, but she didn't. "Dr. Greene says that she seems stable."

"But she's still in a coma?"

April Marlowe nodded. "Yes, but I'm confident the doctors are doing all they can." She paused, dropped her eyes. "Dr. Greene and my brother told me about all you've done. You saved Kathy from the fire, and I know you're still trying to help. Please don't be offended, but I know you're a professional detective; I'd . . . like to pay you."

"I'm not offended, Mrs. Marlowe, and paying me isn't necessary. Kathy's already taken care of my fee."

"Kathy—?"

"Never mind; it's not important. I assume Dr. Greene has asked you about Kathy's medical background?"

She nodded slowly. "Kathy doesn't have any allergies. It seems she's been . . . poisoned." She suddenly reached out and touched my hand. "Mr. Frederickson, how can I thank you?"

"How long have you been here?"

"Three or four hours," she said. "My brother picked me up after he'd spoken with you. Why?"

"Then you haven't eaten?"

She shook her head, clasped her hands together tightly. "I'm not hungry."

"I am. If you don't mind eating with an unshaven dwarf, I'd like you to have dinner with me." She glanced at me quickly, puzzled and perhaps a little frightened. "I know a nice restaurant in the next block," I continued. "I'll leave word at the nurses' station where to reach us if there's a need, but I suspect we could all be in for a long siege. There's nothing to be done here now, so let's eat. I'd like to ask you some questions."

She thought about it, then gave a barely perceptible nod of her head. I took her elbow and helped her to her feet. I left word at the nurses' station that we'd be at the Granada, and wrote down the number.

"Where's your brother?" I asked the petite woman as we headed toward the elevator. "Maybe he'd like to go with us; in fact, I'd like it if he did."

"He won't talk to you," she said softly. "He'll find us if he wants to see us."

It was true that Crandall could always check at the nurses' station to see where we'd gone, but I sensed that April Marlowe hadn't meant it that way. I glanced sideways to see her face, but she was obviously thinking about something else. I guided her into the elevator and pushed the button for the ground floor.

At the restaurant I insisted she have a drink, and she ordered a Dubonnet on the rocks. I felt sufficiently rested to have a double Scotch.

"I can't drink at all," the woman said, flushing at the first sip of her wine.

"It's all right," I said, smiling. "You're in safe hands. Go ahead and drink it; it's good for you."

The waiter took our order, then brought rolls and butter. April Marlowe absently buttered half a roll, nibbled at it. "I must apologize for my brother," she said hesitantly. "I know he must seem . . . strange to you."

" 'Strange' is a polite way of putting it, Mrs. Marlowe. His niece is dy . . . very sick; I'm sure he knows something about this business but he won't say what it is. Now, that *does* seem 'strange' for a loving uncle. There's *prima facie* evidence that a crime has been committed, and I think it would be a good idea if the cops sweated him a little."

"Oh, that wouldn't do any good!" she said quickly, dropping her roll. Her blue-gray eyes were suddenly filled with alarm. "Daniel loves Kathy; he'd no more hurt Kathy—by omission or commission—than I would."

"You're not a loony."

April Marlowe put her elbows on the table, clasped her fingers together under her chin and stared at me. She almost smiled. "Daniel didn't tell you, did he?"

"Tell me what? Your brother won't even give me name, rank and serial number."

"Obviously, he didn't tell you that *I'm* a witch," the woman said evenly. "Wicca has been a way of life in my family for generations." Again she almost smiled. "We lost three ancestors in the Salem witch trials; two were burned, one was hanged."

"I didn't mean to offend you, Mrs. Marlowe," I said quickly, embarrassed.

She took another bite of her roll. As she ate, I noticed that she had a pale brown birthmark on her left cheek; it was a small imperfection that somehow made her even more beautiful. "You didn't offend me, Mr. Frederickson," she said. "You don't know any better because you don't understand. How could you be expected to? There's so much misinformation and prejudice about wicca that you couldn't be expected to know there's more to it than dancing naked around bonfires."

"I'd like to know more, Mrs. Marlowe. Will you tell me about it? It could help me understand what's happened to Kathy."

"I don't think it will," she said distantly. "The people who have done this thing are as alien to me as they are to you. Wicca is *not* evil, Mr. Frederickson; it's *neither* good nor evil, any more than Christianity, in itself, is good or evil—despite the evil that some men have done in Jesus' name. Wicca is simply an Earth religion which emphasizes sensitivity to the natural forces in the world around us. A *Sabbat* is no different from any other religious ceremony."

"Except that your average participant at a prayer meeting isn't trying to do tricks," I said—and immediately regretted it, because I recognized almost as soon as the words were out that I was wrong.

And the woman knew I was wrong. She smiled gently, as at a child. "Wicca, among other things, teaches that you can change your life—and the lives of others—through an intimate relationship with Nature. 'Tricks' aren't really the point; the witch is concerned with that part of human consciousness we refer to as the 'deep mind,' which is really a commonly shared racial consciousness. It's true there are mysteries involved in what we believe—numbers, dates of the year and so on. But that's true of all religions."

She sipped delicately at her wine, patted her mouth with her linen napkin. "It's really very simple," she continued quietly. "Wicca requires no massive organizational structure, no ornate buildings for worship, and no money to sustain it. In this sense, it's very close to what the early Christians practiced. In fact, the reason why witches were burned was primarily socioeconomic, and the church knew *exactly* what it was doing.

"You see, in the 1600s the vast majority of people were peasants, and they practiced wicca. This posed a threat to the social and economic well-being of the rich landowners who controlled the Church; their answer to the problem was to start burning people." She paused and smiled disarmingly. "So much for a *very* biased history lesson. Anyway, we believe that the best way of nurturing and refining our deep minds is through the coven."

"Daniel doesn't belong to a coven."

"That's true, but what Daniel tries to do is far beyond what most witches concern themselves with."

"I've heard him compared to a priest."

"That's a good analogy," April Marlowe said thoughtfully, nodding in agreement. "He works on his own deep mind, and the deep mind of others, alone—without the protection of a group. That can be dangerous. Daniel eventually reached a point where a higher plane of consciousness and control could only be reached by going on alone. That was when he started on the road of the ceremonial magician."

"A hard road, I take it." I felt sarcastic, hoped I didn't sound it.

"Yes," the woman replied evenly.

I picked up a roll, slowly and meticulously buttered it. "Mrs. Marlowe, I don't know anything about the tough life of a ceremonial magician, but it seems to me that your brother is playing spiritual games at a risk to Kathy's life."

"No," she said quickly. "I trust and respect Daniel. Whatever he does, he does for a reason. And he *always* goes his own way, even if that way is incomprehensible to others."

I vividly remembered the force of Crandall's tap on my forehead, and the hypnotic power of his presence. "What if thirteen of these ceremonial magicians got together and formed their *own* coven?"

She thought about it, shrugged. "Well, you'd certainly have a powerful coven—at least, in theory. Who *knows* what would happen? I've never heard of such a thing. I know that's not much of an answer, but it's an odd question. I can't think of any reason *why* a group of ceremonial magicians would want to form a coven."

"Maybe they'd want to burn a man to death and poison his daughter."

April Marlowe's eyes widened. "I don't understand what you're getting at."

"Your brother doesn't talk to you very much either, does he?"

She was about to reply when the waiter brought our food—*paella* for two. April Marlowe ate and sipped at her wine, and she began to look more relaxed. I felt better too. For a few minutes the nightmare I'd been living for almost twenty-four hours was put at a distance, and I was simply having dinner with a beautiful woman. The mood lasted only as long as it took us to finish our dinner; the fact that the woman's daughter was dying only a city block away was too real and terrible to suppress for long.

"There are rumors that a ceremonial magician by the name of Esobus has set up just such a supercoven," I said as I signaled the waiter for coffee.

"I don't think that's true," she said evenly. "There's been talk of this Esobus for years, but I think he's just a myth. *No* one could be as powerful as Esobus is supposed to be."

"Just how powerful is that?"

She considered it for a few moments, then said: "That's hard to explain without getting into a discussion of the 'tricks' that you don't believe in. Anyway, Esobus is supposed to be a 'black' magician dedicated to evil."

"So I've been told. Have you ever heard anyone's real name associated with Esobus?"

She shook her head. "Not with the Esobus we're talking about. Oh, from time to time some witch will adopt the name, but those people are just silly dilettantes. 'Esobus' is a very powerful name. Any ceremonial magician powerful enough to assume that mantle simply *wouldn't;* he'd adopt a name of his own. That's why I doubt this Esobus is anything more than a legend."

"This particular legend may have stolen your former husband's book of shadows."

She put down her coffee cup, frowned. "What on earth are you talking about?"

"Daniel didn't mention that either?"

April Marlowe slowly shook her head. "What would there be to tell me? Frank wasn't a witch. On the contrary, he always thought wicca was a big joke."

Chapter 8

The mysterious, many-mooded creature that is the New York night somehow reminded me of a number of things, including Vincent Smathers; its body was a complex game board of light and dark where there were as many games as there were people and you never knew what move to expect next. Where we were, the beast was feeling good; the block between the restaurant and the hospital was brightly lighted. Children played stickball in the street, using potholes for bases. Older boys and men played basketball and paddleball in a lighted playground in the middle of the block.

As we slowly walked, I told April Marlowe everything I'd learned. She listened with growing agitation, knotting and unknotting the sleeve of the light sweater she'd thrown over her shoulders.

"I just don't understand any of it," she said when I'd finished. "Kathy told you that either Esobus or *Daniel* stole Frank's book of shadows?"

"That's right," I said, gently easing her down on a bench under a mercury lamp in a corner of the playground. "Apparently, she heard him talking to himself."

"Frank certainly did talk to himself, but I wasn't aware he was even *interested* in wicca."

"Well, it's obvious he was. It's also obvious that he was killed—and Kathy probably poisoned—by occultists, most likely witches."

"But *Daniel?* They only met once, at some family gathering, and they didn't show any particular interest in each other. If they ever saw each other after that, no one ever mentioned it to me. Even if Daniel *had* found out that Frank was into wicca, why steal Frank's book of shadows? It doesn't make any sense."

"Whatever happened makes sense to Daniel, Mrs. Marlowe. I'm certain of it. What I told him about your former husband and Kathy *upset* him, sure . . . but I don't think he was really surprised."

She put her head in her hands, rubbed her temples. "I'm sorry," she whispered. "It's all just . . . totally incomprehensible to me."

We sat in silence for a few minutes. I lighted a cigarette, offered her one. She declined. "Please tell me about Frank, Mrs. Marlowe," I said.

"Please call me April."

"All right. If you'll call me Mongo."

She looked up, raised her eyebrows slightly. *"Mongo?"*

"It's a circus name."

"You used to be in the circus?"

"But of course," I said, smiling. "Don't you know that the circus is dwarf heaven?" That usually got at least a chuckle from most people; April Marlowe just stared at me. "I was billed as Mongo the Magnificent," I continued. "The name stuck."

"I'll tell you about Frank," the woman said softly. "But first you have to tell me about the time you spent with the circus."

I did, and was surprised at how easily it all came out. The years I'd spent with the circus were, overall, a painful memory for me. I'd used the money I'd earned to finance my studies. In the course of my earning a Ph.D., the university and I had made the mutual discovery that I was good with students; I'd accepted their offer of a faculty position. The private-detective business had come later. I wasn't rich, but I was reasonably happy. That was what I told April Marlowe.

She'd listened intently, with an interest that I found absurdly flattering. "You're a fascinating man," she said evenly. "From circus headliner to college professor and private detective."

"Oh, just an average superdwarf."

She still didn't smile. "Your self-mockery doesn't always become you," she said somewhat sternly. "You're a very remarkable man. Since you're no longer a circus performer, I think I'll call you Robert—if you don't mind."

I still felt like a performer; I'd always feel like a performer. But I said, "I don't mind, but no one else is going to know whom you're talking about."

"You asked about Frank," she said with a curt nod. "As I'm sure you know, he was a very successful writer. What you may *not* know is that he was a very unhappy one."

"That's not unusual for creative types."

She shook her head. "This is more than that. He'd been unhappy for years with the work he was doing. He considered it all junk—and I suppose he was right. You may not realize this—how *could* you?—but Frank could have been a *good* writer; he had a lot more talent than you'd suppose from just reading those series genre books he churned out. He felt trapped—felt he'd trapped himself, really. He was making a great deal of money from the stuff he was writing. Naturally, his publisher couldn't get enough of it. But more than anything else he wanted to write what he referred to as a 'big book,' by which he simply meant a *good* book. He wanted to write something he could put his own name on and be proud of. It ate at him for years—and it finally cost us our marriage. It must have gotten even worse, because I know he was drinking quite a lot this last year."

The paddleballers on the court nearest us were arguing over one of the players' calls. I'd happened to be looking in their direction while April was talking. When they glanced over at me, I signaled that the ball had been out over the back line. There was some grumbling from the losing side over how I could make a call from so far away, but they went back to their game.

"Why didn't he just *write* his 'big' book, or at least take a crack at it?" I asked, turing back to April. "He certainly had enough money to tide him over."

She thought about it, shrugged. "I really don't know, Robert. He was so *used* to what he was doing. Also, of course, his publisher wasn't interested in publishing the kind of 'straight' book he wanted to do; he was under constant pressure to keep turning out the genre books."

"Again: he had plenty of money. Why didn't he just take a couple of years off?"

"I guess he was under his *own* pressures," she said after a thoughtful pause. "In the end, perhaps he was simply . . . afraid that he didn't have that good book in him." She paused again, ran her finger along the edge of the wooden bench. "As a matter of fact," she continued quietly, "the pressure may finally have gotten to him in another way besides the drinking. He always sent Kathy and me copies of his books—sometimes as many as eleven or twelve a year. We hadn't received *any* for the past year. He must have been blocked, afraid he was drying up." She sighed, put her head in her hands. "Maybe that's why he turned to wicca."

"Maybe. How long have you been divorced?"

"Four years, but we stayed good friends. Frank adored Kathy, and she adored him. As you know, Kathy spent summers with him."

"Did you speak often?"

"Oh, yes. We were always on good terms; we just didn't love each other anymore. He often used the house to store things—tax records, manuscripts, contracts—that sort of thing. Even with all his money, he preferred living in a small apartment, and I have a big attic. In fact, he and Kathy stayed . . ." She choked, put her hand to her mouth, took a deep, shuddering breath. "Kathy and Frank were at the house over the weekend. Frank had driven up to leave something in the attic." She suddenly rose with a start. "I'm worried, Robert; I've been gone too long."

"The hospital's only five minutes away," I said, rising and taking her arm. As we left the playground, two of the paddleballers smiled and waved; the other team scowled. "If Frank wasn't writing," I asked quietly, "what did he want to leave with you?"

April Marlowe looked at me strangely. "I don't know, Robert," she said distantly.

"Can you find out?"

"I suppose so. Do you think it's important?"

"I have no idea, April. It could be."

"Then I'll go back and look for it as soon as I can. But the attic is a mess; I have no idea where he put what he brought, and it will take me hours to dig through . . ." Her eyes grew moist as her voice trailed off. "Right now I have to stay close to Kathy."

"I understand. Do you have a place to stay?"

"Dr. Greene has arranged for me to stay at the hospital."

"Where's your brother staying?"

"I don't know."

I gave April Marlowe my home and office numbers, and

we hurried back to the hospital. Kathy's condition was unchanged.

In the morning I awoke with a start and glanced at my watch; it was ten thirty. I'd slept around the clock. I immediately called the hospital, but the reception desk would tell me only that Kathy's condition was listed as "serious." I asked them to switch me over to the residential room where April Marlowe was staying. April answered on the third ring.

"It's Mongo," I said. "I hope I didn't wake you up."

"Good morning, Robert," the woman said in a heavy, sad tone. "You didn't wake me."

"Were you able to sleep at all?"

"Some. The wine and the dinner helped relax me—as you knew they would. Thank you. And Dr. Greene gave me something to help me sleep."

"Anything new on what's wrong with Kathy?"

"No," April said tightly. "She's still in a coma, and her heartbeat's slightly irregular. The neurologists here are working on her, and Dr. Greene is assembling a team of specialists from other hospitals."

There was an uncomfortable silence in which I found myself with nothing to say. I suddenly realized why, and I felt slightly guilty; beyond my concern for Kathy, I'd thoroughly enjoyed dinner with April Marlowe the night before. I enjoyed hearing her voice over the telephone, and I looked forward to seeing her again.

In some circles, lusting after a comatose girl's mother might be considered a bit tacky.

"Uh, I'll be by later to check on her," I said at last. "You try to get some rest. Do you need anything?"

"No. Thank you, Robert. If I'm not in my room near Intensive Care, I'll probably be having coffee. Be sure to find me, okay?"

"Right."

When I hung up, I realized something was missing; it was the painful knot that had been in the pit of my stomach since early Monday morning. Kathy was in one of the finest medical centers in the world, and the doctor in charge of her case was intensely concerned about her; it would be hard for any group of mere witches to top those odds.

Now, with a full night's sleep in my head, I decided I must have been suffering delusions of grandeur to suppose that Kathy's life could depend on anything I might or might not find out about the gown she'd been dressed in. In the bright morning, I was filled with confidence that Greene and his team of specialists would quickly discover what was wrong with Kathy, and cure her; it was inconceivable to me that they wouldn't. My concern had shifted to wanting to find the people responsible for putting her in the hospital in the first place. I wanted to drum out a few tunes on their skulls.

I checked in with my service and was told that Senator Younger had called the night before and was anxious for me to get in touch with him. The Chancellor had called at eight; he wanted me to come in and see him. Also, Yvonne Mercado had called.

Yvonne could wait. When I called Barnum's office, I was told that he'd be free to see me in a half hour. I said I'd be there. I started to dial Younger's number, then hung up. I remembered all too well the fear and pain in the Senator's eyes, and the confidence Janet Monroe had expressed in me. It would do no good to tell him that something else had come up; it had been four days since I'd spoken with him, and his daughter was also dying. The fact of the matter was that I hadn't even had time to talk to Esteban Morales, much less look into the case against him. I wasn't prepared to tell Younger I'd been weighing the life of his daughter against that of someone else's.

Reluctantly, I gathered up the file I'd started on Smathers based on the information Winston Kellogg had provided me with. I put it into my briefcase, along with the recording of my telephone conversation with Kellogg and a small, portable tape player. Then I drove downtown to the university.

The towering glass-and-stone buildings of the school with its vast, arcane treasury of human knowledge, combined with the ubiquitous murmur of New York's technology, proved a good antidote to the case of creepies Marlowe's death and Kathy's hospitalization had given me. I stood in the middle of the student plaza for a few minutes, armoring myself with the university atmosphere. As a result, I was five minutes late for my appointment.

Barnum was pacing impatiently back and forth across his carpeted office.

"Good morning, Chancellor," I said.

"Good morning, Frederickson," Barnum replied curtly, moving around behind his desk. He lowered his lanky frame into his leather-covered swivel chair. "I appreciate your coming in to see me on such short notice. Please sit down."

I did, placing the briefcase on my lap. "Do you think it's a good idea for us to meet here?" I asked evenly.

"Probably not," Barnum said shortly, "but I hate deceit." He shifted his angular form forward in his chair, began tapping his fingers nervously on his desk top. "In fact, I've been having second thoughts about this whole matter. I'm not sure what I've asked you to do is . . . appropriate." He cleared his throat. His gray eyes seemed cold and distant, as though he blamed me for his discomfort. "I know you've only had a few days, but have you, uh . . . have you found out anything?"

Barnum wanted it both ways. He wanted to find out whatever there was to know about Smathers, but he didn't want to get his hands dirty; in short, he wanted me to decide for him whether or not to continue the investigation. At the moment, that responsibility was resting heavily on my thighs. What my briefcase contained could easily destroy the reputation of a brilliant scientist.

Very carefully, like a man toying with the pin on a hand grenade, I fingered the latch on the case for a few seconds, then abruptly set the case on the floor. "It doesn't make any difference, sir," I said. "I've decided not to take the assignment anyway."

"Then you too feel . . . uncomfortable?"

"Yes, sir, that's part of it. Also, frankly, something more important has come up, and it requires my full attention. I wouldn't be able to continue this investigation in the manner it deserves. That wouldn't be fair to you—or to Dr. Smathers."

He looked at me for a long time, his eyes boring into mine. *"Continue?"* he said at last. *"Have* you found out anything?"

"As you indicated, there are rumors," I answered after giving it some thought. "But that's all." I took Barnum's check out of my pocket and placed it on the desk between us. I wasn't about to destroy a man on the basis of what I'd heard. Neither, apparently, was the Chancellor.

"But you *have* heard something?" Barnum said tightly.

"Yes; but as far as I'm concerned, what Smathers does with his personal life is his business." For all I knew, Smathers had been living like a monk since coming to New York; the brush with notoriety and the law in Boston had to have given him a scare.

Barnum thought about it, nodded. "Please keep the check, Dr. Frederickson," he said, picking up the piece of paper and holding it out to me. "I insist. You have gone to some trouble."

Reacting to the pride in his voice, I took the check. I got up, started for the door, then hesitated and turned back. Barnum was still seated at his desk, staring absently after me. He looked like a man suffering from acute indigestion. I respected the man, and knew that I'd probably left him with an even heavier burden than he'd come to me with. I'd been coy, to say the least, and I felt I owed the man something for his money.

"Chancellor," I said, "I've been up to Smathers' complex, but I couldn't find out anything other than the fact that Kee's Chinese assistant spooks easily. Smathers has everything locked up tighter than a drum. I suppose that's his right—maybe even his responsibility, if he's working with expensive equipment and bizarre types. But I'd think that *somebody* in the administration has a right to know what he's doing—you don't need a private investigator to find out what it is. That's my opinion as a faculty member, not a detective."

"I agree, Frederickson," the man said thoughtfully with a curt nod of his head. "I think perhaps I've been neglecting my responsibilities. I'll look into Dr. Smathers' professional activities myself. Thank you for your time and advice."

Walking out of the Administration Building, I felt a surge of relief; I hadn't wanted to investigate Smathers to begin with. Now I was free of that burden, and I didn't think the Chancellor had been offended. It *was*, after all, Barnum's responsibility to monitor research activities at the university; if he wanted to find out about Smathers' extracurricular activities, he could hire somebody else to do the investigating.

As if to underline my reticence to dig up personal dirt, I glanced up and spotted a Chinese walking toward me. He was tall for an Oriental—over six feet—and stocky. His head was shaven, and he wore heavy horn-rimmed glasses. His dress was rather odd for New York: flowered Hawaiian shirt, ill-fitting blue serge slacks, white socks and wing-tipped cordovans. He looked almost comical, like something out of a World War Two propaganda film. But there was nothing funny about the way he walked and carried himself; his movements and bearing had a distinct military stamp. I was convinced the man was Kee, and I instinctively sucked in my breath. However, the Chinese walked on past me with barely a glance in my direction. That was worth a sigh of relief; I'd been expecting Round Two of Frederickson versus the behavioral psychologists.

My good feeling didn't last long.

"Mongo!" a familiar voice called from behind me. "What luck! I was just looking for you over at your office."

The woman who approached me across the stone plaza was young—twenty-four—and brilliant. Dr. Yvonne Mercado had graduated from the university at seventeen, earned her master's at nineteen and her doctorate at twenty-one. A widely published cultural anthropologist, she'd been around the world several times, charting various cultures. Yvonne also happened to be lovely, with a dark, lusty beauty. She was touted by the university as the successor to Margaret Mead, but I didn't see it that way. Mead had obviously empathized with the people she studied; I tended to look on Yvonne as something of an academic hotshot, seeing people in terms of statistics, books, monographs and awards. She had an unsettling habit of saying exactly what was on her mind. But I liked her, and suspected she might mellow with age.

"Hello, Yvonne," I said, uncomfortable because I was pretty sure I knew what she wanted to talk to me about.

"I tried to call you last night, but your service said you were out."

"I got the message. I was planning to get back to you later."

"Do you mind if I walk with you?" the pretty woman asked. "Where are you heading?"

"To my office; and I don't mind at all."

Yvonne fell into step beside me. "Janet told me you're trying to help Esteban, and she thought you might want me to give you some more background on him. He's such a *precious* man. Have you talked to him yet?"

"Not yet. I'm on my way to make arrangements for that now. I've had other things on my mind."

Yvonne glanced sideways at me, raised her eyebrows. "Mongo," she said reprovingly, "Senator Younger's daughter will *die* without Esteban's help. What could be more urgent than that?"

I told her. Yvonne listened with intense interest, her dark eyes shining brightly.

"My God," she whispered when I'd finished. "That's *fascinating*."

"It is?" I showed her I could raise my eyebrows too. "I haven't had the time to be fascinated; I've been too scared."

Yvonne was impervious to the sarcasm. "You know," she said thoughtfully, "you're only *assuming* that the child's been poisoned. Have you considered the possibility that she's under some kind of spell?"

I stopped walking and wheeled to face her. "What the *hell* are you talking about, Yvonne?" I said impatiently. "For Christ's sake, I'm up to my eyeballs in this mumbo-jumbo garbage. What amazes me is that I'm hearing it from people who are supposed to know better."

The excitement in the anthropologist's eyes turned to hurt. "I've never heard you be intentionally rude before, Mongo," she said quietly. "Why are you angry with me?"

"Forget it, Yvonne. I'm just feeling boorish. I'm sorry."

"No, *I'm* sorry," she said after a long pause. "I can see now that . . . I must have seemed insensitive. I do get carried away with . . . strange situations. But I am concerned, believe me." She hesitated, and her voice dropped. "Will you listen to what I have to say? I've seen this kind of thing before; if there's even a remote possibility that this *is* a spell, the girl's life could depend on what you do. Give me the benefit of the doubt that I wouldn't waste your time."

"C'mon, babe," I said, squeezing her elbow. "Let's sit down."

We moved off the plaza and sat down on the surrounding grass, crossing our legs Indian fashion and facing each other.

"Are you familiar with the concept of 'membership'?" Yvonne asked.

"I belong to the New York A.C.," I said. "Aside from that, I'm not much of a joiner."

"I'm talking about an anthropological concept," she said tightly. It was her turn to be impatient.

"What's your point, Yvonne?" I asked, trying to soften my bluntness with a smile.

She plucked at the grass in front of her as though she were having trouble selecting her words. "You know, Mongo," she said at last, letting the broken blades of grass fall to the ground, "I maintain that it's anti-intellectual to deny that other realities beside our own exist; there's too much evidence to the contrary. The 'membership' I'm talking about is different. You don't consciously join one of these groups; your induction begins at birth. And the terms of your membership are stamped on your conscious *and* subconscious mind."

"All right: so I'm a member of a Western, technological, rationalist society."

"Yes!" Yvonne said excitedly. "My point exactly!"

"Membership" was obviously a subject Yvonne enjoyed talking about, and I had a vision of her anxiously stalking me ever since Janet had told her I might want more information about Esteban. Despite my affection for Yvonne, I wondered how much she really cared about the healer—or Kathy.

"Your *membership* in this society automatically affords you a set of immunities to some anxieties, and vulnerability to others," she continued. "In many ways, we are what we believe."

"Are you implying that Esteban can't heal anyone who doesn't believe in him?"

"Not at all," Yvonne said, shaking her head emphatically. "Esteban is a *psychic* healer. His psyche—his life force—emanates some kind of powerful energy that works independently of the attitude of the person he's working on, the same as an electric light will work regardless of whether the person operating the switch 'believes' in electricity. Esteban's power is mysterious only because we haven't yet been able to codify and label it.

"A *faith* healer is a perfect example of the 'membership' I'm talking about: your tribal shaman, Oral Roberts, President Carter's sister. All can heal, Mongo; make no mistake about it. But faith healers have a selective clientele; *they* can heal only those who *believe* they can heal, through their respective deities."

"They can only affect members," I said quietly. I could see where Yvonne was heading, and I felt a prickling sensation at the base of my neck.

Yvonne slowly nodded. "A faith healer probably couldn't do anything for you or me, because we're not members of charismatic religious groups. I *study* them, yes; but that doesn't make me a member, by any means. You and I believe in *Science,* and that gives us our own special set of vulnerabilities. For one thing, we're liable to end up on a psychiatrist's couch when Science can't otherwise come up with a cure for what ails our souls."

"I know," I said quietly. I'd been there. And I couldn't help thinking of Kathy lying unconscious in a coma that seemed to be intractable to the best treatment modern medicine had to offer. It had never occurred to me that her illness could be one of something other than the body.

Despite the heat of the August sun, I felt chilled.

"Mongo, people *do* die of spells. I've *seen* it; I've seen Cubans withering away in Miami hospitals because they've had 'spells' cast on them. The condition of the body is inextricably linked to the condition of the mind. If you *believe* you're going to die, it's often very hard for the body to resist the suggestion."

"How strong could a seven-year-old's sense of membership be, Yvonne? Enough to *kill* her?"

The beautiful young Puerto Rican thought about it, then said, "Well, I've seen young children in your Southern fundamentalist groups exhibit *stigmata.*"

"Bleeding of the palms isn't dying."

"But the same mechanism may be involved. I think it would depend on how young the child was when she was first introduced to the tenets of witchcraft. Did she grow up in an occult society?"

"Her mother's a witch," I said, feeling ridiculous. Sitting in the sun on a college campus, I found the words totally alien. "But she's into living, not dying."

"Still, the child almost certainly would have been introduced to the concept of spells—forces directed against her by others."

I recalled with stunning impact the story Garth had told me of the two children a pair of witches had turned against their enslaved mother. "What would they do to her?" I asked quietly.

"Oh God, Mongo, I don't know; I'm not an expert on witchcraft. All I'm saying is that people who are truly into witchcraft—those who have 'membership'—are vulnerable to the forces they believe in, precisely *because* they believe in them. That's the price we all pay for our particular belief systems. With the child it could be sheer terror, a form of deep hypnosis or just plain trauma from whatever it was she was subjected to. Neither of us can know for certain—but when you told me your story I just had to give you this perspective. I believe the child's coma *could* have a psychological basis." She paused and squeezed my hand hard. "Mongo, I *do* care!"

"I can see that," I said, squeezing her hand back. "And I thank you." If Yvonne was right, I was left back at the beginning; in order to help Kathy, I was going to have to find out specifically what had been done to her—meaning I'd have to find out *who* had done it. And the nightgown was my only clue.

"Is there anything you'd like to ask me about Esteban?" Yvonne asked softly.

"Yeah. What do you think he could do for my little girl?" The words had come out by themselves, and I wasn't certain myself whether I was serious or indulging in a little black humor.

Yvonne answered very seriously. "What Esteban does is a mystery to me, Mongo. But I am sure he can heal; that's why I was so anxious to have Janet study him. However, as I pointed out, Esteban's power is effective against *disease*. If the girl's condition is . . . a spell, I'm not sure he can help; he's not a member of that belief system. But I really don't know. In any case, I don't see how it could hurt to have him see her. If you can free Esteban, *I'd* ask him to see her."

It occurred to me that Yvonne's notion would be greeted with something less than wild enthusiasm by Dr. Greene and the specialists he was bringing in, but I kept the thought to myself. Yvonne and I got up together. I kissed her hand, then walked to my office, where I called Garth.

"Hey, brother," I said when I got him on the line. "What's happening with John Krowl? Did you get me an appointment?"

"Eight o'clock tonight. Do you have his address?"

"No. Give it to me."

He did, then asked, "How's the girl?"

"The same. I suppose that's something to be thankful for. As long as there's no brain damage, I assume she can be maintained on life-support systems for as long as it takes to find a way to get her out of it."

"*You* sound better."

"I feel better. I had a good night's sleep, and I don't feel quite so much pressure. As long as Kathy's condition remains stable, I have a little more room to move around in. Does Krowl know why I want to see him?"

"Uh-uh. I talked to his secretary. He knows me, so I was able to get you an appointment on short notice. But I wasn't sure you'd want me to go into any kind of detail over the phone. The secretary just assumes you want a reading, and I left it at that. Do you want me to get back to Krowl and fill him in?"

"No," I said after giving it some thought. "I think I'll play Krowl by ear. Let's talk about Esteban. I know this isn't your province, but what do you think the chances are of getting Esteban out on bail? I've got character witnesses up the ass."

"Like you say, that isn't my province. But I know his lawyer's already tried that, and he didn't get too far. He is charged with premeditated murder, and Esteban doesn't exactly have roots in the community."

"Can I get in to talk to him?"

"At your convenience, brother. Esteban and his lawyer don't have any objections, and we couldn't care less. While you're here, there's someone else you're going to want to talk to."

"Who?"

"Weirdo by the name of Richard Crandall. His name's all we've been able to get from him. He knows something about your little friend in the hospital; a security guard caught him in her room at three o'clock this morning. He was doing a witchcraft number; candles, ceremonial robe—the works. Whatever the hell he was up to, he meant business."

Suddenly my heart was beating inside my chest with triphammer speed and force. Crandall's actions during the night were eloquent testimony to the fact that *he*, at least, believed Kathy was under some kind of spell, and that he could undo it.

It also meant Crandall believed time was running out.

"Did he give her anything?" I asked tightly.

"No," Garth replied evenly. "As far as anyone can tell, he didn't even try to touch her."

"What *was* he doing?"

"Ask him yourself. He won't say a word to us. He was dressed in a scarlet robe. The guard found him kneeling at the girl's bedside in the center of a pentagram he'd drawn on the floor with red chalk. He'd surrounded the bed with white candles, and he was passing another candle back and forth in front of the girl's face while he chanted in her ear."

"I'll be right over, Garth," I said quickly.

When I hung up, I found I had what felt like a lead weight in the pit of my stomach, and a lump in my throat. Crandall's chant had been a ceremonial magician's prayer.

Chapter 9

"What the fuck's the matter with you, Crandall? Those cops out there think you're the wildest thing to hit this town since The Flying Nun."

The ceremonial magician called Daniel sat stiffly on the edge of his cell cot. He was dressed in the same conservatively cut gray suit I'd seen him in the day before; his tie was still neatly knotted, and he hadn't even removed his suit jacket. Garth had told me Crandall had been sitting, unmoving, in the same position since being booked. The only incongruities in his facade were a pair of scuffed black shoes and a stubble of beard. Otherwise, his appearance was impeccable.

Daniel slowly turned his head in my direction, and I caught a glimmer of surprise in his steel-gray eyes before they once again assumed their usual inscrutability. "How did you find out I was here, Frederickson?"

"The police lieutenant the hospital security guard turned you over to happens to be my brother. He's in charge of the city's wacko detail, and it's a lucky thing for you he is. If they'd taken you to any other precinct in this city, you'd be sitting in a padded cell in Bellevue right now. I saw your robe and the other paraphernalia out on the desk. You must have really looked smashing in that outfit. Got any pictures?"

"I have to get out of here, Frederickson."

I laughed. "By keeping your mouth shut? You're not going to wish your way out of *here.*" I sat down on the floor across from him, bracing my back against the wall. "There may be something I can do; but first, you and I are going to talk a little turkey—or frog's legs."

"I won't bargain with you," he said stiffly, staring at the section of wall just above my head. "If you want to help Kathy, you have to help me."

"That's what *you* say. We're both thinking of Kathy—and so is my brother. Up to this point, I'd say we've been dealing in a hell of a lot better faith than you have."

"Talk to my sister," he said in the same flat, unemotional tone. "Convince her that she has to go back to Philadelphia. I believe her life could be in danger if she stays here."

"I've given that problem some thought, Crandall. Even if you're right, your sister's not going to leave Kathy's bedside. But I'm not sure she *is* in danger. Marlowe took Kathy to your sister's house the weekend he was murdered; he left some stuff there."

Daniel blinked rapidly, stared at me hard for a moment, then returned his gaze to the wall. I'd just told him something he hadn't known.

"Whoever did this thing to your niece and her father knew a great deal about Marlowe's personal habits," I continued. "They wanted to get Kathy and her father, and they sure as hell did. If they'd wanted to get your sister, there's no doubt in my mind that they would have; they'd have taken all three of them while they were together in Philadelphia. So your sister doesn't seem to be in their plans.

"There has to be a *reason* for the complicated way they did things. Everything has the earmarks of a ritual. Obviously, they were snuffing Marlowe for something he'd done. But why do a number on Kathy? It could be a warning to someone else—or punishment—for something *he'd* done." I took a deep breath, prolonged the silence until the ceremonial magician looked at me, then said: "Would that person be you, Daniel? Is Kathy dying for *your* sins?"

His gaze didn't waver, but I saw his jaw clench and the muscles in his stomach contract and expand under his tight vest.

"*Tell* me, for Christ's sake!" I said. "Tell the cops and me what's going on so we can help!"

"No one can help," Daniel said tightly. "I told you before this is an affair of sorcerers. You couldn't understand then, and you can't understand now."

"Try me again. Tell me why you're the only one who can help Kathy."

"I'm the only one who knows whom to talk to."

"If you'll tell my brother and me, then *we'll* know whom to talk to."

He shook his head. "No. Nobody who matters will talk to you. You'll never be able to find the right people in time, and you'll make it impossible for *me* to find them." He paused, and his eyes suddenly shifted focus as he looked into my face. I felt a curious, empty sensation in the pit of my stomach. It was as though a screen had been rolled away from his eyes, leaving them naked. In that moment he allowed me a brief glimpse into a soul filled with pain, compassion and anxiety.

"April understands," he continued. "I don't have to explain anything to her. For some reason, I feel a tremendous need to assure you—a stranger—that I would do nothing to hurt Kathy, not by omission or commission. It's a terrible weakness for me even to have to say that to you. You're a good person; people like you generate their own special power."

"Flattery won't get you shit with me, Crandall. Why don't you just tell me what's going on?" The screens in his eyes slammed down immediately, and he went back to staring at the wall over my head. "Let's talk about spells, Daniel. I had an interesting conversation with someone whose views I respect. That person tells me it's possible Kathy's condition could be the result of suggestion or trauma—a 'spell,' if you like. What do *you* think?"

Silence. Crandall had already given his answer during the night.

"Come on," I said. "If this thing *is* trauma, the psychiatrists at the hospital may be able to help her; but they'll need some idea of what was done or said to her."

There was still nothing but silence from the man across the cell from me. This time I hadn't even made him blink. "I told Garth that you're the girl's uncle," I continued resignedly. "You're still going to have to deal with the hospital on trespassing charges, but they'll probably drop those. Until they do, you're out on bail."

"You mean I'm free to go?"

"You've got it, pal. The cell door's open. I talked to a bail bondsman before I came in here. I did that because I like your niece, your sister and your nerve. But *you* owe me, and I'm collecting. I want you to tell me what's going on."

"I owe you nothing, Frederickson," Daniel said, rising, "You do what you have to do, and I'll do what *I* have to do."

He made a curiously human gesture of polishing his shoes on the jail blanket, then straightened his tie and headed for the door.

"Daniel!" I shouted. "Who's Esobus?"

He slowly turned. Once more, his eyes were pools of intense feeling. At that moment I thought he had the most expressive eyes I'd ever seen; his ability to express or disguise emotion in them at will was unnerving to me. "I don't know, Frederickson," the ceremonial magician said quietly. "I'm trying to find out; as I told you, I'm the *only* one who can find out." He paused, drew in a deep breath. "Perhaps you're a Christian, Moslem or Jew. There's still power in those ways, despite all their priests have done to suck them dry. If you want to help Kathy, pray for her; from your own deep mind, pray."

My nontalk with Daniel had upset me, and I went to the squad room for coffee and a cigarette. When I felt reasonably calm, I went to find Garth. He took me to see Esteban Morales. I was lucky Morales was still there; the healer was already overdue to be moved to a more permanent holding cell on Rikers Island.

Esteban Morales looked like an abandoned extra from *Viva Zapata!* From under the battered fedora on top of his head, long gray hair streaked with black hung out. Despite his relatively long stay in the cramped holding cell, he looked very clean. He wore shapeless black corduroy pants and a bulky, patched red sweater. There was a tension in his thin, angular, aged body that gave the impression of considerable physical strength. Sitting Indian fashion on the jail cot, his back braced against the wall, he looked forlorn and lonely. He glanced across the cell as I entered, and I found myself looking into a pair of limpid, dark brown eyes. Something moved in their depths as he looked at me. Whatever it was—curiosity, or perhaps amusement—quickly faded. He nodded once in greeting, and his smile was guileless, almost childlike.

"Hello, Mr. Morales," I said, going over to the Mexican and offering him my hand. "My name is Bob Frederickson, but most people call me Mongo."

"Hello, Mongo," Esteban said, grinning broadly. "My lawyer said somebody wanted to see me, but he did not say why. Are you the man who wanted to see me?"

"That's me. Dr. Monroe—"

"Who is Dr. Monroe?"

"Sister Janet?"

"*Si*," he said. "Sister Janet is my friend." He uncoiled his legs and moved forward to the edge of the cot, planting his feet firmly on the floor.

"Sister Janet told Senator Younger about me. I'm a private investigator, and I'd like to help you. Senator Younger believes his daughter needs you to stay alive, so I'm going to try to get you out of here."

Morales gripped his knees with his gnarled hands. I remembered Janet Monroe's Kirlian photographs and wondered just what mysterious force, if any, was in those hands—and what its source might be. "I will be very happy to help Linda if I can get to see her," the healer said quietly. "If *you* can come to see me, why can't the Senator bring Linda here?"

"I don't think he's quite ready to do that yet, Mr. Morales. If I'm going to help you, I have to know the truth. *Did* you kill Dr. Samuels?"

Esteban squeezed his knees so hard that his knuckles turned white under his permanently sunburned skin. "I did not kill anybody, Mongo."

"Okay; I believe you. I've heard Dr. Jordon's version of events. He says he found you next to Dr. Samuels' body. Is that true?"

Esteban nodded slowly, sadly. "I was kneeling next to Dr. Samuels. I wanted to see if I could help. I was trying to stop the bleeding; I did not know he was already dead."

"You know he was stabbed, and that the police found the murder weapon in a bottle of acid. Did you see the knife at all?"

"No, Mongo," Esteban said forcefully. "I did not kill Dr. Samuels, and I did not see any knife." He removed his fedora from his head and ran his fingers through his thick hair. "Terrible, terrible thing," he murmured.

"Dr. Jordan claims that you and Samuels didn't get along. Is *that* true, Mr. Morales?"

"Call me Esteban, please." He paused, and his eyes took on a distant look, as though he were peering back into the past. "I liked Dr. Samuels all right, but he did not like me. I could tell that. He thought I was a big phony." Esteban nodded quickly and smiled. "Still, he let me help his patients, and I was grateful to him for that."

"Do you think you actually helped any of the patients the doctors sent to you?"

The healer smiled disarmingly. "I *know* I did. And the patients—they know. They told me so, and they told the doctors."

"Esteban, did you ever give drugs to anybody? *Any* kind of foreign substance—herbs, potions, plants?"

"*No!*" the old man said, shaking his head vigorously. He lifted his hands, then turned the palms outward to me. "My power is here, in my hands. All drugs are bad for the body."

"If you didn't give drugs to anybody, why do you suppose Dr. Samuels said you did?"

Esteban made a broad, shrugging gesture of bewilderment. "One day the police picked me up at the university. They told me I was under arrest for pretending to be a doctor. It was Dr. Samuels who made the charge; he claimed I gave drugs to patients. I did not understand; I never pretended to be a doctor. Dr. Samuels and Dr. Jordon knew all about what I was trying to do." He sighed and pressed the tips of his long fingers together. "Sister Janet got me out on bail. Then I got a message the same day—"

"That would be last Thursday?"

"*Si.* Last Thursday. The message said that Dr. Samuels wanted to see me that night at seven thirty. I wanted to know why Dr. Samuels lied about me, so I decided to go. When I got to the office, I found him dead. Somebody had cut his throat. Then Dr. Jordon came into the office and saw me by the body. He thought I did it, so he called the police . . ." Esteban's voice trailed off, punctuated by a curiously elegant sweep of his hand that included the cell and the unseen world outside.

"How did you get into the office, Esteban?"

"The lights were on, and the door was open. When nobody answered my knock, I just walked in."

I nodded. Esteban Morales was either a monumental acting talent, or an innocent man; it was impossible not to believe him. "What exactly did Dr. Samuels say when he called you."

"I only talked to Sister Janet's secretary. Dr. Samuels called and left a message."

"So you don't have any idea what Samuels wanted to talk to you about?"

"No, Mongo. I thought maybe he wanted to say he was sorry he lied about me."

"Esteban, how do you do what you do?"

He smiled crookedly. "Do you think I play tricks? Do you think I'm a phony, like the psychosurgeons?"

"What I think doesn't matter," I said evenly.

"Then why do you ask?"

"I'm curious."

"Then I will answer." He again lifted his hands; he looked at them absently, as though they might belong to someone else. "The body makes music, Mongo," Esteban continued. "Not many people can hear, but it does. I hear the music through my hands. A healthy body makes good music; a sick body makes bad music. With my hands and my thoughts, I can make the music better when it is bad; I can make it sound like it should." He dropped his hands into his lap, shrugged. "It is not easy to explain."

"Why were you upset toward the end of Sister Janet's project?"

Esteban blinked rapidly, and for the first time since I'd walked in, his tone seemed guarded. "What makes you think I was upset?"

"Sister Janet told me you were losing your ability to affect the enzymes. She thought you were distracted by something else."

The old man took a few moments to think about his answer. "I don't think it is right to talk about it," he said at last, avoiding my eyes.

"Talk about *what,* Esteban? If I'm going to help you, you have to be completely open with me."

"I know many things about people, Mongo. I see their music . . . but I don't talk about it." He hesitated, then added quietly: "What bothered me had nothing to do with this trouble."

"Why don't you let *me* decide that?"

Once again it took him a long time to answer. "I suppose it does not make any difference now."

"*What* doesn't make any difference, Esteban?"

He looked at me a long time before he finally spoke. "Dr. Samuels' body made very bad music. He was dying; I think he had cancer."

"Dr. Samuels told you this?"

"No. Dr. Samuels did not tell anyone; he did not want anyone to know. But I knew."

"*How*, Esteban? How did you know? You talk about seeing and hearing 'music,' but I don't understand what you mean."

"I do see the music, Mongo," Esteban said, pointing to his eyes. "Other people sometimes call it an 'aura.' Dr. Samuels' aura was a brownish black. It flickered; it was not strong. That is what I usually see in people who are dying of cancer. I knew he had five, maybe six more months to live." The healer wrung his hands, lowered his voice. "I told him I knew; I told him I wanted to help. I told him I could not cure him, but I might be able to ease his pain. Dr. Samuels got very mad at me. He denied he was dying or in pain, and he told me to mind my own business. It upset me; it always upsets me to be around people who are in pain and not be able to help."

My mouth was suddenly very dry. I swallowed hard. "Did you tell this story to your lawyer?"

"No. What would be the point?"

I again thought of the Kirlian photographs I'd seen, and I felt a fluttering sensation in the pit of my stomach. "Esteban," I said, coughing drily as my throat constricted, "can you see *anybody's* music? Can you see their aura?" Esteban slowly nodded, avoiding my gaze as though he anticipated my next question. I asked it. "Can you see mine?"

Esteban had been staring at the floor. Now he looked up into my eyes. It was a moment of unexpected and excruciating intimacy. "I can see yours, Mongo," he whispered.

We stared at each other for a few moments. "Wait a minute," I said at last. "I'll be right back."

Garth was in the squad room having coffee. He saw me at the door, got up and came over. "What's up, brother?" he asked. "You look pale."

"How's the Morales investigation going?"

He shrugged. "It's . . . *going*," he said, sounding

puzzled. "What can I tell you? I said we were looking into it. Believe it or not, I have a few other cases on my hands."

"You still think he's guilty, don't you?"

"Why should I have changed my opinion?"

"Have you seriously considered any other suspects?"

"Who would you suggest? The man was kneeling there with blood all over his hands and the front of his shirt."

"You mean Esteban slashed Samuels' throat, walked away to drop the knife in a vial of acid, then came back to kneel beside the body?"

"Why not? He may have been sorry he did it, or maybe he was just checking to make sure he'd done the job right. Who else besides Morales and Jordon knew that Samuels was going to be in the office complex that night?"

"I don't know, and neither do you. Maybe Jordon did it."

"*Jordon?* Come on, Mongo. It was *Samuels'* practice that Jordon bought into. Would he be likely to kill the goose that laid the golden proverbial?"

"What about the patients that Esteban shared with the two doctors? Maybe one of *them* had a motive for killing Samuels. If you had that list, you could at least verify whether or not Morales ever gave drugs to any of the people on it."

"I can't get the names of those patients, Mongo, and you know it. It's privileged information."

"Well, you could at least *ask* Jordon to give the names to you."

"I did ask, and he won't. He's afraid the people would be embarrassed, and there'd be lawsuits. He's probably right."

It meant I was going to be forced to do something I abhorred; but I was rapidly running out of time and options. Besides, the most important thing was that Garth would *know* what I was doing was abhorrent—and it was essential that I make Garth a believer.

"Will you come back with me to Esteban's cell for a few minutes?" I asked. "I want to try a little experiment, and I need a witness."

"I'm on my way out, Mongo," Garth said irritably. "I've got police business."

"*This* is police business. Come on, Garth, Give me ten minutes."

He hesitated, then gestured impatiently for me to lead the way.

Esteban glanced up as Garth and I entered the cell. His eyes were bright with curiosity. "Esteban," I said, "I'd like the Lieutenant to hear the rest of our conversation." Out of the corner of my eye I could see that Garth had leaned his tall, gaunt frame against the bars on the opposite side of the cell and was tapping his foot rhythmically—a sure sign of impatience. "Esteban," I continued quickly, "will you tell the Lieutenant what a human 'aura' is?"

Esteban described the aura, and I followed up by describing the Kirlian photographs Janet had shown me—what they were, and what they purported to show. Garth's foot continued its relentless tapping. Once he glanced at his watch.

"Esteban," I said, "what does the Lieutenant's aura look like?"

"The Lieutenant looks fine," the old man said, puzzled.

"What about me?"

Esteban abruptly shook his head and dropped his gaze.

The foot tapping behind me had stopped. Suddenly Garth was beside me, gripping my arm. "Mongo, what the hell is this all about?"

"Just *listen!*" I rasped. "Esteban, can you see my aura? Damn it! If you can, say so! I may be able to help you, but you have to do as I ask!"

Esteban slowly raised his head. His brown eyes were moist, filled with compassion. "Why do you want me to say it, Mongo? *You* know, and I cannot help you."

Garth gripped my arm even tighter. I pulled away from him. "Tell me what it is you see, Esteban," I said in a hoarse whisper.

"You are dying, Mongo."

"You have to tell me more!" I snapped. "Be more specific!"

"Your organs are like your body, Mongo; twisted . . . dwarfed. They are not normal. You have a very strong will and life force, but that is not enough. You are still dying."

"Tell me how many years I have left," I said, swallowing hard. I suddenly felt sick to my stomach. "The Lieutenant and I know; let's see if you know."

"Maybe four, five years," Esteban said resignedly. "I do not know for sure. Why do you make me say these things?"

The healer and I stared at each other, our gazes locked. I felt light-headed, even more nauseated. There was no satisfaction in the other man's face—only sorrow. Whatever Morales did, I thought, it was for real. Janet Monroe and Yvonne Mercado were right.

I tore my gaze away from Esteban and spun around to face Garth. I'd caught him at a bad moment; his face was twisted, his eyes full of pain. My brother was rather fond of me.

"Well, brother?" I asked, hoping I had my smile on straight. "It's true that anyone might know that dwarfs aren't long-lived, but how does Mr. Morales' opinion stack up against the medical authorities'?"

Garth's voice was cracked and hollow. "Your clients get a lot for their money, Mongo." He swallowed, looked away. "I'm impressed, sure; but it doesn't prove anything."

"Was an autopsy performed on Samuels?"

"I don't know," Garth said distantly. "Cause of death was obvious. If there was an autopsy, the report's probably been filed away by now."

"Well, check it out. If Esteban's right, Samuels' body was riddled with cancer. He only had a few more months to live, and Esteban knew that. Since Esteban knew Samuels was going to die anyway, why kill him? This man just doesn't have that kind of passion."

"It still doesn't prove anything, Mongo," Garth said hoarsely. "I wish it did."

"It should be enough to raise reasonable doubt that Esteban did it. Look, all I'm trying to do is light some fires under the investigation. Will you do some more checking?"

Garth looked over at Esteban. "I'll have another talk with Jordon about that list of patients." He looked back at me, smiled thinly. "You all right, brother?"

"Of course I'm all right. Hell, we're all dying, aren't we?" My laugh turned sharp and bitter. "When you've been dying as long as I have, you get used to it. Hey, I want to use your phone to make a long-distance call. I'll charge it to my home phone—okay?"

"I'll clear it with the switchboard." Garth nodded curtly, seemed to hesitate, then abruptly turned and walked out of the cell.

Esteban was still staring at me. "I am sorry, Mongo," he said quietly.

"Tell me about Dr. Jordon," I said absently, struggling to get my mind back on business. "You got on well together, didn't you?"

He hesitated a moment, then said, "*Sí.* We got along fine. It was Dr. Jordon who persuaded Dr. Samuels to take part in the experiment."

There was something in Esteban's voice that didn't quite ring true, and I spoke to that. "Do you like Jordon personally?"

He raised his eyebrows. "Oh, I like Dr. Jordon fine. But it was hard to work with his patients. I feel sorry for him. I think he tries very hard, but not everybody should be a doctor."

"Really? Are you saying that Dr. Jordon isn't a good doctor?"

Esteban's eyes clouded. "I am not saying that, Mongo. It is not my place to say that. I think Dr. Jordon is a fine man. He has been very good to me. He tries hard to be a good doctor."

"But you don't think he *is* a good doctor," I persisted.

Esteban said nothing. I kept pressing, but he only sat and shook his head. Finally I left the cell and made a quick call to Washington.

Senator Younger was in his office. He had a number of questions, all of which I finessed in one way or another. The point of the call was to let him know that I was working on the case, and that the police might be a little more interested now in looking for other suspects.

After hanging up, I went outside and lighted a cigarette. It tasted bitter, but that didn't stop me from smoking it down to the end. When I finished that one, I lighted another. I stood motionless on the sidewalk, smoking and playing sponge—soaking up the minutest smells, sights and sounds of the city around me. I missed it already. Dying can be a distraction.

Chapter 10

On my way to my apartment I reflected on the fact that the building where I lived had no 13th floor listed; the numbering in the elevator went from 12 to 14. Black cats, not walking under ladders—and religion—were, of course, part of the culture, but I was particularly struck by the 13th-floor syndrome: the occult—in the form of the magical number 13—had become institutionalized.

After a short nap, I shaved, showered and went to the hospital, where I checked with Dr. Greene. Kathy was still in a coma, and they were awaiting the results of the latest tests. I mentioned the possibility of induced coma, but without using the word "spell." Greene listened patiently, with a straight face, but I could tell he was amused. He promised to let me know if there was any change, and I went over to the Intensive Care Unit. I found April Marlowe sitting idly in a small adjacent waiting room. She was staring off into space, lost in thought. I stood in the doorway for a long time, watching her. She was dressed in boots, straight black skirt and a loose-fitting blouse that didn't quite disguise her full bosom.

April looked up and caught me watching her. She started, then relaxed and smiled wistfully. "Hello, Robert," she said. "You startled me. How long have you been standing there?"

"Just arrived," I lied. I walked across the room and sat down on a chair across from her. She was pale, and her lovely eyes were shadowed with anxiety. "I just talked with Dr. Greene. I understand Kathy's the same."

"I'm worried, Robert," she said in a choked whisper. "I have a bad feeling."

"Of course you're worried," I said gently. "But at least Kathy's not getting worse; and she's getting the best possible care."

She dropped her eyes. "I'm not sure that's going to be enough."

I wanted to reach out and touch her, but I didn't. In different circumstances, if I hadn't been feeling what I was feeling, I would have. But I was embarrassed by my own desire. "Did you know that your brother was arrested here last night?" I asked.

The woman's eyes grew large, then filled with tears. Now I gripped her shoulder; the touch of her sent what felt like an electric shock running down my arm. "I got him out on bail," I continued. "I don't think the hospital will press charges now that they know who he is."

"What was he *doing* here?"

"He was up here in the middle of the night performing some kind of ceremony. That seems to mean he feels Kathy's problem might be something other than physical. He must think she's under a . . . spell. What do you think?"

April slowly shook her head. "I can't answer you, Robert. I don't know anywhere near as much about those things as Daniel does. I just . . . can't say. I have to trust in Dr. Greene and the other doctors."

She smiled wanly and put her hand in mine. Perhaps she felt the tension there, because she moved her hand away after a few moments. We sat in silence for a minute or two. Finally I cleared my throat, balled my fist and extended my ring finger. "April," I asked quietly, "does this gesture mean anything to you?"

"Where did you see that?" she asked, surprised.

"Daniel used it on me."

April's tentative smile vanished, leaving in its wake tension lines at the corners of her mouth. "It's called a 'witch's sword,' or *athamé*. It's an occult gesture—a kind of warning, or curse. Actually, in wicca terms, an *athamé* is a dagger that's been prepared in ritual fashion for certain ceremonies; it's 'blessed.' I suppose you could compare the gesture to a Catholic crossing himself—except in this case the feeling is hostile and is directed against the person the witch points his finger at."

I nodded absently, remembering the curious reaction Daniel had brought about in me when he'd tapped my forehead; I was beginning to understand why people were afraid of him. "April, how long have you been sitting here?"

She glanced at her wrist, but she wasn't wearing a watch. There was no clock on the wall. "I . . . really don't know," she said softly. "There just doesn't seem to be anything else to do but wait. I have this awful . . . premonition."

"Come and have dinner with me. It'll help you relax; besides, I have some more questions."

"Robert," she whispered, "can't we talk here? I'll help you in any way I can, but I'm afraid to leave Kathy."

"We'll eat at The Granada and leave the number at the nurses' station, just like last time. You have to take care of yourself; it's not going to do Kathy any good if you get sick. Believe me, a nurse will call right away if there's any change. We won't be long."

She thought about it, then rose. "You're right, Robert. I'll be happy to dine with you. Thank you."

It was going to rain. The early-evening light was dirty, translucent; the air was moist and heavy, as though the city were about to break into a sweat. Perspiration gleamed on the bodies of the omnipresent paddleball players in the playground, and the *thwack-thwack* of the hard rubber ball against wood paddle and concrete wall seemed unnaturally loud in the thick atmosphere. I asked April if she wanted to take a cab, but she said she preferred to walk. We made our way to the restaurant in silence. I sensed that, unlike the night before, dinner and wine would do nothing to improve April's mood. She was tense, pensive and distracted.

The red velvet and mahogany interior of the restaurant, usually warm and relaxing, seemed oppressive. The air-conditioning level was set too high, and we both shivered as we stepped into the restaurant. The maître d' nodded in recognition, then led us to a good table by the window. The lighted candle in the center of the table made me nervous, and I pushed it to one side.

"What did you want to ask me, Robert?" April asked after we'd been seated.

"Do you know anything about tarot cards?"

"Some," she said. "Why?"

"I have an appointment for a reading in an hour and a half. I'd like to know what to expect."

April cocked her head to one side and looked at me strangely. "*You're* going for a reading? That surprises me."

"Well, it's true that I'm not exactly a believer."

"You might change your mind after a tarot reading—depending, of course, on how good the reader is."

"I'm seeing a man by the name of John Krowl. I'm hoping he can give me a line on this Esobus character."

She looked at me for a long time. "I should have known it would have something to do with Kathy. Thank you again, Robert, for trying so hard to help."

A waiter appeared. April shook her head when I asked her if she wanted a drink, and I didn't press. She ordered *gazpacho* and an omelette. I asked for the same.

"Have you heard of Krowl?" I asked.

"Yes. He's supposed to be very good; only a man by the name of Michael McEnroe is supposed to be better. If you go to John Krowl, you're liable to learn more about *yourself* than about Esobus. Krowl is supposed to be psychic."

"Terrific," I said, flashing a tentative smile. "I need a psychic."

April didn't smile back. "I won't try to convince you of the power of the tarot, Robert," she said very seriously. "You'll see for yourself. Do you know anything at all about the cards?"

"Only that they were supposedly invented by the Gypsies in the Middle Ages; they have pictures, and they're used for fortune-telling."

The waiter brought our *gazpacho*. The soup was good, but April ate only half of it. " 'Fortune-telling' isn't a good word for what happens during a tarot reading," she said, pushing the rest of her soup away. "Despite what you see on Forty-second Street, that's not what the tarot is about. You should think of the tarot deck as a great book of mystical knowledge that uses symbols instead of words. The symbols are very deep. The tarot is one of the occult 'mysteries'—astrology, palmistry and numerology being the occult 'sciences.' Each card is open to a variety of interpretations; the quality of the reading depends on the quality of the channels of communication opened between the querent—the person having the reading—and the reader."

"How does it work?"

"John Krowl will have you shuffle and cut the cards; then he'll use any one of a number of different layouts. What should show up are trends in your life—past, present and future."

"It still sounds like fortune-telling," I said gently.

"If someone can accurately see your past, it's not difficult to predict your future. The tarot deck can change a person's life, if the person truly wants to change; the cards can provide a shock of recognition."

Our omelettes arrived. As we started to eat, April shivered again. I rose and put my sports jacket around her shoulders. She nodded her thanks and pulled the jacket even tighter around her. Seeing her do that gave me an absurd jolt of pleasure.

"You said that the symbols on the cards are inexact. It seems to me that a reader could come up with any number of different interpretations."

"But *you'll* instinctively know if it's a true reading," she said, picking at her omelette. Her mind was back in the hospital with Kathy; her voice was distant, its matter-of-factness masking her anxiety. "A single card may have as many as three or four subtly different meanings; but the specific interpretation of any card is refined by its position in a particular layout. The cards are *intensely* personal, Robert." April paused and smiled thinly. For a moment, she was back in the restaurant with me. "Behind your somewhat flamboyant exterior, I sense that you're a very private man. You shouldn't go to this man unless you're prepared to have your life and dreams stripped bare. He could know all there is to know about you five minutes after the cards are laid out."

"You *are* impressed by the tarot, aren't you?"

"Yes I am, Robert," she said evenly. "Of all the occult studies, I find the tarot the most mystical and beautiful." She had to force herself to eat a few more bites of the omelette, then pushed away what was left. "I'm sorry, Robert," she continued quietly. "I hate to waste food. I know I should eat, but I can't. I'm afraid you've wasted your money on me."

"Don't be silly. Would you like some tea or coffee?"

April shook her head. "The reason I believe Krowl is

probably psychic is that he's been so successful," she said in a low voice. "People wouldn't keep going back to him unless he was telling them something about their lives and helping them to solve their problems. Also, he's been working with the cards for many years. Regular use of the cards can help you develop your own psychic abilities. It's like exercising a muscle, except in this case it's a psychic muscle. I think of the tarot deck as a window into regions of the mind that are beyond the rational."

"Thank you for talking to me, April," I said. "I know it's been hard for you."

As I signaled the waiter for the check, it occurred to me that it would be interesting to see if John Krowl lived up to April's advance billing.

The most spectacular view of the Manhattan skyline, bar none, is from the Manhattan Bridge. I took advantage of a minor traffic slowdown to twist in my seat and look back at the most exciting piece of real estate in the world. Manhattan is, of course, only one of New York's five boroughs, but to me it *was* New York, the city's heart and soul. At that moment the sight of the skyline was probably the only vista in the world that could, if only for a few seconds, lift me beyond my anxiety and fear. Manhattan's tremendous energy can burn a man out, but burning out is not something I worry about.

Traffic began to move again, and I drove down into the amorphous entity of funky culture and parochial defensiveness that is Brooklyn.

Tacky appearances to the contrary, Krowl had chosen a chic area to work out of. Creeping glamour, wealthy dilettantes and accompanying rising rents were driving loft artists out of SoHo, NoHo and the rest of Manhattan's "Ho's." They were migrating in increasing numbers to Brooklyn's DUMBO—"Down Under the Manhattan-Brooklyn Overpass." The area—a montage of dying industries that supplied the artists' lofts and thriving galleries and small businesses that were supported by the artists—even had its own newspaper, the *Phoenix*. It was an apt title; DUMBO was rising from ashes of crumbling concrete.

John Krowl's brownstone was four blocks east of the Manhattan Bridge, in a poor but clean working-class neighborhood. I was a few minutes early, but I rang the bell anyway. It was answered by a young man in his early twenties who looked down at me inquiringly. I introduced myself and said that I had an appointment for eight o'clock. He introduced himself only as Krowl's secretary and told me I'd have to wait a few minutes. He motioned me inside and indicated that I should sit down on one of the three antique chairs just inside the door.

I was in a large circular foyer with a corridor directly opposite me that extended all the way to the end of the house. There were closed doors to either side of me. Around the perimeter of the foyer were a number of old, heavy tables, their surfaces covered with what looked like valuable African primitive sculpture—most of it erotic. The walls of the foyer were decorated with an odd but strangely appealing mixture of garish Haitian paintings and faded Persian tapestries. All of the exposed wood had been stripped to the grain and polished to a burnished glow. In contrast to the rather dreary facade and neighborhood outside, the inside of Krowl's brownstone was like a museum. Krowl had taste.

The art was carefully chosen and interesting, but what intrigued me by far the most in the foyer was a display of at least a hundred plaster hand casts mounted in the spaces around and between the paintings and the tapestries. I got up and went closer to examine them.

The casts had been expertly made, and all of the details in the palms had been meticulously lined in with India ink. The effect was eerie and startling. The names of the hands' owners were inscribed in calligraphic script over the base of the wrist and signed beneath. Most of them belonged to well-known New York and Hollywood celebrities, with a few Washington politicians sprinkled around as if to give the display some respectability, like a heavy bronze identification plaque under a muddy painting. Just about everyone who was anyone seemed to be represented in John Krowl's foyer; it occurred to me that the people represented couldn't all be idiots, and I found I was impressed.

Two names in particular interested me. The first was that of Harley Davidson, at one time the hottest young rock star in the country. I'd known him as Bobby Weiss, a gangling, likable student who'd been blundering his way through college. Criminology had seemed to be one of the rare subjects that interested him, and he'd managed to show up fairly regularly for my undergraduate class.

Bobby had dropped out of school three years before, in the middle of his junior year. A year after that he'd exploded onto the national rock scene as Harley Davidson—Instant Millionaire. He'd signed with Jake Stein, a friend of mine with the William Morris Agency, and I'd kept track of him through Jake. One year I'd even received a Christmas card. I'd thought Bobby spent all his time in Los Angeles, but he'd obviously touched base often enough in New York to hear of Krowl. Seeing the palm print suddenly made me realize that I hadn't heard anything of Bobby for at least six months—no records, no television, not even a gossip item. I wondered what had happened to him.

The second name hit even closer to home, and it gave me a jolt. The name was Bart Stone. Stone was a prolific writer of Western pulp novels who had provided the fictional fodder for dozens of Western films turned out by Hollywood.

I wondered if Krowl, when he'd make the print, had known that "Bart Stone" was but one of the many pseudonyms used by Frank Marlowe. I might ask him.

I wandered down the hallway to the end, where a narrow balcony looked out over a small, exquisitely arranged garden and patio. The area was encircled by plants which seemed to be miraculously surviving in New York's sulfurous air; it seemed a tiny piece of serenity in the middle of the most manic city in the world. Across the way, looming up into the drizzling twilight, was a fifteen-story factory building. The side I was looking at was covered with climbing ivy. The windows had been painted black.

"Mr. Frederickson?"

I wheeled and was startled to find a man I assumed to be Krowl standing almost directly behind me. The door to the left of the foyer entrance was open, and he'd managed to approach me without making a sound.

No one had thought to mention the fact that John Krowl was an albino; his wraithlike, ghostly appearance startled me. Krowl's skin was almost the color of chalk, and he wore his thin, white hair at shoulder length. He wore glasses with tinted lenses, presumably to protect his sensitive eyes from the light. He was five feet ten or eleven, and reminded me of some coloring-book Jesus who hadn't been crayoned in.

I wondered how much Krowl's bizarre physical appearance had to do with the fact that he'd been drawn to—and succeeded in—the occult. Perhaps, in a sense, Krowl and I had something in common; Garth had always maintained that I'd have stayed on our family's farm in Nebraska if not for the fact that I'd been born a dwarf. Deformity—any deformity—can crush, but it can also propel a man beyond his normal limits.

"Is that part of your act?" I asked.

"Excuse me?" Krowl's voice was high-pitched, nasal and raspy.

"I'm Frederickson. I take it you're John Krowl."

"That's right," he said coldly, looking at me intently. "Garth left word with my secretary that you wanted a reading. He said it was a matter of urgency. Why?"

Krowl's chilly abruptness took me aback. I didn't want to offend Krowl in light of the fact that Garth had told me he could be a valuable source of information. On the other hand, something about me obviously put him off; he looked at me as if he were getting ready to ask me to leave. I decided it might be a good idea to get a better feel of his territory before I started asking direction questions.

"I've got problems," I said quietly.

"Really?" He removed his glasses and stared at me with pink, washed-out eyes. "How do you think I can help?"

I shrugged. "I thought that was obvious. I was hoping you'd read the tarot for me."

Krowl put his glasses back on and smiled thinly. "Frederickson, why do I get the feeling that you think I'm full of shit?"

I felt myself flush. I had to give him points for frankness. "Let's say I'm *hoping* you can help me," I said, trying to sound humble and offering up my most innocent smile.

"My fee is forty dollars."

"Fine."

"Very well," Krowl said abruptly. "Come with me, please."

He turned and walked back down the hall. I followed

him through the open door, which he closed behind us. I found myself in a kind of parlor/sitting room carpeted with the finest Persian rugs. There were more Haitian paintings and faded antique tapestries on those sections of the walls not covered by oak bookcases filled with leather-bound volumes. The room was dominated by a round mahogany table in the center. Over the table a stained-glass Tiffany lamp hung like a sparkling jewel in the middle of the room's dark, earth colors. Although the table was not particularly large, its magnificently carved legs and edges lent it an air of massiveness. There were two chairs.

Krowl took a small bundle wrapped in black silk out of a drawer in the table, unwrapped it to reveal a deck of tarot cards. He sat down and motioned for me to sit in the chair across from him.

"Aren't you going to look at my hand?" I asked.

He shook his head and began to shuffle the cards. "Not now," he replied softly. "Perhaps later. Frankly, I get very bad vibrations from you, and I'd like to see what the cards reveal."

"I'm sorry you feel that way," I said, resisting the urge to add something sarcastic.

Krowl put the deck back together, shoved it across the table to me and indicated that I should shuffle.

"I still don't feel that you believe there's anything to be gained from this," the albino said, watching me closely as I manipulated the cards. He made a clucking sound of resignation. "You should try to keep an open mind. As you shuffle the deck, meditate on some problem or question you'd like the cards to speak to. By the way, are you involved with a woman by the name of Amy? Or Abigail?"

"What?" I stopped shuffling and looked up at him, startled once again. The names *Amy* and *Abigail* were very close to *April*. I found Krowl's question distressing for a number of reasons, and I wasn't sure I wanted to confront any of them. I tried to smile, but it felt like a grimace. "Is that a preview?"

"You'll have to tell me."

"Don't you think you should check out my cards?"

"You're carrying a woman with you," he said, looking at me intently. "I thought I saw one of the names mentioned."

"No," I said curtly.

"All right," he said easily. "The *presence* of the woman is what's important, not her name. Are you right- or left-handed?"

"Right," I said, actually having to think about it. My mind was wandering, and I was having trouble concentrating.

"Then the left hand is the hand of your subconscious. Use it to cut the deck into three piles, then put them back in the opposite order."

When I'd done as he'd instructed, Krowl looked through the deck, without disturbing the order, until he found a particular card, which he placed face up on the table between us. The card showed a young man stepping off a cliff.

"This card is the *Significator*," he continued. "It will represent you in the read. It's The Fool."

"That doesn't sound very complimentary."

He wasn't amused. "The Fool is an innocent," he said. He spoke softly, but his voice had an edge of disdain. "I often use The Fool as a *Significator* for people who come to see me for the first time. As you can see, the young man is about to step into an abyss; it's the first step in a journey of the consciousness. Whether you succeed on this journey or are dashed on the rocks below is up to you."

"That seems fair enough."

Krowl quickly laid the cards out between us. He placed a card on top of The Fool, then another card crossing them both. Moving in a counterclockwise direction, he laid out four more cards, one at each point of the compass around the center cards. Finally he laid out four cards in a vertical line to his right.

I found myself staring at the cards. The predominant symbol in a number of cards seemed to be swords; I didn't find that encouraging.

Krowl sat in silence for almost five minutes, absently tapping his fingertips together as he stared at the cards. He seemed very much interested in whatever it was he was seeing.

"This is an unusual layout," Krowl said at last in a soft, clipped voice. He looked at me inquiringly. I felt a fluttering in my stomach, but said nothing. Finally Krowl returned his attention to the cards and exposed the card that had been covering The Fool.

"The Queen of Swords," Krowl continued. "We say that the card in this position 'covers' you. It represents the general atmosphere surrounding your question. As you can see, it *is* a woman. The Queen of Swords may be a widow. I'm certain she's the woman I mentioned—the one in your thoughts."

He pointed to the card he had laid across The Fool. "This 'crosses' you. It's the Two of Cups—Desire. You have a very strong attraction to this woman.

"Frankly, the rest of the layout is confusing. The card at the bottom is The Devil. In this position it represents something which has happened to you in the past—and which is important to the matter. The Devil is a powerful card. And evil." He hesitated, rapped his knuckles once, hard, on the gleaming surface of the table. "There is evil surrounding the woman," he said forcefully. "Black magic. Does that mean anything to you, Frederickson?"

"You're doing the reading," I said tightly.

Krowl took off his glasses and stared at me with his pale eyes. "The Devil can also indicate the psychic. Something dark. Have *you* had a psychic experience lately?"

Krowl had shaken me with his comments about a woman; now I felt as if I'd been hit between the eyes with a hammer. The dream. As much as I'd been resisting thinking about it, I *had* had a "psychic" experience: Transcending all the laws of logic and science, a comatose child had somehow reached out across an unmapped abyss of the spirit and touched my mind in order to tell me she was in danger. The dream had been vivid and complete, from the flames surrounding Kathy to the gown she'd been wearing. The dream had enabled me to save Kathy's life—but it was an experience I still wasn't psychologically prepared to examine.

"Finish the reading," I said tautly, struggling to keep my voice steady. "Then maybe we'll see how it all ties in."

Krowl made a harsh sound in his throat and started to rise. "You're uncooperative and hostile," he said, anger sparking on the hard flint of his voice. "I don't understand what you're doing here."

"I *would* like you to finish the reading," I heard myself saying. "I'm curious."

Krowl hesitated, then shrugged and sat back down again. He continued in a perfunctory, almost apathetic, tone. "The card on the left side of the cross shows an influence which may be just passing away: it's the Page of Swords, reversed. It's a sick child—perhaps the woman's daughter.

"At the top is the Five of Wands. It represents something that may happen in the future. This is a card of violence. There's violence around you; I can feel it, as well as see it in your cards."

A large, invisible hand planted itself on my chest and pushed me back in the chair. My gaze rose to the Tiffany lamp over the table; more than half the shards in its glittering surface were the color of blood. The hand reached inside my chest, wrapped itself around my heart and squeezed. Images swam in the glass; the faces of people I'd known—some good, some evil, all dead. In an age when most detective work was sterile and boring, done with computers and phone checks, I continually found myself involved with high-fever cases that grew into epidemics of death. It seemed wherever I went in my career, I left a foaming, bloody wake filled with bodies; whatever garden I set out to till ended up Golgotha. But I survived. I was a carrier. Now Kathy and April had been exposed.

My neck and ears felt hot. Krowl had been reading my mail, and I found that the fear I'd initially felt was rapidly metamorphosing into anger. There could be any number of explanations for what seemed to be the deadly accuracy of Krowl's reading; he could very well have read about me and the violence that usually attended my investigations. What Krowl could not possibly know—because I hadn't realized it myself until he'd pointed it out to me—was the importance April Marlowe had suddenly assumed in my life. Krowl had hit that target dead center. The truth was that April Marlowe distracted me as much as—or more than—the plight of her daughter, or the Senator's. It was ugly, hard for me to admit; but it was true. It made me feel ashamed.

Krowl pointed to the card on the right side of the cross. It showed a dog baying at the moon. A large, ominous-looking crayfish was crawling out of a pond at the dog's feet. "The Moon," Krowl said, placing his forefinger on the card. "Its position represents something that may happen soon. The Moon may stand for deception, unforeseen *perils* . . . secret enemies." He pursed his lips and squinted at me. "Possibly bad luck for one you love."

"What kind of bad luck?" I asked quickly. My voice sounded strange in my ears, shrill and strained.

Krowl smiled broadly, as though he'd won a major concession from me. "I don't know," he said quietly. "The woman is sad now; I pick that up from you. She's surrounded by trouble, and I sense that *you* carry much of that trouble with you; you bring it to her."

"What do the rest of the cards tell you?" I asked, pointing to the vertical line of cards on his right. I hoped my voice was steady, put I'd experienced an unnerving flash of the "bad luck" I'd brought to others in the past. Like Garth: A woman *he'd* loved had died in the desert sands of Iran, six thousand miles away. Garth himself had fired the bullet that killed her.

"The Nine of Swords," he said, pointing to the card at the bottom of the vertical line. "Its symbols speak for themselves. The card is in the position representing your fears—in this case suffering and illness, possibly the death of one you love." He frowned and suddenly swept his hand over to the Page of Swords on the opposite side of the cross. "Or the woman's *daughter*," he added quietly. "It's the woman's *daughter* you fear for. And—" He abruptly stopped speaking and stared intently at the cards, as though looking for something. Finally he shook his head, continued.

"The next position represents the opinion of family and friends. As you see, the card is Strength. All it means is that you know they have faith in you.

"The next card is the Six of Swords, and it's in the position of your hopes. The card is a logical one for the 'hope' position. A man—you, obviously—ferries a woman and her daughter across a lake toward a more peaceful place.

"The last card represents the outcome. It's the Ten of Swords: disaster."

Krowl let the prediction drop perfunctorily, then removed his glasses, leaned back in his chair and crossed his hands behind his head. The light from the overhead lamp danced eerily in his pink eyes. "Normally, at this point I'd try to be upbeat," he continued casually. "I'd try to assure you that the trends shown by the cards don't necessarily have to come to pass. I'd tell you that the cards reflect your present state of mind, and what *could* happen if you don't change your present behavior patterns. But I don't think you care about what I have to say. I still think you came here for some other reason."

"You're very perceptive, Krowl," I said, meaning it. My stomach was churning, and I felt light-headed. I hoped it didn't show. I found I disliked Krowl; he was arrogant and—to judge by the way he'd handled my reading—cruel. He was also, as I'd been warned, damn good.

"Thank you," Krowl said with a thin smile. "Now, why don't you tell me what it is you really want?"

"I came to see you because I wanted to see what the tarot cards are all about, and you've shown me," I said. "But it's true that I had another reason for coming here. I need information."

Krowl rose stiffly from his chair. "I don't give out information," he said coldly. "I never discuss my clients. You owe me forty dollars."

I stood up, counted out the money from my wallet and placed it on the table. "I don't want to talk about any of your clients; what I need to know involves one of mine. The sick child you saw in the cards; that could be her. She's dying because something was done to her; I have to find out exactly what's wrong with her."

Krowl's gaze dropped to the layout on the table, and he stared at the cards for a long time. Finally his eyes flicked back to my face. "What are you talking about?" he asked tightly. His face was flushed to the point where it almost matched his eyes.

"The girl's father got himself involved in some bad witchcraft business," I said, watching Krowl carefully. "I think his new friends killed him and did something to the girl. She's in a coma. It will help if the doctors can find out *what* was done to her. I'm trying to find the people responsible. Garth said that you might be able to help me. I have to find a ceremonial magician who uses the witch name 'Esobus.' Have you ever heard the name?"

Krowl quickly reached for his glasses and put them on. "What makes you think I'd know anything about this?"

"I just told you: Garth told me you might know who Esobus is."

The albino started to put the cards in the layout back into the deck. Both his hands were trembling now, and he looked sick. Suddenly he pushed the cards away and walked quickly to a bookcase filled with occult icons and books. He leaned against it, arms outspread and forehead touching the leather-bound volumes, as though drawing strength from the symbols and words there. He spun around as I started across the room toward him.

"Get out!" Krowl said firmly. His flesh had returned to its normal parchment color, and he'd stopped shaking. It was quite a transformation. "What right do you have to come to me under false pretenses and start asking questions?"

"Hey, buddy; I'm just asking you to help a little girl who's dying. Esobus works out of your bailiwick, not mine. I can see that you're afraid; okay. I absolutely guarantee that no one will ever find out you gave me his real name."

"I don't know anything." He half-turned toward a louvered door behind him. "*Jonathan! Come here!*"

"Bullshit," I said quietly. "You sure as hell know something; you looked like you were about to toss your cookies when I mentioned the name. Come on, Krowl. Anything you tell me will be kept in the strictest confidence. Nothing is going to happen to you. Tell me Esobus' real name."

A huge man, almost seven feet tall, appeared in the doorway, and Krowl motioned toward me. "Get him out of here," he said to Jonathan. Then to me: "Don't come back here again."

I waved an embarrassed, reluctant Jonathan off and headed for the door, where I paused with my hand on the knob, turned. "I don't know what your problem is, Krowl," I said softly, "but I want to make a prediction of my own. I'm betting that I can be an even bigger pain in the ass than Esobus. I'm making up a creep list, and it looks like you're on it. If that girl dies because the doctors don't have information you could have given me, I'm going to be back. You think on that, you son-of-a-bitch." I took a card out of my pocket and handed it to the bemused Jonathan. "Here's my number; you call me if you want to talk."

I made a point of slamming the door behind me.

I walked to a phone booth at the end of the block and

called Garth. I let the phone ring ten times and was about to give up when Regina finally answered.

"Hi, Regina. It's Mongo. Let me talk to Garth, please."

Garth came on the line a few seconds later. "*Jesus,* Mongo," he growled. "You pick the most *incredibly* inopportune times to call."

"Think of me as your conscience."

He grunted. "How's the little girl?"

"The same."

"Did you get anything from John?"

"A hard time. He doesn't like me; I don't like him."

"That's too bad. He's a great contact. If anyone knows who Esobus is, I'd have laid odds it would be John."

"And you'd win. Krowl knows something, all right; I thought he was going to pass out when I mentioned Esobus. The problem is that he threw me out. He's afraid of something. If Krowl won't tell me about Esobus, I'm going to start finding out about Krowl. How well do you know him personally?"

"Not well enough to tell you anything useful. I met him through some of my other contacts."

"Okay. I want you to do something for me. Have you heard of Harley Davidson?"

"The motorcycle or the singer?"

"Ho-ho. I thought he was out on the Coast, but it turns out he's one of Krowl's clients. He may have digs here in the city. If so, some of the Special Details boys may know where to find him. Make a couple of calls for me in the morning, will you? Davidson used to be a student of mine, and he may be able to give me a better line on Krowl."

"Will do. Incidentally, a friend of yours has been very busy lately."

"Who?"

"Daniel—or Crandall, or whatever the hell his name is. He's been cutting a pretty wide swath through the underground here. You've got company; the word is that he's looking for Esobus too. The difference is that those nice folks are afraid of *him.* I hear he's scaring the shit out of people."

"Yeah? Well, good for him. Get back to me on Davidson as soon as you can, okay?"

"Check. May I go now?"

"You may go now. Listen; save some energy, will you?"

Garth cursed good-naturedly and hung up. I dug another dime out of my pocket and called Madeline Jones. Madeline had also known Bobby Weiss before he'd become Harley Davidson. Weiss had enrolled in my class because he was interested in criminology; I was sure he'd taken astronomy because he'd lusted after Madeline.

"Hello?" It was a stranger's voice—hollow, thin and strained.

"Uh . . . is Dr. Jones there?"

"This is Dr. Jones speaking. Mongo?"

"Yeah. Mad? God, you sound terrible."

"I . . . have a cold. And I'm very tired."

"Sorry to be calling so late."

"It's all right. Is something . . . wrong?"

"First of all, I just saw John Krowl. I'm sure he knows something about Esobus, but he won't talk to me. I'm afraid our relationship got off to a rather rocky start."

"What . . . makes you think John knows anything about Esobus?"

"Big reaction when I mentioned the name. Anyway, I was hoping you'd talk to him for me; assure him that I'm relatively straight and that anything he tells me will be in strict confidence. I know you think Esobus is a myth, but it looks like you're wrong. Hearing the name definitely upset Krowl. I just don't have the time to lean on him. Will you talk to him?"

There was a long pause at the other end of the line, and I repeated Madeline's name.

"Yes, Mongo." The stranger's voice was barely a whisper. "I'll talk to John, but I don't think he'll have anything to say to me."

"Well, I'll appreciate your making the effort. And I may have another lead. Do you remember Bobby Weiss?"

"Uh . . . vaguely."

I wondered; rumors around faculty circles had it that the student and the middle-aged woman had been lovers. "I think he may be in New York," I said. "I was wondering if you'd heard anything from him."

Again there was a long silence; again I repeated her name.

"I'm sorry, Mongo," she managed to say at last. "I'm

just so . . . exhausted I can't think. I don't know what's the matter with me."

"Mad, have you seen a doctor?"

"No. I just need . . . some rest. I haven't heard from Bobby. I'm sorry I can't help you there."

"It's okay. Listen, sweetheart, you take care of yourself. Okay?"

"Yes," Mad answered dully. "I will. Thank you, Mongo. Goodbye."

When I hung up, I found that I was concerned about Madeline. I quickly reminded myself that I had enough other things to worry about, and that Madeline—to say the least—was a strong woman who could take care of herself.

There was nothing more to be done that night. I went home, took a hot bath, then fell asleep as soon as I lay down on the bed.

Nightmare time. I'd have expected something to do with werewolves and goblins, but it wasn't like that at all. I was at the bottom of some desert valley in which the colors were all wrong; low, green plastic sky, gray cactus and sagebrush, purple sand and stone. I was surrounded by figures that looked like people, but weren't. As if to confirm my suspicion, one of them pulled back his lips to reveal long snake-fangs. Slowly, in ballet-unison, all of the figures lifted their arms and wriggled their fingers: suddenly the air was filled with the deadly, rustling song of rattlesnakes. Then the figures began to change into snakes. A few, unable to complete the transition, exploded soundlessly. The rest completed their metamorphosis—almost; I was ringed by rattlesnakes with human faces.

It was all too absurd to take seriously. I knew I was dreaming, and I decided to wait patiently until I woke up.

My patience became a little strained when the snakes started to crawl toward me. Dream or not, the human faces on the scaled, limbless bodies repulsed me. I didn't want to be bitten. I instinctively reached out for a rock; one of the snakes hurtled through the air and buried its fangs in my right thumb. It hurt far more than such dream-things should, and I was relieved to feel the heavy-lidded, swirling sensation of vertigo that was always my passport to consciousness. The screen inside my head went blank and I slowly became aware of my bed, my pillow, the sheet over me, the hum of the air conditioning.

I was definitely awake, but my thumb still hurt. Something was wrong.

Something was gnawing on my thumb.

Tiny needles of fire and ice were vibrating in my flesh, grinding down to the bone. I sat bolt upright in bed and shrieked when I saw the dark, fluttering shape hanging from my thumb. I jumped out of bed and violently shook my hand, but the thing wouldn't come off. Bony, cold wings flapped against my hand, and I knew with sudden, chilling certainty what it was—and what was wrong with it.

Groaning aloud with revulsion and terror, I reached over with my left hand, wrapped my fingers around the bat and yanked it off my thumb. It took all my willpower to hang on to the writhing animal, but I knew I had to keep my head. My entire body was quaking, oozing sweat, but I managed to walk across the room, turn on the light and examine the bat. It had worked one cold, skin-covered wing free and was flapping it against me in a mindless, disease-powered frenzy. Its body kept churning, and I could feel its tiny, clawed feet scratching against my palm and wrist. The maw with its tiny needle teeth was covered with froth and blood. The flesh on my right thumb where it had been chewing was shredded; blood and flecks of saliva covered my hand.

I gagged and tasted sour bile in the back of my throat. Desperately hoping that it was all a dream-within-a-dream, I screwed my eyes shut and waited to wake up. But I was awake. The tiny, muscular body squirmed; I could feel its soft, throbbing belly, wirelike veins, slimy feces lubricating my hand. In a few more seconds it would wriggle its way free.

Fighting off a strong compulsion to vomit, I staggered back across the room and used my free hand to remove the pillowcase from my pillow. I dropped the bat into it, then beat the shape to death with a shoe. Groaning and whimpering like a maniac, I kept pounding the stained pillowcase long after the creature inside it was dead.

I wrapped the package in plastic, washed off my hands with alcohol and bandaged my thumb as best I could. I tried to keep my mind off what I knew was inevitably before me as I dressed, picked up the plastic bag and went down to my car. I couldn't stop shaking. With the bundle on the seat beside me, I careened through the night streets of Manhattan to the university Medical Center. I didn't want to die *that* way, and I tried not to think of the deadly germs coursing through my system at that very moment, being carried by my bloodstream toward my brain.

Chapter 11

"It's rabid," Joshua Greene said. "I'm sure you suspected it."

I gripped the edge of the examining table on which I was sitting, winced as pain streaked through my freshly cleansed and bandaged right thumb. I was in my shorts, and felt cold. "Of course," I said. "Healthy bats don't normally make a habit of chewing on people's fingers."

"You know what has to be done, don't you?"

"Yeah. I know. How many shots am I going to need?"

"I'm not sure. We'll start off with one a day, vary the dosage and take blood samples as we go along. Maybe we can get away with six or seven. I'll start you off, and your regular doctor can give you the rest."

"My doctor's away for a month. I'd just as soon you took care of it, if you don't mind. I'm beginning to feel at home here. How's my little friend?"

"The same," he said stiffly. "My team of specialists is setting up a new battery of tests for this afternoon. Right now, let's concentrate on you."

Greene asked me questions about my height and weight, then left the room for a few minutes. He returned with a hypodermic needle that looked at least nine inches long. He prepared the syringe and came toward me. I lay back on the examining table and stared at the ceiling.

"Antirabies serum is injected directly into the abdominal wall, Dr. Frederickson—"

"Yeah, yeah, I know all about it. If you're going to start sticking needles into my gut, you may as well start calling me Mongo."

"Very well. And if you're going to continue an investigation on behalf of one of my patients, you may as well call me Joshua. Now that we've broken down the social barriers, let's get back to the matter at hand."

He paused, narrowed his eyes and stared at me hard. "There is no cure for rabies once the symptoms have appeared," he continued. "That can be anywhere from two to eight weeks, depending on how well the victim handles himself. *No cure.* I emphasize this because I suspect you could be a difficult patient."

I sighed, shook my head. "You've got to be kidding. Order a stool specimen, and I'll meekly ask you what color you'd like."

"Good. You sound very cooperative. Since there's no cure for rabies, we use the classic Pasteur treatment. I'll be injecting a weakened rabies strain into you. Your system will then build up antibodies in time to defeat the main strain that the bat infected you with. The serum I'll be giving you is prepared from duck embryos. We have some synthetics, but I still consider this the best."

"Lord love a duck."

"Please listen," Greene said evenly, but with absolute authority. I listened. "The point is that you must *rest* in order to let your system build up the necessary antibodies. Do you understand?"

"I understand."

"Good. You've probably heard that the shots you're going to get are painful. It's true. Besides pain, you'll probably experience nausea and extreme fatigue as a result of the injections. As I said, you should rest as much as possible if you want to get away with the minimum number of shots; but then, you'll probably be happy to. Here comes Number One."

I put my hands behind my head, closed my eyes and clenched my teeth as Greene daubed on some local anesthetic, then slowly slid the tip of the needle into my abdominal wall. He worked slowly, expertly, negotiating the needle through the tough, striated muscles. When he had the needle properly inserted, he slowly pressed the plunger. My stomach felt as if it were being filled with hot metal. He finished, slowly removed the needle. When I started to get up, he put a hand firmly on my chest.

"Take it easy for a few minutes," he said. "You'll be able to contain the nausea if you eat small amounts, fairly often. If your stomach hurts, take aspirin."

"What are the odds I could end up with rabies anyway?"

Greene shrugged. "Very slim, since we've started the injections within hours of your being bitten. That's assuming you do as I tell you. Where did you manage to find a rabid bat?"

"In my bedroom," I said, swallowing hard. My mouth tasted like something purple. "A more interesting question is how it got there, and I've been giving that some thought. It occurs to me that the bat might be a small memento from the same people who put Kathy into a coma."

Greene frowned. "Are you serious?"

"I may be rabid, but I'm not paranoid. I live on the fourth floor of an apartment building. How many bats do you find flying around Manhattan?"

"They're here, and they're quick. Did you leave your window open at any time during the past few nights?"

It was true that I had—to air out the apartment after a particularly smoky party. Still, I wondered: I had a chain on my apartment door, but someone could have slipped the bolt lock, let the bat in, then closed the door again. It was a Wednesday morning, and in the past three days my name had undoubtedly been added to a few enemy lists. It was *possible* that a rabid bat had flown in through a window I'd left open over the weekend, but the potential relationship between being bitten by a bat and the occult business I'd been investigating was just too poetically neat to ignore.

"Have you eaten anything since last night?" Greene asked.

"Uh-uh. Seeing that little critter hanging off my thumb seems to have taken away my appetite."

Joshua Greene smiled. It made him look quite handsome. "You're pretty peppy for a guy who's just had his first antirabies shot. Would you like a lollipop or a cup of coffee?"

"Actually, Joshua," I said, sitting up, "I'd like some information?"

"Really?" he said quizzically. "Are you thinking of becoming an M.D. in addition to your other accomplishments?"

"Only if the shots don't work and I end up howling at the moon. What's your opinion of healers?"

He gave me an amused grunt. "You trade me in for a

healer and you'll find yourself howling at the moon and frothing at the mouth in a very short time. Does that answer your question?"

"I'm not sure."

He thought about it for a few moments. "A faith healer is fine for someone whose illness is psychosomatic," he said seriously. "That's assuming, of course, that the sufferer is a believer."

"What about a psychic healer who's supposed to be able to heal in a way that has nothing to do with religion?"

"Nonsense," Greene said evenly.

"That's straight enough," I said, and almost doubled over with a spasm. I waited, and after a few moments the twitching stopped.

"I'll have the nurse bring you some coffee," Greene said. "Then you should get something to eat. After that, you may want to go home and sleep. You're going to be very tired."

"Thanks," I said, getting down off the table and starting to dress. "Tell me: do you know Dr. Jordon?"

When I didn't get an answer, I looked up at him. "Eric Jordon?" he asked guardedly.

"That's him."

"Is he your regular doctor?"

"No."

"A friend?"

"An acquaintance. He's affiliated with the Medical Center, isn't he?"

Greene looked uncomfortable. "I . . . uh, I don't believe he's been affiliated here for five or six months."

"Oh? What hospital is he affiliated with now?"

Greene looked nervously at his watch and cleared his throat. "I'm not sure he's affiliated with any hospital at the moment," he said quietly.

"Isn't that odd? I'd think it would be tough going for a doctor who didn't have hospital privileges somewhere."

Greene put his hands in his pockets and lowered his head. "These sound like the kind of questions a private detective might ask. Are they?"

"Yes," I said quietly. I liked Greene and wanted to be up-front with him. Besides, I didn't have time to be clever; I'd tried that with Krowl, and had probably lost an important source of information as a result.

"Malpractice suit?"

"No, Joshua. I can't go into detail, but it involves a case I've been working on simultaneously with the Kathy Marlowe matter. Believe me, I wouldn't be asking you about Dr. Jordon if this other case, in its own way, wasn't just as important. It involves a woman's life and a man's freedom. Dr. Jordon has access to information that might answer some important questions, but he's being very uncooperative. I'm trying to find out why. That's all I can say, except to assure you that anything you tell me will be held in strict confidence."

"Is Dr. Jordon being . . . charged with anything?"

"No. I'm just trying to understand his behavior."

Greene shook his head and shoved his hands deeper into his pockets. "Look . . . I appreciate your frankness, but you have to understand that professional ethics prevent me from discussing a colleague."

"Sure, Doctor," I said with a sigh. "I understand perfectly." I finished dressing and started toward the door.

"Wait a second," Greene said tensely.

He disappeared out into the corridor, and I waited impatiently, in a hurry to be on my way. Greene returned five minutes later with coffee in brown paper cups. He motioned for me to follow him into a small office just off the emergency room. He closed the door after us, then offered me a cigarette. It tasted like chalk. I ground it out and sat down in a straight-backed chair.

"How's your stomach feeling?" Greene asked casually as he sat down on a leather divan across from me.

"It hurts."

He nodded. "You're the first private detective I've met," he said easily, stirring his coffee with his little finger. "It must be interesting work."

"Sometimes," I said curtly, putting down the cup and starting to rise. "I'd love to chat with you, Joshua, but—"

"*For example*," Green said forcefully, still stirring his coffee. "I imagine you have procedures for finding out things about, say, a doctor you are interested in."

"Sure," I said softly, slowly settling myself back down into the chair. "We clever, real-life private detectives have procedures for finding out absolutely anything. But some procedures are more time-consuming than others."

"I thought so," Greene said, refusing to meet my questioning gaze. "And of course, almost all your time at present is being used to try to find out what's been done to Kathy." He covered his mouth with a long, tapering hand, coughed drily. "Assuming you did have the time, how would you go about checking on a physician?"

I stared hard at the doctor, but he refused to look up from his coffee. By then the liquid had to have grown stone cold, but he kept right on stirring. "I'd start by asking questions of his patients and colleagues—if they'd talk to me. After that, I'd use my contacts in the various Court Clerks' offices to see if there'd been any malpractice suits filed against the doctor; how many, if any, and what their disposition had been. That's exactly what I *will* do—when I get the time."

Greene lighted a cigarette, took two quick, deep drags, then ground it out. "I see," he said, carefully wiping an ash smudge off his index finger. "After a lot of digging, you might very well discover that this particular doctor *had* had a number of malpractice suits filed against him; enough, in fact, to eventually cost him his hospital affiliation. Then you'd investigate further and find that he hadn't been able to get another one. Of course, it would probably be helpful if you could find out about the relationship this particular doctor had with his partner." He cleared his throat. "Assuming, of course, that the doctor you were investigating *had* a partner."

"It would be helpful," I said tightly. "Also very time-consuming. Doctors don't like to talk about each other."

"Oh, I know all about that. But, if you persisted, you just might discover that the senior partner was dissatisfied with the relationship and was taking steps to dissolve this partnership. I'm not sure what any of this would have to do with your investigation, but it certainly might answer a few of your questions about the doctor."

"It certainly might," I said, fairly springing up out of the chair. "You've got my number; you'll let me know right away if there's any change in Kathy's condition, right?"

For the first time since we'd entered the room, Greene lifted his eyes to meet my gaze, smiled easily. "Right."

"In the meantime, I'm going back to work on finding out what's been done to Kathy."

Greene raised his eyebrows. "I told you: you're going to find that you're very tired and sore. And you *must* rest."

"Yeah. Well, I'm just going to have to put it on remote control. I'll walk and talk very slowly."

Joshua sighed. "Any leads at all?"

"My cup runneth over with weirdos, but I can't say for sure that any of them qualifies as a lead. You still don't think there's any possibility Kathy could be suffering from some psychological trauma?"

He shook his head. "Forget that notion. There's no witchcraft involved in Kathy's condition, Mongo. Whatever's wrong with her has a physical cause. I'm sure we'll have the answer as soon as we learn what the question is."

On the way out, I raised my bandaged thumb in the air. "Thanks for the tender loving care, Joshua. And thanks for the discussion on private detectives."

Joshua Greene had been absolutely right: I was exhausted, and it felt as if I had a permanent cramp in my stomach. I tried to eat some breakfast, but I couldn't even get started on it. I went back to my apartment and lay down, but I couldn't find anything even remotely resembling a comfortable position. I got up and took three aspirins, then sat on the edge of the bed and idly rummaged around in my emotions.

Despite Greene's assurances, I was still very much afraid of the deadly germs that were loose in my system. I was more than a little angry, and I was beginning to feel sorry for myself. That wouldn't do at all. If I couldn't sleep, I had to do *something*. I picked up the phone and dialed Bill Younger's private number. The Senator answered on the first ring.

"Senator, it's Frederickson."

"Frederickson," Younger said gruffly, his voice strained. "I was just getting ready to call you."

"How's your daughter?"

"Linda's . . . worse. I'm . . . not sure even Esteban will be able to help her if she has to wait much longer. I'm getting ready to hold that press conference you suggested in the first place."

"That could cost you your career, and it won't necessarily get Esteban out."

"I have to do something, Frederickson. Have you been able to find any new evidence?"

"No, but I think I may be able to raise some new questions. At the outside, how much time do you think we have before Esteban won't be able to help your daughter any longer?"

There was a long silence on the line, then: "A week, maybe ten days. She's deteriorating rapidly now. She . . . she—" His voice broke, and I heard him sob. After a few moments he cleared his throat and brought his voice back under control. "It takes her most of the morning to clear her lungs. Her medication helps some, but only Esteban seems to be able to affect her condition for any length of time."

"All right, Senator. Here's what I've got—and it's not much. I don't want to get your hopes up, but maybe—just maybe—I can raise enough questions and doubts to get Esteban a sympathetic bail hearing. But I'm going to have to get my facts straight, and that's going to take some more time. Hold off on your press conference for a couple of days. In the meantime, either bring your daughter with you to New York or leave a number where I can reach you twenty-four hours a day. It's next to impossible to get bail in a premeditated-murder case; if I *can* arrange a hearing based on new information, I may want you here—fast. I'll try to arrange for any hearing to be held *in camera*, but I can't promise anything."

"Linda and I will be in New York this evening," Younger said tensely. "We'll stay at The Plaza. You can reach me there whenever you need me."

"Very good. There's one other thing, and you probably won't like it. If I run into any road jams, I may need a little unethical political pressure brought to bear. If you've got any juice in the city, start getting your contacts together. Okay?"

"I'll do whatever you say, Frederickson."

When I hung up, spasms of pain and nausea rippled through my belly. I wasn't looking forward to the hours I was going to have to spend talking to court reporters and combing through the public trial records. And I was going to have to conserve enough energy for some fast talking.

I started to stand up, but another spasm put me on my back with my knees drawn up to my chest. I breathed deeply, trying to relax. The deep breathing helped some, but it also made me return to the question of just *how* a rabid bat had ended up in my bedroom. It *could* have flown in a few days before, during the time when I'd left the window open; it could have holed up in some nook or cranny. Maybe. But I was finding my discomfort and the fact that I could *still* die of rabies—not to mention the general inconvenience of being bitten by a rabid bat—somewhat distressing. If someone *had* sicced the animal on me, I definitely wanted to find out who so that I could repay the kindness.

Assuming the bat had received human help getting in, it was obviously a kind of deadly game-playing, and probably had something to do with the Esobus matter. I had no way of knowing who'd been talking to whom, or who could be responsible.

I picked up the phone and started to dial Krowl's number, then thought better of it and hung up. I assumed that coming up with a rabid bat in the middle of Manhattan was no particularly easy task. Krowl had been shaken enough to blow someone's whistle after he'd talked to me; but unless Esobus had a private cave full of rabid bats, it wasn't likely that the little critter who'd bitten me could have been conjured up in the few hours that had passed since I'd left his house. In any case, I doubted that Krowl would talk to me, and a call would only telegraph the fact that I was suspicious.

It suddenly occurred to me that there was someone else who'd had the time; also, to judge by his background, he was crazy enough to come up with just such a nasty gift for somebody he was unhappy with. He might not have any connection with Esobus, but at the moment I didn't feel picky. I called the Chancellor's office. Two secretaries later, I got him on the line.

"Good morning, Dr. Frederickson," Barnum said. He sounded a lot better than he had the last time I'd talked to him; controlled and self-assured. "How are you?"

"Actually, I'm feeling a bit tacky."

"Oh? I'm sorry to hear that. Incidentally, I'm glad you called. I've been feeling rather embarrassed about that . . . matter we discussed."

"I don't know why you should be embarrassed. You have a legitimate concern."

"Well, thank God you're a discreet man. You were absolutely right to back away from it, and I appreciate your good judgment. I should have handled it myself from the beginning."

"You've talked to Dr. Smathers?"

"Yes, I have," he said firmly. "Yesterday morning, right after you left."

"Did you talk about the rumors?"

"No," Barnum said, sounding a little less sure of himself. "I didn't feel I had the right. But I did ask him where all his money was coming from." He laughed shortly, and his voice brightened again. "It seems Dr. Smathers has been getting a number of grants on his own, and you know what sloppy bookkeepers these scientists are. Very commendable of him, I think—the grants, I mean."

"Very commendable. Did you find out what he's up to?"

"Well, I've been through most of his complex. It seems Dr. Smathers has received grants to study certain forms of psychotic behavior. The equipment they use is very expensive, and there *are* potentially dangerous people on the fourth floor from time to time. That explains the need for tight security. Actually, Dr. Smathers was quite gracious."

"Chancellor, did my name come up?"

Barnum cleared his throat. "I'm afraid it did, Dr. Frederickson. Not that *I'm* indiscreet, but Dr. Smathers seems to have put two and two together. He jokingly asked me if I'd hired you to check up on him."

"Jokingly."

Barnum laughed nervously. "I didn't confirm or deny, but I think Smathers guessed. Actually, he seemed more amused than offended."

"Amused," I said. "I'm glad to hear that." I added a good-bye and hung up. The phone rang almost immediately. It was Garth.

"Hey, brother," he said. "Your phone's been busy for a half hour and it's only nine in the morning. What's up?"

"Somebody's been driving me batty. That's a punch line. Want to try and guess the joke?"

"What the hell are you talking about?"

"Never mind. Have you got a line on Harley Davidson?"

He grunted. "Yeah, and it's bad news. If you want to

get anything coherent out of him, every second counts. And I'm not kidding."

"What's the matter with him?"

"Your friend Davidson's a junkie, and it seems he's in a bad way."

"That doesn't sound like Bobby."

"Well, unless there are two rock stars going by the name of Harley Davidson, this is your man."

"How long's he been on junk?"

"According to my sources, about a year," Garth replied. "Once he started to go, he went downhill fast. I've seen it before. He hasn't sung a note in six months, and his band's broken up. No promoter will touch him, even if he *wanted* to perform, which I understand he doesn't. For a while he was moving around a lot, staying with friends. Now even *they* don't want him."

"Have you got a current address on him?"

"Try 38 Farrell Street. You know where it is?"

"Yeah," I said, feeling a little chill. "Off The Bowery. Thanks, Garth. I appreciate the information—and the speed."

"Let me know what you find out."

"Will do. Any further information on Daniel?"

"Still kicking ass, from what I hear."

"If the two of you cross paths, tell him I want to talk to him. About bats."

"What's with the bats?"

"I'll talk to you later, brother. Thanks again."

After hanging up, I eased myself over the side of the bed. The pain in my stomach had eased to a kind of dull throb; now it was my thumb that burned. I managed to get dressed; I needed a shave, but decided to save my energy for what looked to be a long day. I wanted to talk to Davidson, then start pulling together my other contacts.

I opened my apartment door and was startled to see April Marlowe, her hand raised as if to knock. We both jumped, then laughed. She was dressed as she'd been when I'd first seen her, in jeans and the steel-blue silk blouse. She looked tired, but still stunning.

"Robert!" she said breathlessly, reaching out and gently touching my right hand. "I saw Dr. Greene this morning and he told me what happened to you. Are you all right?"

"Just a little sore, April. Thanks."

"*Sore?* Dr. Greene told me you were in pain and that you'd probably be in bed all day!"

"I'm surprised you're not at the hospital."

April looked at me oddly; something like a cloud passed across the surface of her blue-gray eyes. "After all you've done for Kathy, I thought it was time *you* got a little tender loving care."

"Thank you," I said quietly, covering her hand with mine. As before, the touch of her flesh was like an electric shock, making it hard for me to breathe. This time she didn't draw her hand away. I squeezed her fingers, then quickly drew my own hand back, embarrassed by even this small intimacy. I felt like a shy schoolboy—even more so since Krowl's reading had made me intensely aware of just how much April Marlowe fascinated me. "I appreciate your coming to see me, April," I continued, resisting the impulse to look at my feet. "I know how hard it is for you to leave Kathy. You can go back now. I'm all right."

"They're running more tests on Kathy this morning," April said softly. "I told Dr. Greene I'd be here, so he knows where to reach me. I did want to get out of the hospital for a little while. I thought I'd come over and make you something to eat, and here I find you on your way out. At least you can let *me* take *you* out to breakfast."

The fact of the matter was that there was nothing I'd have liked better than to spend a leisurely hour or two with April Marlowe; but it was also a fact that the depth of my feeling toward her was beginning to frighten me. I was, when all was said and done, a dwarf. I didn't want to make a fool of myself. It wasn't that I lacked self-confidence: I didn't lack for female company, platonic or otherwise. But April was different; she was creating an emotional climate in me that I feared was blowing out of control. I didn't want to do or say anything that might jeopardize our relationship—whatever that relationship might be.

April was a woman I wanted badly—and could love.

"Uh—I can't hold anything down, April. And I have to keep moving; I have to find somebody."

"It has something to do with Kathy, doesn't it?"

"Maybe; I'm not sure. I feel like I'm chasing a ghost, if you'll pardon the outrageous analogy, but I have to keep after this Esobus. At the moment, I'm trying to get more information on John Krowl. I'm on my way to talk to a man by the name of Bobby Weiss. You may have heard of him as Harley Davidson."

"The singer?"

"He *used* to be a singer. Right now he's on the skids."

"Robert, may I go with you? I . . . really don't want to be alone today."

"Where I'm going isn't exactly Park Avenue, April. It's ugly; very ugly."

She shook her head. "I'd still like to go—as long as you don't think I'll be in the way. I'll wait in the car; just as long as there's a phone nearby so I can check in with the hospital."

Against my better judgment, very conscious of Krowl's reading of the tarot cards, I nodded my assent.

I drove across town on 72nd Street, turned south on the East River Drive and exited in lower Manhattan on Houston Street. The pain in my stomach persisted, as though Joshua Greene had left part of the needle there; but my weariness had vanished, chased by the excitement of being near April Marlowe. The late morning and afternoon no longer loomed as a nightmare of forced endurance; the woman beside me made everything all right, and I had to remind myself of the seriousness of the errand I was on.

Cars were jammed up in the left lane, waiting to get onto the entrance ramp for the Manhattan Bridge. Krowl, of course, lived just across the river, and it occurred to me as I pulled into the right lane to pass that I was driving at a right angle to the problem. Looking up Bobby Weiss in order to get information on the palmist and tarot reader might well be a waste of precious time. I felt a surge of rage at Krowl for holding out on me—if he was holding out on me.

April must have had similar thoughts. "How did your reading with John Krowl go?" she asked.

"Ummm."

"What does '*ummm*' mean?"

"It means you were right: I was impressed."

"How did the two of you get along?"

"Not too well." I glanced over at her. "I think he knows something about Esobus, but he isn't likely to tell me what it is. The man I'm going to see had his hand cast on Krowl's wall; I want to find out what it takes to get into the Inner Sanctum, and what it means once you get there. By the way, your former husband's cast was there too."

April half-turned in her seat, touched my arm. "*Frank* went to see Krowl?"

"As Bart Stone; at least that's the way the cast is identified. Krowl may not have known his real name when the cast was made."

"Perhaps not," April said distantly. "On the other hand, 'Bart Stone' was far more famous than Frank Marlowe; that was one of the things that bothered Frank. He wanted to produce something he could be proud to put his own name on." She paused, shook her head. "If you knew Frank, you'd realize that a tarot reader would be the *last* person he'd have gone to see."

"You also said he was the last person you'd have expected to be involved in witchcraft," I reminded her gently. "And the person I'm going to see is the last person I'd expect to become a junkie, but that's what he is. I don't think I'll recommend this occult business to any of my friends."

She looked away. "It's not all like that, Robert," she said sadly. "You've seen so much . . . evil. I guess you can't be expected to understand."

"I've met *you*," I said, brushing the back of my hand across her forearm. "And that makes me think wicca can't be all bad."

I stopped for a traffic light, and two bleary-eyed members of The Bowery's vanguard looking for the day's first bottle of Thunderbird or cheap rotgut whiskey stumbled off the divider and proceeded to "clean" the lights and windshield of the car with the filthy rags they carried. I rolled down the window and managed to slip a dollar to the man nearer me before he'd smeared the entire windshield.

"Thank you," the man said. His smile was vacant, but his voice was surprisingly clear, with precise diction. "You're probably curious about me. I used to be an engineer. It's not that people haven't tried to help me. Don't you believe it. I'm here because I'm a loser. I *want* to be here; I'm a bum because I *want* to be a bum."

I glanced into his face and was startled to see that he

was a fairly young man who only looked old. I always gave money to the street-working winos when I passed through this section, but I rarely *looked* at them. Now, when I did, I was shaken, not only by the wasted human being who lived from one bottle to the next, but by the research which seemed to indicate that there was no solution. As the man had said, he was on The Bowery because he wanted to be, and all the king's psychiatrists probably couldn't keep him away. Put him in the hospital, dry him out, buy him clean clothes, get him a job . . . he'd be back in a week, just like the shopping-bag ladies in midtown.

I wondered if the man thanked all his "customers" with his confession.

April had rolled down her window and given the other man a dollar. The light changed, and I stepped on the accelerator.

"What do you hear from your brother?" I asked.

April, who'd been looking back, sighed and turned around to the front. "Nothing. I think he's spoken to Dr. Greene on the phone to ask after Kathy, but I haven't seen or spoken to him since you saw the two of us together at the hospital." She pointed out the window to the dirty summer streets. "I know he hasn't gone home. He's somewhere out . . . there."

"Oh, you bet he is. *My* brother tells me Daniel's scaring hell out of every warlock in the city. What's he *doing* out there, April? What does he think he can accomplish?"

"The same thing you're doing," she said softly. "He's trying to help Kathy."

"Then why won't he cooperate with the police? Or with me?"

"I told you: he has to do things his own way."

"Membership," I said quietly.

"Excuse me?"

"Nothing. I was just talking to myself."

I turned left on The Bowery, the quintessential "skid row"—a thoroughfare of dead dreams, drunks and wholesale appliance and lighting stores. The Bowery is the catch basin for the city's human dregs. This street is as far into the spiritual sewer as the drunks can flow. Having resisted the best ministrations of everyone from the toughest troops of the Salvation Army to flying squadrons of social workers, they are tended to in soup kitchens and flophouses, but, for the most part, left alone in their special circle of hell, like bits of human garbage moldering in the wind, snow, sun and rain, apathetically waiting for death. Those men who'd begun cleaning windows early—or who'd had some coins left from the day before—were already sprawled on the sidewalk, or huddled in doorways drinking death disguised as bottles in brown-paper bags. Of late, they'd been joined by a new breed of derelict: hopeless, wild-eyed crazies dumped on the streets under New York State's new "enlightened" program of releasing the mentally ill from the hospitals and returning them to "neighborhood care."

It was a bad place to be looking for a friend.

Farrell Street was narrow and litter-strewn, bounded on both sides by gutted, decaying buildings. I parked in front of the address Garth had given me; it was a rotting hulk that looked a month or so away from disintegration. April asked if she could come along, but I insisted that she stay in the car. I locked the car doors, then went up to the entrance.

The front door of the building was half off its hinges. I pushed it to one side, stepped over an unconscious drunk and walked down a hallway that reeked of urine and garbage. The door to Bobby Weiss's apartment was locked, but a terrible stench emanated from the room on the other side. I knew what I was going to find even before I went in. The lock broke easily; I pushed open the door and entered.

The floor of the room was littered with glassine envelopes and needle-works. Bobby Weiss/Harley Davidson was out, and he wouldn't be back. He'd left his half-naked body behind, a dirty needle stuck in its thigh, on the filthy bathroom floor. From the smell, I judged that he'd been dead at least two days.

The odor wasn't helping my stomach any. I put a handkerchief over my mouth and nose and began looking around the apartment. There wasn't much to look at; Bobby had apparently hocked most of his possessions during the course of his addiction, or had simply left them behind in the string of places where he'd flopped.

There was one thing he hadn't been able to pawn, and it

occupied a place on top of a stained orange crate next to a bed with grease-stained sheets.

The book had been put together with skill and great care, with inscribed metal covers and leather thongs for binding.

My stomach muscles fluttered as I opened the metal cover and began to leaf through the book. There were about thirty pages; the writing at the beginning was neat and concise—the handwriting of the Bobby Weiss who'd been one of my students. The last twenty pages were almost totally illegible, obviously scrawled under the influence of heavy drugs. But there was more than enough in the first few pages to tell me that I'd stumbled over much more than I'd expected to find.

I felt wounded and very tired as I put the heavy book under my arm and walked from the room. I was leaving behind the wasted body of a boy who, to judge by the strange manuscript he'd authored, had been shot by invisible bullets of superstition; Bobby had exploded under their impact, plunged from the rarefied atmosphere of celebrity to end as a cold, gray hulk, like a falling star.

My thumb throbbed painfully, a not-so-gentle reminder that the same gunsights were undoubtedly being lined up on me.

Chapter 12

"Is that a book of shadows?"

April nodded, closed the book and handed it back to me. "Yes," she said softly. "But it's a very simple one. That's the work of a beginner." She paused, put her hand on her forehead. "It's so *evil;* the sex orgies and drugs, the . . . animal sacrifices."

"You describe Bobby as a beginner; yet Esobus is mentioned in there a number of times—twice as leading a ceremony. Bobby was obviously a member of Esobus' coven. No mythological figure there: Esobus himself." I hesitated, then added, "I'm sure Frank was a member of the same coven."

April looked away, and her shoulders began to tremble. I thought she was going to cry, but she didn't. The trembling stopped. She turned back to me, sighed deeply. "No, Robert. I'm sorry, but it just doesn't make sense. You're right when you say that Esobus must exist: Frank mentioned the name, and it's in this boy's book of shadows. But the Esobus you hear stories about would never share a coven with beginners like Frank or the boy who wrote this book."

"Don't covens accept novices?"

She shook her head emphatically. "Any coven that Esobus headed would have only thirteen members, and every one of those members would be a sophisticated and highly skilled adept. By rights, neither Frank nor this boy should even have been able to *meet* a ceremonial magician, much less participate in a ritual with one."

I absently traced my index finger along one of the symbols inscribed on the book's cover. The metal felt greasy and warm. "What's 'scrying'?" I asked. "It's mentioned in here a number of times."

April smiled wanly. "Scrying is a method of divination—looking into the future. It usually involves crystal gazing, but flame or water can also be used. The person who kept this book would have been nowhere near a point where he could even begin trying to scry."

April's matter-of-fact tone surprised me. "You're saying you believe there *are* people who can divine the future?"

She took a long time to answer. "Yes," she said at last. "I believe Daniel may be able to. *I* scry, but I use it for meditation. You'd be surprised how deep into your mind flame or water can take you." She blinked, added distantly; "Maybe that's where the future is anyway—inside ourselves." Suddenly she shuddered and gripped my arm tightly. "Robert, can we find a telephone? I want to call the hospital."

"Right. And I have to call the police about the body."

I put Bobby Weiss's book of shadows on the floor of the car and drove out on Houston, where we found a pay phone. When April got out to make her call I leafed through the book again, thinking of amateur witches in a supposedly top-secret supercoven of ceremonial magicians. From the notes in the book, it was clear that the corruption and decline leading to Bobby's death had begun with his admittance to the coven.

Suddenly I was startled by a banging sound at the side of the car; April was pounding on the window, struggling frantically to open the unlocked car door. The concern and grief that had been etched in her face had turned to panic, as though she had just passed from one nightmare into another even worse. In her panic, she couldn't even operate the door latch. I quickly reached across the seat and opened the door. April fell into the car, bumping her head on the frame.

"Robert!" she gasped in a strangled, breathless voice. "My daughter's dying!"

Daniel—gaunt, disheveled and hollow-eyed—was already at the hospital when we arrived. I had no idea how he'd learned about the emergency, and he wouldn't even look at me when I spoke to him. He put his arms around his stunned sister, and they both sat down on a small, worn sofa in a corner of the waiting room outside the Intensive Care Unit. April sobbed on his shoulder while he stared vacantly at the floor. This particular ceremonial magician had lost at least twenty pounds since I'd seen him last.

A half hour later, Joshua Greene emerged from the room where he and his team of specialists had been working on Kathy. Greene's face was haggard, and his surgical smock was stained with sweat. He motioned us into a smaller, more private anteroom. Daniel, walking very stiffly, led the way, with April leaning on his arm. I hesitated, feeling like a stranger now, but Greene indicated with a nod of his head that he wanted me to join them.

"We understand and accept, Doctor," Daniel said evenly as I entered the room and closed the door behind me. "Kathy's dying, and there's nothing you can do to save her."

Greene slowly shook his head. "We—"

"It's not necessary for you to say anything, Doctor," Daniel said abruptly. "We don't need your comfort."

"What's happened, Joshua?" I asked quietly.

Greene shifted his gaze to me. "We don't know," he said, his voice almost cracking. "A few hours ago Kathy's heart began beating arhythmically. There doesn't seem to be anything we can do to control it. We've tried drugs, but they don't sustain her. She gets weaker after each episode."

"You can't help her?" I asked tightly.

Greene slowly shook his head. "The problem is systemic. Whatever was given to her has worn down her resistance to the point where her body is giving up. We're doing all we can to save her, but in all likelihood . . ." He took out a handkerchief and wiped his forehead. His black flesh was chalky. "I'm sorry, Mrs. Marlowe," he continued in a choked whisper. "In all honesty, we don't think Kathy will . . . survive much longer. I feel you . . . should prepare yourself for the worst."

"We are prepared," Daniel said evenly.

"How long?" I asked.

Greene thought about it for a long time, then said, "Perhaps twelve hours, if Kathy continues at her present rate of decline."

"What—" My voice caught, and I swallowed, trying to work up some moisture in my mouth. "What would Kathy's chances be if we could still somehow find out what's wrong with her?"

"I don't know, Mongo," Greene said hoarsely. "I just don't know."

Daniel came across the room and reached out for me. I instinctively shied away, but his hand gripped my shoulder and held. "Frederickson," he said softly, "I thank you for all you've done—and tried to do—for my niece. I'd offer you money, but I know you wouldn't accept. I hope you will accept my friendship; April will tell you that my friendship is the most precious thing I can offer you." He released my arm, stepped back and smiled almost gently. "This matter is finished. April and I are a part of wicca; we can accept death as a part of life. *You* accept it. Leave us in peace."

"We've still got twelve hours, Crandall."

The ceremonial magician shook his head. His smile was gone. "No. The battle is over; I feel it. Now I wish you'd leave us alone."

"April?" I said, turning to the woman.

She'd been softly crying. Now she looked at me, tried to smile but couldn't. "It is over, Robert," she sobbed. "Daniel knows these things." She moved closer, kissed me, pressed her wet cheek against mine. "*Thank* you, Robert. You must go now. Leave Daniel and me alone; we know how to console each other."

I couldn't think of any of my more traditionally religious friends who could have taken Greene's kind of news better than April and her brother. Yet the serenity these two witches seemed to enjoy in the face of Kathy's approaching death only served to transform my own frustration and desperation into anger. "She's not dead yet!" I shouted, wheeling on Daniel. "We still have time! Twelve hours, one hour—what difference does it make? Let's use the time! Work with me! We'll go out—"

"*No!*" Daniel said firmly. "I've talked to everyone there is to talk to!" He sighed angrily and shook his head. Now he made no attempt to hide his pain. "I couldn't find out anything, Frederickson. If I can't, you can't."

"This time we'll work together. I think I've got some leads that—"

Daniel stepped back and cut me off with a wave of his hand. His eyes had gone cold. "Go! You're not family. April and I don't want you here!"

I glanced back and forth between the brother and sister,

the witch and ceremonial magician. I knew there was nothing more I could say to them, nothing more either of them wanted to say to me. Joshua Greene, his head down, was holding the door open for me. I wheeled and walked through it.

I went down to my car and drove across town toward Garth's precinct station. It was one o'clock in the afternoon, and the crosstown streets were plugged with traffic that I hardly seemed to notice. I knew that every minute counted, yet I felt strangely serene; all of my options had been narrowed down to a very small set of choices, and it was almost a relief. At the moment, there was nothing I could do about the traffic, and I didn't waste energy worrying about it. I felt as though I were looking down a tunnel twelve hours long; at the end, brightly illuminated, was the answer to the question of how I was going to spend those hours.

I knew I couldn't hope to find Esobus in the time I had left—not after both Daniel and I had been beating the bushes without success for three days. What I needed was more time, and there was one person who just might be able to give it to me.

Esteban Morales was absolutely the last button I had to push. It was a decision I'd unconsciously made the moment I'd walked out of the hospital. Either Esteban could heal, or he couldn't. It made absolutely no difference what I believed.

I needed Garth *at* the station house—Garth and Garth alone. There was no time to go looking for him. Wallowing through the traffic, I was surprised to find I had—at least temporarily—renewed a lapsed membership of my own; for almost twenty minutes my lips had been moving in a silent prayer that Garth would be there.

I made it—by a few seconds. As I pulled up to the curb, Garth was just coming down the steps with Johnny Barnard, his partner. I nodded to Barnard and pulled Garth to one side.

"Jesus," Garth said, real concern in his voice. "You look like hell. What did you do to your finger?"

"Harley Davidson's dead. His body's in that apartment on Farrell Street."

"You always bring such interesting news," Garth said

wryly. "Who'd have thought that the Messenger of Death was a dwarf?"

"That's not funny," I snapped.

"You're right," he said after a thoughtful pause. "I'm sorry. That's what comes from hanging around with cops all day."

"I need an hour or two of your time. Now."

He ran a hand through his thinning, wheat-colored hair, then glanced toward his partner, who was waiting beside an unmarked squad car. "I work for this city, Mongo. Sorry, but I'm on a call. Grave robbers. We've got three teen-agers with an apartment full of skulls they stole from a cemetery over in Queens. That's not funny either."

"Two hours, Garth," I said, struggling to keep my voice even. "I need you. If you feel you owe me, I'm cashing it all in now. If I owe you—well, I'll owe you some more. Two lives are at stake."

We looked into each other's eyes for a few moments; then, without another word, Garth went back down the steps and spoke a few words to Johnny Barnard. Barnard shrugged, got into the car and drove off. Garth came back up the steps slowly.

"What's the matter with you, Mongo?" he asked quietly, peering at me through narrowed lids. "You look and talk like a stranger. If I weren't afraid you'd yell at me, I'd say you look like you'd seen a ghost."

"I'm goosing one. I want to spring Esteban on bail, and I need your help."

"What? You think I'm going to smuggle Morales a file inside a cake?" He slowly shook his head. "Go home and go to bed, brother; you've got to be running a fever. We've had this conversation before. The man's charged with premeditated murder. If that weren't enough, he's considered a transient. Forget it."

"Two hours, Garth. That's all I want. I'm going to try something; if I can't pull it off in that time, it'll be too late anyway. Okay?"

"First tell me what you plan to do."

"What kind of lawyer does Esteban have?"

"I told you: Legal Aid."

"He'll need better."

"No, he won't. The guy's name is Herman Spiegel. I

know him; he's young, enthusiastic, and he's damn good. You won't find better."

"Call Spiegel and get him over to the Criminal Courts building. The two of you have to round up a judge to hold an emergency bail hearing." I glanced at my watch. "It's one thirty now; let's make it for three thirty. I'll need you as a witness to tell what you saw and heard yesterday in Esteban's cell. Was there an autopsy performed on Samuels?"

Garth nodded curtly. "You were right; he had cancer."

"*Esteban* was right. He knew about Samuels' cancer, and he knows about my condition. You can testify to that."

"You'd better come up with more than that, Mongo. A judge—if I can find one to listen to you—will laugh you right out of the hearing room. If you don't mind, I'd just as soon my colleagues didn't get a chance to spread the rumor that you and I are idiots."

"I know I'll need more; if I can't come up with it, the whole thing's off."

"What kind of evidence do you think you're going to find?"

"I don't want to say yet."

"Aw, c'mon, Mongo," Garth replied wearily. "I said Spiegel was good, but F. Lee Bailey couldn't get a judge to stand by for two hours with the kind of tap dance you're showing me."

"I've got somebody better than F. Lee Bailey; I've got Senator Bill Younger."

That impressed him. "*The* Senator Bill Younger, I presume. What does he have to do with Esteban?"

"You'll find out at the hearing; or sooner, if he wants to tell you. He'll be here ten minutes after I make a call. He'll help you and Spiegel find a sympathetic judge. What about it? Are you with me?"

Garth grinned crookedly. "Aren't I always? Hell, I'm your biggest fan."

"Thanks, brother." Baby time: the first props for my magic act were in place, and the pressure that had been building up inside me emerged as tears. I quickly wiped my eyes, blew my nose. "Is Esteban still inside?"

"Yeah." Garth slapped me lightly on the back and

glanced at his watch. "He's being transferred to Rikers Island at four."

"I want to talk to him."

We went into the station house, and Garth took me back to Esteban's cell. As before, the old man was squatting on the cot, his back braced against the wall. He looked up and smiled broadly as I entered. His face was still serene and peaceful; perhaps there was a bit more sadness in his large brown eyes.

"Hello, Mongo," Esteban said, getting up from the cot and placing a gnarled, mahogany-brown hand on my shoulder. "It's good to see you again."

"It's good to see you, Esteban. I don't have much time, so I'll get right to the point. Senator Younger is in town with Linda. She needs you badly. And there's a little girl who also needs you to give her the strength to stay alive a few days longer."

Esteban lifted his hands from his sides, then let them drop loosely in an elegant gesture of helplessness. "I will do anything I can, Mongo. But I am here—"

"Well, I'm going to try and get you out on bail. But I have to ask you some questions. You may not want to answer them, but you're going to have to if you want your freedom. First, is Dr. Jordon a negative healer?"

Esteban looked puzzled. "I do not know what you mean, Mongo."

"You seem to have some kind of positive effect on people; being around you helps them to get better. You once said Dr. Jordon shouldn't have become a doctor. What did you mean?" When he hesitated, I stepped close to him and gripped his arm. "Esteban, two people are going to die in a very short time unless you can give me some answers."

"Dr. Jordon had a bad effect on patients," Esteban said quietly. "I saw it in his patients that I treated. It was harder for them to get better when he treated them."

"How did Samuels and Jordon get along?"

"They were . . . not friendly," he said with obvious reluctance. "They tried not to show it in front of me, but I sensed tension when they were together."

"Thanks, Esteban," I said on my way out of the cell. "I hope I'll be seeing you again in a couple of hours."

I hurried to my apartment, where I had a miniature cassette recorder. I taped the machine to my body, then called Janet Monroe. She wasn't home, but I finally reached her at her university office.

"Mongo!" she said. "Senator Younger called me; he told me—"

"Babe, I haven't got time to talk. I need you."

"I'm here," the nun said quickly.

"Get over to the university Medical Center; sixth floor. The patient's name is Kathy Marlowe. She's dying fast, but from what you and Mercado say, Esteban just might be able to maintain her long enough for me to get information that could save her life. I need you to set things up. Younger will be bringing his daughter over there. We'll need another bed set up in the Marlowe girl's room so that Esteban can work with both of them. The doctor you want to speak with is Joshua Greene. He's going to be pretty incredulous. I need you as a scientist to talk to the physicians, and as a nun to talk to the girl's mother and uncle."

"Are they Christians?"

"Hardly; but I suspect the three of you may have something in common: you take your beliefs seriously. Concentrate on the mother; right now she's trapped by the notion it's all been written, and that it's a waste of time to try to change the ending. If the big weirdo with her gives you any lip about accepting fate, kick ass. Okay?"

"When do you want me to go?"

"Right now. I don't know when I'll be there, but there isn't a minute to spare."

"I'll do my best, Mongo."

"I know you will, Janet. Thanks."

I made my second call to Senator Younger. I told him to meet Garth at the station house, then quickly filled him in on what I hoped to do.

Now I had to make the crucial decision whether to call Eric Jordon or go directly to see him. If I called and he simply refused to see me, my show closed out of town. I preferred to confront him directly, without any prior warning. On the other hand, his office was about thirty minutes away, allowing for traffic. He could have an office full of patients; he could be out on a Long Island golf course; he could be in Bermuda. In which case, precious hours would be wasted. I decided to call; it might give me a slight advantage if I could start him stewing before I got there.

I dialed his number and got his nurse. I was told that Dr. Jordon was in, but that he couldn't be disturbed. I asked her to tell him I wanted to talk to him about his dead colleague. She sniffed, informed me that she'd see if he'd come to the phone. He did.

"Dr. Jordon here."

My stomach picked that moment to heave, and I tasted bile in my mouth; a burning, acid sensation undulated back and forth across the inside of my belly. I couldn't afford any show of weakness; I had to appear cold, confident. I crouched down on the floor and pressed my fist into my stomach. The nausea passed. I activated the tape recorder and put the tiny microphone up against the receiver.

"This is Robert Frederickson," I said, blinking sweat out of my eyes.

"Who?"

"Right now I'm the most important person in your life," I said, trying to imagine how Laurence Olivier would handle it if he wanted to sound casually menacing. "I've been doing some checking on your operation, and I've found out some interesting things. I thought I'd talk to you before I went to the police."

I winced when a new spasm of nausea hit me, and shoved my fist even deeper into my stomach. I felt short of breath. There was silence on the other end of the line. All Jordon had to do was laugh, or be outraged, or hang up, and the play was finished. If there was a play.

Finally Jordon said, "What *things* have you found out?"

The curtain was going up. I covered the receiver with my hand as my breath came out of me in a whoosh. I took a deep breath, said evenly, "I don't think you want me to go into it over the phone."

"What do you want, Frederickson?"

"We can talk about that when I see you. I'll be over in a half hour. Be sure you make yourself available."

Hanging up quickly, I doubled over and waited for the spasms to pass. Then I left the apartment, got into my car and began to drive to Jordon's offices. Despite the adrenaline pumping through my system, I suddenly felt exhausted, unable to keep my eyes open. I lighted a cigarette.

That helped some, but the smoke made me sick to my stomach. I pulled over to the curb, opened the door and retched.

Thirty-five minutes later I walked into the offices Jordon had once shared with Robert Samuels. I paused and hyperventilated. The nausea and pain in my stomach had subsided, and I was grateful for that: I was about to do the most important Command Performance of my life.

There were no patients in the waiting room. Jordon's nurse-secretary directed me down a narrow connecting corridor to a wood-paneled office, where I found Eric Jordon sitting in a leather-backed chair behind a massive oak desk. He was wearing a starched white lab coat. He'd crossed one ankle over the opposite knee; he held his hands in front of his chest and was gently tapping his fingertips together. If he was surprised to discover I was a dwarf, he didn't show it; his face didn't show anything. His mouth seemed frozen in a kind of grimace, and his pale flesh looked the color and consistency of plaster of Paris. I reached inside my pocket and activated the tape recorder as I walked up to his desk. I was feeling light-headed again; it wouldn't do to pass out on my co-star's floor.

"Dr. Jordon," I said with a curt nod.

"Say what you have to say Frederickson," he said tautly. He sounded as if he were talking through a thick gauze mask, and he was breathing shallowly. His thick brown hair was tousled, greasy. He seemed to be looking straight through me.

"All right, I'll lay it on the line for you. I lied to you on the phone; I haven't been doing any investigating. I haven't had the time, which is a subject I'll get back to in a minute. The point is that I'm *going* to be doing a lot of digging, and I'm here to tell you up front what I expect to find. I know you were a brilliant medical student, and you're probably a great diagnostician. But I expect to find that you're not a very good physician. Patients just don't respond to you. As brilliant as you are with facts, figures and computer readouts, you screw up when it comes to people."

Suddenly my head spun. I leaned heavily on his desk and tried to cover the pause with a cough. The room straightened out. Judging from Jordon's glazed expression, I wasn't even sure he'd noticed.

"I think I'll find that a number of malpractice suits were filed against you—and won," I continued quickly. "You lost your hospital affiliation, but you weren't really concerned about that because you still had your main meal ticket—a partnership with Robert Samuels in this medical-services conglomerate. I think I'll find that you're very good at what you're doing, which is attending to the business side of medicine. But that wasn't enough for Samuels. After all, it was *his* business he'd brought you into, and he had a controlling interest. Samuels was a good physician, and when he found out you weren't he wanted to dissolve the partnership. If that happened, you'd be finished. After all those years of medical school—not to mention the financial investment—you saw yourself being cut out of the profession. Something in your head snapped—if I may be generous. You couldn't let that happen. I think I'll find that the two of you insured each other's lives—a common business practice. So you had to kill Samuels to protect your future. When Janet Monroe approached you concerning the Esteban project, you saw your chance. Somehow you managed to talk your partner into cooperating, but Esteban was a setup from the beginning. *You* were the one who went to Samuels with the story about Esteban drugging one of your patients; a lie, but Samuels bought it. He hadn't wanted to work with Esteban in the first place. Now he blew up and filed a complaint with the police. You'd established a motive. Then it was a simple matter of *you* leaving a message for Esteban saying that Samuels wanted to see him that Thursday evening. You killed Samuels, then waited around for Esteban to show up. Everything just fell into place. Esteban's too passive to be outraged, and he's considered a bit peculiar to begin with; everyone just assumed he was guilty."

I paused. Jordon hadn't batted an eye during my speech, and it didn't look as though he intended to say anything now. I needed him to react so that I'd have something on the tape; a word—a tone of voice—anything to indicate, however tenuously, that I'd struck a nerve, and that what I was saying *could* be true. It was the only thing that could provide a bail situation for Esteban.

Jordon wasn't exactly being cooperative; he continued

to sit and stare like a robot. I wasn't even sure he'd been listening.

"You're thinking that all this is going to be hard to prove," I continued, not having the slightest idea what he was thinking—if he was thinking at all. I was fighting off a growing sense of panic. "True. But there have to be records somewhere; records and insurance policies. I'll get to it, Jordon, I assure you. Maybe I won't find out anything, maybe I will. But if you *are* guilty, you've got an opportunity few murderers do: you can almost square things by giving yourself up. The reason I haven't had time to do any real investigating on you is because I've been working on a case involving a little girl who's dying. Now she's slipping fast, and if there's even a *chance* that Esteban can give her a few more days, I want her to have those days. *You* can give them to her. Personally, I doubt that the old man can do her any good. But you'd know better than I would if Esteban has any healing gifts; you kept records on the patients he worked with."

I paused to give Jordon a chance to say something; anything. He sat as rigid and silent as a catatonic. My mouth was dry and puckered, and there was an acid, burning taste at the back of my throat.

"Here's the bottom line," I continued, my voice cracking. I licked my lips and swallowed hard, trying to work up some moisture in my mouth. "If you killed Samuels, I'm going to prove it anyway. If you're guilty, come with me now and give yourself up so that we can get Esteban out of jail. First, you'll be doing yourself a favor; second, you'll be doing *me* a favor—and I'll do what I can to help you; most important, you'll be doing the child a favor. A friend of mine can—and will—bring a lot of political juice to bear in order to get you the best possible deal. What about it, Jordon? What do you have to say?"

He still didn't have anything to say. He sat in the same position, unmoving, bloodless fingertips pressed tightly together. His face was a pale, ashen gray, and his eyes shone fever-bright. It was then that I knew I was right; but Jordon's appearance was useless to me, because it would be worthless at a bail hearing.

I tried to think of something else to say that might prod him, but came up empty. And my stomach took that moment to knot with the worst pain I'd experienced yet. I gasped and doubled over. At the same time, Jordon abruptly uncrossed his legs, leaned forward and opened a drawer in his desk. When his hand emerged from the drawer, it was holding a small automatic. I tried to bunch my legs under me as I looked for some place to dodge or run. It wasn't necessary; he was no longer interested in me.

In one swift motion, Dr. Eric Jordon put the barrel of the pistol into his mouth and pulled the trigger.

Chapter 13

The judge was not happy with me.

He was particularly unhappy with the way I'd pressured Jordon, and he made it clear that he considered me partly responsible—in a moral, if not legal, sense—for the physician's death. He was unhappy with the fact that I'd left it to Jordon's hysterical nurse to call the police, and had left the offices before the investigating officers had arrived. Most of all, the judge was unhappy with the fact that no one had told *him* that Jordon had committed suicide before he'd been startled by the gunshot on the tape recording. He was also unhappy about what he considered the irregularity of the *in camera* proceeding.

That was for the record. Off the record, he told us he personally did not believe in psychic healing, but was impressed by Senator Younger's sincerity and the fact that Linda Younger was, after all, still alive. The judge attributed this to God's mercy, but conceded that God just might be working through Esteban. He understood the unusual circumstances and the pressure I'd been working under. More important, he agreed that the tape recording represented enough circumstantial evidence to justify a reexamination of Esteban Morales' situation. Esteban was free on cash bond that Senator Younger had put up, on Younger's responsibility.

I could hardly believe I'd pulled it off. In fact, I was in such a mental haze that I remained in my seat, staring at the bench, after the judge had left. People were talking excitedly around me, but I was having trouble connecting words to their meanings. Garth grabbed my arm and started to help me up. I shook him off, rose and followed him out of the courtroom.

Garth drove Younger, Esteban and me to the hospital in a squad car. I was exhausted and in pain, and everything around me segued dreamily into and out of focus. The tension of my confrontation with Jordon had made me temporarily forget just *what* was the matter with me; now the realization that I was infected with a disease that tore up men's minds before it killed them washed over me like an icy wave. I wasn't exactly following doctor's orders, and I was afraid. I knew I should go home and go to bed, but Kathy was in even worse danger; I had to know what was happening at the hospital, which meant I'd have to hold myself together for another hour or so.

There was something approaching a crowd outside Kathy's room, and there was a palpable tension in the air. Joshua Greene was there, along with three other doctors who I assumed were the team of specialists he'd called in. Flanking the physicians were three men in dark, pin-striped suits with name tags that identified them as hospital administrators. None of them looked happy. On the opposite side of the corridor, as if facing off against an opposing team, were Janet and April.

I anticipated problems, but Janet had done her job well; Linda Younger had been given a bed in a private room with Kathy. Indeed, it was Janet who seemed to be in charge of the whole operation—probably understandable since, obviously, no one associated with the hospital wanted to assume responsibility.

As soon as we arrived, Janet took Esteban by the arm and led him into the room. Through the open door I watched him as he stopped between the two beds and stared down at the girls. He spoke cheerfully to Linda Younger, then had a whispered conference with April, who'd followed them in. She nodded, and Esteban came back out into the corridor.

"I can still help Linda," Esteban said to the Senator. "With her, we have more time. But I must work with the little girl immediately."

"I understand," Younger said in a hoarse voice. "Go ahead and do what you have to do. I'm just so grateful—" He turned to me with tears in his eyes. "Frederickson, I'm so . . . *grateful.*" He broke into sobs, covered his face with his hands and hurried down the hall toward the men's room at the end.

Esteban went back into the room and turned off the lights. He took off his jacket and shoes, then lay down on the bed next to the pale, comatose Kathy. To me, Kathy already looked dead, but occasionally her chest would rise almost imperceptibly, then fall again as she clung to life.

One of the administrators started to object. April came out into the corridor and silenced him with a reminder that she'd signed a paper releasing the hospital from any responsibility for what Esteban did to her daughter. Then she nodded to Esteban, who, taking care not to disturb any of the tubes connected to her body, picked Kathy up and placed her on his chest. He put his cheek against Kathy's, closed his eyes and began to stroke her body. In the silence I thought I could hear him softly humming to himself. April came over to me, put her arms around me and squeezed hard. Then, without a word, she went into the room and knelt next to the bed on which Kathy and Esteban lay.

"You're making things worse, Mongo."

I turned to face Joshua Greene. The rest of the local medical establishment stood slightly behind him, grimly nodding their agreement like a Greek chorus. "The girl is going to die," he continued tightly. "All you've done is raise false hopes. The mother and uncle were accepting. You should have left them alone with their grief; now they'll only have to go through that phase all over again."

"It seems to me that that decision is the mother's."

Joshua sighed. "How do *you* feel? You look terrible."

"I feel like shit. I've got stomach cramps, and I constantly have the sensation that I'm going to throw up. Is there something you can give me?"

He slowly, firmly, shook his head. "Within the past twenty-four hours you've been bitten—damn good—by a rabid animal. You've got rabies coursing through your system right now. You've had the first in a series of rabies shots that are painful and are *no* guarantee, in the circumstances, that you won't develop the disease anyway. The injections have side effects, and you're feeling them; I can tell by your eyes that you have a fever. If you don't rest and let the serum take effect, there's a very good chance that you could die of rabies. I don't think you're aware of just how dangerous your situation is."

He was wrong. I was very much aware of what I was risking. But I heard myself saying, "I have to keep going, and you know *why* I have to keep going. Give me something to prop me up."

"*No,*" Greene said, a slight tremor in his voice. "I won't help you kill yourself; offhand, I'd say that's what you're trying to do. Rabies is a horrible way to die, Mongo."

He paused, stared at me with his compassionate, soulful eyes. "First, your vision will begin to blur. Then your throat will begin to constrict to the point where you can't even swallow your own saliva; you'll slaver all over yourself and howl like an animal because you'll crave water but won't be able to drink it. Of course, by this time your mind will be gone. We won't be able to do anything but isolate you, strap you down and wait for you to die. And once you start to develop symptoms, it's over. And you *are* going to develop symptoms unless you do as I say. Think about it."

"Oh, I will Joshua," I said softly. "I have." My mouth already felt dry. Greene had told me that symptoms wouldn't normally appear for several days, at least. But then, I was a dwarf—and the bat had really enjoyed a picnic on my thumb; I had to be carrying an extra-large dose of pathogens in my system.

A glacial wind rose from somewhere in my mind, chilling me; regardless of the consequences, I *couldn't* rest—not just yet. I had only a few years left anyway; Kathy had a lifetime.

I wanted to talk to Janet, but she was involved in what looked like a heated conversation with one of the hospital administrators. I walked quietly into Kathy's room, paused beside the first bed and smiled at Linda Younger. The frail twenty-four-year-old woman was resting serenely, her hands folded peacefully across her stomach. Suddenly she opened her violet eyes, saw me and smiled. She reached out and gripped my hand.

"Thank you, Dr. Frederickson," she whispered weakly. "My father told me what you did."

I blew her a kiss, then moved around behind the kneeling April and put my hand on her shoulder.

"Thank you for not letting me give up, Robert," she said quietly, taking my hand.

"Hey, there's no guarantee," I whispered in her ear. "I just had to take this last shot at buying some time."

"I understand. Even Daniel seems to believe that Esteban can help. Otherwise, he wouldn't have permitted it."

"Where is he now?"

"He's back out . . . hunting."

"When did he leave?"

"I don't know; I've lost track of time." She put her cheek against my hand, gently kissed my bandaged thumb. "You have to rest, Robert. You should see what you look like. You're killing yourself."

"I'll take it easy, April, but I've got to get back out on the streets. If I don't, getting Esteban down here will be a wasted exercise. Maybe we've got a little more time now, but not much." I gently pulled my hand away and looked at my watch. It was almost five, and the sand in Greene's original twelve-hour estimate was running out. "I've got to go. I'll be in touch."

Janet was waiting for me out in the corridor. "Thanks, love," I said to her. "You came through with flying colors. I can imagine the talking you had to do. I owe you a big one."

"Mongo!" she called after me as I headed for the elevator. "Where are you going?"

"Hunting."

It was five thirty by the time I got to the William Morris Agency offices in the MGM building on Avenue of the Americas. Despite the late hour, I was fairly certain Jake Stein would still be at his desk, talking on the phone to Los Angeles: such is the life of a high-powered talent agent.

The receptionist buzzed Jake, and a minute later I was on my way past a sliding glass partition into the honeycomb of inner offices of the largest talent agency in the world; William Morris, with its worldwide network of offices, represented about half of all the name actors, writers, directors and singers in the world. They'd represented me during my later years with the Statler Brothers Circus. Now I wanted to talk to Jake about Bobby Weiss.

Jake was twenty-eight; with a full head of bushy blond hair, he looked younger. When I walked into his office he was talking up some kind of deal into a telephone receiver that was part of a ten-button console; five of the ten buttons were lighted and flashing. He hung up, swung around in his swivel chair, saw me and grinned broadly. His grin faded as he rose and looked me up and down.

"Hello, sweetheart," Jake said. "For Christ's sake, what's the matter with you? You look like the lead in a cancelled pilot."

"Overwork. You know how it is with us hotshot private eyes. Don't you watch television?"

"No shit, Mongo; you look terrible."

"I'm all right," I said, shaking his hand. "It's good to see you, Jake."

"Likewise." He drew a long, thin cheroot from a plastic container in the pocket of his double-breasted sport jacket. He lifted the cigar and waved smoke away from his milky blue eyes. "You want a drink? I've got some Chivas in the drawer."

"Yeah . . . uh, on second thought, no thanks." I had no idea how Scotch and antirabies serum would mix, and it didn't seem like a good time to experiment; the way I felt, I'd probably come down with instant bubonic plague. "I want to talk to you about Harley Davidson."

"Davidson? Christ, I haven't seen anything on him in six months. He left us, you know. What do *you* hear?"

"He's dead. I found his body . . ." I had to stop and think; time was collapsing in on itself, and it seemed inconceivable to me that only a few hours had passed since I'd walked into Bobby's rotting apartment. "I found his body this morning."

"God damn," Jake said thoughtfully, shaking his head. He took a deep drag on his cheroot, breathed out the smoke with his words. "I'm really sorry to hear that. I liked that kid. What happened to him?"

"He killed himself. In slow motion."

"Drugs," Jake said, nodding. "I heard things, but I hoped they weren't true." Eight of the ten buttons were flashing now. Jake glanced at the console unconcernedly, looked back at me. "Poor son-of-a-bitch," he continued quietly. "The air's thin up there where he was, and it's stone fucking cold."

"He seemed fine while he was with you, Jake; top of the charts, and a network show in the offing. And he looked healthy enough in his pictures. What happened between the two of you?"

Jake shrugged and ran a hand through his thick blond hair. "His contract was up; he decided he wanted to leave so that he could sign up with a guy by the name of Sandor Peth. What the hell? Harley wanted to leave, it was his right."

"Peth's name was dog shit when *I* was here. Why would Davidson want to leave the people who'd taken him to the top in order to sign with a creepy second-rater like Peth?"

Jake shook his head. "It's tough to figure, isn't it? Peth *is* a creep, and a rip-off artist. It looks like Harley went straight downhill after signing with him."

"He may have started sliding slightly before that."

"I don't follow you."

"I think he got involved with some nasty people who specialize in giving bad advice. I was hoping you might know something about it."

Jake stared into space for a few moments, then ground out his cigar and popped a mint into his mouth. "Well, Harley had an absolutely enormous ego-occupational requirement, you know. He was easily influenced by anybody who knew how to play up to that ego. That's about all I can say."

"Jake, it's important for me to find out who greased the skids under that kid—if that's what happened. It could tie in with a case I'm working on."

Jake nodded thoughtfully and began drumming his fingers on the cluttered desk top. I was beginning to worry about the flashing buttons on his telephone console; Jake obviously wasn't. "Harley was getting pretty deeply involved in the occult a few months before he left," Jake said at last. "Could that be any help?"

"It certainly could," I said, feeling my blood pressure go up a few notches. My face felt hot. "The problem is that an interest in the occult wouldn't make him any different from ninety percent of the other people in the business, right?"

"Sure; it's the Age of Aquarius, you know. But Harley had gone past the point of comparing sun signs at cocktail parties. At the beginning he seemed to be on an astrology and palmistry trip. He was really manic about it, you know?" Jake clucked his tongue disapprovingly. "Then, I think he got into witchcraft. He didn't talk so much after that."

"And then he left you to sign with Sandor Peth. You think Peth's a witch?"

Jake's laugh was high-pitched, boyish. "Peth's a son-of-a-*bitch*, for sure, but I don't know anything about his being a *witch*." He shook his head, laughed once more, then grew serious. "Peth personally insures the lives of everyone in his stable. I'll bet that shmuck is going to make a bundle off Harley's death."

"Did Davidson ever mention the name John Krowl?"

"Christ, yes," Jake said with an expansive wave of his hand. "Harley was one of Krowl's favored clients—and very proud of the fact. That's a status symbol in this town." He suddenly rose and walked quickly to a filing cabinet near his desk. "I just remembered: Harley left something here that might interest you," he continued, opening a sliding metal drawer and quickly riffling through a bank of files. "It was during his manic phase that I told you about. He brought me in a copy of a horoscope he'd had done. He was really riding high at that time, and something about the horoscope amused him. He said it was terrible."

Jake found what he was looking for, drew it out of the file and handed it to me. The paper was heavy bond. In the center were two concentric circles divided into twelve sections by intersecting lines. Each section was filled with what I assumed were astrological symbols. They were meaningless to me. The margins of the paper were filled with more symbols—also meaningless. What *did* mean something to me was the heavy, block-print handwriting; I'd seen it before.

The signature at the bottom of the page read *Jones*.

"Can you make a copy of this for me, Jake? I asked tightly.

"Keep that," the agent said. "I don't want it. I wouldn't even have it around if I weren't such a compulsive filer." He grinned sardonically. "I guess Harley was right; his horoscope wasn't so good after all."

"Definitely not," I said, pocketing the paper. "Thanks, Jake."

"Hey, sweetheart, I hope you're going home to bed."

"I have miles to go before I sleep." I was trying to be funny. I promptly banged into the doorjamb and ricocheted out into the hallway.

It was after six, but Madeline Jones often worked evenings in her lab and I thought I might reach her there. I used a pay phone in the lobby of the MGM Building to call her. The phone rang eight times before Mary Szell, Mad's assistant, answered.

"Hello?"

"Mary, is Mad there?"

"Who's this?"

"Mongo."

"Mongo? I didn't recognize your voice. Do you have a cold?"

"Something like that. Is Mad around?"

"You haven't heard?"

"Heard what, Mary?"

"Mad's in the hospital. She's had a nervous breakdown. She collapsed here yesterday afternoon."

A hot flush started somewhere between my shoulder blades, flashed down my spine, then turned icy. I shivered spasmodically. Everyone was full of surprises.

Someone was banging a gong; I listened hard and it turned out to be Mary's voice calling my name.

"All right, Mary," I said. "Thank you."

After hanging up, I sagged against the side of the telephone booth and tried to think. Mad had lied to me about not being in touch with Bobby Weiss, and I wondered why. I was probably the last person in the world she'd want to talk to at the moment, regardless of the reason. On the other hand, Kathy Marlowe was suffering from something a lot worse than nervous collapse, and I had absolutely no time to be considerate.

I shook off my chill, put another dime in the slot and called the Medical Center. The reception desk informed me that Madeline Jones was seeing visitors, and gave me her room number. My watch read six fifteen, which left me an hour and forty-five minutes before visiting hours were over. I didn't feel strong enough to walk out the door, but I managed. On the way out I caught a reflected glimpse of myself in a wall of polished marble, and immediately understood why everyone was asking about my health; if not for the fact that I was the only dwarf in the lobby, I wouldn't have recognized myself. I was going to have to do something about my light-headedness; nausea or no, I had to try to eat something and hope that it stayed down.

There was a good seafood restaurant down the block. I went in and immediately made my way to the men's room in the back. I filled the washbasin with cold water and used my good hand to splash my face and neck. I began to feel better. Now all I had to do was manage to keep something in my stomach.

I sat at a corner table, ordered some fish chowder and broiled shrimp. The food tasted good; I probably could have eaten more, but I thought it was a good idea to wait and see how that settled. I finished off with a cup of black coffee, then went out into the street and hailed a cab; I didn't think I could handle a car.

Fifteen minutes later I was at the Medical Center, visitor's card in hand, on my way up to Madeline's room on the second floor. It occurred to me that I was spending so much time at the hospital it would save time if I simply opened up an office in the basement.

Madeline was propped up in the bed, reading a magazine. She looked pale and drawn—older. She was wearing a quilted pink robe with a white-and-pink floral design. The robe looked strange on her, dowdy and unbecoming. I was used to the more severe, tailored look that shaved years off her. There was a vase filled with yellow roses on the night table next to her.

Madeline glanced up as I entered. "Mongo!" she cried, startled.

I went over to the side of the bed and kissed her on the cheek. "Hello, babe. How you doing?"

She smiled shyly, self-consciously patted her silver hair, which was hanging loose around her shoulders. Her blue eyes looked watery and tired. "Oh, I feel so *silly* being here."

"What's the matter, if it's not impolite to ask?"

"Just nervous exhaustion," Madeline said, a slight tremor in her voice. "Things . . . just started to catch up with me. I . . . well, I just passed out in the lab. God, I *do* feel silly. I'll be out tomorrow."

"To rest, I trust."

She nodded. For the first time, she looked directly into my eyes. "*You* look like you need a—" She suddenly gasped and put a hand to her mouth. "The little girl! How is the little girl?"

"She's still dying, Mad; I'm still working on it, and I'm still short on time. Now it may be down to a matter of hours—or even minutes. At the moment, I'm scraping the bottom of the miracle barrel with a psychic healer who's trying to keep her alive long enough for someone to find out what's wrong with her."

"You shouldn't have taken the time to come and see me," she said hoarsely.

I took a deep breath and started to reach inside my jacket pocket for the horoscope Jake had given me. Mad suddenly reached out and grasped my hand. "What happened to your thumb?"

"It was gnawed on by a rabid bat."

Mad's eyes widened. "You're joking!"

"Nope. It just happened to be winging its way around my bedroom in the middle of the night. I have a strong suspicion that it didn't mosey in by itself. I don't suppose any of your mysterious friends keep rabid bats around the house, do they?"

Madeline looked at me a long time. I watched in horrified fascination as her face suddenly fell apart and she started to giggle in a high-pitched, girlish voice that frightened me. Then, without warning, the giggles abruptly turned to racking sobs. She turned her face away and buried it in the pillow. Uncertain of what to do, I tentatively reached out and touched her shoulder. Gradually her sobbing eased. She groped toward her nightstand and found a Kleenex. She wiped her eyes, then blew her nose.

"I'm sorry, Mongo," Mad said in a harsh, strained voice. "I guess you can see why I'm here."

"Hey, babe, *I'm* sorry," I said, meaning it. "I shouldn't be here asking you questions. I wouldn't be bothering you if I wasn't running out of time."

"I know," she said quietly. "And your question was perfectly reasonable. For the past few years I *have* been spending a lot of time with some very strange people. It's—" She started to sob again, but quickly brought herself under control. "It can be so evil."

"Is that why you're here, Mad? Did this occult business finally get to you?"

I thought she took a long time to answer. Finally she

lifted her eyes again and looked directly into mine. "I don't know, Mongo; I honestly don't know. I *am* a scientist, and most of my scientific colleagues consider—or *would* consider, if they knew about it—my interest in the occult idiotic. After a while, I suppose, the internal pressure starts to build. You begin to doubt, to wonder just what it is you're doing. You start thinking that maybe it *is* all superstition, and that you're a fool."

It was time. I cleared my throat, said, "You seem to have been right on target with at least one of your astrology clients."

Something like a shadow muddied the surface of her pale blue eyes. "What do you mean?" Mad asked breathlessly.

I removed the horoscope from my pocket and handed it to her. Mad glanced at the paper and grew even paler. She slowly crushed the paper in her fist and screwed her eyes shut. Tears oozed from beneath her lids, slowly trickled down her cheeks like tiny, transparent slugs. "Where did you get this?"

"Bobby's agent," I said, touching her arm again. "Believe me, Mad; I wouldn't be asking you about this if it weren't for the child."

Madeline slowly opened her eyes and stared at me. "What does this horoscope have to do with the little girl?" she asked in a strangled whisper.

"Bobby's dead from an overdose of drugs. I found him this morning. He'd been going downhill for months, and it very much looks like *he* was involved with Esobus. He was definitely into witchcraft, and he had a book of shadows that mentioned Esobus' name. Bobby may have killed himself, but I'm certain someone gave him a good push to get started."

Madeline swallowed hard. "And, of course, you want to know why I lied to you about not being in contact with Bobby since he left the university." It wasn't a question.

"I want to know anything you can tell me—anything you may have left out the last time we talked that might lead me to Esobus. If you're frightened, I understand; I've seen enough of the wreckage Esobus leaves in his wake to understand why people are afraid of him. I'll keep anything you tell me in absolute confidence."

She bit her lower lip and slowly shook her head. "I really don't know any more than I've already told you, Mongo. I was ashamed to tell you about . . . this. I knew what had been happening to Bobby since I cast that horoscope. I guess I was afraid you'd think . . . *I* was the one who'd given him a push. I just wasn't thinking clearly."

I grunted noncommittally. "It looks like Bobby created a self-fulfilling prophecy from that piece of paper you gave him."

Madeline shook her head again, this time more vehemently. "No, Mongo. The trend was there right from the beginning, exactly as I interpreted it. Please believe me; I *saw* how his life was about to change, and I hoped the horoscope would serve as a *warning* to alter his living patterns." She passed a trembling hand over her eyes. "Bobby didn't take it seriously."

"Can you interpret that horoscope for me exactly as you did for him?"

Madeline hesitated, then finally nodded. She slowly smoothed out the crumpled paper. "The inner circle is the natal horoscope," she said wearily. "It represents the positions of the sun, moon and planets at the time of Bobby's birth. It shows a strong talent in art or music, with the talent used in a superficial, popular vein. The chart indicates considerable success."

Again she swallowed hard. I poured her a glass of water from a covered carafe on the nightstand. She drank it down, smiled shyly. Her eyes seemed clearer. "The outer circle is a synthesis," she continued in a stronger voice. "It's the horoscope projected up to the time when Bobby came to see me, and extrapolated into the future. Saturn—an evil, tearing influence—is in the worst possible conjunction with the other planets. There's a bad grouping in Scorpio—the sign of the occult. And there are a number of other afflictions indicated, including a bad conjunction in what we call the 'house of the secret enemy.' Bobby had reached a critical, very dangerous crossroads in his life. That's what . . . I told him."

She took a deep, shuddering breath, then carefully folded the paper into a small square and dropped it on the nightstand. "It *was* accurate," she whispered. "Deadly accurate."

"Mad," I asked quietly, "how did Bobby find out that you were an astrologer?"

"John Krowl recommended me to him. Bobby had become one of John's clients."

"How long had Bobby known Krowl before he came to you?"

"I don't know," Madeline said softly.

"Maybe Krowl was the 'secret enemy' you saw in Bobby's horoscope."

"Maybe," she said, staring at the ceiling and blinking back tears.

"What do you think?"

She rolled her eyes toward me without turning her head. "Why do you ask me that, Mongo?"

"Could Krowl be a member of Esobus' coven?"

"I'd have no way of knowing the answer to that question. If he were a member, he'd never even drop a hint to an outsider."

"What about Bobby? Could he have been a member?"

Mad shook her head. "That would be impossible. If there is such a supercoven, all of the members would be ceremonial magicians—like Esobus."

"So much for your Wizard of Oz theory, Mad. Esobus definitely exists."

"The Wizard of Oz is dead," she said in a dry, quaking voice.

There didn't seem any more to be gained by talking to Madeline. In fact, it appeared I'd accomplished nothing but managing to further upset a sick friend. "I'm sorry I bothered you, babe," I said, placing a yellow rose from the vase on the pillow next to her head.

"Please don't apologize, Mongo," she said, biting her lower lip, obviously fighting back tears. "I do understand. The child is here, isn't she?"

"Two floors above us."

"You'll . . . let me know what happens with her, won't you?"

"Yes, babe. I'll be in touch. Feel better." I kissed her and left the room.

As soon as I turned down the corridor, I knew I was in trouble. Searing pain swept around inside my stomach like sloshing waves of acid. My vision blurred, and a silent scream of terror wriggled free from a primitive part of my brain and filled my head with banshee wailing; Joshua had told me that that was how it would begin.

But another part of me kept functioning in the psychic din; at this point, another day probably wouldn't make much difference one way or another. If I'd gone over the edge and now had to die, I wanted to do it on my feet, at full gallop. I knew I was going to faint, and I didn't want to do it in the middle of the corridor. I'd end up with a team of doctors and nurses poking at me, and I couldn't afford the time.

I staggered blindly down the hall, running my hands against the wall until I felt a knob. By squinting, I could read UTILITY ROOM on a plate just above my head. I opened the door; in the light from the corridor I could just make out a pile of clean towels stacked up just inside the doorway. I closed the door, sprawled on the towels and promptly passed out.

Chapter 14

I woke up groggy and disoriented, and it took me almost a full minute to figure out I was in a hospital bed. The first thing I felt was an immense, warm surge of relief to find that I was seeing 20/20, and wasn't drooling or belting out the Top Ten to imaginary moons. I sat up with a start and looked at my watch. It was eleven o'clock; I'd been asleep for fifteen hours.

I got quickly out of bed. A wave of dizziness hit me, and I steadied myself by holding on to the metal headboard of the bed until it passed. I was in my shorts; my clothes were nowhere to be seen, and the wardrobe in the room was empty. I cursed softly, marched out of the room and down the corridor toward the nurses' station. A group of patients walking in the hallway stopped and stared at the angry dwarf in his Jockey shorts; they looked at one another, then broke into laughter. The reaction of the nurse on desk duty was quite different.

"Dr. Freder—"

"Kathy Marlowe," I said quickly, forcing the words out through lips that felt like stiff leather. "The girl in—"

"Kathy's still alive, sir," the nurse said, smiling.

I sighed, pressed my face into my hands. "Where are my clothes, nurse?"

"Dr. Greene left strict—"

"Nurse!" I shouted, taking my hands away from my face and slamming them against the desk. "I want my fucking clothes! *Am I getting through?!*"

The woman jerked her head back as though I'd hit her, sniffed through her thin, aquiline nose. "Dr. Greene has your clothes," she said archly. "He left specific instructions to be called as soon as you woke up."

"Well, it looks like I'm awake, so you can call him

wherever he is and tell him to get his ass over here. Got it? Otherwise, I'm going to run out in the street like this, and I'm going to sue! *Sue!*"

She sniffed again as she reached for the telephone in front of her. "I'm sure he'll be right with you, Dr. Frederickson. Perhaps you'd prefer to wait for him in your room." She surprised me by winking. "I wouldn't want you to catch cold."

I wheeled and marched back to my room, where I sat down on the edge of the bed and fumed. However, the news that Kathy was still alive made it difficult to stay angry. Relief and gratitude soon swept away my rage.

Greene arrived five minutes later. He was holding my folded clothes in one hand, a huge, familiar-looking hypodermic needle in the other. "Kathy's still alive," he said, tossing my clothes on the bed.

"I heard. *How* is she?"

"There's no improvement, but her condition has stabilized. Under the circumstances, I consider that a minor miracle." He motioned me backward on the bed. "Lie down, Mongo. The only reason I kept your clothes was to make sure you didn't run off without getting your injection. Remember: you need one of these *every* day. I want you back on the street, but I don't want you returning here through the Morgue entrance."

I lay back, closed my eyes and grimaced as Joshua slid the needle into my abdomen. "Don't you ever sleep?" I asked through the sick, yellow pain.

"I have a resident's room here." He injected the serum, then slowly withdrew the needle. I fought off the impulse to vomit. "Your brother was here asking about the girl," he continued. "I told him you were here. He didn't want to wake you up, but he wants you to call him." He smiled thinly. "I take it you didn't bother to tell him that you'd been bitten by a rabid bat."

"Garth tends to worry about me."

"I can see why." He cleared his throat. "Mrs. Marlowe's also very concerned. She'd like you to stop by her room before you leave."

I tapped my watch by way of an answer. "We're still on borrowed time, right?" I sat up on the edge of the bed and began dressing. "How the hell did I end up in bed?"

"One of the nurses found you. Most of the hospital personnel know about Kathy—and you." He almost smiled. "You're on the verge of becoming a legend in your own time—at least, around here. The nurse called me, and I carried you here. You're considerably heavier than you look. I don't know why I didn't call an orderly; I think I may have strained my back."

"I'm compact," I grunted. "I seem to detect a change in your normally inflexible attitude."

The black doctor shrugged his frail shoulders. "You've slept for fifteen hours, which is all I asked you to do in the first place. You want to get out on the streets; *I* want you out on the streets. Kathy and I need you. Like I said, I just don't want you to *die* out there, or end up developing rabies. So investigate, and work as quickly as you can. But you *must* take it easy, and you *must* make sure you get back here every day for your injection. Clear? You obviously have a high pain threshold, not to mention incredible endurance. But your mind and body can only take so much. *Pace* yourself, and we'll get along just fine."

"Got it," I said, pulling on my jacket and heading for the door.

"Mongo," he said. I stopped at the door, turned back. The doctor smiled wanly. "I've been waiting for your questions—or comments—on Esteban."

"What's to say, Joshua? Kathy's still alive, and that's the only important thing. I'm sophisticated enough to know that doctors aren't wizards or sages. Esteban may have nothing whatsoever to do with the fact that Kathy's still alive. It's irrelevant. I don't care what's keeping her alive—so long as she's alive."

"I'll drink to that," Joshua said quietly. There was an odd, questioning tone to his voice. "Esteban hasn't slept at all; the man doesn't seem to need it. He just lies there with Kathy, rocking back and forth humming to her. He spent an hour with the Younger woman. During that time we monitored Kathy, and she started to slip again; Esteban had to go back to her. It's the most incredible thing I've ever seen."

"You sound impressed."

"I *am* impressed, and I wanted you to know. *You* impress me. It was quite a feat, the way you smoked out Jordon to free Esteban."

We stared at each other for a few moments, and I finally nodded. "Thanks, Joshua. I got lucky. Let's just hope that Esteban *continues* to impress. Thanks for taking care of me. I'll be in touch."

The sleep orgy had left me groggy, but my body seemed to be tolerating the second shot better than it had the first. The pain in my belly was more of a dull, throbbing ache than the acid burn it had been, and my vision was clear. I left my car where it was and took a cab to Times Square, where the phone book had told me Sandor Peth had an office. I bought two hot dogs with sauerkraut from a Sabrett vendor and washed them down with a Coke. I waited ten minutes to see how they'd settle, then went looking for Peth.

Appropriately enough, Peth's office was on 42nd Street, New York's mecca of polymorphous sex, gimcrack novelty stores and Instant Sleaze, just off Times Square, a floor above a porno movie house. To judge by the score or more of facsimile gold records tacked to his walls, Peth had to be making tons of money; as a manager, he was getting a flat twenty percent of the artist's take from each one. However, his wealth wasn't reflected in his office space. Old coffee cartons, sandwich wrappers and grease-stained paper bags overflowed a flowered metal wastebasket and littered the floor.

Peth seemed to be wearing most of his money. He looked like his reputation; he sat behind his scarred wooden desk like a bloated spider, alternately talking into two telephone receivers. Despite the fact that it was a muggy August day and the office lacked air conditioning, Peth was wearing a three-piece suit that must have cost at least four hundred dollars. He was sweating, and he would occasionally remove a silk handkerchief from his breast pocket and wipe his brow. He had a globular face in which two small black eyes were set like raisins in a clump of rising dough. The fringe of dark hair that circled the bumpy bald dome of his head was cut short. Every finger on both his hands, including the thumbs, had a diamond ring on it. In his own way, Peth was a striking figure. If you were into sloth and repulsion.

There was no secretary, so I simply walked into the office and waited by the door. Intent on his dual conversations, riffling through what looked like a pile of contracts on his desk, Sandor Peth took some time to notice me. His voice was croaking, phlegmatic, his conversation rapid-fire and punctuated with references to network shows, "The Coast" and "thou's." He suddenly wheeled in his chair, saw me and arched his eyebrows inquisitively. He curtly finished his conversation on one line, talked for another minute or two on the other, then hung up.

"A *dwarf!*" he coughed, letting the pudgy fingers on his left hand hover over the telephone-console buttons as though waiting for them to decide on their own which button he should push next. "I love it! What the hell do *you* do?"

"Snoop," I said evenly. I wanted his undivided attention.

"Snoop?" His fingers continued to hover indecisively over the buttons, wriggling like fat worms.

"My name's Frederickson. I'm a private investigator. I'd like to ask you some questions."

Peth leaned back in his swivel chair and roared with laughter. His body shook, but the laughter never reached his eyes, which were like blotches of thick paint, with no light or life. "*Great*! A stand-up comic!" His laughter tapered off to an obscene chuckle. Peth was a bit overcooked, I decided, like a refugee from one of the fifth-run movie houses on the street below. But he was real and sitting in front of me, raw and rancid at the center. "Jesus Christ," he continued absently when his laughter had run its course. "Who the fuck do I know that would be playing practical jokes on me?"

"How about Harley Davidson?"

Peth had started another chorus of laughter; now it shut itself down in stuttering dribbles until finally he was looking at me soberly. "Frederickson," he said thoughtfully. "A dwarf. Seems to me I've heard . . . You used to be with the Statler Brothers Circus? Mongo the Magnificent?"

"You've got it, sweetheart."

"Jesus fucking Christ," he said, thin white lines appearing at the corners of his mouth. "You *are* a private detective. And you're heavy."

"That's the nicest thing anyone's said to me today."

Peth scowled; on his face, a scowl was a formidable expression. "What the fuck do you want with me?"

"I told you: I want to ask you some questions about Harley Davidson."

"What do *you* know about Davidson?"

"For openers, he's dead."

Peth made an effort at projecting surprise and grief, but gave it up after about ten seconds. "Son-of-a-bitch," he said casually, tapping a fat, bejeweled index finger on his desk.

"Yeah. Son-of-a-bitch."

Peth shrugged and started to pick up the phone. "Well, that's tough; but show biz is tough."

"Funny how Davidson started sliding after he signed with you."

"What the fuck does that mean, dwarf?"

There was no way Sandor Peth was going to give me information voluntarily, and with his street smarts he'd be almost impossible to trick. I knew I was probably wasting my time confronting him directly, but he was one more button that had to be pushed. On the other hand, he could be a very big button; there was no telling what might pop out if I pushed hard enough. There was no doubt in my mind that Peth was in some way—no matter how peripherally—responsible for Bobby Weiss's death, if only because he had passively stood by while it happened. For that reason alone, I wanted to kick him a few times and see which way he bounced.

"That's the talk around town," I said.

"*What's* the talk around town?" he shouted, half-rising out of his chair. Peth obviously had a hair-trigger temper.

"The talk is really a question," I said evenly. "What did you promise—or do—to that kid to get him to leave William Morris and come over to a guy who operates out of a shithouse like this one?"

"Watch your mouth, dwarf," Peth said menacingly. "There's a simple answer to your question: Davidson felt I could do more for him than Jake Stein."

"Oh, *yeah*," I said, emphasizing the sarcasm, watching him. "Everyone can see what *you* did for him. What *did* you offer him, for Christ's sake?"

Peth was not about to enlighten me. "I'm going to sue you, dwarf!" he shouted at me. "I'll sue you for slander!"

"So, sue. From what I hear, you'd be a tough guy to

slander." I smiled. "How much money are you going to make off Davidson's death? I know you had him insured."

Now Peth was having to make a considerable effort to control himself. His knuckles were white where his hands gripped the edge of his desk; he held the tight grip until he stopped shaking.

"I'm a businessman," he said in the tone of a man who was just trying to be reasonable. His voice sounded as though it were being filtered through a thick wad of cotton, and his face was blotched with pink and white patches. "It costs money to build these people up; I personally insure everyone in my stable. After seeing which way Davidson went, you can understand why. Not everyone can handle success. I have to protect my investments; it's just good business."

"What about all the money Harley Davidson earned? What happened to it? When I found him, he was living in a sinkhole. He couldn't have spent *all* the money he made on junk."

Peth scowled again. "Hey, *I* don't know what he did with his money; I wasn't his mother. I got twenty percent, period. What he did with the rest was his own business." He smiled almost sweetly, like some grotesque, poisonous cherub. It suddenly occurred to me that the man was mad. "Look," he said quietly. "I don't suppose you want to tell me who you're working for?"

"I don't suppose I do."

"It can't be his folks; they wrote him off months ago because they didn't want a junkie for a son. I assume that's what he died of."

"You assume right. I don't suppose you want to tell me the real reason why the kid left William Morris to sign with you?"

Peth squinted at me. "We can make a deal, dwarf. Whatever your client's paying you, I'll go better; a *lot* better. I can make you a rich man."

"What the hell could I possibly do for you?"

"One thing: tell me who sicced you on me. That's all. Tell me the name, forget about all this, then go off and enjoy your money."

"It's a tempting offer, but I think you'd better clear it with Esobus."

Peth's control snapped like a rotten string. He was up

and out of his chair with a quickness that amazed me, skittering on his fat legs around the desk to stand in front of me. I found myself staring up into his florid face. His right fist was clenched, the ring finger pointed at me in the warning gesture April had described as the witch's *athamé*.

"You're working with Daniel, aren't you?" he squeaked.

"Daniel who?" I asked, my heart starting to pound.

Peth slowly put his hand down and heaved a deep sigh. "Look, Frederickson," he said in a lower octave, reaching out with one thick hand, "maybe we can still . . ."

I was sick, and my reflexes were only half what they usually were. Before I could back away, he'd wrapped the fingers of his right hand around my bandaged thumb and begun to twist. Now, for the first time since I'd walked into his office, Peth's eyes showed signs of life; they glowed like banked coals fanned by winds of hatred and sadism.

Searing pain arced through my finger, then scorched its way down to the pit of my stomach. I shouted with surprise and pain and reacted instinctively, rolling away from the torque of his grip to release the terrible pressure, then trying to twist free. Peth grunted with amusement at my feeble efforts and moved with me, maintaining and tightening his hold. He started to twist my thumb in the opposite direction, at the same time raising his jeweled fist in preparation for a blow on the top of my head that was guaranteed to crush my skull.

With Peth hanging on to my thumb, there was only one way to go—and that was where I went. I got my feet under me and pushed up hard, slamming my head into his groin. He shrieked, let go of my thumb and crumpled to the floor. The air exploded from his lungs and he lay there, gasping for air and cradling his genitals with both hands.

Holding my thumb, I struggled to my feet once again and stood over Peth. I wanted to see his teeth on the floor; I reared back, ready to smash the toe of my shoe into his mouth. Suddenly the muscles in my stomach contracted with the worst pain I'd known yet. I groaned and doubled over with pain, then stumbled backward until I came up against the wall. I sat down hard, clutching at my stomach and fighting off spasms of nausea.

Peth, still rolled up in a fetal position with his hands in

his crotch, looked over at me and cackled insanely. "You're a dead man," he wheezed, his breath whistling in his lungs.

"What's wrong with the girl, Peth?" I was doing a little wheezing of my own. We were two sidelined cripples, glaring at each other across an abyss of agony and hatred.

"What girl is that, dwarf?" His words triggered a new spasm of insane, high-pitched laughter. "*What girl?* Oh, you are a *dead dwarf!*"

I stared into the leering face, desperately wanting to kick at it and keep kicking until the laughter had stopped and he'd told me what I wanted to know. But I knew that wasn't the way the scene would play. I was helpless; Peth could—and would—kill me as soon as he recovered. I had to get out of the office.

I finally managed to struggle to my feet and wobble out the door, leaving Peth rolling on the filthy floor in his three-piece suit. He was giggling hysterically. "*What* girl?" he kept repeating in his high-pitched whine. "Oh, man, you're one dead fucking dwarf!"

I couldn't stand straight. Sliding against the wall, I made it around a corner, then hunched down on the floor until the spasms of pain and nausea passed. I was sweating heavily, and it was ten minutes before I could straighten up. All the while I could hear Peth cackling in his office down the hall. I walked shakily down a rickety stairway to the street, then went to a phone booth on the corner of 42nd and Broadway. I was suffering a bad case of blurred tunnel vision, but I was determined not to waste time worrying about symptons. I had to do what I had to do, and what would be would be.

Garth had just come in. "Hey, brother," he said, real anger humming in his voice, "why didn't you tell me you'd been bitten by a rabid bat? For Christ's sake, why did I have to hear it from the doctor who treated you?"

"Garth . . . I need you."

"What's the matter, Mongo?" he asked tensely. "Where are you?"

"Corner of Forty-second and Broadway. I've got someone I think has the information we need."

"Who?"

"Sandor Peth; Harley Davidson's manager."

Garth's voice was thick with excitement and tension. "What makes you think he knows anything?"

". . . Witch," I managed to say. "Knows about Daniel. Garth, he's a crazy. We're going . . . to have to beat it out of him. That's why I need you. Can't . . . handle it by myself."

There was a long silence on the other end of the line. Then: "Mongo, did you try to do a physical number on this guy?"

"Fat chance; I'm so weak I can hardly fucking walk. You've got to get over here."

"Stop talking crazy, Mongo," Garth said quietly but firmly.

"Garth, there's no *time*!" I shouted into the receiver. "If you won't help me beat it out of him, I'll have to go back up there and try again myself!"

"Hold it!" Garth commanded sharply, as if sensing that I was about to hang up. "Just listen to me! Don't panic; it's not like you."

"Garth," I mumbled, screwing my eyes shut against an awful dizziness that threatened to sweep me away with it. "Kathy's on the verge of dying. What else can I do?"

"It's what you've already done that worries me," my brother said evenly. "Let's hope you haven't given this Peth cause to swear out a warrant on you."

"He knows I know he's involved with that coven. He won't make any noises to the police."

"You *hope* he won't. If he does, you're going to be hung up good. You wait right there; I'll come over and pick you up. We'll put a little heat on Peth together. But no rough stuff. You *wait* for me. Got it?"

"Yeah," I said after a pause. I really had no choice. "Hurry it up, will you?"

"I'll be there in a few minutes. Sit tight."

I hung up, took a few deep breaths to settle my nerves and stomach, then went fishing in my pockets for another dime. I only had a nickel. Getting change in Manhattan is one of the most difficult feats known to man, and the newsstand on the corner was inexplicably shuttered. I hit four porno movies before I found a cashier who took pity on me and gave me change for a dollar. Armed with the precious coins, I went back to the phone booth and called the Medical Center.

"Reception."

"What's Kathy Marlowe's condition?"

"Uh . . . may I ask who this is?"

That was a new wrinkle, a little frightening. "Dr. Robert Frederickson," I said tightly.

"Just a moment, Dr. Frederickson," the woman said. There was an odd ring to her voice that made my stomach contract painfully with anxiety. "There's someone here who wants to speak with you."

I waited, breathing shallowly and tapping my fist impatiently against the glass. A few moments later April came on the line. She was crying, and for one terrible moment I feared I was about to get the dreaded news that Kathy was dead. But then I realized that she was crying with happiness, and her weeping was punctuated with joyous laughter.

"Robert!" April cried. "We've all been waiting for you to call! Dr. Greene says he thinks Kathy's going to be all right!"

Someone was banging a gong inside my skull again, and there were tears in my eyes. "Have they found out what's wrong with her?"

"Yes!"

"How? *What's* wrong with her?"

"I don't know all the details, Robert. Who *cares*? Just get *over* here, will you? I want to *hug* you!"

Garth pulled up just as I was flagging down a cab. I got into his car, told him the news, and we drove off toward the Medical Center.

Garth kept asking questions, which I fended off. At the moment, I was too tense and tired to talk; but in that small part of me that wasn't totally drained, I felt elated. If Kathy was going to live, we were all home free. Almost. The sky had grown overcast, and the city was awash in a dull bronze glow. I kept telling myself that the poor light was the reason I didn't seem to be able to see too well.

Chapter 15

True to her word, a beaming April grabbed me as I walked into Kathy's room. She joyfully mauled me, then started on Garth.

"Where's Kathy?" I asked, nodding toward the empty bed.

"They have her a floor below, in a special-treatment center," April said, wiping away tears of happiness. "Dr. Greene said something about lithium poisoning. The point is that they can clean the poison out of her body now. He's convinced she's strong enough to survive." She paused, put a hand to her mouth and hiccuped, then laughed and hugged me again. "You saved her life twice, Robert. First from the fire in the apartment, and then when you brought Esteban to her."

"Where's Esteban now?"

"He's gone with Senator Younger and Linda to their hotel suite; he can work with Linda there."

"What about Daniel?"

April's eyes clouded for a moment and she shook her head. "I don't know where my brother is," she said distantly. "I haven't heard anything from him since he was here last." She sighed, brightened. "But that's not unusual for him. *God,* I can hardly believe that Kathy's going to be all right!"

I accepted April's kiss on the mouth, and felt a thrill shudder through my body as I kissed her back. I caught Garth watching us, a bemused smile on his face. I flushed, cleared my throat and looked away. Garth knew.

Joshua Greene emerged from the elevator at the end of the hall, saw us and fairly skipped down the corridor. His dark eyes and white, even teeth shone in his ebony flesh. "Good news, huh?" he asked, grinning broadly.

"To say the least," I replied. "Is Kathy . . . really going to be all right?"

Joshua nodded. "She'd been poisoned with a massive dose of lithium. Lithium occurs naturally in the body, and it's hard to trace without a specific test for it. She should be regaining consciousness soon."

"A nice piece of medical detective work, Doctor," Garth said admiringly. "We all thank you."

"I'm afraid we don't deserve the credit," Joshua said thoughtfully. "As a matter of fact, Officer, I'm glad you're here. There's something I'd like you all to hear."

The doctor led us down a side corridor to a small office. Garth, April and I went in, and Joshua closed the door behind us. "We'd have discovered the lithium eventually," Joshua continued, "but perhaps not in time. The information that saved Kathy's life came to us in a tape recording. That's what I want you to listen to."

Joshua opened a drawer and took out a small tape cassette, which he placed on a playback machine he'd already set up. There was about fifteen seconds of silence; then a voice began speaking. The voice was eerily distorted into a metallic, wailing tone, a kind of electronic falsetto which made it impossible even to tell whether the speaker was a man or a woman. The voice quickly described what had been done to Kathy: a large dose of lithium injected anally so that no needle mark would show. The approximate dosage was given, and then the tape abruptly went silent.

"That's it," Joshua said, shutting off the machine. He ejected the cassette and handed it to Garth.

"How did you get the tape, Doctor?" Garth asked, putting the cassette in his pocket.

"It came this morning, by Special Delivery. I'm sorry if I've ruined any fingerprints on it."

Garth shook his head. "I doubt there would be any fingerprints on it to begin with. Whoever sent this is too clever to leave obvious tracks."

We all stood in stunned silence for a few minutes. It was Garth who finally broke the silence.

"Does the voice on the tape mean anything to you, Mrs. Marlowe?"

April slowly shook her head. "No," she said softly. "It sounds like some kind of *machine*."

"It means that someone in Esobus' coven got cold feet," I said.

"I'll take Kathy away from here," April said with a heavy sigh. "We'll go someplace where no one can ever hurt her again."

"We'll get whoever is responsible, Mrs. Marlowe," Garth said tautly. "We don't want any other little girls to be hurt." He turned to me. "It looks like we have you to thank for smoking out whoever made this tape."

"Maybe we should be thanking Daniel," I heard myself saying. I was distracted by all the new questions raised by the recording. "Then again, this tape may have been sent for an altogether different reason."

Joshua cleared his throat. "Excuse me, but I must get back to Kathy now. Mongo, don't forget to come in for your shot tomorrow."

"Thank you, Doctor," Garth said as the thin black man walked from the room.

April turned to me and took my hand. "*Now*, at least, you can rest and take care of yourself."

"And *I'll* take you home," Garth added, putting one of his large, strong hands on my shoulder.

"Hey," I said, pulling away and almost falling over. "I've still got a client."

Garth frowned. "What the hell—? *Who*?"

"Kathy," I said evenly. "She gave me all the money she had to find her father's book of shadows. I figure I haven't earned my fee yet."

Garth walked me out of the hospital. "You know," he said wryly, "that remark about the girl giving you all her worldly goods in order to help her father sounds like the punch line from a Christmas story."

"Yeah. I'm a sentimentalist."

"You want a beer?"

"Not really." The excitement surrounding Kathy's pending recovery and the strange tape recording had made me temporarily forget my aches and pains. Now they all came back; I felt as if I were collapsing in on myself. My thumb and stomach were beating an excruciatingly painful rhythm, in unison. "Christ, Garth, I'm *tired*. I think I'll go home and sleep for a week."

"That sounds like a remarkably intelligent statement,

coming from you. What are you going to do when you wake up?"

"You know the answer to that."

He grunted. "I do. That's why I want to talk. Come on. You should eat something, anyway. Try to stay awake long enough for a little conversation."

We walked two blocks to a diner, where we sat in a back booth. Garth ordered two club sandwiches and coffee, while I settled for poached eggs and tea. Garth seemed unusually thoughtful.

"I think you're right about the tape," he said at last. "Someone in the group had second thoughts."

"Sure. The question is—who?"

"You've been ahead of us on this thing from the beginning, Mongo. Now I guarantee you're going to see a little more action from the Police Department. This tape is the first real evidence we've had that a crime was committed."

"That's profoundly debatable; I just haven't had time to jack you guys up."

Garth smiled thinly. "Let's assume you did flush someone out. Who would it be?"

"Christ, Garth, I don't know. And I'm too sick and tired to think about it now."

"Who have you been talking to?"

"You know who I've been talking to," I said with a shrug that caused a painful jolt in my stomach. "I'm certain Peth is in this up to his triple chins, and that's who I plan to start working on when I feel stronger."

Garth shook his head. "Leave Peth alone. Let us handle him. We'll put a tail on him and see which way he crawls. At the moment, all we have is the fact that he mentioned Daniel."

"He attacked me."

"That too. But I don't want you stomping around and messing things up."

"Hey, brother; Peth's the only real lead *I've* got, and *I'm* the guy who found him. I don't know who Daniel's contacted, and I'm not likely to find out."

Garth nodded. He finished his first sandwich and started on the second. "We're going to be looking for Crandall, too," he said around a mouthful of sandwich. He reached across the table and punched me lightly on the arm. "Don't you think you've had enough?"

"For a few days; until I feel better, and the doctor tells me I'm out of danger from the rabies. But then, like I told you, I've got a client." I lifted my throbbing, bandaged thumb and waggled it at him. "I've taken a personal interest in this case."

"You take a personal interest in every case. Have you got any other candidates besides Peth?"

"Sure. Krowl could know something—in fact, I'd bet a year's salary on it. But he's not going to crack easily."

Garth stared into his coffee for a long time, then pushed the remaining half of the second sandwich aside. "Krowl's going to have some explaining to do for me," he said at last.

"Meaning what?"

Garth looked up at me and smiled crookedly. "In honor of your corny Christmas story, I'm going to give you a little gift: information." He laughed when I made a gesture of mock astonishment. "Try not to have a stroke. I got a call from one of the men who searched that rathole where your friend died. As a matter of fact, he called me just before you did. Have you been wondering what Davidson did with all the money he earned while he was on top?"

"The question occurred to me."

"They found something interesting in Davidson's clothes," he said. "It was a will; meaningless, because he died without any assets—at least, none that we've been able to find. Apparently he was too far gone to realize that."

"What did the will say?" I asked, leaning forward.

"He was leaving everything he thought he had to an outfit calling itself the Mystic Eye Institute. Now, I just happen to know that Mystic Eye is a group headed by our mutual friend John Krowl."

I fell asleep in the car on my way back to my apartment, and Garth had to shake me awake when we arrived. I got out and made it up to my apartment, then fell onto the bed without even taking off my shoes.

I woke up at seven in the evening, my thumb throbbing painfully. I got up, took three aspirins, then tried to go back to sleep. It was no use. I still felt rotten and exhausted, but the few hours' sleep had been just enough to juice up my mental circuits to the point where all the events of the past few days came flooding back into my thoughts. I knew for certain that I wouldn't be able to truly relax until the case had been wrapped up and I'd looked into the faces of the people responsible for trying to kill a seven-year-old child. I decided it couldn't hurt to *think* about it. And maybe just walk around a bit, if I felt I absolutely had to.

My head felt dizzy, but I was hungry. I made myself soup and a sandwich; the food stayed down, and I started to feel better. I shaved, showered and put on my bathrobe, intending to relax for a few hours with some music and a book. I called the hospital and was assured once again that Kathy was in satisfactory condition. When I asked to have my call switched to Madeline's room, I was told that the scientist had been released that morning. I reached Mad at her apartment.

"Hello?" Her voice sounded normal.

"Hi, babe. It's Mongo. How are you feeling?"

"Much better, my friend. Thank you. What about you?"

"I'm feeling about half. Listen; I just wanted you to know that the little girl is going to be all right."

"Thank God," Mad whispered intently. "Were they finally able to diagnose what was wrong with her?"

"Yeah. Believe it or not, somebody sent a tape recording describing exactly what the problem was. Pressure was felt somewhere. I don't know whether I had anything to do with applying it, but I want to thank you again for supplying me with the information you did."

"It was nothing," Mad said, sounding immensely relieved. "I'm just so glad the girl is going to live."

"Mad, have you ever heard of the Mystic Eye Institute?"

"Why, yes," she said after a moment's hesitation. "It's an occult-studies school run by John Krowl. Why?"

"Just curious. Can anyone join?"

"Yes, as far as I know," she replied, sounding puzzled. "It's just a school. John and a few other people give lectures and conduct seminars on the occult arts."

"Then there's nothing particularly secretive about it?"

"No. As a matter of fact, it's listed in the phone book. Mongo, are you still investigating this Esobus thing?"

"Yeah. Do you have any idea how Mystic Eye is funded?"

"I don't know for certain, but I assume it's supported by membership and lecture fees. I've never had much to do with it; too public." She paused, added, "Mongo, do you think *John* has something to do with the people who harmed the girl?"

"I don't know, Mad. That's what I'm trying to find out."

I tried to relax with a book, but I couldn't remember what I was reading from one page to the next. The pain in my stomach and thumb seemed to be calming down, and I was hungry again. I ate another sandwich and felt even better. I knew I should stay home and rest as I'd planned to do, but I couldn't. I was restless, and easily convinced myself that a little ride and chat couldn't do much damage. I got dressed, went out into the night and took a cab to Krowl's brownstone in Brooklyn.

It took some talking to get past Krowl's surprised secretary, who told me that *no* one ever came to see John Krowl without an appointment, and that he'd have to call the giant Jonathan if I didn't leave. I told him I was sure Krowl would want to see me, as I had some information about Esobus and the Mystic Eye Institute. I purposely put the two names in conjunction just to see what Krowl's reaction would be.

The ploy got me in to see Krowl. The albino was waiting for me in his sitting/reading room, his long white hair and parchment flesh forming a striking contrast to his purple Oriental smoking jacket, black slacks and shoes.

"What do you want, Frederickson?" Krowl snapped, his pink eyes flashing angrily. "What's this nonsense about Esobus and the Mystic Eye Institute?"

"I don't know; I thought I'd ask you. What *is* the Mystic Eye Institute? I thought maybe I'd join."

"You're not welcome," Krowl said evenly.

I opened my eyes wide in mock horror. "Don't tell me you discriminate against dwarfs!"

"You're not interested in the occult; your only interest is prying into other people's business."

"Harley Davidson must have found the curriculum fascinating. I understand he gave you all his money. When he was working, that must have amounted to a million dollars or more."

Krowl frowned. "Who told you that?"

"It doesn't matter. It's true, isn't it?"

Krowl shoved his spectral, chalk-colored hands into the pockets of his smoking jacket and began to pace back and forth. "Harley Davidson thought enough of our work to make a few sizeable donations," he said at last. "But that's not unusual; a number of my clients have joined Mystic Eye and donated money. What of it?"

"I don't know, Krowl," I said, trying unsuccessfully to look into his eyes. "But I'll tell you the real reason I came here: I keep stumbling over victims who started out as hand casts on your wall."

Krowl stiffened, quickly drew his smoked glasses out of his breast pocket and put them on. Now he looked at me. "Get out of here, you little bastard!" he snarled. "And don't come back! The next time you show up here, Jonathan will meet you at the door. You and I have nothing more to talk about. You seem to think that I have something to do with these people you're after!"

The smoked glasses resembled two huge insect eyes on his colorless face. "I never said that," I replied softly to the eyes.

"And I'll sue you if you do, Frederickson! I don't involve myself with witchcraft at all."

"Maybe not, but I'm betting you know a lot of people who do. Did you talk to Esobus after I left here the other night?"

He laughed thinly, without humor. "What are you talking about?" he snorted. "Esobus is a fairy tale."

"Bullshit. I'm betting that particular fairy tale is damn well upset right now. Somebody in his coven doesn't quite live up to the going standard of nastiness. The hospital received a tape recording explaining what was wrong with the child. Thanks to whoever sent it, the girl's going to live."

I watched for a reaction; there was none. The black insect eyes simply stared back at me. Finally, Krowl said: "I'm glad the child is out of danger, but I'm going to give you a warning. I have no idea who the people are that you're after, but there's no doubt that you're on a fishing expedition—and you're fishing in my home. This time you came close to making accusations: I resent that. I've told you I know nothing about this matter, but you don't believe me. Have it your way: If you think I'm involved, prove it. Otherwise, I advise you to stay away from here. And keep your mouth shut." He paused, coughed dryly; it was a soft, slightly menacing sound. "I'll have your license, Frederickson. Believe me; I have very powerful friends."

I believed him, and I knew I'd probably made a mistake in coming to see him. I *was* on a fishing expedition, and Krowl didn't have to be a genius to know it. If he was involved with the coven, he was now definitely on notice that I was looking him over. The powerful friends he'd mentioned could easily chew me up and spit me out in the various regulatory agencies I was responsible to. I was going to have to back off until I could gather more evidence.

Of course, there was always the possibility that Krowl *was* totally ignorant of Esobus and his works, as Krowl claimed. I doubted it. He'd never even bothered to ask what had been wrong with Kathy.

After a good night's sleep I rose at ten, feeling fairly decent. I ate a light breakfast and went over to the Medical Center for my shot. On the way it occurred to me that exactly one week before I'd been happily drumming away, planning to while away the rest of the summer nibbling at the Big Apple. I'd ended up with a mouthful of worms. It seemed years since I'd rolled up my practice pencils into the Tchaikovsky score and filed the package away in my drawer.

Kathy had been moved from Intensive Care into a private room. She was out of the coma, but under heavy sedation as a result of the washing-out process she was undergoing. I was allowed to look in on her; as I stood next to her bed looking down on her peacefully sleeping body, I felt tears of gratitude well in my eyes. I waited a few minutes, hoping that April would show up. She didn't, and I went downstairs to keep my appointment with Joshua Greene.

By now the injection procedure was becoming a familiar—if no more pleasant—ritual. After the shot, a nurse brought me tea and Joshua left me alone to dress. On my way out of the room I almost bumped into an excited and flushed April who was carrying a shopping bag that looked heavy. As always when I saw her, I experienced a small rush in my stomach and chest that had absolutely nothing to do with rabies shots.

"Robert!" she cried. "I was just on my way over to your apartment. I met Dr. Greene in the elevator and he told me you were down here."

"Ah, and you come bearing gifts," I said, smiling and pointing to the bag.

"It may be something better," April said, her voice taut and humming with excitement. "After you left yesterday, I drove home to Philadelphia to look for those things of Frank's I told you about. Now that Kathy's going to be all right, I thought it was time I tried to help you and Garth." She used both hands to lift the bag. "Here's what I found."

My heart began to pound as I took the bag from her and carried it over to an examining table. "Is this all there was?"

"I don't know, but this is definitely what he brought last Saturday. I recognized the bag. There may be more in other parts of the attic, but I wanted to bring this to you as quickly as possible."

Slowly and carefully, I began to take the items from the bag and lay them out on the table. There were a number of books on witchcraft, most of which looked academic and sophisticated. Many of the pages were heavily annotated in what April confirmed was Frank Marlowe's handwriting. There were also three notebooks, which I skimmed through quickly. They consisted of research notes on witchcraft and the occult in general. There was no mention of Esobus, or a supercoven.

At the bottom of the bag was a leather carrying case which contained a tiny tape recorder of the sort a person can strap to his body in order to make surreptitious recordings. There was also a small spool of recording tape.

"Have you listened to this yet?" I asked April, picking up the tape.

She shook her head and gripped my arm. "I'm not sure how the machine works; I was afraid I'd break the tape, or erase it."

I put the tape in the machine, turned it on.

"Black Bull of the north, Horned One, Dark Ruler of the mountains and all that lies beneath them,

Prince of the Powers of Earth, be present, we pray Thee, and guard this circle from all perils approaching from the north!"

The chant was repeated twice. April whispered in my ear: "It's an invocation of protection. It may be the coven!"

I nodded as another, lone voice came on the tape.

"Whence come you?"
"I travel east in search of light."
"What passwords dost thou bring Esobus?"
"Perfect love and perfect trust."

April gasped, and I shut off the machine. "It's Frank, isn't it?" I asked softly.

She slowly nodded, her eyes wide with shock. "Yes. It's Frank's voice. What we're hearing is an initiation ceremony."

"Frank's initiation ceremony."

"And the other voice . . ."

I turned the machine back on.

> "I, the Guardian of the watchtower of the north, forbid thee entrance. Thou canst not enter this holy place from the north, save thou first be purified and consecrated. Who vouches for you?"

A third voice came on the tape; it was distant and muffled, barely audible.

> "I, guide of souls, do so. Let Bart Stone be one of us."

The tape ran out; I rewound it and played it over again twice. April went to a corner of the room and stood leaning against the wall, her hands to her temples. The third voice that had come in was totally unrecognizable. Obviously, Frank Marlowe had wired himself for his initiation ceremony, but the tiny recorder had picked up only the sounds of the group's chanting, Marlowe's own voice—and the voice of the coven leader. That voice had been amplified and distorted.

"The leader," April said tensely. "It sounds just like the voice on the tape that was delivered to the hospital."

"That's right. It *is* the same person."

"Robert, what does it mean?"

"It means you were wrong about Frank not being a part of Esobus' coven." I paused and carefully started replacing the items in the shopping bag. What I was thinking was so off-the-wall that it threatened to turn the entire case inside out, blowing away a major assumption I'd been operating on up to that point. Yet the evidence offered by the two tapes appeared to point to one, inescapable conclusion. I finally put my thoughts into words, if only to hear how insane they sounded when spoken aloud. "It also means—or seems to mean—that the person responsible for saving Kathy's life is Esobus himself."

Taking the shopping bag with me, I got into a cab outside the Medical Center and gave the driver directions to take me to Garth's precinct station house. I got there just as Garth came hurrying out the door. I intercepted him on the way to his car.

"Hey, brother," I said, hoisting the bag in his direction. "Wait up. I've got something here you're definitely going to want to check out."

"Not now, Mongo," Garth said tensely, brushing past me. He started to slide into the car, then motioned for me to get in beside him. "Come on. I guess you've earned the right to see this—if that's the way to put it."

"What are you talking about?" I asked, knowing from Garth's tone that I wasn't going to like it.

"Our elusive friend Crandall got himself lost permanently. He's dead."

Chapter 16

It was not yet noon, but the temperature had to be approaching ninety. The heat and the drugs in my system were poking at my brain, making it hard, despite my respect and feeling for this victim, to concentrate on the fact that we were on our way to a pre-luncheon meeting with Daniel's death. As if bodies weren't found, and people didn't die, on hot mornings. Then too, I may have been distracted by the pastoral surroundings—The Ramble, a heavily wooded area of Central Park notorious as a trysting place for homosexuals, but in fact freely used by lovers of all colors, creeds and sexual persuasions. Even heterosexuals.

Neither of us spoke as I followed Garth along one of the many trails cutting through woods, around ponds and across the strong spines of granite mini-cliffs that sparkled in the heavy white sunlight. We passed a number of late-rising bird-watchers, tweedy men and women with necks bowed under the weight of huge binoculars that looked powerful enough to track an ant at three hundred yards.

A uniformed cop was waiting for us a half mile or so down the trail. He led us off the main trail, up over a small outcropping of rock and along a narrow path that was incongruously marked with NYPD posting signs. We went around another outcropping. What I saw made my mind snap back into focus with such force that I involuntarily groaned and snapped my jaws shut.

Daniel's body was in a tiny clearing in the center of a secluded, dense copse of trees, surrounded by uniformed cops and police technicians. It wasn't pretty. Daniel had been stripped naked and staked spread-eagled, face up, to the ground. He'd been tortured, and a cat's head had been stuffed into his mouth as a gag. The immediate cause of death looked to be an ornate ceremonial sword that had been plunged into Daniel's heart, but he'd been expertly carved up first. Occult symbols had been scratched into the rocky soil around him: it had been a ritual torture and murder.

"It looks like Crandall finally found the people he was looking for," Garth said softly.

I nodded slowly, but could think of nothing to say. Despite his brusque stubbornness, I'd liked Richard Crandall, and had come to respect his strange, unyielding demand for solitude. As April had said, he was, by nature of his beliefs, a loner who had to do things his own way. It occurred to me that his hunt had been a kind of spiritual exercise. The ceremonial magician was dead, and I wondered who would pray for this strange priest of the occult. I decided I would.

We waited for the police photographers to finish their business, then went back to Garth's car, where I played the tape for him. When it had finished, I turned the machine off. He didn't say anything, and I asked, "You want to hear it again?"

Garth shook his head. "I'll give it to the lab boys. They may be able to clean it up and raise the levels so we can try for some voice identification." He paused, added, "So that's Esobus. It's the same voice we heard on the hospital tape. You can tell that, even with the distortion."

"Yep. It was Esobus, the *leader* of this shithead crew, who backed off and supplied the information that saved Kathy's life. Interesting, huh?"

"To say the least," Garth replied quietly. "There's something else that's interesting: this tape proves that the distortion on the two tapes wasn't done *after* the recording. Only Esobus' voice is distorted; except for poor quality, all the other voices on the tape are normal. What the hell do you think is going on?"

"It's electronic," I said. "You can get that effect with certain kinds of microphone and feedback setups. Obviously, Esobus masks his voice from his own coven, which could mean *they* don't even know who he is."

"Christ, that's hard to believe. Wouldn't they try to find out?"

"Some weird people here, brother, which I don't have to tell you. Everyone I talk to who's ever heard of Esobus speaks of him as a legend. If Esobus wanted to keep his identity secret, even from his own coven, he just might have the muscle to get away with it. The rest of the coven might view it as some kind of ritual source of power."

Garth stared out the side window for a few moments, then made a sharp, hissing sound of disgust. "What the hell was that girl's father doing with this bunch of creeps? You gave me the impression you thought Marlowe was pretty straight—at least morally."

"I still think he was. And Marlowe isn't the only one who doesn't seem to fit this picture. Bobby Weiss—Harley Davidson—wouldn't have hurt a fly, unless he accidentally dropped his ego on it. Neither of those men was a torturer nor murderer. Not only that, but I've been told over and over again that Esobus is a ceremonial magician who wouldn't form a coven with anyone *but* other ceremonial magicians who are almost as heavy as he is. Obviously, that isn't true." I hesitated as a thought flitted up from some dark corner of my mind. I tried to look at it, but it ducked out of sight behind drug-shadows of weariness and confusion. "Maybe," I added feebly.

"What 'maybe'?" Garth said scornfully. "A coven has thirteen members, period. In this case, there would be Esobus and twelve others. So Marlowe and Harley Davidson turned out to be closet pussycats."

The thought came back for a return run. This time I grabbed it and flopped it over on its back. Its face was ugly. "Unless Marlowe and Bobby Weiss were marked as victims from day one. They only *thought* they were members of the coven; the *real* members were doing a number on them."

Garth was still staring out the car window, idly tapping his knuckles against the glass. "I like it," he said at last. "Go ahead."

"All right, let's noodle on it together. Try this for openers: Thirteen members of the coven *are* heavies, and all very kinky—with Esobus himself the only question mark. They prey on vulnerable people who are sucked in and made to *think* they're members. The suckers are given all the sex, drugs and anything else they want; and all the while the *real* coven is going to work on them."

"Milking them dry, like they did to the kid."

"Sure; they took Bobby's money, but there are other things the coven could want—and get. Power; political influence. God knows we've got enough closet screwballs at all levels of government. Can you imagine what this coven could do with a senator or two in its pocket?"

"Shit, yes," Garth said softly, slowly nodding.

"And they may have them," I said, thinking of the hand casts on Krowl's wall.

We sat quietly for some time. Out of the silence another idea began to emerge, and I voiced it. "I think they may have found one joker in the deck," I continued, poking my brother in the side. "Frank Marlowe, with his research notes and tape recordings; he was the joker. Maybe he was trying to do a number on *them*. Check this out: Marlowe was initiated as Bart Stone—only one of a dozen different pseudonyms he used. The coven members thought they were initiating a rich and famous Western pulp writer. I don't think they *knew* that wasn't his real name. If they *had* known his real name, why not use it at the initiation ceremony?"

I thought about it some more, and was pretty sure I had the answer. "April told me Marlowe hadn't written anything in almost a year. But he damn well *was* working. Somehow, he fell into the coven situation—and he knew what to do with it. He was researching this outfit, and he planned to write a book about them. *This* was going to be his big book—*his* 'book of shadows.' "

"And the coven found out about it," Garth said, giving the window a single, hard rap that rattled the glass. "They took all his notes, then killed him. It means everything he wrote, with the exception of what we've got in that shopping bag, was destroyed."

"I'm not so sure." Something about the whole thing still didn't sit right. I tried to pin it down in my mind, couldn't, and let it go.

"Somebody's going to have to tell Crandall's sister," Garth said, looking over at me.

"I'll do it," I said quietly. "Drive me over to the hospital."

Garth glanced sideways at me again as he leaned forward to start the car. "She's under your skin, brother, isn't she?"

I grunted noncommittally. "Good-looking woman."

"Damned if I don't think you're falling in love."

"Come on, Garth; I've known the woman less than a week."

"You should see your face when you look at her; your eyes actually get glassy." He paused and chuckled at the thought. "Come to think of it, I don't believe you've ever been in love before, have you? I know you do all right with the ladies, although I'll never understand what they find lovable about a smart-ass dwarf. But this is different; this one scares you. Knowing you, it's only logical that your first real love would be a witch."

"Shut up, Garth, and mind your own business." I'd meant it to sound light and joking, but the words and tone came out serious. The fact of the matter was that the power April Marlowe exerted over my muscles, glands and mind *did* frighten me.

I hadn't forgotten John Krowl's reading.

"Hello, Kathy."

"Mr. Mongo!" Kathy squealed excitedly. She was still pale, but healthy patches of color had appeared in her cheeks, and her blue eyes were clear. "What have you *got?*"

The enormous stuffed panda I carried on my shoulders was as big as I was. I dropped it on the bed next to Kathy with an exaggerated sigh of relief. "His name's Horace. He wants to be adopted by a little girl."

"Hello, Robert," April said quietly from where she was sitting on the edge of the bed. "How are you feeling?"

"Okay," I lied, already feeling self-conscious in her presence. I squeezed April's hand and kissed Kathy on the forehead. "You look just great, sleepyhead," I said to the girl. "But it's about time you woke up; you've been asleep a long time."

Kathy giggled, then suddenly frowned. "Have you found my daddy's book of shadows yet, Mr. Mongo?"

I glanced quickly at April, who gave me an almost imperceptible shake of her head; it meant Kathy hadn't yet been told of her father's death. It was the right decision, I thought. "Not yet Kathy," I said. "But I'm still looking."

"I know you'll find it, Mr. Mongo. You'll make everything all right." She hugged the bear and me at the same time. "Mommy says you brought me here when I got sick, Mr. Mongo. Thank you."

"You're welcome."

She frowned again. "Why didn't my daddy bring me?"

"I'll explain it to you when you're feeling better," April said, gently smoothing her daughter's hair.

"Kathy," I said, "I have to talk to your mother. It's very important. May I borrow her for an hour or so? I'll bring her right back when I'm finished, and you can spend the time getting acquainted with Horace."

Kathy solemnly considered the proposition, then finally nodded her assent. I took April's arm and guided her out of the room. "How long will Kathy have to stay in the hospital?" I asked as we rode down in the elevator.

"Dr. Greene says he wants to keep her around for three or four more days. The poison hasn't been completely flushed from her system, and you can see she's still very weak."

"I talked to Janet Monroe before I came over here. Now that Kathy's out of danger, she'd like you to stay with her until Kathy can go home. She lives only a few minutes away. You must be tired of that hospital room."

"I'll think about it, Robert. What is it you want to talk to me about?"

"I'll get to it," I said, avoiding her eyes. "Let's walk over to Janet's."

At Janet's apartment I told April of Daniel's death, omitting the gruesome details. April wept for a few minutes in my arms, but she wasn't hysterical; she almost seemed to have anticipated her brother's death, and was prepared for the news.

Janet came later, as I'd asked her to. April cried some more, then began to talk of her and Daniel's childhood in a witch family and community. Some of the stories were funny, others sad; all were fascinating.

April finished by saying in a firm, proud voice: "My brother was a good and strong man who understood the ways of the human heart. Struggle was his life. He lost this battle, but he will always live in the hearts and memories of those who loved him. So mote it be."

The ceremonial magician had received his memorial service.

An hour after returning to my apartment, I received a phone call. The voice on the line was clipped and heavily muffled. The message was brief and to the point.

"Be at The Cloisters at midnight. Esobus wishes to speak with you. Don't contact anyone. Come alone. The lives of the child and her mother will depend on your following these instructions to the letter."

Every word had struck me with the force of a blow, dazing me and making me short of breath. I was more drained of feeling than afraid; I moved like an automaton, forcing myself to eat some steak and eggs for strength. The food stayed down, and I stretched out on my bed to rest. I didn't think I'd be able to sleep, but I set the alarm for ten just in case. Then I closed my eyes and breathed deeply and regularly, trying to empty my mind of everything; I knew I would need all my energy and concentration in the long night ahead.

At ten I rose and dressed. I took out my Beretta, checked the firing mechanism and magazine, stuck the weapon into my belt by my spine. I planned on being early, so I started to leave at ten thirty. I hesitated, walked over to the telephone and stared at it. I desperately wanted to call Garth, clearly aware that in most situations like this it was a sucker play not to bring in the police. But this case had some unusual, deadly wrinkles; their numbers and the place they'd chosen for the meeting gave the coven members all the advantages. There was no doubt in my mind that I would be walking into a trap; I was liable to end up staked to the ground and whittled on, like Daniel. Still, it seemed I had no choice but to play this round by their rules. There were thirteen members of the coven, and the entire area surrounding The Cloisters would be easy enough for them to cover. Even if the police did manage to catch whoever might be lying in wait for me, the others would certainly find out about it and act accordingly; they'd demonstrated that they didn't make idle threats. I had no qualms about blowing the brains out of my hosts, but I wanted to make certain April and Kathy weren't casually killed by default; there was no guarantee that the police could make anyone they captured talk before some kind of action was taken against the mother and daughter. But I was certain *I* could; I had a few spells of my own to cast.

Traffic in midtown and on Riverside Drive was almost

nonexistent. It was a clear night illuminated by a full moon. The Hudson River, on my left, had taken the cold light, shattered and rewoven it into a brightly spangled robe that stretched, swelled and glittered to the New Jersey shore on the opposite bank.

It took me only fifteen minutes to reach the north entrance to Fort Tryon Park, where The Cloisters is located. It struck me as I drove slowly up the lower driveway how appropriate the setting was for communing with a bunch of witches. The Cloisters is one of New York's landmarks, an enormous castle structure which is a museum housing prime examples of Medieval European art and architecture. There is a great deal of church art, and the very name conjures up visions of pious, ascetic men and women devoting their lives and talents to their Deity. And, of course, the witch in the Middle Ages carried as much weight as the priest. Now, in the twentieth century, the church had revered landmarks and the occultists had sidewalk scam parlors. It looked as if Esobus were trying to turn the clock back a few centuries, at least symbolically.

I didn't want any cruising patrol cars to spot my Volkswagen and come looking for me, so I parked the car on the shoulder of one of the parking areas, between two trees. There was always a chance that my reception committee had arrived even earlier, but I doubted it. I walked in the darkness up toward the Medieval castle. The Cloisters had always been one of my favorite places; now, at night, it was different and threatening, like a gentle friend who has without warning turned neurotic and vicious. In the night, under the full moon, it looked eerie, haunted, with its stone balustrades jutting like blunt teeth chewing a sky bleeding midnight blue.

I had no idea who was supposed to find whom, but I wanted to make certain that I saw my hosts first. To that end, I climbed up on one of the ramparts circling the vast lawn and walked up to the museum. Then it was Circus Time. I managed to human-fly my way up the rough stone wall of The Arcade until I was on the roof of the building. I walked across the pebbled surface and positioned myself behind a balustrade above the Fuentiduña Chapel. That gave me a view of the main approach road. I crouched down, gun in hand, and waited.

And waited.

By twelve fifteen I was anxious. Staying low so as not to show a silhouette, I'd already been around the perimeter of the roof several times, checking out the surrounding area below. There was no sign of life. Twenty minutes earlier a patrol car had cruised up, turned at the head of the drive, then headed back. By twelve thirty, I was soaked with nervous sweat. It occurred to me that *they* could be watching, waiting. If they thought I hadn't followed their directions . . .

I clambered back down the side of the building the way I'd come. Once on the ground, I began making a circuit of the museum. My stomach was beginning to cramp again—not only from the antirabies serum, but from fear and tension. I started whistling to attract the attention of anyone who might have trouble seeing a dwarf in the dark. I was convinced that if the coven had said they intended to kill April and Kathy if I didn't show up, they'd do it.

One circuit completed, I sat down on the stone wall near the entrance and whistled some more, louder. By one thirty, I knew no one was coming. I walked back to my car, distracted and tormented by the thought that Kathy and April could now be in jeopardy because of my game-playing. If I was lucky, the night's exercise had been only a run-through to see if I *would* show up alone; if I was lucky, they hadn't noticed that I'd spent two hours holed up on the roof trying to get the drop on them. If I was lucky.

Bad luck to one you love, Krowl had said.

With my state of mind what it was, my senses and reflexes weren't quite what they should have been. Also, I was suffering from a bad case of the stupids not to have thought of where *else* they might try to ambush me. I was seated in my car, turning the key in the ignition, when I felt the skin on the back of my neck begin to prickle. But it was too late. I tried to twist away, but the man in the back who'd picked the lock on my car door reared up and sapped me expertly. There was a loud thud inside my skull, which kept ricocheting around inside my head. I tried to follow the sound's bounces, and suddenly one echo became a white ball of fire that rushed at me. I tried to duck away from it, tripped over another echo and plunged down into a sea of red-tinged darkness.

Chapter 17

I seemed to be trapped in some strange, nonvisual dream; there was no light, no images—only lucid thoughts. What I was thinking was that I had to get up and go to the hospital for my daily shot. Without my injections, I would go mad and die in agony. It occurred to me that something had happened, a problem had arisen, which could prevent me from going to the hospital. I tried to remember what it was, and couldn't. I decided it was nothing; I wasn't hurt, and I couldn't imagine anything aside from injury that could keep me from going for my medication. That would be suicide. It was simply a matter of waiting to wake up.

Something was tapping softly on the inside of my head—not painfully but persistently, with a sound like a pencil eraser bouncing on soft wood. Then I realized with astonishment that it was only the blood pulsing through my veins. I listened for a few minutes until it faded away and I was once again left alone with only my thoughts. I couldn't move, which seemed to reaffirm the fact that I was dreaming after all. That was all right; I was resting, as Joshua had told me to. I would rest a little while longer, then wake up and go to the hospital.

I didn't seem to be able to wake up. I kept waiting for the phone to ring, or Garth or someone else to come and wake me up. No phones rang, and no one came. Time lost any meaning; after a while I couldn't tell whether I was awake or asleep. My thoughts were my only companions, and I couldn't shake off the feeling that something terrible had happened to me. Or *was* happening. I fought against a growing sense of panic by carrying on long internal monologues, telling myself old jokes over and over again, laughing without sound inside my mind. The line between sleeping and waking became increasingly blurred, then seemed to disappear altogether.

I remembered. A low moan started somewhere in the back of my mind and exploded in a silent, breathless scream punctuated by terror-filled images: My attacker had fractured my skull and I was in a deep coma. Or I was paralyzed. I had no head, no toes, no legs, no fingers—no body at all. There was only the theater inside my mind, and I wondered how long that was going to stay open. Or perhaps what I was experiencing was but a split-second journey that all men must travel between life and death.

I choked back my terror and tried to think. Obviously, I wasn't dead yet. I felt no hunger or thirst, and it occurred to me that I could be in a hospital, being fed intravenously. Garth, Joshua and April could be at my bedside. Janet might be there, praying for me.

Maybe the doctors didn't know my mind was working; maybe they'd pull the plug on whatever machine was keeping me alive. Or, maybe I was simply lying in a ditch at the side of some road.

Maybe I'd be buried alive.

Waiting; silence; a constant struggle against a terror that, once out of control, would devour my mind before the rabies that was now coursing unchecked through my system. I tried to think of other things, but "other things" always ended up April—and I knew I loved her. I longed for her. That made me cry. I couldn't feel tears, couldn't hear my sobs, but I knew I was crying—at least, inside my mind. Every thought was filled with emotion, and emotion was my only link with reality. Suddenly my mind screamed again, and I backed down into myself, away from the terrible need to see and touch someone I loved, and who loved me.

My mind blinked, and I found myself on a gray plain stretching endlessly off to—nothing. There was no horizon, only a black pit directly in front of me. I backed up . . . and the pit moved forward, like some living thing stalking me. It yawned before me like a dark hole on a silent planet. There were sounds in the hole—wailing winds, screams, groans; and I realized the hole was myself, the deepest part of me. It was an abyss, a tear in my psyche I knew I must, at all costs, avoid falling into; at the bottom was madness.

I was crying again. I thought of April, then of my mother—a beautiful, willowy woman who'd loved me, and who, with Garth, had kept me whole during the nightmare years of my childhood and adolescence.

Still waiting; still locked in combat with my fear. At the moment, that battle was a standoff. I kept waiting for something to *happen*.

Once I must have fallen asleep, because I found myself slipping like a slab of molten plastic over the edge of the hole; the hole was closing over my head, and I struggled desperately to pry open its jaws and climb out. The sides of the hole were dotted with faces; lips curled menacingly, baring long fangs and froth-specked teeth; there were large red holes where the eyes should be; hands studded with thousands of snakelike fingers curled around my throat and tore at my eyes.

Madness. I wondered how many seconds, minutes, hours, days had gone by since I'd been hit on the head. Perhaps rabies was percolating in my brain tissue, carrying me along its foaming crest into the terrible dark hole. I could stay in a coma indefinitely, until my brain became totally infected and I died screaming—to myself.

Suddenly my mind blinked again and I found myself out of the hole, my mind cast adrift on a vast, eerie sea of quivering rubber. I wept again; not as a man weeps, but as a child caught in the grip of nameless, nighttime terror.

My mind was closing in on me, eating itself; there were other things in my mind with me, and they were alien. The whisper of snakes that poison and crush; a world of giants that laughed and mocked; things that would hurt a dwarf and not even notice.

It suddenly occurred to me that the fears were somehow familiar, like a scarred rocking horse uncovered in the corner of some dusty attic of the mind. In this case the terrors were old, half-forgotten memories from the storage bin of my childhood. My mind had turned cannibal and was gnawing through the protective membrane of the subconscious.

"Hello, Bob."

The voice was soft, and seemed to originate from some alternative universe inside my head. It came from everywhere and nowhere, starting from somewhere behind where I thought my eyes should be, then undulating out to fill my skull. I waited desperately for something else to be said, but there was only the terrible silence—now even more maddening.

After a while I decided I'd only imagined the voice.

"Hello, Bob. This is a friend."

The voice was definitely real. For one long, terrifying moment I was afraid it would go away, as it had before. But the voice came again—very soft and soothing, with a slight accent. I couldn't place the voice, but its owner had made a mistake—perhaps spoken too soon, or for too long a time. My mind paused in its self-destructive feast, looked around, and growled with anger as it struggled desperately to make connections.

> *"You have been with us . . . some time now. I am going to help you. I know how lonely you are. I know you are sick and need medicine. I know . . . you need love. I can give you all these things, but first you must be alone a while longer so that you can think. You will learn to love my voice. Then you will learn to love me."*

There was a prolonged, aching silence. Then:

"Goodbye for now, Bob."

Suddenly I knew where I was, and who had put me there. In that moment my breathing stopped as countless pieces of thought and memory fused together to form a conscious idea that burned somewhere behind my eyes with whitehot, searing certainty.

I was being subjected to sensory deprivation.

It meant my old friend Vincent Smathers and his buddy Kee were charter members of Esobus' coven. They'd arranged a special demonstration of their work just for me. After my initial reaction of mindless shock, I felt almost relieved; the realization of what was happening to me gave me a frame of reference, eliminating the horrible fear that I was in a coma and paralyzed, buried alive inside my own mind.

All that was left was the equally horrible reality. I was a helpless captive of the scientists, who, for their own arcane reasons, were keeping me alive simply so that they could drive me crazy. The irony was that, without my daily shots, the strain of rabies in me would be bubbling away, cooking me toward madness and death. Smathers and Kee were competing for my mind against the disease in my body; it was a race I couldn't win, and perhaps had already lost. I had no idea how many shots I'd missed or, if I'd missed a lot, what was keeping me alive. It was all enough to depress me.

I tried to keep my terror at bay by concentrating on what I'd read about sensory deprivation. I thought I could visualize my surroundings; I'd be floating in a large, water-filled tank. The saline solution would be warmed to body temperature; my arms and legs would be restrained by straps, loose enough to allow for circulation but sufficiently tight to restrict any kind of movement. I imagined my head was encased in some kind of hood which was wired for sound and into which oxygen was pumped. There were probably tubes stuck into my body through which I was begin fed intravenously. I didn't feel any pain in my thumb or stomach—indeed, I had no physical sensations whatsoever. It could have been the cumulative effect of the womblike environment, or they might have given me just enough of a paralyzing drug, like curare, to damp down my nervous system.

The next thought that occurred to me was that I'd be in the tank until I died, living like a mental mole in absolute darkness. Smathers and Kee would never take me out, even after they'd squashed my will and mind; the tank was my stakes in the ground, Kee's voice my ceremonial sword.

I was only a floor above dozens of people who knew and cared about me, yet they had no way of knowing where I was, or what was being done to me. My captors would one day grow tired of the madman they'd created; the ritual would be completed, and they would go away and lock the steel doors of the laboratory behind them. I would be left suspended in the water—floating forever until I died and rotted and my bones sank to the bottom of the tank.

That image unleashed my panic; it pounced on me like a huge, shapeless beast. I shrieked soundlessly under its weight and gnashing teeth. I kept shrieking until I passed out, or slept, or simply short-circuited.

"Hello, Bob. This is your friend again. I know how you've missed me; I know how terribly lonely you are, and how badly you need to hear a human voice. But you must be left alone still a while longer to think things out. There has been a great misunderstanding on your part. You hate Esobus and his servants. You have spoken to people and said incorrect things. You have done me a great disservice. But you will become a servant of Esobus, and you will do his will. You will love me and want to undo the damage you have done. Listen to my voice, and you will understand. I will leave you alone now, Bob. You should give a great deal of thought to what I have said. I am Esobus, and you will learn to love me as you love the sound of my voice."

I seriously doubted that, but I waited for more anyway. There was only silence. For the first time, I tried to speak out loud. I cursed slowly, methodically—or imagined that I did. It seemed to me that my voice came back to me muffled, as from a great distance.

Through the timeless silence I clung to my rational thoughts like a finely spun life raft; they were all I had. I'd accepted the fact that my situation was hopeless, and an unexpected benefit was the temporary suspension of my terror and frustration. Now I was involved in a ritual of my own. The idea of a bunch of witches killing me when cholera, a psychotic Russian and the Iranian SAVAK had failed made me angry enough to want to hold out as long as possible. It had become a matter of pride.

I tried to fight off the oppressive loneliness by finely focusing my thoughts. For a while I concentrated on April, but that was too painful and only made matters worse. I shifted my concentration to Esobus and the coven, mulling over everything that had happened, everyone I'd talked to, all I knew or could reasonably conjecture: Daniel's behavior, Marlowe's immolation, Kathy's poisoning—I kept it all rolling, in living color, on an endless loop in my mind.

It didn't take me long to come to the conclusion that Smathers and Kee had been carrying out experiments in sensory deprivation at the university from Day One. They'd probably been scooping Bowery derelicts up off the sidewalk to use as subjects, then putting them back—or burying them—when the experiments were finished. The money for the equipment had come from their piece of the coven action in milking wealthy victims like Bobby Weiss.

Also, I was now positive that the rabid bat *had* come from Smathers. The Nobel Prize winner had unlimited access to the research facilities of the university's medical school, and that was undoubtedly where he'd scrounged up the diseased animal. Ironically, his reason at the time had probably been personal, completely divorced from the Esobus investigation. The bat had been Smather's offbeat revenge on me for investigating *him*.

Every so often I tried to move. Perhaps because I finally had a fix on the nature of what was being done to me, I imagined I could occasionally feel an arm or leg move, my chest expand and contract. Once I even felt pain in my thumb, and I'd never experienced a more welcome sensation. But then it disappeared, which seemed to confirm that they were using curare in the intravenous solutions they had to be feeding me.

Waiting.

It went on and on, the terrible, crushing silence filled with my personal demons. Despite my acceptance of my death and my desperate efforts to focus my thoughts, the impact of the sensory deprivation was devastating. Knowledge of my situation was at once my greatest torment and my only defense; but it wasn't enough of a defense. The total lack of stimulation was tearing away the scabs on my psyche, releasing every pustule of fear and frustration I'd ever known, bringing it all up in one lump to sore and fester in my conscious mind; soon a flash point would be reached.

With increasing frequency, I found myself waking from periods of unconsciousness to find myself slipping down into the black hole. I fought back, but I was getting progressively weaker. Soon, I knew, I would fall down there and not be able to climb out. I'd be a zombie, a slave to Esobus, willing to do anything that was asked of me.

Until the rabies killed me.

The next time I emerged from semiconsciousness, I discovered that the black hole was far in the distance, and I felt on fairly solid mental ground. It took me a few seconds to realize what had brought me back.

My left foot was resting against something solid. I could *feel* it, and it was as if this delicate sense of touch were the greatest gift I'd ever received.

Slowly, tentatively, I sent a message from my brain down to my left leg, very politely asking it to move. It did. My toes wiggled, and my foot slid back and forth, touching the smooth, slightly slimy side and bottom of the tank. I tried the other leg. It too moved, as did my arms.

I was floating free.

I twisted around and felt my knees bang against the slate bottom. I stood, reached up with my hand and felt my fingers curl around a steel edge. I gave a mental whoop, pushed off the bottom and pulled with my arms. Buoyed by the salt water, I soared like a slightly dopey flying fish over the side of the tank. Needles tore from my flesh, and I landed hard on my back on a bare, hardwood floor. That stunned me for a moment, but nothing had broken. I ripped the rubber mask off my head. The light from the fluorescent lights in the laboratory slashed into my eyes like razor blades. I screwed my eyes shut and took deep, shuddering breaths. My skin was a kaleidoscope of sensation, as if every nerve fiber in my naked body were thirstily drinking up the feel of the water and the cold wood. My sensory floodgates were open, and *living* was gushing through them.

They hadn't killed me yet.

I tried to rise, but couldn't. My legs felt like warm putty. After spending an unknown length of time in the water, I knew it was going to be some time before everything worked properly.

I propped myself up on one elbow and opened my eyes to slits. The light still hurt, but the pain was tolerable. I was surrounded by a tangle of wires and plastic feeding tubes. A metal stand from which the intravenous feeding bags had hung was directly to my left. A huge electronic monitoring machine a few feet off to the right blinked merrily, as if welcoming me back to the world of light and the living.

When I moved my head, I found something else watching me. My flop on the floor and the tearing out of the feeding tubes must have tripped some warning device; Kee's Chinese assistant had appeared, and he was holding a large .38 in his hand. The sight was just what I needed to cheer me up.

The Chinese advanced toward me. I rolled over on my back, closed my eyes and moaned. When I felt him standing over me, I opened my eyes, grabbed the metal stand and pulled it toward him. The Chinese ducked, instinctively raising his gun hand to ward off the steel bar. The .38 went off, and a bullet shattered the glass tank above me. Several thousand gallons of water cascaded over us, knocking the Chinese off his feet and sloshing me across the room to come up hard and painfully against the monitoring machine. I sputtered and coughed water. My vision cleared in time for me to see the dazed Chinese get up on his knees and retch; fortunately, he'd swallowed more water than I had. The gun had fallen out of his hand and was about twenty feet to his right, near what looked like the main power switch for the floor. I began crawling toward the weapon on my hands and knees.

I'd just got started when the rest of the entourage arrived. Smathers and Kee, probably alerted by the sound of the gunshot, rushed in through the door on the opposite side of the room.

Things didn't seem to be going too well for me.

Seized by terror, and not a little self-pity at the *injustice* of it all, I felt my heart hammering inside my chest, paralyzing me; all I could do was stay kneeling and stare at the two scientists.

Kee was wearing a plaid work shirt, shiny chinos a size too small for him, and green, high-top sneakers. But he didn't look funny to me. His eyes behind his horn-rimmed glasses were great dark pools of oil set in flesh that might have been made of fine yellow porcelain. He made a hissing sound behind his teeth.

Smathers' emerald-green eyes were filled with hate. He

swore in frustration, then barked orders. The assistant quickly rose to his feet, spotted the gun and started to walk toward it.

The realization that I was about to be shot—or dumped back into the tank—proved remarkably therapeutic. It seemed a good time to do *something*; like turn around, scramble back the way I'd come, climb up on top of the monitoring machine and pull some wires.

The machine whirred and popped, sending up clouds of black, acrid smoke. The live wires in my hands sputtered like deadly Fourth of July sparklers. I figured it was time for something to start going my way; I spun a mental prayer wheel, something concerning proper insulation in the machine I was squatting on, then tossed the wires into the water on the floor.

Kee had excellent reflexes. He leaped at the same time I dropped the wires and managed to land on a dry, warped, upward-sloping spot against the wall on the opposite side of the room. Smathers and the assistant weren't so lucky—or fast. They both tried walking on water, but didn't get far. Their screams were burned out of their throats by a few hundred thousand volts of electricity. Already dead, they danced around for a few seconds, then fell; their bodies gradually stopped twitching as the electricity locked their joints and muscles. There was a smell in the air like that of fried pork rinds.

The gun was still in the middle of the floor, surrounded by the electricity-filled water. That was just fine with me, because Kee was having troubles of his own: the water was gradually working its way up the increasingly narrow shores of his island of dry wood. Kee was backed up against the wall, his arms splayed out to either side of him, his fingers clawing at the plaster. Rabies or no, dunking or no, at the moment I felt—good. I sat down, crossed my legs and smiled at him.

"Tough batshit," I said easily. "Win a few, lose a few."

For the first time, Kee's eyes reflected real emotion. There was fear of the liquid death seeping toward him, and there was hate. A lot of hate. I shouldn't have goaded him; it had been too inspirational.

The main power switch was a good fifteen feet away, but I'd already seen the strength he had in his legs. Kee gave a tremendous yell, then leaped straight up in the air;

he planted his feet against the wall and dived for the power switch.

I knew he was going to make it, and he was closer to the gun than I was. Kee's fingertips hit the control switch, plunging the floor into darkness. His body hit the water a split second later, and I jumped to the floor. Waddling like a drunken duck on legs that felt as if they belonged to a toddler, pumping my arms for momentum, I staggered down the corridor toward the stairs. I could hear Kee splashing furiously along behind me, and there was no doubt in my mind that he'd remembered to pick up the gun. I caromed off the wall at the end of the corridor, fell down the stairs and hit the steel door at the bottom. Naturally, the door was locked.

There wasn't going to be any naked dwarf running through the hallowed corridors of Marten Hall.

I spun and crouched in the darkness, trying to make myself as small a target as possible. With two bodies in the laboratory to explain or somehow get rid of, I expected Kee would no longer be concerned with making me a servant of Esobus; he'd want to dispose of me as quickly as possible. It was going to be like shooting a dwarf in a barrel.

I held my breath and waited for the crash of the gun. All I heard was a dull click; the water had fouled the gun's firing mechanism. I waited.

I could hear Kee slowly and cautiously descending the stairs. I'd taught him some respect, but that wasn't going to be enough. Even if I hadn't spent an unknown number of hours underwater, semi-paralyzed by drugs, I'd probably have been no match for the powerful Kee I'd watched flit across the floor and walls of the laboratory like Superman. On the other hand, I couldn't just sit still and wait for him to beat my brains out.

After waiting a few seconds for him to descend further, I lunged up and forward, sweeping my hand through the general area where I hoped his legs would be. I got lucky. I caught his ankle and yanked. Kee yelped with surprise and went backward, landing on his back on the stairs.

There was no way of getting by him. I was very weak, and I assumed Kee was a karate expert. He'd probably break every bone in my body by the time I got halfway past him. But I had an angle on his midsection, and I drove my fist into his groin. That took the power out of a kick that could have killed me; his heel bounced painfully off my rib cage, but did no damage.

Kee was doubled over with pain, his shape just barely visible in the darkness. I could get past him now, but that would just mean playing cat-and-mouse up in the darkness of the laboratory; that was a game I eventually had to lose. I had no choice but to attack.

Grimacing against my own pain, I moved up and clapped my hands over Kee's ears. He screamed and half-rose. That was the position I wanted him in; he was off balance, his concentration shattered. I grabbed hold of both his ears and dropped. Kee flew over me and plummeted down into the darkness. He came up hard against the steel door, and there was a single, sharp cracking sound. I didn't have to go down and feel his pulse to know that Kee was dead, his neck broken.

I tasted blood, and I was very dizzy. I slumped down on a step, braced myself against the wall and waited for my head to clear. Eventually I would go back upstairs, find a phone and call Garth. At the moment I was thinking of something else. The fact that I was still alive was nothing short of miraculous; I should have felt elation, but I didn't. I felt hollowed out. Now that the danger was past, I felt strangely split, not caring about anything at all; I felt a stranger to myself.

I told myself it was just the aftermath of terror, the effects of shock and exhaustion. I was sure the strange feeling of emptiness would pass.

Chapter 18

It didn't.

It had taken me only a few hours to realize that the long submersion in the tank had resulted in much more than a temporarily wrinkled and squeaky-clean dwarf. Smathers and Kee had gutted me, scraped me out, using my own mind against me as a razor-sharp scalpel. I'd lost something in the tank. I wasn't sure *what* it was I'd lost, which meant I wasn't sure how to find it. I'd sensed the beginning of a psychotic episode; I felt as if I were a bag of skin loosely inflated by a few weak, random thoughts.

I'd decided that I needed at least a mini-vacation before the bag of skin deflated and I spent the last years of my life in a psychiatric ward at Rockland State. Still unwilling to leave New York with so many questions remaining, I'd packed a bag and moved into the Waldorf. It was a move I'd made before when I felt the need to decompress; I enjoyed the luxury. Also, I'd solved a difficult case for the manager some years before, and there was always a suite waiting for me, at a large discount. But the move had been a mistake; the newly decorated rooms reminded me of a Baskin-Robbins ice cream parlor. A phone call to the desk would have gotten me another room, but I couldn't manage the call. I couldn't manage anything. Moving into the hotel was the last purposeful action I'd taken.

Someone was knocking on the door. It had to be a mistake, since no one other than Garth, Joshua and the hotel staff knew where I was. Garth or Joshua would have called first. Room Service, which, at Garth's insistence, had been leaving sandwiches and milk at regular intervals outside my door, rapped only once.

I ignored the persistent knocking and stayed in my chair before the window, staring out over the city. I would pick out a car coming up Park Avenue below me, follow it with my eyes until it was out of sight, then pick up another car and repeat the process. That was what I'd been doing with my days. When I felt tired, I slept; when Joshua showed up to give me an injection, I let him in; if I felt hungry, I'd open the door to get whatever Room Service had left me. The rest of the time I sat and stared.

Garth had responded to my call four days before. He and Johnny Barnard had broken down the laboratory door, wrapped me up in a blanket and taken me to the university Medical Center, where I learned that I'd been in Smathers' sensory-deprivation tank for about three and a half days; it had felt like years.

Apparently, there'd been more of a safety cushion built into the series of rabies shots I'd already been given than Joshua had led me to believe; he'd simply given me an extra-large dose to make up for the shots I'd missed, then told me I'd be all right as long as I rested and got the remaining shots. The wound on my thumb had healed to the point where the immersion in the water hadn't done any lasting damage. I was told that there was nothing wrong with me physically, and that I could go home after Garth had taken my deposition. Later, I'd checked into the Waldorf.

The next morning, a Wednesday, I'd tried to get up to go to the Medical Center for my shot; I couldn't. It had taken me almost two hours to *care* enough to call Greene and ask him to come over. A bag of skin has no desire, no fear, no will. I'd intended to brush my teeth, bathe, put on clean clothes, go out into the sunshine. Now it was Friday, and I still just couldn't seem to get around to any of those things. The PLEASE DO NOT DISTURB sign still hung on the knob outside.

I picked out another car, followed it up the avenue. It was some time before I realized that the person on the other side of the door was shouting.

"*Robert! It's April!* I know you're in there, and I'm not going away until you open the door!"

April Marlowe was the last person in the world I wanted to have see me. Indeed, just the sound of her voice induced my most violent reaction in four days; I jackknifed forward in the chair and clapped my hands over my ears.

"*Robert!* There are a lot of people out here in the hall,

and they're staring at me! *Please!* It's terribly embarrassing, but I'm *not* going away until I see you!"

Finally I rose and went to the door. I opened it, then quickly stepped back into the dim light of the room. In that instant I'd seen that April was telling the truth: at least a dozen people had been standing around in the hall, watching her pound on the strange dwarf's door. It made me feel even sicker.

April stepped into the room, and I quickly closed the door behind her. Dressed in a white jumper embroidered with red and green flowers, worn over a pale blue sweater, she seemed in that moment the most beautiful woman I'd ever seen. The light scent she was wearing drifted into my nostrils. I dropped my eyes and turned away in shame: I knew what I looked and smelled like.

"Robert? What's the *matter* with you?"

"Hard . . . to talk," I mumbled. It was as if each word had to be carefully searched out inside my head, practiced, then forced through my mouth.

"Robert . . . ?"

She started toward me, and I cringed. She stopped and stared at me intently. "Don't . . . don't want . . . to talk."

"Okay," April said softly, after a pause. "Let's just sit down and be together."

I shook my head. The movement brought tears to my eyes; they rolled freely down my cheeks, dripped from my chin to the floor. "Please . . . go away."

"Nope," she said easily. There was the slightest trace of laughter in her voice. "If you want me to go, I'm afraid you're just going to have to throw me out. Judging from the way you look, I think I can handle you."

"Garth . . . tell you I . . . was here?"

"No. It was Dr. Greene. I persisted. He says there's something wrong with you, and that you won't let anyone help you."

"Wants me . . . to see a psychiatrist. I've . . . been there. I'll be . . . all right. Just . . . need to be alone."

"That is *not* what you need at all," April said firmly. She paused, then added quietly, "The coven got hold of you, didn't they?"

"Greene . . . has a . . . big mouth. Didn't he . . . tell you about it?"

"No. He just said that you needed help desperately."

"Bullshit," I said, and was immediately sorry. I said so.

"You can curse if you want to, Robert. You can say anything you want to that will make you feel better. Just talk to me."

"Want . . . to be alone." It wasn't true. I wanted to be with April, wanted to fall into her arms. I wanted to sob aloud, and couldn't. It was as though my bag of skin were encased in a rubber sheet that was shrinking, making it hard for me to breathe.

There was a long silence. Finally April's voice drifted over to me, very softly. "Garth said something about you doing battle with your own demons, but I didn't understand. Now I think I do. You're a lot like Daniel. It has to do with pride, Robert, doesn't it? Your will—your deep mind—against the combined will of the coven."

"Nothing . . . really the matter with me."

In a sense it was true. I knew enough about sensory deprivation to appreciate its psychological effects—the reason why research into it had been banned in the first place. Smathers' dunking—on the surface—had been nothing compared with what a Russian by the name of Kaznakov had done to me. Kaznakov had physically tortured me to the point where I'd ended up nearly psychotic. Victor Rafferty had helped bring me back from that. But then there had been terror—endless, omnipresent fear of everything from ringing telephones to being alone; most of all, there had been the fear that the hulking torturer would return, find me and finish the job he'd started.

There was no terror now. The problem was that there was *nothing*, not even anger. There was only terrible lassitude and apathy. In one corner of my mind, I badly wanted to get back out and finish the job on the coven; I wanted to find Frank Marlowe's book of shadows, if it hadn't been destroyed. Yet I couldn't move. It was as though submersion in the silent world of water, the terrifying sensation of floating over the black hole at the bottom of my psyche, had mortally wounded me in a way that physical torture couldn't. Something that had been in me had drained out through that hole; my body was still around, but *I* was gone. I'd kept telling myself that a three-and-a-half-day soak couldn't be all that serious. Every minute I sat in the darkness staring out the window confirmed the fact that I was wrong. Smathers and Kee had pulled my plug good.

Lost in my thoughts, I hadn't even been aware that April had left the room. Now I heard the sound of running water. Part of me was curious about the water—but not very. The next thing I was aware of was April's hand on my arm, firmly guiding me into the bathroom. The tub was filled with steaming water.

April matter-of-factly began to undress me.

"What are you doing?" I mumbled.

"I'm a witch, remember?" April said somewhat smugly. "I'm working a spell." She clucked her tongue. "No talking while the witch is at work."

She finished undressing me, made a face and threw my filthy clothes into a corner. I stood before her naked and unmoving. I thought I should feel embarrassed, but I didn't; I simply felt terribly vulnerable and helpless. If April had told me to go up on top of the hotel and jump off, I probably would have. For some reason, her warmth and mothering only made me feel emptier, more in need. Again I wanted to cry.

"Get in," April commanded evenly, pointing to the steaming water. When I just stood there, she added, "Get in or I'll push you in."

I stuck a toe in the water, winced and pulled it back. "Too hot," I said.

"Aha! Signs of life! You said that quite clearly."

April put her hand on my back and pushed me inexorably forward. There was no way I could resist the pressure of her hand; I finally stepped into the tub and sank down into the hot water. The heat jolted my nerve endings, yet the shock was oddly comforting; it made me feel secure, perhaps because it gave me something besides myself to think about. For a moment, the rubber sheet encasing me seemed to expand.

April firmly shoved my head under the water, then pulled it up. She shampooed my hair, then found shaving cream and a razor in the medicine cabinet. Sitting on a towel on the edge of the tub, she went to work on my beard. It was awkward and uncomfortable for her to shave me from that position, and I knew I should do it myself—yet I couldn't move. I could barely even turn my head. I leaned back and closed my eyes, afraid that if I stared at her hard enough she would disappear—or I would cry. I lay passively in the water and steam until she'd finished.

"That concludes Part One of the spell," April said cheerfully, rinsing off the razor and replacing it in the medicine cabinet. "You're going to have to wash the rest of you yourself."

April winked at me, then walked out of the bathroom and closed the door behind her. I surprised myself by reaching out for a bar of soap and washing the rest of my body. But then I started to slow down again as my mind shifted gears, went out of focus and began replaying blurred images from the nightmare I'd lived inside my head while I was in the tank. I wanted desperately to finish bathing, dress in clean clothes and greet April with the announcement that I was taking her and Kathy to dinner. But I couldn't move, and my mind blurred even further out of focus as the heat left the water.

April returned to find me sitting listlessly in a tubful of water that had gone cold. I managed to smile wanly as she shook her head disapprovingly. She drained the tub, pulled me up by the arm and wrapped me in a large bath towel.

"Sorry," I croaked.

"Shhh." She cocked her head to one side, put her hands on her hips. "This is going to be tougher than I thought," she said after a few moments. "I can see how difficult it is for you to talk, Robert, so don't try. Just be silent and let me take care of you."

She guided me into the bedroom, where she took the spread off the bed and turned back the sheets, which I could see had been changed from an extra supply in one of the closets. She stripped the towel from me. Suddenly very tired, I flopped on the bed, and April covered me. Then, with the same lack of self-consciousness she'd displayed when undressing me, April began to take off her own clothes. When she'd finished, she carefully folded her clothes and draped them over the back of a chair. Again, April struck me as the most beautiful and desirable woman I'd ever seen. Her skin was smooth and creamy, in striking contrast to the large, earth-brown nipples on her full breasts. Bathed in the early-afternoon light, she glowed golden, like a Rembrandt painting.

She came around to the other side of the bed, slid under

the covers and unhesitatingly wrapped me in her arms. I knew that her actions had nothing to do with lust, and that absolutely no demands were being made of me. In my exhausted state, sex was the farthest thing from my mind. April was offering me her wholeness, her *self*. Lying in her arms, my face pressed against the soft flesh of her breasts, I could hear her heart beating; I felt safe.

Then, suddenly, I was hard. Under the circumstances, my erection embarrassed me; but April smiled, reached down and gently began to stroke me. After a few moments she threw back the covers, lay on her back and spread her legs. With a surge of energy that amazed me, I mounted her and hungrily thrust myself into her body. It occurred to me that I was being serviced; in my present state of mind, I couldn't imagine anyone—much less April—wanting me. Offering me her body was an *act* of love, not making love. Yet, surprising to me, she was ready, the inside of her body warm and wet.

The insistent pressure of my lust built up inside my groin very quickly. I came in her with a groan, then collapsed on her chest. April held me in her with her legs wrapped around my body, gently rocking me back and forth like a baby. Finally she sighed and unlocked her legs. I rolled to the side, but clung to her while she stroked my head. Now I felt even less of an inclination to talk—but it made no difference. There was no longer any need for words. I was still lost inside myself, but my anxiety was gone, and the state of my psyche was no longer important; April was all that mattered. In that state of mind, I drifted peacefully off to sleep.

When I awoke an hour or so later, I found that April still lay beside me with her arms wrapped around my body. When I glanced up, I found her smiling, and I knew she hadn't slept. I began to stroke her breasts and immediately grew hard again. This time we made love quickly, hungrily. April, her eyes closed and lips slightly apart, moaned softly as she moved under me in perfect rhythm with my body and mind. I came again, slept again.

The next time I awoke, April was no longer beside me. Perhaps she'd sensed in some way—*occult* was the only word I could think of—that I no longer needed her so desperately. The smell of food drifted in from the other room, making my mouth water and stomach growl. I was filled with an almost overwhelming sense of gratitude. April had offered me herself to give me back myself. By taking me into her body, she'd brought me back into the world. I was whole again.

I quickly showered, then dressed in my robe and went into the living room. April was dressed, singing softly to herself as she adjusted the burner flame under the warming cart Room Service had brought. The sight of her made a lump rise in my throat.

"Voilà!" I cried, my voice cracking with emotion. "It speaks!"

April turned and grinned. I wanted to go over to her, but something held me back. Garth had been absolutely right: I'd never experienced these emotions before, never felt so vulnerable. April seemed to sense that; she came to me and kissed me lightly on the mouth. "So I see," she said. She gave me a wicked leer, added, "Now it looks as if *everything* is in working order."

"Nobody has ever given me such a gift," I said quietly. "Thank you."

"Bite your tongue," April said, going back to the warming cart to examine the Chateaubriand. "Offering charity has never given me orgasms."

"That was some spell. I think you've inspired me to study for the ceremonial magician-hood."

She finished basting the steaks with butter sauce, then turned back to face me again. She was no longer smiling. She came back across the room, put her hand over my heart, then placed my hand firmly on her left breast.

"It's no joke, Robert. Any witch—good or evil—recognizes that love is the most mysterious and powerful force in the universe. The human heart is its home, and that makes the heart the ultimate book of shadows. Today, for a short time, we opened and read ours together. We performed a ceremony, and we felt the power of that which cannot be put into words. It was a mutual celebration—the only way this ceremony can be performed properly. Both our lives are richer for it. The 'spell,' you see, is really very complex at the same time that it's very simple."

"It's a nice thought, April," I said quietly. "But the bad guys cast spells from the same book."

She patted my chest, smiled again. "Ah, yes. This book of shadows is very complex indeed. But we were fighting the combined forces of one of the most theoretically powerful covens that has ever existed. They've been beating at your consciousness, believe me; and they emptied you. All it took was one poor, little old witch to fill you up again. It's not that I'm stronger than they are; *love* is. Love is stronger than hate, good more powerful than evil."

"I'm sorry, April, but I don't believe it," I said softly, preferring frankness to condescension. "At best, I think it's an even struggle."

"*Believe?* Robert, my love, I just *proved* it to you, didn't I?" She playfully punched me on the arm. "I *know* it sounds simplistic, but it's also true." She shrugged. "I can't explain the existence of evil when good is so obviously superior a force. It's an occult mystery. Evil usually gets faster and more immediately usable results; it's a much *easier* force to stalk and wield."

"I'll bet you and Janet have some interesting discussions."

"Actually, we spend most of our time together discussing the care and feeding of African violets. Come on; lunch is ready. How's your stomach?"

"It'll feel a lot better after I get some real food in it. I only have two more shots to go, and I think my body's finally getting used to the stuff."

I set the table. April served the food, and we sat down to eat. "Well," I said around a mouthful of succulent steak, "the bad guys are short two members of their coven. Three, depending on how much pressure Garth is putting on Sandor Peth."

April shook her head. "I don't have any idea what you're talking about, Robert. I'm completely in the dark as to what you've been doing. Neither Garth nor Dr. Greene wanted to tell me what's happened to you until *you* wanted to talk about it." She reached across the table and squeezed my hand. "But you don't have to tell me anything if you're not ready."

"It's not a problem," I said, and proceeded to fill April in on everything that had happened up to that point. It had all begun with my being hired to investigate the strange behavior of a Nobel laureate, and ended with my escape from one of his oversize fish tanks.

"A *Nobel Prize* winner?" April interjected.

I nodded. "It seems winning a Nobel Prize is no guarantee that you're a good guy. Smathers and Kee were almost certainly real members of the coven. Peth is another member. These nice folks have been exploiting famous, wealthy and influential people. There's no telling how many men and women they have under their control, offering them God knows what."

"They've been offered secret power," April said evenly. "They've been fooled into believing that they can control anything and anyone they want, through witchcraft."

"That's incredible. How can they be so damn stupid?"

April looked at me for a long time, her eyes reflecting curiosity and, perhaps, a touch of impatience. "Robert," she said at last, "sometimes you can seem incredibly dense. Don't you see, even now, that it *works?* Those people you're talking about are *being* totally controlled. They just don't *realize* it—which is how most control works anyway. You've already *proved* that the coven has been able to corrupt, manipulate and destroy people, and then you say that you doubt your own proof; you still doubt the existence of the force they're able to bring to bear on the deep mind."

She sighed and cocked an eyebrow. When I didn't say anything, she continued: "You see, the white magician cultivates love because he or she knows that love is ultimately a more powerful force. The black magician stalks and wields evil because it offers quick results. Love offers freedom; evil offers slavery. *You* think the choice is simple, but it's not. Most people unconsciously prefer to be slaves to their secret desires, rather than control and define their lives through love."

I smiled thinly. "The bad guys weren't quite so subtle with me."

"What did they do to you, Robert?" April asked quietly.

"Sensory deprivation," I replied, surprised at how easy it had become to talk about it. "They put me in total isolation in what's known as a hydrohypodynamic environment. They made a slight mistake by placing me in a situation that I could—and eventually did—associate with Smathers, but they obviously didn't care; they figured they'd have me there as long as it took to break me." I paused and carefully folded my napkin, placed it on the table in front of me. "You were right about pride. I remembered what you'd told me about the deep mind, and coming back by myself became a challenge for me." I smiled. "If the truth be known, I much prefer your method."

"They killed Daniel," April said softly. "Why do you suppose they didn't simply kill you?"

"I'll give you a guess—but I think it's a good one. No matter what Daniel found out—and I'm convinced he knew a lot to begin with, and found out even more—he didn't talk to anyone outside his own belief system. His contacts were very strictly limited, so the coven could afford to kill him. With me, they had a different problem. They knew I'd smoked out Sandor Peth, and they knew I was in constant touch with the police, through Garth. What they couldn't be sure of was just how much I really knew, or whom I'd told. They wanted to find out, then use me—if they could—to cover their tracks. And if they wiped me out in a bizarre fashion to make it a kind of rite, so much the better."

"But you got away," April said intently.

"Sure did," I said with a grin. "*Poof!* Disappeared right into thin air; flew out on a broomstick I found in the janitor's closet."

She didn't laugh. "*How* did you get away, Robert?"

"I was cut loose," I replied seriously. "They had me bound with leather straps around my wrists and ankles. Somebody sliced through them, but I was either asleep or too zonked-out to realize what was happening at the time."

"But who would . . ." April paused, and I could see that she knew the answer. "*Esobus,*" she whispered.

"Right. Esobus again. It had to be. Who else but a member of the coven would know where I was, and what was being done to me? It looks as though Esobus is turning out to be my guardian angel as well as Kathy's. Kee tried to tell me that *he* was Esobus, but that's nonsense. He was trying to get me to identify with Esobus and the coven; since it was his voice I was listening tc, he played Great Pumpkin."

"It all seems so . . . *strange.*"

"I assume that's meant to be an understatement."

"But *why* would Esobus . . . ?" April's voice trailed off into puzzled silence.

"I'll find the answer to that question when I find Esobus."

"Oh, Robert," April sighed, "you're not going on with this, are you?"

"Of course I am; I still have a client."

"Kathy is *not* your client," April said with real exasperation. "She's too *young* to hire you! She's a minor, and I *forbid* you to look on her as your client!"

"She's not too young to give me everything she had in order to help someone she loved. She hired me to find her father's book of shadows, and I don't want her to be disappointed. Besides, needless to say, *I'm* curious about that book, and about Esobus. I can't back off now."

"But if you're right about Frank's book of shadows being an exposé of the coven, it must have been stolen and destroyed by them."

"Probably. I want to find out for sure; and I want to find out who Esobus is."

"But you're *ill*, Robert!"

"I'll be all right. I'm going to nail these bastards."

"The police will take care of it now."

"I know; it's probably only a matter of time. I just want a piece of the action."

April only shook her head, whispered, "You're crazy."

"No. Just slightly put out."

"I'm afraid they'll kill you, Robert," April breathed. "After all you've done for us, after all you . . . mean to me . . . I don't think I could bear losing you."

"Hey, it's *their* side that's losing. I've got momentum, and I absolutely guarantee you they can't kill me. Your spell has cloaked me with invincibility for at least a hundred years."

"Words!" April said with sudden anger. "Words, and stupid pride! Death can come in an instant! You'll be killed, and all that will be left will be your stupid words! I don't want to have to remember you as a wonderful, *stupid* man!"

"I'm sorry you feel that way, April," I explained quietly. "I just have to follow this thing through to its conclusion. If you can't understand, there's no way I can explain."

April sighed again. "Kathy's recovering beautifully, but I'm exhausted—and *you're* exhausted. I was hoping that in a few days we could all . . . go off somewhere together.

Kathy would like that so much." She winked, and growled playfully. "So would I, lover. Want to think about it?"

"*Think* about it? My God, I want to go *now!*" I reached across the table and took her hand. "But I can't just leave this thing hanging."

"I can see that," April said, looking at me hard. "I was just hoping."

"Can I get a taking-care-of-business check?"

"You've got a postponement."

"Where's Kathy now?"

"With Janet."

"How's she getting along with Horace?"

April smiled warmly. "Just fine, but she'd love to see her best friend, Mr. Mongo. She's been asking about you all week, and she doesn't understand why you haven't come to see her."

"Does she know about . . . her father yet?"

April nodded. "She knows that Frank died in the fire you saved her from, but not the details. She doesn't remember anything about what happened before the fire. All she can say is that she fell asleep in the car coming home from my house; that's all she remembers until she woke up in the hospital."

"It's just as well. Are you and Kathy doing anything this afternoon?"

"No. Why?"

"I have to drop by the hospital for my shot, and then I'd like to do something with the two of you. Like go to the zoo. Can Kathy leave the house?"

"She can, and I know she'd *love* to go to the zoo."

"I'm a zoo freak—if you'll pardon the pun."

April giggled. "I'll ignore the pun—and I'm a zoo freak too. I love orangutans." Her smile fluttered and faded. "Does this mean that at least you're not starting back to work right away?"

"Certainly not before we go to the zoo," I said, getting up to clear away the dishes.

But I would right afterward, as soon as it got dark. And I had a pretty good idea where to start looking.

Chapter 19

The lights were on in Krowl's brownstone, and the shades were up. I didn't want anyone inside looking out and seeing me, so I stayed across the street in the night shadows. I walked to the end of the block and went down the side street. In the shadows between the glows cast by two street lights I crossed the street to the warehouse behind Krowl's house. The warehouse still looked abandoned, but I didn't think it was; the coven had to have a private and secure place to meet, and the warehouse looked like a perfect spot.

All the windows I could see were painted black, and the glass looked as if it were reinforced with wire mesh. Considering the neighborhood, the building looked in good shape and seemed to be maintained well. In the front was a stainless steel door with a heavy padlock. I was reasonably certain I could work my way through the lock, but the street was too exposed.

I had better luck in a side alley. I had the same problem with a heavy door and padlock, but in the alley I was shrouded in darkness. There was always the danger of setting off an alarm, silent or otherwise, but there didn't seem to be any way of getting around that risk if I wanted to get inside the building—and I most certainly wanted to get inside. The drop-bolt lock was expensive and sturdy; beyond the skills of the average burglar, nervous and in a hurry. It took me almost an hour and my entire set of custom-made lockpicks to get through it.

I stepped inside the door and found myself in pitch darkness. I fumbled along the wall, found a light switch and flipped it. Fluorescent lights came on, throwing a stuttering, soft glow over a narrow stairway. I slowly climbed the stairs, paying close attention to where I stepped in case the setup was booby-trapped. I could find no wires or mechanical devices that would indicate an alarm rigging, and I assumed I was home free.

At the top of the stairway I found myself on a catwalk which circled a broad concrete area on the first floor below. Occult symbols had been painted on the concrete between the perimeter of a large black circle and twelve smaller circles surrounding it. Black draperies encircled the entire area. There was a sloping, sunken area in the center of the floor. The depression was scorched, and I thought I could see three small metal outlets that were probably gas jets. They would make a clean, gas-burning bonfire; all the conveniences of modern covenry.

To my right was a narrow platform constructed of reinforced concrete and jutting out over the ceremonial area below. At the end of the platform was a small enclosure draped in crimson velvet. Assuming I was right about Esobus keeping his identity secret even from the members of his own coven, the cubicle would probably be where the ceremonial magician held forth. A look inside the cubicle confirmed it. There was what I assumed to be a one-way mirror overlooking the area below. In front of the glass were a bare wooden writing desk and a straight-backed metal folding chair. The walls were bare, except for a small sign that had been lettered with India ink on heavy bond paper. It was neatly taped to the smooth wood just to the left of the glass, and read:

> THE SEARCH FOR TRUTH IS NEITHER MORAL NOR IMMORAL: IT IS THE PREREQUISITE OF A CIVILIZED SOCIETY.

It seemed a curious motto for the leader of a coven that went around killing people and poisoning little girls.

I took the paper from the wall, folded it and put it in my pocket. Then I turned my attention to the small console of electronic equipment in the corner to the right of the desk. There were a tape deck, a microphone and equipment for voice distortion. I was certain that the message Joshua Greene had received in the hospital had been recorded on the machine I was looking at.

I went back out on the catwalk and walked around it. The gutting and reconstruction of the building was far from complete. There were a number of dusty corridors radiating off the catwalk to other sections of the building. I walked down one corridor and found myself in a large, bare area that looked as if it had once housed heavy equipment. I didn't have time to explore all the other sections, and I was anxious to examine the main floor. I returned to the catwalk.

There was probably a stairway leading downstairs if I looked long enough for it, but I was in a hurry. I found some heavy rope on a scaffold that had been left in a corner. I anchored the rope, then dropped it over the railing and shinnied down. At the bottom, just in case I wanted to get back up in a hurry, I coiled the rope end and hid it behind a section of black drapery. On the other side of the drapery, on the concrete apron of the main area, I discovered a large cubicle whose walls and ceiling seemed to have been constructed from prefabricated materials. A quick swing around the area behind the drapery showed that there was a total of twelve such cubicles.

I stepped into one, found the light switch and turned it on. Again, fluorescent lights flickered on. My heart almost stopped as I heard a sudden, pneumatic hissing sound. I wheeled and dived for the entrance. In a way, I was lucky that my reflexes were slightly off; if I'd been a split second faster, I'd have been decapitated or cut in half as a steel plate dropped from a hidden niche above the cubicle doorway and hit the floor with a solid, loud clang.

I got my arms up just in time and absorbed the force of my hitting the plate with my forearms. Panicked at being caught like an animal in a trap, I leaped up and hurled myself against the steel; the plate set me right down on the floor again. This time I stayed down, held my head in my hands and tried to calm nerves that were shrieking with fear. The plate was solid, and all I'd get from banging against it would be a broken shoulder and a headache.

If I had to play rat, I decided I might as well try to be a smart one: I got to my feet and carefully examined the surface of the plate. Fifteen minutes of this convinced me there was no way to escape; obviously, one had to make arrangements for walking out before walking in. That, I thought, didn't seem to bode well for my future—which could be very short. But I knew that the terror generated by dwelling on the fact would only sap my strength. There was nothing I could do but wait and see who—if anyone—was going to show up. I took out my gun and looked around.

The cubicle had been designed as an all-purpose private retreat for one of the coven members. There were a cot, a small library of sorts with an esoteric collection of occult books; there was even a black-draped altar with black candles. In the center of the altar was a large, hand-bound book with hand-tooled leather covers and thick parchment pages. A book of shadows. Having absolutely nothing better to do and needing something to keep my mind off my situation, I sat down on the edge of the cot, placed my gun next to my right thigh and began to leaf through the book.

It belonged to a man by the name of Jan Watson, a ceremonial magician from North Dakota. There were numerous pages of mystical diagrams, recipes for herb medicines and poisons, records of dreams and their magical interpretation in an occult framework. There was also a record of what Watson referred to as altered states of consciousness reached during coven ceremonies—most of which seemed incredibly ugly and vicious.

Apparently, I hadn't been the first persistent burglar to force my way into the coven's headquarters; according to Watson's book of shadows, three other men had been trapped as I was, then put to death in sacrificial rites. It seemed an effective, if somewhat tacky, method of cutting down on the neighborhood crime rate. It also made me feel slightly better. It seemed to mean that they wouldn't simply leave me there to starve to death. Also, I much preferred waiting around for a sacrificial rite to being gassed or shot from some hidden aperture in the walls or ceiling.

The most intriguing sections of Watson's book of shadows were those dealing with the formation of the coven a year and a half before; there were detailed records of the group's activities and proceedings. It made fascinating reading—right up to the point when the plate sighed open and John Krowl stepped into the room. I started to grab for my gun, then froze with my hand in the air.

Krowl was wearing a red, hooded robe with black occult symbols embroidered across the front. Dressed in the robe, his white hair framing the ghostly-pale flesh of his face, he made quite a striking figure. But it wasn't his costume that impressed me as much as the enormous black .45 automatic in his hand. The lights had been turned off in the main chamber, and there was a loud hissing sound from the activated gas jets. Behind Krowl, courtesy of Consolidated Edison, firelight flickered and danced like heat lightning.

Moving very deliberately, keeping the .45 aimed steadily at my chest, the albino came across the room, picked up my gun from the cot and threw it skittering behind him into the darkness. Then he moved back to a safe distance, by the entrance.

The only way out was through Krowl, but he'd have to be set up first. I'd have to try a little game of Concentration; to see just how good he was.

I closed Watson's book, crossed my legs, looked up at Krowl and tried to smile. "Dr. Livingstone, I presume?" I was grateful for the fact that my voice came out steady, but with what I hoped was just the right amount of underlying hysteria. The hysteria wasn't difficult.

Krowl looked at me for a few moments, puzzled, then grinned crookedly. "You're a tenacious fool, Frederickson."

"The gun and the gas fire are rather newfangled, aren't they?" I asked, giggling inanely. "I don't mean to offend you, but, frankly, it spoils the image."

"The advantages of living in the twentieth century," he said smugly. With the heavy artillery in his hand, at what he obviously—and with good reason—thought was the end of the matter, Krowl was showing that he could be positively droll.

"I can't believe you're going to kill me with a gun," I said in the same thin, breathy voice I'd been using. "I mean, a shooting would be so *déclassé* for a big, bad ceremonial magician." I shrugged nervously, uncrossed my legs and planted my feet firmly on the floor. "Why don't you just try spelling me to death?"

It was time to try for the secret square and hope it didn't turn out to be a rubber duck—or a dead dwarf. I lunged forward, hitting the floor and rolling, aiming at Krowl's legs. The gun exploded in my right ear, partially deafening me; concrete splinters sprayed my face. Even as I came up into a crouch, I knew I'd missed. Krowl was standing over me, holding the gun steady with both hands. The barrel was inches away from my head, and I stiffened, closing my eyes and biting into my lip in anticipation of the next shot—which I doubted I'd even hear. It didn't come. I opened my eyes, wiped the blood off my mouth.

"You'll die, Frederickson," Krowl snarled, "but you'll die in a way *we* choose—by fire and *athamé*. The only decision you have to make is whether you want bullets in your kneecaps and elbows when we kill you."

Krowl motioned me back. I sank to the floor, bracing my back against the wall, cursing silently and methodically at myself for missing the only chance I'd probably ever get, and at drug-and-disease-wasted muscles that wouldn't work properly. "You're missing a couple of members," I said, trying desperately to think, to plan. "I'd hate to be sacrificed at anything less than a full-blown offical gathering."

Krowl almost smiled. "You're tough, Frederickson. And you have personal power. I respect you."

"Fuck you, you creep son-of-a-bitch."

Krowl looked at me strangely, his pinkish eyes slightly out of focus. "Down through the centuries, dwarfs have always been considered receptacles of power," he said distantly. "They were kept as consorts, for good luck, in the Medieval courts. Maybe that's what we should do with you. We could chain you, keep you here in a cage. No one would ever know."

"Krowl," I whispered, "come Mental Health Week, I'm going to nominate you for Poster Child."

I was rather hoping he'd get mad; if he got mad, he might get sloppy. He disappointed me.

"Keeping you with us was just a thought," Krowl said with a shrug, his eyes coming back into focus on my face. "You're going to die."

I sighed. "Where's the rest of the coven?"

"They'll be here—except for Smathers and Kee, of course. It seems their power was not equal to yours."

"Will Esobus be here?"

"Yes."

"Spouting electronic bullshit from his own private cabin," I said, watching Krowl carefully, waiting for another chance at him. In order to get it, I'd just about have to put him to sleep; I couldn't generate much momentum from my seated position, and Krowl looked as though he were paying attention. "*You* don't even know who Esobus is, do you?"

Something like chagrin or embarrassment moved in the albino's eyes, but he didn't speak. I motioned toward the book of shadows left open on the cot. "Come on, Krowl," I continued. "Your coven-buddy Watson didn't know, and he indicated that he was pretty pissed off about it. The only reason he went along was because he'd been asked to by the man who'd recruited him. That was Smathers, a fellow weirdo and pervert Watson had known for years. In fact, you *all* joined by invitation, and the hosts for the party were Smathers and Esobus. Smathers vouched for Esobus, and one of the conditions for joining was that Esobus be allowed to maintain absolute secrecy about his identity." I slowly planted my hands on the floor at my sides. "I think you've all been witched-out, Krowl; Smathers was just jerking around the bunch of you."

Krowl's pale eyes glinted. He noticed my position and wiggled the gun. I put my hands back in my lap. "Esobus is the greatest ceremonial magician alive," he said intently. "He made it possible for all of us to join together. Tonight, we—or one of us—will be asked to share the secret of his identity."

"Smathers was the liaison between Esobus and the rest of the coven," I said. "But Smathers is dead, and you just told me there was no backup man. There won't be a new messenger boy until tonight. How will Esobus know about this meeting?"

"Tonight's meeting was scheduled beforehand," Krowl said softly. "You picked the best of all possible times to visit us."

I most fervently *hoped* Esobus would show up. It was Esobus who'd saved Kathy's life, Esobus who'd undoubtedly cut my bonds in Smather's lab—and Esobus who was going to have to get me out of this one. Esobus was my last potential ace in the hole—a possible secret ally. It was a paper-thin chance, especially in view of the fact that he was going to have to pull this particular dwarf rabbit out of a hat in full view of the other coven members, but it was the only hope left on the shelf.

A movement to the left caught my eye. A robed figure

had appeared and was standing just outside the entrance to the cubicle. The hood covered the man's face, and his hands and arms were folded inside the flowing sleeves of the robe. He nodded to Krowl, but didn't speak. Number Two had arrived, and we were obviously in a holding pattern. My stomach muscles knotted painfully, and for a moment I was afraid I was going to be sick.

Krowl acknowledged the other man's presence with a brief movement of his head, then turned his attention back to me. "It was all in the tarot cards," he said absently. "Except that you almost brought *me* bad luck."

"I remember something about disaster," I said tightly.

"For you, Frederickson; not for me."

"I'm not dead yet," I said, and was sorry I'd spoken. It was false bravado, to say the least, and it sounded desperate and silly.

"You will be soon."

"Christ, you're a bunch of sickies!" I said with a lot more feeling than I'd intended to show. I knew that I had to stay calm and look for my best chance; but I vividly remembered what Daniel's body had looked like. Krowl, with his gun, and the gathering, robed assemblage outside the cubicle did tend to make me nervous. A rational part of me kept insisting that dead was dead, and it didn't make any difference how you died. But I didn't want to be tortured, cut, burned; I didn't want a dead animal stuffed in my mouth, or to be howled over by men in crimson robes. Their "spell" was working as it was supposed to: I was very much afraid, and my fear had a paralyzing effect. They were working my head over before they began on my body. I didn't really have much hope that Esobus or anyone else was going to save me. At least, I hoped to die with some dignity, which meant I'd have to try to mask my fear for as long as possible.

Krowl gestured with the barrel of his gun toward Watson's book of shadows. "You've been doing a lot of digging, and now you've read a genuine book of shadows. Have you finally satisfied your curiosity?"

Something in his voice—or perhaps the question itself—struck me as odd, and for a moment curiosity displaced fear. It suddenly occurred to me that there was something Krowl wanted from me. I certainly hoped so;

from where I was sitting, I didn't look like a man with too much bargaining power.

Three more hooded, red-robed figures had joined the first man outside. That left five more to go—assuming Garth hadn't picked up Sandor Peth.

"I know you're all full of shit," I said, trying to keep my voice steady as I fought my mounting fear with words. "Your supercoven is shit. Men who are supposed to be the best ceremonial magicians in the country are brought together into one coven, and what do we get? People raised from the dead? Darkness at noon? Lead turned to gold? Nope. We get a bunch of nasty little boys dressed in Halloween costumes ripping off gullible people. It would be mildly funny if not for the fact that you're murderers. You're still all absolutely ridiculous, you know, and killing me won't change that."

That struck a nerve. Krowl's eyes flashed angrily, and the muscles in his jaw clenched and fluttered. "You miss the point, Frederickson," he said, his voice rising a notch.

I snorted. "They've been selling the Brooklyn Bridge to idiots like the people you've conned ever since we bought Manhattan from the Indians."

"We're committed to the accumulation of power through the conscious pursuit of evil," Krowl said in the tone of a slightly wounded professor correcting a dense student. "I won't even try to explain states of consciousness, or the inner journeys of the mind that we're able to achieve together."

"Spare me. I can take you on a tour of Bellevue and show you other people with altered states of consciousness." I paused, waited for my heartbeat to slow down; the longer we bantered, the longer I'd stay alive, and I was talking too fast. "Besides," I continued in a more measured tone, "the way I see it, *you* do all the work, Krowl. You've got a talent. Maybe it's just supersensitivity; whatever it is, I accept the fact that you gain tremendous insight into people, with your cards, in the wink of an eye. You can see their hopes and their secret terrors. But *you're* the one with the talent, and I suspect you're the single piece of flypaper that holds this wormy outfit together."

"Your analogy aside, I'm flattered," Krowl said. He obviously was.

"Don't be," I snapped. "I haven't finished. You know

what I think? This alleged 'supercoven' of yours, with possible exceptions of Smathers and a leader who won even tell you his real name, is, in fact, the B group; you're second-raters." I paused, then asked softly, "What did you and Michael McEnroe fight about?"

Krowl stared at me for a long time, then slowly blinked once. "What do you know about McEnroe?" he asked tensely.

"I know he is—or was—your mentor. Your entire operation, including the hand casts, is patterned after his. I know McEnroe's very heavy, and that he taught you everything you know. My guess is that people like him and Daniel would have made up the A group; they were the *first* ones invited to form a coven. Smathers used the name of Esobus as bait to dangle in front of the *real* heavies. They may have laughed at him; more likely, they simply ignored him. So Smathers and Esobus had to widen the list. God, they really had to scrape the bottom of the cookie jar to come up with a madman like Sandor Peth. But they managed to bag *you*, Krowl. You certainly weren't Michael McEnroe, but you'd have to do. For the rest, Esobus and Smathers had to settle for more dumbies—like you—who'd be willing to accept a squawk box as a leader."

It was all speculation, a barrage of words fired in a wide scatter pattern, and I paused to try to gauge Krowl's reaction. I decided I must be pretty close to the target; the albino's mouth was slightly open, and his breathing had grown rapid and shallow.

"You're the conduit," I continued. "You're the key to this operation. People come to you for help and advice in your capacity as a palmist and tarot reader. With your talent, you can hit a moving vulnerability a mile away. Then you reel them in. Also, of course, there's the prestige the suckers feel from being in secret association with the great John Krowl—in a *coven*, no less; that's the clincher. You suck them in, then farm them out to other members of the coven—like advising Harley Davidson to leave Jake Stein at William Morris and sign Sandor Peth as his manager. Right up to the moment they die—or are milked dry—they continue to believe that they're members.

"I'm betting the rift between you and your teacher came when McEnroe found out what you were up to; he heard *you'd* been extended an invitation and were going to join. He also knew that, despite all your talent, you were evil and could be exploited. That's when he dumped on you." I paused, leaned slightly forward and smiled. "As far as I know, you only messed up with one man—but that was some screw-up."

"You don't know what you're talking about," Krowl said defensively.

"The hell I don't. Frank Marlowe had you turkeys in his sights from the beginning."

Krowl's eyes flashed. "The man you're referring to didn't survive long, did he?"

"You murdered him, but you didn't control him. You cast Bart Stone, big-shot Western writer, in the role of sucker, and all the time Frank Marlowe was playing Exorcist. He was planning to rip *you* off. I think that's funny as hell. Who knows? Before you killed him, Marlowe may even have found out who Esobus is."

Two more figures had joined the group outside. The cubicle was beginning to heat up, but I couldn't tell whether it was from the fire outside, or the fear inside me. Krowl motioned for me to get up.

"It's not going to do you any good to kill me," I said quickly, my voice too high-pitched. "I put my brother on to Peth. If I end up dead or missing, you're going to learn a new definition of the word, 'pressure.' "

"Peth is dead," Krowl said smugly. "In our world, the slightest mistake is paid for with death. Peth's mistake jeopardized us all, and he had to be eliminated. Now there's no proof of our existence; when you're dead, there'll be no one to lead the police to us." He smiled broadly, triumphantly. "In any case, we have many people, who think they're members, in a position to protect us."

He was probably right. The book of shadows I'd read was proof of a sort, and there were undoubtedly others lying around in the other cubicles; but no one was ever likely to find one, any more than they were likely to find my ashes.

"There is one thing you can tell us," Krowl continued. His voice seemed slightly off-key.

"Why should I tell you anything?"

"Because if you do, we'll spare the lives of the girl and

her mother. I give you my word on that. We do have our own code of honor, and I offer you that."

"You can stick your word and your code of honor up your ass, Krowl."

"You were searching for what you thought was Frank Marlowe's book of shadows. I want to know if you found it; if you did, I want to know what you've done with it."

The question struck me with the force of a blow to the stomach. It confirmed that the *coven* hadn't taken Marlowe's book of shadows, and they were very much afraid of what it might contain. Marlowe's diary was the last threat to them.

"I never found it," I said quietly. "I could play games and tell you I did; but I didn't."

Krowl studied me for a long time, then nodded brusquely. "I believe you," he said at last.

"Good. It's the truth. So lay off the Marlowe woman and her daughter. There's no power for you in hurting them."

"I am ready."

The sound, shrill and distorted, filled the building.

> *"O pentacle of power, be thou fortress and defense for Esobus against all enemies, visible and invisible, in every magical work."*

"It's time," Krowl said quietly, motioning with the gun for me to rise.

When I tried to stand, my condemned man's legs almost gave way under me. "I've got one more question," I said thickly, easing myself up by bracing my back against the wall. "You talk about a code of honor: What the hell did the little girl have to do with it? You killed Marlowe because you found out he was on to you and investigating your operation. Okay. But why poison the child? What kind of *honor* is that?"

Krowl hesitated, then said, "Debts must be paid; betrayals must be avenged."

"You *did* avenge Marlowe's betrayal when you killed him. Why take it out on his daughter too?" Krowl remained silent, staring. "Did someone *else* betray you, Krowl?"

Something dark moved across his eyes, but before I could chase it the voice came again, this time more forcefully.

"It's time!"

Krowl nodded toward the others waiting outside. As one, their right hands came out of their sleeves; each hand was holding a large, glittering blade. With a precision that would have made the Rockettes envious, the robed figures moved into the cubicle and surrounded me, the points of their daggers pinning me in the center of the circle they'd formed. Now Krowl put away the gun and took out his own knife.

Surrounded by sharp steel, I was herded into the huge outer chamber, close to the fire. Fueled by adrenaline, my legs were working all right, but there was no way I could duck away from or under the knives without being run through—which was what I suspected was going to happen anyway. At a word from Krowl or Esobus, eight blades would slice into me.

I glanced up at my last refuge of hope—the platform over my head. The mirror at the front of the elevated cubicle stared back at me like a baleful, pupilless eye reflecting the firelight.

As if to acknowledge my attention, Esobus began to chant.

> *"Black Bull of the north, Horned One, Dark Ruler of the mountains and all that lies beneath them. Prince of Evil, be here, we beseech thee, and guard this circle from all enemies!"*

The group repeated the chant, then went into a series of other invocations in some archaic tongue that I couldn't understand. At one point I thought they might be sufficiently mesmerized to have lost track of the ceremony's *pièce de résistance;* I tensed, ready to move. Suddenly, as if reading my mind, Krowl stuck me in the stomach with the point of his blade. The needle tip went through my shirt and into my flesh, drawing a dribble of blood that ran warm down my belly and into my groin. I stiffened and stayed that way. Krowl had nicked me without missing a word.

There was a long silence; then the mechanical voice intoned:

"Robert Frederickson."

"Present; but I'd like to be excused."

> *"I conjure thee; by night your eyes are blinded, by day your ears are stopped, by earth your mouth is sealed, by rock your limbs are bound!"*

"Fuck you!" A little chant of my own. It was beginning to sound as though Esobus, my hoped-for secret ally, were reading my epitaph, and that we were nearing the end of this particular ceremony. But if Esobus was concerned that I was going to start shouting out accusations that he was a closet goody-goody, he gave no indication of it. His voice droned on without interruption.

> *"Twist and tangle, never to rise up again. Your eyes grow dimmer, your limbs grow numb. The angel of death now draws near . . . Wait! . . . There is an intruder among us!"*

The last was definitely not part of the ceremony, and I grimaced as I felt the points of eight blades dig into me.

Suddenly I heard a familiar voice chanting, the words echoing through the chamber.

> *"O pentacle of might, be thou fortress and defense for Robert Frederickson against all enemies, seen and unseen, in every magical way!"*

On the flickering outer edges of the firelight I could just make out the figure of Madeline Jones standing at the railing of the catwalk, above and to the far left. Her arms were stretched out to either side, and her eyes were closed in fierce concentration.

The sweat on my body turned ice cold, and I almost stumbled. My head spun, and for a moment I thought I had to be hallucinating. But I wasn't the only one in a state of shock: Krowl's mouth drooped open in astonishment.

"*Damn* you, Madeline Jones!" Krowl shouted. "This isn't your affair! Be gone from this place, or die! So mote it be! *So mote it be!*"

Madeline's voice came again, soft in contrast to Krowl's rasping shout, floating in the dry, heated air like a sonic feather.

> *"Four corners in this house for holy angels. Christ Jesus, be in our midst. God be in this place and keep us safe."*

There was a short silence; then Madeline continued: "You know who I am, John Krowl. I am of the belief and the society. Robert Frederickson is under my protection. Let him go unharmed. *So mote it be!*"

Krowl had apparently tired of chants. The curious battle of sorcerers was over, and it was Technology Time: Krowl was reaching inside his robe for his gun.

But Madeline had given me what I most needed: distraction. Having overcome my initial shock at seeing Mad, I sucked in a deep breath as though I were diving underwater, then dropped to the floor. A knife tip slashed my shoulder, but that was all. I rolled backward through a pair of legs, at the same time kicking my toe up into their owner's groin. Then I got up and sprinted around the edge of the fire toward the place where I'd left the rope. With a little luck, it would still be there.

"Be careful, Mad!" I shouted as I ran. "Krowl's got a gun! And watch out to your left! Esobus is up there somewhere!"

Three gunshots rang out, and the wooden beam over Madeline's head splintered. Mad ducked away, looked around in desperation, then started running—in the wrong direction.

"Not *that* way, Mad!" I yelled as I saw her racing toward Esobus' cubicle.

The rope was where I'd left it. I swung out and shinnied up it into the darkness. Krowl got off a shot at me, but the dancing firelight must have distorted his vision, because he didn't even come close. I was up the rope in world-record time; but it was too late to stop Madeline. As I clambered over the railing I heard a scream, then a body falling heavily to the floor.

Below, I heard the sound of feet racing in all directions. Although I hadn't been able to find any, I was certain there was at least one stairway leading up to the catwalk, and probably two or three. The coven members would be on us soon, and they'd be shooting.

I raced down the catwalk, expecting a figure to leap out at me from the darkness at any moment. But Esobus was gone. Madeline was crumpled into a heap on the narrow platform leading to Esobus' cubicle. For a moment I thought she was dead, but when I turned her over I could see that she was still breathing. However, what Esobus had done was almost as terrible for a beautiful woman like Madeline; a cross had been carved into her forehead. Blood was flowing freely from the crosshatch wound, covering Mad's face. She began to moan softly, her hands fluttering like wounded birds about her face, as though she feared to touch it.

"Oh God, Mad," I said, lifting her head. "You have to get up. They'll be here any minute."

I quickly tore off my shirt and pressed it to her bleeding forehead. Madeline slowly raised her right hand and held the impromptu bandage in place. With my hand under her arm, she struggled to her feet. Directly in front of me was one of the corridors I hadn't explored; that would be where Esobus had gone. I started to lead Madeline back the way I'd come.

"Where are you going?" Madeline whispered in a hoarse, cracking voice.

"We can get down to an alley. It's the way I came in."

Mad shook her head, moaned with pain. My shirt was already stained crimson with her blood. "Better . . . to go . . . my way."

"You can't see, and I don't know how you came in."

Running footsteps echoed throughout the factory. The acoustics of the building made it impossible to tell who was where, but the hollow, popping sounds were definitely coming closer, converging on us.

"Where . . . I was standing," Mad whispered. "Corridor leads to . . . window. Fire escape."

There was no time to argue; one or two men had undoubtedly covered the doorway leading to the alley. "I won't ask you if you can run, Mad. You *have* to. They'll kill us if they find us."

"I know," she murmured. "Go ahead. Just . . . don't let go of my hand. Straight . . . down the corridor."

Gripping her wrist tightly, I raced back down the catwalk. Madeline, pressing my shirt to her wounded forehead with one hand and holding on to me with the other, staggered after me. I found the corridor, turned down it.

The part of the warehouse we were in consisted of abandoned, dust-filled offices. At the end, as Madeline had indicated, there was a black-painted window which was ajar. The lock on it had been broken, and a crowbar lay off to one side. I pushed the window open, then helped Madeline through the aperture and onto the metal grate outside. The fire-escape ladder, held aloft by a counterweight, led down into the small garden/patio behind Krowl's brownstone.

There was a wail of approaching sirens.

"Damned if that doesn't sound like the cavalry," I said, taking Madeline's elbow and guiding her down the rusted steel steps. "Our cup runneth over."

"Garth," she whispered in the same pain-filled voice.

"Good. He'll be able to get you to a hospital fast."

We reached the bottom, and I looked up, involuntarily flinching as I half-expected to see the flash of a gun from the open window. But it looked as if we were home free. Wherever the coven members were searching for us, it wasn't in the corridor we'd come down. I started leading my rescuer toward a gate leading out to a side street.

Madeline held back, squeezing my hand hard. "Can't let police . . . see me, Mongo."

"Why not? Garth knows about you."

". . . Called anonymously," Mad said, her voice barely audible behind a terrible curtain of pain and shock. "Garth doesn't . . . know I'm here. They'll have the coven. But if they . . . find me here, I'll have . . . to testify in open court. It will ruin me, Mongo. You know that. I'll . . . lose everything that means . . . anything to me."

"Krowl and the other members will tell the police."

"No. They won't, Mongo. No matter what . . . happens, they won't tell how you escaped. Occult . . . business."

Of course they wouldn't, I suddenly realized. And not only because it was "occult business."

"Mad," I said quietly, "we could have a problem here. The coven will have time to destroy their books of shadows. Without those personal records, I'm not sure what can be proved against them; without evidence, there's just a bunch of guys in an empty building celebrating Halloween early. I'm sure they've got a lot of politicians and judges in their pockets; the coven could blackmail those people, if they have to. The DA may need you to corroborate my testimony before a grand jury. That crew has killed a number of men, ruined the lives of dozens of others, and tried to poison a little girl. And don't forget that Esobus ran a blade across your forehead. Don't you want to see them permanently put out of business?"

Madeline swallowed hard, sobbed. "Mongo, if I testify, everything about me will come out. I'll be laughed out of the scientific community and never be taken seriously again. Teaching is my whole life. *Please* don't take that away from me."

It occurred to me that *I* was going to have legal problems if I tried to protect Madeline: I would have to perjure myself. But perjured was better than dead, and dead was what I would be if not for Madeline.

The sirens were very close now. "All right," I said quietly. "But I have to get you to a hospital."

"My car's just down the street. Thank you, my friend."

Chapter 20

I took Madeline to the nearest hospital, where she was immediately admitted through the Emergency Room. An intern cleaned and bandaged my shoulder, and even managed to find me a shirt left behind by some boy. Then I was allowed to sit with Madeline while the cross-shaped wound was washed, and pressure pads applied. The medical staff's best plastic surgeon was called in to do the stitching. It was the only logical thing to do; but I knew that the best plastic surgeon in the world wasn't going to be able to leave Madeline's forehead free of a scar she'd carry with her for the rest of her life.

I could think of nothing to say to Madeline except a simple "Thank you."

The surgeon indicated she'd be under the knife and needle for an hour or two. I told Madeline I'd stay close by, kissed her on the cheek and went out into the waiting room.

As with the sensory deprivation, there was none of the exhilaration I felt I should be experiencing after narrowly escaping being carved up and barbecued by the coven. What I did feel was a deep gratitude to Madeline for saving my life, sorrow and regret at the price she'd had to pay. Underlying it all was a profound sense of dissatisfaction at things left unfinished. But I knew there was one piece of business that had to be taken care of right away. I got up and went to a pay phone by the entrance.

Garth was still at the coven's headquarters, but I convinced the station's desk sergeant that my brother would want to talk to me right away. I was patched through to his car radio.

"Mongo! You all right? We got a call—"

"I know, Garth. I was there, but I'm all right."

There was a pause, then: "*Well?* Where the hell are you *now?*"

". . . Taking care of some business," I said, feeling like The Fool in the tarot deck. Stepping off a cliff. Except that I was no innocent.

"How'd you get away?"

"Dwarf cunning," I said, hating myself for the smart-ass lie, but thinking of the woman a few rooms away having her face sewn back together. "Listen; Sandor Peth's dead, and you've got what's left of the coven there—except for Esobus." I swallowed hard, trying to rid myself of a sour, seaweed taste in my mouth. "Uh . . . you didn't happen to pick up anyone in the street outside the building, did you?"

"No." Now Garth's voice was strained. "Tell me what happened."

I did, omitting only Madeline's role in helping me escape. I finished up by saying, "You'll find all the evidence you need in the books of shadows they keep in their cubicles."

"Sorry, Mongo," Garth said tightly. "We didn't find anything—and we probably couldn't hang on to it if we had. Whoever called said the coven was about to kill you; it wasn't exactly the kind of situation where I felt like waiting around for some judge to swear out a search warrant. *We* could conceivably be in trouble, if they want to press it."

"Krowl and the others . . . weren't dressed in ceremonial robes?"

"No robes, Mongo."

They would have been consigned to the gas fire, along with the books of shadows and any other incriminating evidence in the coven's possession. I felt sick.

"Well, you'll just have to make do with my story. *I'm* telling you they're behind the whole thing. That factory is the coven's headquarters. What the hell did they say they were doing with a mini-crematorium in the center of the floor?"

"Hey, brother, I believe you. The point is that we don't have any physical proof. Krowl swears that the complex was started as an adjunct to his Mystic Eye Institute, then left unfinished when he ran out of money."

"Then what were they doing there?"

"As far as the law is concerned, it doesn't *matter* what they were doing there. Krowl *owns* the place. Anyway, it would help if we could find the woman who called in. She probably knows a lot. You don't have any idea who it was, do you?"

"No," I lied. I was beginning to feel light-headed and nauseated again, and I knew the feeling had nothing to do with antirabies shots. "Like I said, you'll just have to make do with my testimony."

"Right now I'll make do with just *finding* you. Where are you, Mongo? I'll come around and pick you up."

". . . I'll be at the station house in a couple of hours."

There was a long silence on the other end of the line. When Garth finally spoke again, his voice was hard and cold. "You're holding out on me, Mongo. What the fuck do you think you're up to?"

"I'll talk to you later, Garth," I said, and hung up.

Feeling as if I were wrapped in a bale of wet cotton, I went to a canteen down a corridor from the Emergency Room and got a cup of coffee from a vending machine. I sat down, lighted a cigarette and stared down into the brown depths of the coffee. The steaming liquid reminded me of the hole I'd seen in the floor of my mind, and I recalled how I'd gone over and over the facts of the case in an attempt to keep from falling into that hole. Now, with the coven experience behind me, there were more elements to add. I was convinced that if I stared hard enough, mixed everything together and stirred hard enough, the rest of the answers would break free and float to the top, like clots of rancid cream.

The cigarette end burned my fingers. I stubbed the butt out in a standing ashtray while continuing to stare into the coffee, thinking. I was still staring when I felt a hand on my shoulder. It was Madeline. Her entire forehead was bandaged, but her lovely blue eyes were free of pain. To me, she still looked beautiful; she wouldn't look so beautiful to others when the bandages were removed.

"Hello, babe," I said softly. "Shouldn't you at least be staying here overnight?"

Mad shook her head, and winced. "The blood made the wound look worse than it really is. I'm all stitched up, and the plastic surgeon says there won't be *too* much of a scar." She smiled and made a small curtsy. "I'm betting it will look sexy. How about getting me a cup of coffee?"

I brought her coffee from the machine, sat down across from her. "Thank you again for saving my life."

"You're welcome again. Now let's forget about it, okay? Having you around is worth a little slice on the forehead. Remember what you said? We're the only two people who have anything to say to each other at those boring faculty parties."

"Why did you run the way you did, Mad? Didn't you know Esobus was there?"

She grinned wryly and gently touched her bandaged forehead with her fingertips. "I knew; I guess I'm just a damn fool. Call it the curiosity of the scientist. I wanted to see who Esobus was."

"Did you get a look at him?"

Madeline shook her head. "He was dressed in a crimson robe, like the others, with a hood over his head. He was just running out when I came up. He was tall—over six feet, I'd say. I didn't see the knife until it was too late; it just kind of flashed out at me. His hand was big, and I think he was wearing a diamond ring on his index finger."

"Mad, how did you know they had me? How did you know where I was?"

She blinked rapidly, and her eyes went slightly out of focus as she absently touched her cheek. "Didn't I tell you?"

"No, you didn't."

"I received a telephone call. This voice—"

"Was it a strange voice? Distorted, like Esobus'?"

"Yes," Madeline said, sounding confused. "How did you know?"

"It doesn't make any difference. Go ahead."

"The voice told me where you were," Mad continued in a quiet, subdued tone. "It said that the coven planned to kill you. I was told to call the police right away, and even told where the window would be open. When I called Garth, I was told he wasn't there. The police said I'd have to give my name before they'd listen seriously to anything I had to say. I gave them the information and told them it was a life-and-death emergency, but I just *couldn't* give my name. Then I panicked and came myself." She paused and sipped at her coffee. "Do you have any idea who might have called?"

"It was the same person you heard leading the ceremony tonight," I said tightly. "Esobus."

"The man who *slashed* me?"

I slowly nodded, still staring down into the coffee. Now my stomach was tying itself into knots of nervous tension. At last, one more answer had come boiling up from the mixture of questions in my mind; the face of this one was leering and obscene.

"Mad," I said, looking up at her, "I owe you my life, so I really don't have any right to ask you for more. But I will anyway. If you'll help me, I think I may be able to clear this whole matter up."

"You mean you think you can find Esobus?"

"Maybe," I said, pushing my cold coffee to one side. "I just may be able to produce physical evidence that will pin murder and extortion on those happy coven brothers." I paused, added, "The police are going to need it; there was nothing worth anything left in the coven headquarters by the time Garth got there."

"I'm sorry to hear that," Mad said, lowering her gaze. "Did you . . . tell Garth about me?"

"No, and I don't plan to. If you'll help me, there won't be any need."

"You know I'll do anything I can, Mongo—as long as I don't get any publicity."

"I want you to go for a ride with Garth and me. Garth already knows about your involvement with the occult, so that won't be a problem. You'll eventually have to make up a story about what happened to your forehead, so it may as well be sooner as later." I lighted a cigarette, squinted against the smoke. I suddenly felt very tired. "There's another woman I'd like to ask to come along. I'll need her expertise, as well as yours."

Mad's blue eyes clouded, and she frowned. "I don't know, Mongo," she said hesitantly. "My career is *so* important to me. Lately, I've begun to regret that I ever became involved with the occult."

"I know. But this woman's a witch to begin with—and she's a friend of mine. You have my word that she'll keep your secret."

Mad gave a slight toss of her head, then brushed her silver hair back and smiled easily. "Your word's good enough for me. Where are we going, and what do you plan to do?"

"Let's wait on that until I get everything absolutely straight in my own head. When will you feel up to going out?"

Mad shrugged. "I'm ready to go *now*, if it will clear this business up once and for all."

"Tomorrow morning," I said. I rose, took Mad's arm and helped her to her feet. "If you change your mind and want to wait a few days, let me know."

"All right. But I won't. What time?"

"I have to check with Garth and the other woman, but let's say eleven."

"Eleven it is."

I walked Madeline to her car and drove her home. Later, I called Garth and April. My stomach wouldn't stop churning.

The city was aglow with copper light, and the late-morning air was oppressively thick, dirty and hot. Black-bottomed clouds had been scudding low across the sky for hours, phantom freighters impatient to unload their wet cargo. It was going to rain soon—and hard.

Despite the impending downpour, no one had suggested that we put off the trip. Events now seemed to be moving with a momentum of their own. Garth, Madeline and April seemed to sense that; I knew it. To put off this journey would only postpone the inevitable, and it was best to get it out of the way as soon as possible. That was what I kept telling myself. I was, after all, responsible for whatever was going to happen, and at the moment I was the only one who carried the burden of knowing just how ugly was the face of the secret we hunted.

The tires on Garth's car whined as we went down the entrance ramp and entered the maw of the Lincoln Tunnel. There'd been little conversation; everyone was waiting impatiently for me to explain what we were supposed to be doing, and the atmosphere inside the car was tense. Garth was driving his Pontiac, and Madeline sat with him in the front, staring moodily out the side window. April sat in the back with me, holding tightly to my hand. Her palm was wet and clammy. I was slouched down in the seat, wishing I were even smaller than I was. I puffed mechanically on a cigarette, blowing the smoke out the side vent.

"Are you sure you're all right, Doctor?" Garth said quietly to the woman sitting next to him.

"Yes, thank you," Madeline said evenly. "I'm just paying for my own stupidity. If I hadn't been so impatient and yanked on the chart, the rack wouldn't have fallen on me."

Garth inclined his head back. "Are *you* all right, Mongo?" he asked with heavy sarcasm. "Are you *alive*, Mongo?" Anger and hurt hummed in his voice.

"I'm alive."

"You're being *very* mysterious, brother, even for you."

"Lay off for a bit, will you, Garth?"

"Come on, Mongo!" Garth snapped. "The party's under way, and you're the host. It's time you told us where we're going, and *why* we're going."

We passed out of the tunnel, into New Jersey. I flicked my cigarette out the window and straightened up in the seat. I'd run out of time. "We're going to Philadelphia to look for Frank Marlowe's book of shadows."

"What the hell?" Garth said, accidentally hitting the brake and almost sending us into a skid. Madeline had turned in her seat and, like April, was staring at me with astonishment. Garth started to pull over to the shoulder of the road.

"Keep going, brother," I said curtly. "At the moment, I'll feel better if we're moving."

"*Where* in Philadelphia?" Garth asked, accelerating up past the speed limit and moving into the passing lane. The anger in his voice had been replaced by curiosity.

"To April's house—with her permission, of course."

April gasped and put her hand to her mouth. "Robert? *I* didn't take Frank's book of shadows!"

"Of course you didn't," I said to April, squeezing her hand. "I think your former husband put his book—or at least, the bulk of it—in your attic. That's what we're looking for."

"Explain, brother," Garth said quietly.

"Frank Marlowe wasn't working on a 'book of shadows' in the witchcraft sense of the term. This was his big book—the one he'd always wanted to do. And it *would* have been big; maybe it still will be. A coven: witchcraft, murder, extortion and sex—it had everything, up to and including some very big names in show business and politics. *That* was his book of shadows; he was probably even going to call it that. He'd been working on it from the first day he became involved with the coven."

The rains came; or, rather, they attacked. The sudden cloudburst was a thick wall of water falling on us with the force of a giant wave. Sheets of rain swept over the car, instantaneously reducing visibility to zero. Huge droplets banged against the roof and windshield like the foot slaps of millions of running soldiers; their supporting artillery could be heard close by—laser rockets of lightning, explosions of thunder, their percussive vibrations felt through the body of the car.

Garth immediately turned on the wipers, but, despite the fact that he had them on at high speed, they had little more effect on the blurred windshield than someone swishing his hand through the water of a pond looking for something on the bottom. Garth slowed the car to a crawl as dozens of taillights, glowing like red wounds in the day, suddenly appeared on the road before us.

A few minutes before, I would have been glad for any excuse not to talk, Now I resented the storm's interruption, the way in which it had wrenched my audience's attention away from me. My certainty, and the words it generated, were building up with inexorable force, like poison in an infected wound.

After fifteen minutes of creeping along, watching Garth hunched over the wheel, I could stand the pressure no longer.

"April," I continued, raising my voice so as to be heard over the snare-drum beat of the rain and loud *flop-flop* of the wipers, "you were the one who told me Frank used to periodically drop manuscripts off at your home for storage and safekeeping. That's what he'd been doing with his book. The early parts of his research—the meat of what we want, including the names of the coven members and records of their activities—is probably still up there in your attic. That shopping bag you brought me was the *last* thing he brought up. I'm sure that, if we really look around up there, we'll find more than enough to put Krowl and the rest of the coven away permanently."

April shook her head. "I don't understand. You said that Frank told Kathy his book of shadows had been *stolen.*"

"Only part of it—the sections he had in his apartment. The main work had been done, and I'm betting he was just researching background material on witchcraft in general in order to flesh out the book. Those sections didn't have anything in them to identify the members of the coven; but when they were stolen, Frank knew his secret was out and that he was in deep trouble. It was those minor sections that Daniel stole."

"Daniel?" April whispered breathlessly.

Garth was concentrating hard on the road, but at the same time listening intently to the conversation. I nodded to April and leaned forward so that my brother and Madeline could hear over the roar of the storm.

"It had to be him. Kathy said her father told her that either Esobus *or* Daniel had taken his book of shadows. Well, let's assume he knew what he was talking about. I know the *coven* didn't take it, because Krowl asked *me* where it was. Admittedly, since Esobus has obviously been playing some kind of double game, it's possible that Esobus took it and didn't tell the others; but I don't think so. My money's on Daniel, and if April will take us to his house after we search her attic, I think that's where we'll find the missing sections."

"I'll take you anywhere you want to go, Robert," April said. "But why would *Daniel* take Frank's notes?"

"A good question, and I think I have the answer. Daniel wanted to scare Frank off the project. Hypothesis: Esobus and Smathers were the seminal force behind the formation of the coven. Smathers was the front man, and Esobus provided the name that—theoretically—would attract the best ceremonial magicians. Like Michael McEnroe—and Daniel. Daniel was certainly one of the first men asked to join, but he turned the invitation down. *All* the real heavies—at least, all the ones Smathers knew of—turned it down."

"But then, Daniel would have known about Smathers' involvement from the beginning, wouldn't he?" April said.

"Not necessarily. Smathers was the front man, but I think the original contacts would have been made through unsigned letters; Smathers wouldn't have wanted to be *too* up-front. Besides, the fact that the writer knew the identities of the ceremonial magicians in the first place would have lent the project—and the invitations—a certain air of legitimacy. Only if they responded—say, to a post-office box number—would Smathers come out of the closet. As I said, Daniel probably ignored the whole thing."

Suddenly the taillights before us became brighter brake lights, an unmoving, twin smear of crimson stretching off into the blurred distance. Garth brought the car to a halt and pulled the emergency brake. There was no way of telling what was causing the solid tie-up, but it was undoubtedly an accident—and a big one. The situation had a feel of permanency about it, and I cursed under my breath. My nerves were raw with anticipation, guilt and anxiety.

"But Daniel would have known about the *coven* from the beginning," Garth said thoughtfully, absently shutting off the wipers and ignition. "That would be dangerous information to have."

"Right," I said tightly. "Knowledge of the coven—and, later, information about what they were up to—probably made Michael McEnroe nervous enough to skip town by taking an extended trip to India. Now, considering the fact that we've been dealing with a bunch of crazies who make a fetish out of ritualistic behavior, Kathy's poisoning could begin to make some sense—if that's the word for anything these people did. It certainly didn't in the beginning: They'd already killed Marlowe, so why bother with Kathy? I got the definite impression from Krowl that there was a *double* betrayal—Marlowe's and someone else's. Who *else* did the coven think betrayed them? I think it was *Daniel*. The coven poisoned Kathy to get back at Daniel—to punish him in the most evil, devastating way they could think of. They were torturing him, while at the same time warning him that they could do the same thing to *anyone* he loved if he betrayed them again."

Madeline had been half-turned in her seat, staring at me intently. Now she turned around and stared at the rippling, shifting sheets of water on the passenger window. "How did Daniel betray them?" she asked distantly, her voice barely audible.

"He didn't, Mad. They only *thought* he did. But he anticipated the problem and tried to head it off by taking those parts of the book that Frank Marlowe was working on in his apartment. Daniel probably didn't know that he didn't have all of it, and by the time he found out it was too late anyway."

"Sorry, brother," Garth said, shaking his head. "I've lost you somewhere."

"I understand," April said in a breathy whisper. "Oh, my God."

"When Marlowe was first approached, the coven didn't even know his real name," I continued. "He was initiated as Bart Stone, the Western writer. Somehow, the coven finally found out that he was researching their entire operation for an exposé. About the same time, they found out his *real* name. From there, it was only one small step to finding out that Marlowe had been married to a witch who came from generations of occultists, and that his ex-brother-in-law was a famous ceremonial magician . . . who'd ignored their invitation. They figured Daniel had turned Marlowe on to them."

There was a prolonged silence, filled only with the wash, bangs and roar of the storm. Finally, Garth said, "I like it, Mongo. It *could* be the way you say it is—but you're only guessing."

"True. But I've had a lot of time to think about this—above and under water. The problem has always been finding an overall theory that will fit the available facts; this is it. Daniel eventually found out about the research project when Frank Marlowe approached him directly for information. Daniel immediately knew there was going to be a problem for *him* if they ever found out what Marlowe was up to, and he tried to warn Marlowe off. When that didn't work, he stole Marlowe's book of shadows as a warning."

"I still don't understand why Daniel didn't come to the police after his niece was poisoned," Garth said.

"He was afraid they'd drop the other shoe," I said. "On April. His only chance was to find them himself and convince them they'd made a mistake."

"Yes," April said very softly, slowly nodding. "But there's more to it than that, and you'd understand if you'd known Daniel. He was a priest—and he behaved as a priest. Besides, if Robert's right about the bulk of Frank's book being in my attic, my brother really had nothing to tell the police; involving them could only make matters worse."

"Assuming you're on target all the way," Garth said to me, "do you think we'll find Esobus' real name in Marlowe's manuscript?"

"I don't know." I paused and lighted a cigarette; my hands were trembling. "Frank might have spotted her if he'd hung around the warehouse long enough, but I'm not confident about that. I'll bet Esobus missed an awful lot of coven meetings—the real ones as well as the phony ones. Esobus is a very busy woman. In any case, I'm hoping she'll confess of her own free will."

April put a trembling hand on my elbow. *"She?"*

I reached into my pocket and took out the paper I'd removed from Esobus' cubicle. My stomach muscles fluttered as I read it aloud. " 'The search for truth is neither moral nor immoral: it is the prerequisite of a civilized society.' " I slowly crumpled the paper and jammed it back into my pocket. "Mad," I said softly, "I found that little homily tacked up inside Esobus' cubicle. What do you make of it?"

"It sounds strange," Madeline said in a choked voice. "On the surface, it sounds a little academic. For the leader of *that* coven, it sounds incredibly self-serving."

Madeline breathed a deep sigh and rested her head wearily against the side window. Up until that moment, I'd hoped I was wrong and that I'd simply misread all the clues. But now I realized with a sudden, sickening jolt that I was right, and I groaned inwardly. Garth hissed through his teeth and quickly glanced at Madeline. April was staring at me, her eyes wide.

"You're Esobus, Mad," I said softly, feeling short of breath. "You knew it had to come to this one day. 'The Wizard of Oz is dead'; remember when you told me that?"

"Facts, Mongo," Garth said tightly. "Where are your facts?"

"I don't have any facts, and there's still a great deal that I don't understand. Madeline is going to have to fill us in on the details."

Mad shook her head; her silver hair rippled and cascaded over the back of the seat. Then slowly, like a tree toppling in a forest, Mad fell sideways until her cheek came to rest on Garth's shoulder. Garth started to bring his arm up to put it around her shoulders, then uttered a startled grunt. There was a swirl of movement in the front, with Madeline sliding back across the seat and flinging open the door. Suddenly the roar and spit of the storm was in the car. Garth grabbed for Madeline and missed as the woman leaped out of the car and was swallowed up in the deluge.

"She's got my gun!" Garth shouted, scrambling across the seat and diving into the storm after her.

"Stay here!" I snapped at April as I opened the door on my side and stepped out.

I was soaked through to the skin within moments after getting out of the car. The fury of the wind and rain was even greater than I'd imagined listening only to its voice; a sudden gust of wind threw me against the car's trunk, spinning me around and momentarily disorienting me, robbing me of precious seconds. By the time I got around to the other side of the car, neither Garth nor Madeline was in sight.

Shielding my eyes from the driving rain with my hands, I could see that I was at the foot of a fairly steep embankment that rose off the right shoulder of the turnpike. There was a flash of lightning, and in that moment I could see the tops of trees whipping violently back and forth along the top of the embankment.

Suddenly I felt a hand grip my arm. I spun around and found April standing next to me. Her hair was matted to her cheeks and the top of her head, and tiny rivers of water cascaded down her face, blurring her features.

"Get back in the car!" I shouted, spitting water.

"No! She'll need me!"

"She's goddamn likely to *shoot* you, woman! Do as I say!"

"No, Robert! No matter what you say or do, I'm going to help search for her. Even if Dr. Jones *is* Esobus, she's not evil. She saved Kathy's life—and yours. She's a woman; I'm a woman. I'm going to her. You can't stop me, so take me with you!"

There was no time to argue. April's voice rang with determination, and I couldn't have her wandering alone in the storm. Nor could I drag her back; the decision to expose Madeline in this manner had been mine. What was happening was my responsibility, and I couldn't leave Garth and Madeline alone in the storm.

I started to scramble up the embankment, gripping April's hand tightly and pulling her up after me. The force of the storm was tearing away loose patches of sod, turning the face of the hill into a checkerboard of ice-slick patches of grass and slimy, clinging squares of mud. We slipped often, breaking our slide by digging our fingers into the ground. We would rise again, resume climbing; within seconds, the rain would strip the clots of mud from our clothes and bodies. It was a difficult climb for anyone, not to speak of an injured fifty-year-old woman. Logic dictated that Madeline had not attempted it, that she had run parallel to the highway. Somehow, I knew she hadn't. I sensed instinctively that, driven by desperation, Mad would want to be alone, to seek the natural sanctuary of the trees—and that she had made it. Madeline was too intelligent to believe she could get away; there was no place to go. And I did not believe that she intended to shoot us. Instead, I believed she had something else in mind—a ritual; an epilogue to the strange book of shadows that was her life. For some reason, that thought frightened me more than the idea of being shot myself.

But I could be wrong. At that very moment, Madeline could have Garth—or us—in her sights, pressing her finger on the trigger . . .

Perhaps Garth had caught her. Garth was young, strong. But he was also a logical-thinking policeman. If he had not seen her start up the hill, he would be searching up and down the turnpike.

April and I reached the top of the embankment and fell to our knees, leaning against each other and gasping for breath. Rain cascaded and swirled around us, making it impossible to see more than a few feet in any direction. It was difficult to breathe, almost as if the air were filling with water and we were drowning.

There was a loud, sharp crack, and I cringed, thinking it was a gunshot. But it was only thunder.

Suddenly, as if a switch had been thrown, the wind began to subside. Through the translucent sheets of rain I could make out a thick growth of tall grass and brush a few feet in front of us. There was a low retaining fence;

beyond that was the wooded area I'd glimpsed from below.

"Robert," April gasped, "she couldn't have come this way. She must be down on the highway."

I shook my head. "No. She's somewhere near," I half-turned, put my face very close to hers. "Go back, April. Please. I'm afraid for you."

"I can't, Robert. Don't waste time arguing."

I pulled April to her feet and led her toward the fence. I held the wire strands apart for her to climb through, then followed. The foliage and trunks of the trees provided some cover from the lashing elements, and we ran ahead. I shouted the names of Garth and Madeline, but my words were sucked up and extinguished by the storm.

The stand of trees was only a few hundred feet wide; on the other side of the wooded strip, thick factory stacks speared the black sky. Between, forming a buffer zone perhaps a half mile wide, was an ugly no-man's-land of rolling, lumpy landfill, garage dumps and occasional oases of grass.

Madeline, her figure barely visible through the curtains of rain, was kneeling in one of those oases which formed a small basin a hundred yards away from the foot of the embankment. Her body was bent forward at a sharp angle, and both her hands were pressed hard into her stomach. For one horrible moment I thought she had shot herself. But she was sitting too still, too steady. Her stiff immobility was statuelike, as though she intended to kneel there in the open, exposed to the pelting rain, for as long as it took to cleanse herself—perhaps forever.

With April clinging to my arm, I began to move down the slippery face of the hill, heading toward the basin where Madeline knelt. Suddenly, April drew her breath in sharply and squeezed my arm. I looked in the direction she was pointing and saw Garth emerge from the woods, perhaps fifty yards away. He immediately took in the scene, motioned to us with a single, terse wave of his hand, then began moving down himself, angling to his left in an attempt to approach Madeline from the rear.

But Madeline wasn't going to be taken by surprise. Suddenly, as if sensing our presence, she lifted her head. I winced when I saw that the rain and wind had stripped the bandage from her forehead, exposing the cross-shaped wound. Blood oozed from the raw flesh between the crusted stitches, mixed with rain and covered her face in a pink wash. Shaking, I raised my arms—more as a calming gesture than to show I was unarmed—and continued moving toward her, keeping my body in the line of fire between Madeline and April. Garth had almost reached the bottom of the embankment. He stopped to wait for us, and we cautiously converged on Madeline together.

When we were about ten yards away from Madeline the wind abruptly abated even further, until there was only the steady drumbeat of the rain, much lighter now. I had an eerie, chilling sensation that the storm was no more than a special effect; the tens of thousands of buildings, the millions of people, the hundreds of square miles surrounding us, were a backdrop for a movie. Our movie. All the master shots had been made, and now we had arrived at center stage. The camera was moving in for an Extreme Close-Up. I shook off a chill.

"Please don't come closer," Mad said evenly. Her voice was soft, but could be heard clearly in air that now, almost stripped of wind, suddenly felt too thin, drained of oxygen.

April, Garth and I squatted in a semicircle before Mad.

"Give me the gun, Dr. Jones," Garth said quietly. "You're hurt. Let us take care of you."

There was no answer, and Garth started to reach out toward her. Madeline tensed and straightened to show us that the barrel of the gun was turned inward, pressed against her stomach. Garth slowly sank back down on his haunches.

"That's a .38 Police Special, Dr. Jones," Garth continued in the same quiet, even voice. "If you shoot yourself like that, you're going to put a big hole in yourself. But you may not die right away. Don't do it; don't gut-shoot yourself. You'll suffer terrible pain, and there'll be nothing we can do to help you."

"Please, let's go, Dr. Jones," April said. "Come back with us. This is a bad place. I feel it; you feel it."

Madeline looked at April for a long time. "It's the right place, April," she said at last.

"Talk to us, Mad," I said. "Get it out of your system."

"You talk," she replied in a dark, stranger's voice.

"Can we go someplace out of the rain? We're cold."

Madeline shook her head and seemed to tighten her grip on the gun.

"I'll talk, Mad," I continued quickly. "I think you want me to." I took a deep breath, wiped the water off my face and formed a shield over my eyes with my left hand. "You saved my life last night—for the second time. The first time was when I was floating in Smather's fish tank. You also saved Kathy's life—after you found out what had been done to her."

"I don't understand, Robert," April said in a shuddering tremolo. "If Dr. Jones is Esobus, wouldn't she have known everything the coven was doing from the time they planned to do it?"

"Knowing Mad as I do, I don't think so," I replied to April, at the same time watching Madeline carefully—very conscious of the gun in her hands. "In fact, I think that, of all the members of the coven, Madeline—or Esobus—knew the least. Like I said, she *is* a busy woman, traveling all over the world in her role as a leading researcher in cosmology. I think Mad began this coven business as some kind of experiment. One day she discovered it had all gotten out of hand, but she didn't know what to do about it. Am I right, Mad?"

Madeline said nothing; instead, she raised her face to the sky—as though she were looking or listening for something. She made no sound, and the rest of her body didn't move; with all the water on her, it was impossible to tell for certain, but I was sure she was crying.

"You see," I continued, "Esobus' image was an all-powerful, mystical and supersecretive inspiration. But Esobus was a *leader* only in name, not a person the other coven members could sit down and plan things with. The coven meetings Esobus attended probably consisted almost entirely of *ritual*—there was no practical business discussed. Besides, Esobus was a fraud—not a ceremonial magician at all. But only Madeline and Smathers knew that."

A giant chill squeezed me in its icy hand and shook me. April held me tightly until it had passed.

"In Mad's mind, she was probably conducting an experiment in witchcraft that would finally reveal some kind of truth about the occult to a very suspicious scientific community," I continued, forcing the blurred words out through stiff lips that felt paralyzed. "These were the same people who'd laughed at her because of her ideas about astrology. Madeline's obsessed with the occult; in setting this whole thing in motion, she saw herself as a kind of pioneer. She's been looking for the lost Atlantis of the mind, if you will, but she found that she couldn't control it. Maybe she couldn't even decide if she *should* control it, considering the fact that it was an experiment; for a little while, she may have had trouble deciding whether to remain an aloof scientific observer, or intervene. Fortunately for Kathy and me, the human being in her won out over the dispassionate scientist. But right up until this morning, she was still trying to hedge her bets and get out of this whole."

The wind was rising again, as if the storm had regrouped its forces and was returning for another major assault.

"I'm so sorry," Madeline whispered softly. Incredibly, her voice could be heard clearly in the rising cacophony, as though her words had slipped through cracks in the wall of wind. "So sorry."

"A big question," I said, raising my voice in order to be heard. "I doubt that you were originally interested in witchcraft. What's the connection between you and Smathers? How did you find out that Smathers was a ceremonial magician, and how did you get him to set up the coven for you?"

"He was my . . . lover," Madeline said in a voice that was suddenly strangled. "I was his mistress for months before I found out about . . . the other things. Then I became intrigued with the question of what *would* happen if a coven of ceremonial magicians was formed—and with the problem of how I could become a part of it. Vincent was . . . amused by the idea; we planned the Esobus thing together. You've guessed the rest. Vincent took care of all the planning. I really *didn't* know about . . ." Her voice trailed off.

"Smathers was a madman," I said, making no attempt to hide the disgust I felt. "And he was a pervert. How could you ever get involved with a man like that?"

"Powerful," Mad said distantly, her voice still mysteriously overriding the wind. "Vincent was . . . so strange and powerful. You wouldn't understand, Mongo."

But I thought I did. The darkness beyond the light of

science, the void of night that Mad had been trying to explore, had finally swallowed her up.

Madeline slowly rose to her feet, and we rose with her. For a moment I thought—hoped—that it was finished, that a catharsis had been achieved and Madeline was ready to give up the gun and come with us. It was a false hope. She still held the gun in a reverse position, its barrel pressed even more tightly into her stomach, one thumb resting against the trigger. Again she raised her face to the sky and cocked her head, as though listening to voices in the storm that only she could hear.

"I've seen a lot of things in the past few weeks, Mad," I said quickly, driven by a sudden, terrible need to fill the space between us with words, as if I could filibuster away the dreaded sound of a gunshot muffled by Madeline's flesh. "Maybe most of the things I've witnessed are beyond scientific measurement. People like you and Krowl have strange talents, and most of us don't know how to deal with them. But some of these things bite if you don't handle them correctly, and you finally came to realize that. As much as you kept telling yourself you were simply being a scientist by keeping a foot in both camps, you wanted out; you wanted to be saved from the coven you'd created. You had a nervous breakdown because of your guilt—right after you'd made the recording that saved Kathy's life. My God, you've been dropping clues on me all along with those references to the Wizard of Oz. You once told me you were interested in the pursuit of knowledge, not personal power; it started to come together for me when I saw that sign in Esobus' cubicle. But you were never willing to come all the way out. You kept hoping right up to the end that you could run around putting Band-Aids on something that had to be amputated."

"Shut up, Mongo," Garth snapped. "You're being too hard on her. She's also helped a lot of people."

Madeline shuddered with cold, slowly shook her head. "No. Let Mongo finish. He knows I . . . need to hear it all."

The catharsis would come, I thought, and felt immense relief. That was what Mad seemed to be telling me: say it all, get it out in the open, and she would come back with us.

"You ran back to the cubicle in the factory building because you had to retrieve the tape you'd put on to cover your movement to the other end of the catwalk." I smiled tentatively and tried to establish eye contact, but Mad's gaze kept slipping away. I considered trying to knock the gun away, but rejected the idea. I couldn't assume that risk. "You took the tape off and threw it away somewhere into the darkness. A fleeing man might have stuck a knife *into* you, but it's highly unlikely he'd take the time—or be accurate enough—to carve a perfect cross on your forehead. No, Mad. The cross is your own, self-inflicted, mark of Cain: disfigurement as a form of expiation. It isn't enough, Mad; it's dues time for the Wizard of Oz."

"I couldn't live with it any longer, Mongo," Mad said evenly.

"I know. Now you don't have to. And Garth will tell you there are extenuating circumstances. You've saved lives."

I began to seriously doubt the old chestnut about a man's entire past flashing before his eyes at the moment of sudden, violent death. Or perhaps I wasn't really dying, because it wasn't that way at all. Quite the opposite. I was seeing things that had not yet happened, as though the thunderous explosion had blown my own book of shadows open to pages that had not yet been written.

Now Mad looked at me directly. She smiled as she said something, but she had lost control of the wind, and her words were lost. I watched her lips and thought she said, *"Thank you,"* or *"I love you";* or it may have been simply *"Goodbye, Mongo."*

Garth was with April, Kathy and me at the zoo, laughing at the orangutan. Ironically, Garth—the biggest and strongest—seemed to be the only one who had sustained a lasting injury. He was hobbling around with his right foot and ankle in a walking cast.

Madeline suddenly stiffened, as though an invisible metal rod had risen from the ground and skewered her. She flipped the gun around so that it was facing away from her, then raised both arms above her head. She slid up on the skewer, balancing on her toes, extending her arms even higher, bowing her head until her chin rested on her chest.

Now the camera began to grind in ultra-slow motion. Madeline's body had become a ramrod-straight, steel-tipped spear thrusting itself up into the air. She was offering herself, and I knew she was going to be taken.

My brother knew too. Garth and I leaped as one toward April.

But we were moving so *slowly*, divers straining every muscle to trudge along the bottom of the sea.

April and I had finished making love while Kathy napped. We lay in each other's arms, watching snow gather on evergreens outside some mountain lodge. It struck me that months had passed, and we were still together.

I desperately hoped it was more than death's anesthetic dream.

Straining, but still moving in slow motion. Garth grabbed one of April's arms; I grabbed the other, and we dived.

There was an exquisite sensation of floating, totally out of control and thus free of the terrible responsibility of thinking and making decisions. There was nothing to do but ride.

As I slowly flipped over in the air, I saw the bolt of lightning poke its sharp head from its black home. It seemed to hesitate, looking around. Finally it saw Madeline and began to drift lazily down a jagged route toward the gun in her hand.

I wanted to shout a warning to my friend, tell her to throw the gun to one side and float with us away from the lightning. There was time; everything was happening so unbelievably *slowly*. But when I tried to yell, my voice was no more than a deep rumble, like sounds from a record being played at very slow speed. I could *see* the words come out of my mouth, explode and stick to my face.

Beyond my horror was a childlike fascination with how *pretty* everything was—the way the lightning passed through the air, firing the surrounding molecules into a lovely, shimmering white glow. The smell of ozone was pleasant in my nostrils, something like burning leaves on a cold fall afternoon.

But I was losing sight of the spectacle as I rotated in the air. Garth and I bumped into each other, then drifted apart again as we both tried to protect April with our bodies.

I was actually auditioning for an orchestra—but not the New Jersey Symphony. Too bad. It was a pickup group of extremely talented Juilliard students interested in playing modern music. There was plenty of Boulez and Messiaen, but no Tchaikovsky. The incredibly complex rhythms were driving me crazy, but I was having a perfectly marvelous time. April was sitting in the first row of the auditorium, smiling broadly at me while Kathy excitedly pounded her mother's thigh.

Garth was in the back of the auditorium, grudgingly—very grudgingly—nodding his appreciation.

At least, the bone-cracking, wet cold was gone. It had been supplanted by a sharp, tingling sensation that hurt my joints, but had an overall warming, *liquid* feel. The electricity coursing through my body was oddly invigorating, and made me feel as though I could run for hours without getting tired.

If only I could stop floating and get my feet on the ground.

I'd lost sight of Mad during one half turn. Now, as I came out of a slow spin, I could see that the lightning had completed its journey to the barrel of the gun. Mad was softly aglow, like a fluorescent bulb; she would have been beautiful, except for the way the electricity made her hair stand out from her head, each individual strand vibrating like a sliver-thin tuning fork.

Then Madeline began to burn, and I didn't want to look anymore. I didn't want to remember her that way.

I closed my eyes. Holding tight to both April and Garth, I let myself float away into the velvet darkness behind my eyes.

9 780967 450391